Elusive Wisdom

"...a beautifully intelligent, irresistible legal thriller, full of energetic and lively characters. The "good guys" are real people, with flesh and blood fears and hopes. There is hard work, with lots of plot machinations that draw the reader deeply into the story and take the reader across the country and back again. There is love fulfilled, and old lust enjoyed in remembrance and in denial and loss. There is perseverance and perspicacious deducing. There is indefatigable pursuit of justice, using both brains and brawn, both incorporating some sneaky maneuvering. There is a plethora of weapons available to all characters. There are gun shot wounds. And all this is in the pursuit of justice. The best part of the yarn may be the tackling of a conspiracy, luckily involving Mississippi and a variety of those who have promised to use the shield of justice for the public good. Add all the legal excitement, the crime-solving puzzle, and the sex toys, and you have a riveting read that is hard to put down. This is a great book for a long airport wait, for a wonderful stay at the beach, or when waiting for court to begin. It is exciting, absorbing, legally compelling, and basically covers the Seven Deadly Sins—and then some!"

—Verna MacCornack, Ph.D

"As a trial lawyer who practiced in San Francisco for thirty years, I find Mr. McCray's novel a most enjoyable and excellent read. His understanding and knowledge of the craft of the civil and criminal trial lawyer is evident throughout this fascinating story. He weaves a gripping tale of mystery and machination. The characters he has created fairly jump off the pages. By the time you reach the surprising conclusion you feel that DD O'Neil and all of the principle actors in this dramatic story are familiar friends and acquaintances. Although the matters presented in this tale of legal intrigue are at times complex, Mr. McCray's facility for telling a good story make it all eminently readable and understandable. From jury tampering to blackmail to murder, this novel has it all. While the wisdom in this fine novel may be elusive it is certainly enlightening and compelling. I highly recommend *Elusive Wisdom* to anyone who enjoys a fine mystery wrapped in compelling human drama."

—John Davids, San Francisco trial lawyer

Elusive Wisdom

**A NOVEL BY
JOE McCRAY**

Red Caboose Tales

Published by Red Caboose Tales
22703 NW Reeder Road
Portland, OR 97231

ISBN 978-0-9837748-3-9

A Note From the Author

The general rule, not to be lightly ignored, is that a novel must stand by itself – be whatever it is. Bolstering its contents with comments by the author is seen as self-serving claptrap. But...

Fiction generated for the last two or three decades under the supposed genre of "Legal Thriller" has, I think, more often than not misrepresented lawyers and the private practice of law. Even novels, in my view, have to accurately reflect life and institutions. Stories, like this one, that take place within the context of something as present in American life as the law need to account for what really goes on. To do otherwise fails the fundamental obligation of literature to illuminate.

This story includes reference to cases and tasks of its central characters other than the case that occupies the center of the story. That is because, among other things, no lawyer in private practice spends all of his time on one case. Here, these "other cases" are presented as a means to see how the system works and to express some of the values the principal character holds dear.

With this exception, this story is fiction. The names and events are a product of my imagination, if inspired by my experience.

—Joe McCray

Table of Contents

Part 5: Wisdom

Part 6: Elusive Wisdom

Part 1: Discovery

Most people want to do the right thing.
Some don't care. Others think it is foolish.

Joe Cleary on the reason for trial lawyers

CHAPTER ONE
1979-A Dip In Perfidy

MR.O'NEIL: Ladies and gentlemen, Judith Pavlone must depend on you to apply the law and good sense fairly. She is otherwise helpless. Whether she can spend the rest of her days with the best that can be had when she can't move her arms or her legs is dependent on you being what the law expects you to be – caring, thinking human beings. The defense is counting on you being something else.

Jack Curly is far and away the most informed and respected highway safety engineer in the country. In his role as the head of the Ohio State University Traffic Safety Institute, he was retained by the European defendant, *Internacionale,* to evaluate the performance of their products. That is a fact which led them to the knowledge that twenty years ago – twenty years, ladies and gentleman – Mr. Curly went a few rounds with the bottle and, after only six weeks of intense treatment, managed to win. This, Mr. Keislor would have you believe, is enough for you to question Mr. Curly's credibility. To do what Mr. Keislor suggests, ladies and gentlemen, would require you to be something other than the caring, thinking human beings the law needs.

It is simply without question that La Strada's design was defective. The fact that the Federal Automobile Safety Standards do not include a standard for roof strength is not relevant, as the Judge will instruct you is the law. What is not disputed is that the auto industry itself has established a roof-strength standard that La Strada never met. Herr Hoffler, from *Internacionale,* has testified that his company actually makes a small, fuel-efficient car which is tested for roof strength and it passes all applicable industry standards. The difference? – $150, ladies and gentlemen, $150.

It is unreasonable to risk the catastrophe that Judith Pavlone experienced for a mere $150. It is, I submit the very definition of recklessness.

Watching and listening from the spectator seats of the Court, the Honorable Vincent Alphonse Muzio of the United States District Court for the Northern District of California was satisfied that his long ago observation about Daniel Dermot O'Neil remained accurate:

"This kid is one of the best I've seen. A gambler, but with a fiery commitment to justice."

A short while after Judge Rowland committed the case to the decision of the jury, O'Neil sat with friends at Number 9 Jones throwing back Irish whiskey and ice, feeling spent – emotionally and physically. Trial-mate, Rick Esquivel, over his vodka gimlet, too, was spent.

"That was a great closing, DD – a great closing. I can't think of anyone who could do it as well. Here's to the jury."

Raising his glass of Irish as well was Joe Cleary, DD's lifelong friend, both being raised in and around Butte, Montana.

"You decided not to mention that lying sack of shit Kurt Meinor. You're probably right. But, I think you got 'em."

Of course, DD would not dare think Cleary was right. He never did. As miserable as waiting for a jury always is, he always knew he'd do it again – and he always predicted he would lose. "What could I do? Explain that our own expert is a sanctimonious teetotaler? Hardly."

On Friday afternoon, four days later, the call came. Grabbing his suit jacket, and with Rick right behind him, DD's heart was in his throat as he stepped quickly onto Turk Street.

"Whoa! DD, f'crissake we've been waiting for these people for three months. They can wait a few minutes for us. Take it easy. We have to wait for Judith anyway."

Finally slipping his jacket on, DD stopped and looked at Rick. "You're right. You're absolutely right. Thanks."

Whereupon, the warriors walked slower – deliberately – but slower. *Why do I do this? Why do I put myself through this over and over again? Exposing myself to pain and anxiety, rejection and embarrassment. No, it hasn't happened yet, but I know it will. Can I take it if it happens?*

Collected and composed, DD and Rick pushed open the swinging doors to the courtroom. Keislor and Dru Lacey were already there; Judith had not arrived. Nearly three months of battle – intense, minute-by-minute battle. Three years of preparation – New York, Frankfurt, Veracruz. It comes to this. Everyone anticipating the moment of conclusion, even Jerry the bailiff, sitting nervously with his belly spread over his gun belt, and the lovely, shy Fiona Danby, Judge Rowland's clerk, pretending to be busy at her desk in front of the bench. Finally, Judith rolled in with her new electric wheel chair. Smiling – god, she always smiles.

She whispered: "DD, I want you to relax. It doesn't matter what anyone decides, you did a great job – you and Rick – and I'm so very proud of you."

All of DD's edges melted a little, then the Judge took the bench and Fiona announced the fact. She called the case.

Looking at Jerry, the judge issued the order, "Bring in the jury Mr. Bailiff."

The rigamarole DD had seen so often was repeated. A kind of slow march to something – wholly devoid of meaning to DD- something he would just as soon avoid – *oh, to be someplace else.*

They had known that Ella Mae White was the foreperson of the jury. Once the Judge had inspected the verdict papers, they were returned to her. A tall woman with milk-chocolate complexion, a sizable bosom, short-cropped hair, and wearing bright brass earrings, her voice was commanding.

"On question one, 'whether the LaStrada was defectively designed', the answer is 'no'."

It came to DD's consciousness as a hot bullet might – striking somewhere around the temples.

She continued: "On question four, 'whether *Internacionale* was negligent in designing the LaStrada', the answer is 'no.'"

Crushing rejection. Abject loss. Trying desperately to hang on to the notion this was not all about him, DD felt the blood rush to the pain in his head. Judith, mustering all of her strength, hoisted her helpless arms toward him and managed to grab him at the shoulders.

"I'm so sorry Judith. I don't know what happened." It was all he could do – a barely audible explanation.

DD was in his office the next morning, by himself, trying to do something positive. Joe appeared at his office door. "Pretty miserable. I guess you – we – just have to go through it. You – we – have been pretty lucky 'til now."

"Joe. I've been going through all that shit since yesterday. I can't feel sorry for myself – that's ridiculous, f'crissake. It's my job – it's part of my job. If I can't take it, I gotta get another job. But jesus, it hurts. I don't think I've felt this way since my mother died – I was nine years old; I could be expected to cry."

He paused. Then returned his attention to Joe. "That could happen any minute. All that work. All that right. They said 'no' – they said 'no' twice!"

Stepping inside the door, Joe looked out the window into the courtyard garden so fastidiously kept by Ramon.

"You've had a tough year, partner. This case sucked up pretty much every waking hour except the few you spent divorcing Melanie."

"Yeah. That's more like a bad dream, this is a nightmare. Getting Melanie out of my life was actually a relief."

"DD, you and women. I don't know what the problem is, but jesus, it sure produces drama."

Joining Joe at the courtyard window, DD said, "Joe, I gotta get out of here. I can't face all this right now. There's just enough money to pay Jeannie for the month and maybe my tab at Tony's. I don't know what I'm going to do with what I owe on this case. I'd just like to go home, see Mick, and maybe stalk a whitetail."

Joe turned to DD and put his arms around him. "Good idea. Say hello to Moonshadow for me."

***

CHAPTER TWO

High Mountain Sojourn

A cold wind was biting his right eye and cheek, but DD didn't relish turning east to face its ferocity. Neither, he was sure, did Loop. The flying snow would then be bouncing off the horse's magnificent chest.

But once DD turned dead into the wind, the howling ceased. The dull thud of Loop's gloved hooves was the only sound and it was almost no sound at all. Loop did pierce the quiet with an occasional heroic snort, letting the elements know his contempt.

It was only two miles now. The last would be out of the wind where the trail dropped down Alice Creek to a sheltered nook in the rock where his father had built his house.

"Today," DD thought, "...God, I could do this every day..."

All of his childhood was lived here. Today was like then. Did it matter what else was going on the world?

The good-sized body of a whitetail buck was tied to the travois DD had fashioned from a scrub pine near where the animal fell. This way, the loaded travois slipped along the dry snow in Loop's track – not a difficult burden for the big chestnut.

In his childhood here, DD's companion was Dig, the predecessor to Loop. It seemed they were always together and for generations, but the reality was they ran through the mountains and parks only for six years before DD went off to Seattle and Dig died for the loss.

Raymond Little Beaver had wanted so badly to make it up to O'Neil – the loss of Dig – that when his prize mare gave up a strong colt, he made it a gift to DD.

Marialena Moonshadow removed the cigarette from her lips, and shouted as DD and Loop approached the gate:

"Damn. You did real good for a city slicker DD! If I had enough teeth, I'd chew that hide all soft to make you a jacket." DD wondered at Moonshadow's vigor after consuming the better part of a fifth of bad bourbon last night. Maybe that's what kept her able to stand there in the bitter wind in a sleeveless cotton shirt and jeans drawn over her skinny rump and outsized belly.

"Jeesus! You even gutted the thing. Guess you are one of us yet." Moonshadow laughed obscenely as DD swung the blooded body of his prize off the pine branch and onto the lower rail of the corral fence. He then proceeded to the barn to unsaddle his horse.

Moonshadow had been around Mick O'Neil's place since DD's last year in elementary school. She cooked, cleaned, and kept up the place for Mick, DD's dad. At some point, there was more to the relationship between them, but time and the ravages of booze and cigarettes gradually led Moonshadow to go to bed in the extra room on the first floor of the house. Mick's physical infirmities may yet bring them again to the same bedroom, when he can't climb the stairs any longer. For now, he still climbed, and the household remained amiably laid back, if seemingly sexless.

Johnny Fox emerged from the shop at the near end of the barn. His long, black ponytail instantly covered with snowflakes as did the broad rim of his leather hat jammed on his head. "DD, I'll skin that in the shop. You go on in and warm up."

Johnny's thick hand grabbed the deer's body just under its head and swung it up on his shoulder.

"Wait a minute Johnny. I want to do it. I haven't done it for twenty years," DD shouted, and shuffled through the snow after Johnny. Mick's forge was roaring and its heat pleasantly stung the near-frozen cheeks and hands of DD as he entered the dark space. Johnny was past the forge and hanging iron at the back of the shop, where he impaled the buck's rear legs on hooks on the cross beam, suspending it upside down.

"Every time I visited and got a buck, you always did the skinning. I felt like a white hunter and you were a dark skinned bearer. I don't like that feeling."

The two busily cut and scraped the hide from the meat, Johnny on the right side and DD on the left. "Well, DD you sure are white, but I ain't so dark skinned and this ain't Africa." He chuckled and continued to move quickly, outpacing DD's halting efforts. "Why do you want to get back into this skinnin'? It's just hard work unless you do it all the time."

Johnny had liberated the foreleg and a quarter of the right front of the animal while DD labored at the opposite foreleg.

"You gonna stay so you can get used to this?" Johnny paused a moment to watch his out-of-practice friend hack away with the skinning knife.

DD stopped and stood up, looking into the bright, black eyes of his lifelong friend, Johnny Fox. "Probably not. Sounds good right now, though."

Ultimately, Johnny overwhelmed DD's effort and neatly finished the job in about a half hour.

"You still bleed these guys in the field, don't you?"

Johnny leaned against the stall, patting the whitetail's exposed meat.

"Yeah" DD replied as he walked out into the daylight, "white man squeemishness, I guess."

"Wasted food," grumbled Johnny, as he joined DD for the snowy walk to the house.

Moonshadow had prepared gravy from onions and hog fat cooked with her own bird sausage, a mixture of meat and blood from quail, duck, pheasant, and chukar. This over buttermilk biscuits and scrambled eggs made a hearty breakfast – a mainstay around Mick O'Neil's.

The old man came through the door from the stairway. "Mornin' folks! Lena, you notice that kid of mine still rises early and gets going, always did."

Mick's patter was soft, with more than a hint of West Irish brogue. His thick hair was black but generously striped with gray and white. Nothing of his hard life dulled his blue eyes; they virtually flashed with energy and wit. Through an impish smile, he looked at DD

"Ah see you stumbled across that buck I tied up for ye last night! Was it a struggle, son?"

Without interrupting the loading of his plate with Moonshadow's fixings, DD smiled and replied, "Da, that one got away for lack of a decent knot. This one I had to chase down on foot and bash it with the butt of me rifle – bein' out of bullets and all."

Moonshadow squealed in laughter. Johnny chuckled quietly and Mick smiled broadly:

"Well then, ye didn't spoil the meat, did ye?"

Mick then turned to business. "Preston's gotta get that damn dapple out of here. She's fine, she's shoed, and she is eating us out of all our feed. The sonofabitch probably won't be able to pay me everything he owes me and now I gotta fix his horse trailer so he can pick her up. That's first on the list today, son. Wanna help?" There wasn't a hint of rancor in any of this, and Mick was speaking as if he were in a library.

"Sure," DD anxiously replied, "but I've been away for a long time."

"Well," the old man sighed as they headed for the shop, "you can be a holder."

Mick was still bigger than DD – probably four inches taller and forty pounds heavier. Certainly, much of that weight was the consequence of metabolic changes occasioned by age, but Mick was always big and heavily muscled. Father and son were similarly freckled on pale skin and both sported ample hindquarters.

Mick removed his bright, clean, white flannel shirt and carefully hung it behind a door of a closet intended to be free of smoke and dust from the fired iron. He donned a leather apron over his black undershirt and set to stir the fire. He turned suddenly and grabbed the rear door of Preston's horse trailer and with one hand held it up for DD to take. Once it was in DD's grasp he removed the hinge and rod with one move and gestured to DD to put the door down for now.

The hinge Mick had made the night before had cooled and now he hammered out the couplets that would secure it. Preston's trailer would be ready to go in two hours and the dappled grey mare on her way to be fed elsewhere.

As the last couplet lay cooling, Mick wiped his blackened and sweating face to look at his son. "Not a clean way to make a living, but cleaner than most, don't you think?"

He turned to hang the tongs and drop the hammers in the bucket.

"I suppose that's what happened, isn't it? A blacksmith's son gone to the City and the City wouldn't bend; is that it?"

At the sink in the closet, Mick washed and scrubbed.

"Someone named Vincent Muzio telephoned whilst you were chasin' down that whitetail this mornin'. Says you should call him at 11 this morning, San Francisco time."

"Judge Muzio, what's up?"

"Well, I just want to know if you're coming back anytime soon. A friend of mine has a problem that will likely require a trial. I recommended you and told him I'd ask you. Could be an answer, right now, DD – it's a business case and he can pay your fee."

"Jesus, I don't know your honor. Does the guy know I just lost a big case?"

"DD, f'crissake, no one expects any lawyer to win all his cases. This guy needs a good trial lawyer. That's what you are and you should do it and quit feeling sorry for yourself."

He was right, DD thought. I've got to get these bills paid and I've got to keep going. If this client could pay fees....

"You're right Judge. I've been fooling myself. The next plane out of Butte is on Wednesday afternoon. I won't get back until very late Wednesday out of Salt Lake. I'll see you Thursday. Thanks...as usual."

Vincent Alphonso Muzio was a senior judge of the United States District Court for the Northern District of

California. A native San Franciscan, he was widely respected as a trial lawyer and judge throughout the City. He presided over two trials of Joe Cleary and Dan O'Neil and befriended them as they built their reputations.

The Judge was right. The client needed a trial lawyer and he was both willing and able to pay one.

Slowly, DD worked his way out of his crushing debt. Within a few months, he was broke again, although not nearly as much in debt.

Feeling foolish was not something that Daniel Dermot O'Neil was used to. Yet, after the Pavlone verdict and the divorce from Melanie Langley, he felt foolish. The swagger that was so characteristic had not gone away, certainly, but the self-confidence was eroding, even with the improvement in fortune.

Six months being married to the "drop-dead" gorgeous Melanie Langley were miserable. She and DD never really got on the same page except in the frequent and often long sexual sessions. An heiress to an insurance fortune, Melanie had become an apparent hippie and was frequently seen at so-called radical political rallies – particularly anti-Vietnam War gatherings. When she showed up as the owner's agent when DD was looking for a place to live on Telegraph Hill, the deal was probably sealed.

But Melanie Langley was her father's daughter, and he was a long-scheming insurance executive without a whit of social consciousness. Melanie was fascinated by the insurance business and pursued her career in it with a perverse glee.

Ultimately, neither Melanie nor Robert Langley approved of DD's take on the legal profession, and that was what led to the sudden and complete break-up of the couple. Melanie had never been rejected by a man in her life. When DD announced he wanted a divorce she couldn't believe it. Then, when it became real with the service of the divorce papers she announced to him and anyone who would listen that "he isn't getting a dime of Langley money!" The suggestion was that was the whole reason for the divorce. It was a while before it occurred to Melanie that – if that were true – it was also the reason for the marriage in the first place. Of course, DD's petition to dissolve the marriage specifically asked for nothing from her and offered her nothing. Bitter pills for the self-centered beauty to swallow.

***

CHAPTER THREE

1983–Mississippi Calling

"Someone named Glen Allen McNaught of Indian County Mississippi for you."

Jeannie's tone revealed this was another call that held no particular prospect of income or challenge.

"What's it about?" DD responded with only vague interest – unwilling to interrupt what might be a fruitful foray among volumes of Federal court decisions.

"Wouldn't say. He got your name right. Insisted on speaking with Daniel D. O'Neil"

Giving up, he marked the page, closed the volume and picked up the telephone.

"Dan O'Neil."

A deep voiced drawl came over the line.

"Mistah O'Neil, I am the older brother of Ella Mae White."

The name was one that DD seemed to recognize, but could not bring it to mind.

"Ella Mae," McNaught continued, "died here las' week and I got this package with your name and the like, hand wrote by Ella Mae. We, that is, her sisters and me and Norrie Nash, the pastor, want to know what to do with it."

Still not able to bring the woman to mind, DD said, "I don't believe I know Ms. White"

As soon as he uttered those words, he realized in fact he did recall Ella Mae White.

She had not immediately caught his attention when meeting the eighty-three prospective jurors dispatched to Department 12 of the San Francisco Superior Court three years earlier. It was not that Ella Mae was ordinary. She was buxom, with a creamy light chocolate-colored complexion and flashing green eyes. Her bearing was one of command and determination.

But, she was among an eclectic assembly of local citizenry, so there simply was no ordinariness. The mix was startling to the eye and ear. Cantonese, Mandarin, Tagalog, street jive, Mexican, Salvadoran, Harvard, Berkeley, Stanford, and New College. The wide range of styles, combinations of sexual orientation and wealth, along with the diversity of races, always made DD wonder how such a small place as San Francisco could be so accommodating.

When DD was playing the great roulette wheel called jury selection, Ella Mae White first made her appearance in his consciousness – a tall woman, seemingly resolute and, at the same time, melancholy. To the point where she was called as a potential alternate juror, the box was occupied by some pretty weak people. Every potential leader and every engineer had been excused peremptorily by Keislor.

Of note was a small black man, maybe forty-years old, expressing himself in street jive and clearly "of the street" – Reginald Renfro, seated as juror number four. He gave his address in the Tenderloin. DD waited for Keislor to challenge him, but strangely, he never did.

When DD entered the courtroom the morning after he had delivered his opening statement he found Drucinda Lacey and Darla Reid of defense counsel's staff arranging exhibits for Keislor's opening statement. Keislor himself was oddly calm and seemingly with nothing to do. The appointed hour arrived and Mr. Renfro had not – the seat for juror number four was empty. Fifteen minutes passed. Judge Rowland appeared from his chambers unannounced and hailed counsel to join him behind closed doors.

"I don't know why the hell you two let this guy stay on the jury. Couldn't you tell this would likely be the result?"

The judge was miffed.

" I'm going to have Jerry go over to his hotel and see if he can find the guy. It's only ten minutes away. In the meantime, I'll release the jury to return in an hour."

Jerry, the Judge's horribly overweight bailiff, hustled off through the swinging doors of the courtroom. DD grabbed his first witness in the hallway and told him what was happening, making sure he hung around. Keislor, usually a flurry of kinetic energy, sat quietly at counsel table not saying a word to his staff .

DD could hear the telephone ring in the Judge's chambers about a half hour after Jerry left. He heard the judge talking, but could not hear what was said. A few minutes passed and the judge appeared at the door to his chambers, once again hailing counsel.

"Gentlemen, I am afraid that Mr. Renfro is dead. He was found when Jerry asked the hotel management to look in on him. Although we are a long way from knowing the cause of death, Jerry says it looks as if he overdosed on heroin."

DD had no choice, it seemed, unless he wanted to wait another two and possibly three months to try the case. He had run out of money. Judith would likely not receive any more disability benefits, and who knew what havoc such a delay would cause the case he had put together.

"Let's go with one alternate and try like hell to keep the thing moving so we don't lose him," DD finally conceded.

Thus, Ella Mae was on the jury in 1979.

"We kinda figured, you being a lawyer, that maybe you knew about this lawsuit where Ella Mae got the money."

"She had a lawsuit?"

DD did not remember that Ella Mae had reported that when she was being questioned during jury selection.

McNaught continued, "Well, that's what she said. I couldn't figure it out myself because those things usually take a long time. She said that she had sued her boss, but never explained what it was about."

"Mr. McNaught, I think your sister was on a jury in a case where I was the lawyer back in 1979. But I can't imagine why she would address anything to me."

"Well, Mistah O'Neil, we don't know either, but the thing is there's a whole lot of questions about Ella Mae. And it may be that none of this is really our business, but there is this envelope and it may have some answers."

Having spent three years trying to forget the <u>Pavlone</u> case, DD was completely convinced there could be nothing relevant to him in this envelope/Ella Mae White business. He started to tell McNaught he couldn't help when the agony of the jury's verdict came rushing into his belly, along with the incomprehensible fact that this seemingly open and generous woman was the forewoman of the jury that rendered that verdict.

McNaught continued, "When Ella Mae was out there in San Francisco, she'd send us letters from time to time. I remember she told us she was the executive secretary to the president of some technical company. I always thought Ella Mae was smart."

"How long was she out here?" DD interjected.

"Hard to say." McNaught was struggling to remember. "She left here in about 1970 when she was 28 years old and went to N'Orleans."

There was a melancholy about McNaught's report of his dead sister's history, or what he knew of it.

"When she did that, she left her boy, Donald, with our mother. I think he was about twelve years old at the time. Then we didn't hear from her for some time."

Beginning to feel like an intruder, O'Neil tried to cut off the revelations.

"Did she ever mention my name since she returned to...where is that in Mississippi?"

"Indian County, just northwest of Jackson," McNaught patiently supplied. "No she never did, but then she never talked much about her time in San Francisco and neither would Malvina."

DD didn't want to know but felt expected to ask, "Who's Malvina?"

McNaught cleared his throat, a seemingly stage-clearing.

"Ella Mae's friend, she brought from San Francisco."

He would say no more, but DD felt there definitely was more.

"Mr. McNaught, I really don't know why Ella Mae would write to me, but why not just send me the letter and I'll open it?"

"Maybe..."

McNaught's tone and cadence was suddenly less soft and more aggressive,

"I haven't made myself clear, Mr. O'Neil. I'm not just Ella Mae's brother, I am the sheriff of Indian County. We could probably open this envelope without your permission, legally, that is. But we really don't feel that 's right and, I think I need you to explain the contents as part of my murder investigation."

**

CHAPTER FOUR

Welcome Back to Mississippi

This was DD's second trip to Mississippi. The first was in 1963 under the auspices of the Student Nonviolent Coordinating Committee. No one understood why he made that trip and he didn't really understand why he was making this one. At least this time he was flying to Memphis, rather than struggling to keep a 1954 Plymouth on the road from Seattle. Maybe while he was here, he could look up a couple old buddies from those days.

Things must have changed pretty dramatically in Mississippi. No one in 1963 could have imagined a black sheriff. In fact, blacks weren't even allowed to vote back then.

Aside from musing over the ironies of history, DD pondered what McNaught had said. It wasn't an envelope with a letter; it was a package weighing "a couple pounds." Ella Mae had built one of the largest houses in the county. She was found dead in it – a hole in her forehead made by a bullet from a small caliber firearm. Nothing in the house had been disturbed, that is nothing except Ella Mae's forehead. Whether anything had been stolen had not yet been determined.

In one sense DD's curiosity motivated him. Probably more importantly, he got a whiff of the possibility of vindication for Pavlone. Either way, DD's compulsive personality would propel him headlong.

Nevertheless, there was little that this trip could do for his financial problems. He certainly couldn't afford its expense, let alone being away from the office. Ironically, he was as broke as he had been the first time he came to Mississippi.

Jeanie had rented the car for him, using her credit card. Jean A. Jureau's loyalty was undaunted but frequently strained over the seven years she had worked for DD. In all the tough times of late, she remained DD's friend – critical, but dedicated. She was mad as hell about this trip, but had committed her credit card to the plane fare and the car. Rick had loaned him $500; had insisted on it.

South from Memphis on the interstate, one is quickly out of the sprawling urban sameness that makes virtually every American city look like every other. Northern Mississippi's rolling hills spreads before the traveler – thinly wooded with slender pines. Here and there DD could see scattered farm buildings that disappeared as the highway split a swamp of lily pads and dead trees.

Having identified the exit from McNaught's directions, DD followed it under the interstate and headed east to the Indian County seat of Magnolia City. The road was narrow and not well maintained. It twisted through the low hills covered with cotton crops and past wide, dusty spots where country stores squatted under worn and rusted Coca-Cola or Dr. Pepper signs. Around one only blacks could be seen. Around the next, only whites. Maybe, DD thought, Mississippi hadn't changed all that much.

On the other hand, as one approaches Magnolia City, smoke stacks appear – paper mills and other industrial operations can be seen as one enters the mid-size town. There are a couple of new housing tracts just to the north – the town was growing and modernizing, but there were still the farm trucks on the main thoroughfares, and cotton enterprises from gins to warehouses.

Nearer the center of town, the streets were tree lined. The houses were mostly brick with neatly-painted window frames and well-trimmed yards. It appeared to DD many of these homes were occupied by blacks. DD doubted that was true back in 1963.

It was mid-afternoon and hot as DD drove into town looking for the building that housed the sheriff's office. There were very few people on the street, but it turned out that one of them was Sheriff Glen McNaught. He was tall, slim, and dark skinned – clothed in a crisply pressed tan uniform, topped by a broad-brimmed hat and seemingly impervious to the heat and humidity.

27

"Mistah O'Neil."

McNaught emphasized the "O" as he stepped up to the rental car and extended his big hand in greeting. DD shook the sheriff's hand and felt strangely welcome to Magnolia City. He followed McNaught into the building and the refreshingly cool sheriff's office.

"We got more than one surprise for you, Mistah O'Neil. C'mon back here."

They walked past a uniformed white officer sitting in front of what looked to be a radio communications console and into McNaught's large office.

"Son of a bitch! Is that you Sonny?"

DD's face lit up in delight as he embraced, and was embraced by, a muscular black man about DD's age dressed in a white linen suit and tie.

The man laughed. "It is indeed Didiyo, it is indeed."

In 1963, Sonny Elliott was assigned by SNCC with DD to establish a "freedom house" in Greendale, Mississippi, on the Mississippi River. Elliott was older than DD and had resigned from the Green Berets to return home and join the civil rights effort.

"What the hell are you doing here? How did you know I was coming?"

They both kept laughing and hugging.

"Man, don't you ever gain weight?," DD said. "Look at you, man, look my fat ass. Jesus it's good to see you."

Sonny was as overwhelmed as DD.

DD declared "Damn it, you answer my questions first. "

The mutual welcoming hilarity subsided and Sonny caught his breath:

"Didiyo, believe it or not, I am an assistant Attorney General for the State of Mississippi. Glen, here, told me about the envelope and I suggested that he call you without letting on that he knew me. I knew, you crazy Irish bastard, that you'd drop everything and come."

McNaught interrupted the reunion. "Mattie is on her way to supervise the openin' of the envelope; that is, if you don't mind openin' it with all these people around, Mistah O'Neil. "

DD turned to his old friend. "Sonny, what is going on here? Why is the State's Attorney General involved?"

"I don't know what's going on, Didiyo, not yet. What I know is that Ella Mae White was murdered in her house. We don't know who did it or why, but suspect that envelope, or at least its contents, just might help us along with the answers to those questions."

"Second," Sonny was mimicking the style he observed in DD many years before, "'the right thing' just doesn't jump out at you. There is no will that anyone knows about. I don't know that this envelope and its contents belong to you just because your name and address are on it or whether it is just part of the estate of the decedent. What I am suggesting is a compromise between those two possible legal niceties. You get to open the envelope and Mattie and G.A. get to share the surprise with you."

"G.A.?"

DD pointed to the sheriff and Sonny nodded in the affirmative.

"Mattie?"

"She's the Public Administrator for this county. Until the family gets around to having a court appoint one of them to handle the property, Mattie Deare is it."

DD shrugged.

"And DD," G.A.said pointedly, "there's a lot of money and property for my sisters and me to fight over."

DD shook his head and leaned on the desk behind him. "I can't figure that out. As far as I know, Ella Mae worked for secretary's wages. That couldn't be more than $40,000 a year. What amounts are we talking about here?"

"DD, I am going to tell you because I want to impress on you that we have a very strange murder case on our hands. We get murders, but not like this. So far as we can tell from looking just in local banks and Ella Mae's personal financial papers that we could find, she had more than $200,000 in investments – stocks, bonds. There is another approximately $200,000 plus in cash in each of two bank accounts. She paid cash for her house and cash for the Cadillac and the Porsche."

"Gentlemen, I understand you-all summoned me. Well, here I am."

Looking toward the door to the sheriff's inner office, DD felt a jolt in his loins when he saw what turned out to be Public Administrator Mattie Deare. She didn't exactly walk into the room. She floated on an erotic force field that addled the men.

G.A. cleared his throat and blushed a bit in fraternal bonding with Sonny and DD. "This here is Mattie Deare."

"And who might these distinguished gentlemen be, G.A.?" she sang as she removed her broad brimmed, ribboned hat. DD was transfixed. All he could think of was satin, lazily folded, smooth satin over secret places.

Bravely, G.A. took over, "This here is Sonny Elliott from the Attorney General's office down in Jackson. Over there is Daniel D. O'Neil from San Francisco."

"Tch, tch – very impressive."

She strode across the room to the window and her sarcasm flowed like warm molasses.

Mattie Deare probably toyed with men like this all the time. She was a fantasy of beauty. If she was black, she was very light skinned. If she was white, she was tawny. Her skin had an unreal tone and sense of softness to it. Her spaghetti strapped summer dress provided a substantial clue to the elegance of her breasts and that they were free of the usual foundational garment. Not tall, not short. Slim – not skinny.

After an exchange of knowing looks between Sonny and DD, each reached the unspoken conclusion that this was not what one would expect as a Public Administrator.

"So, Mistah O'Neil, you came all the way from San Francisco just to see what poor, miserable Ella Mae White left in that package with your name on it? Well, let's get to it. It will be interesting."

G.A. produced a locked steel box from his evidence locker. It was labeled "White, E.M., deceased June 16, 1982" With a key from the ring attached to his belt, G.A. opened the box and retrieved a large, brown envelope, closed with a heavy metal clasp. In addition to the clasp, the flap was taped and across the front in heavy black ink was written DD's name, office address and telephone number.

Sonny asked DD to open the envelope, which he did with a letter opener produced by Mattie. Glancing at the contents he dumped on the desk, it did not seem that any mystery was being solved, but, rather, that another was being created.

There were several sheets of photocopied bank checks – each made out to Ella Mae White in varying but large amounts, drawn on an account of what the printed checks said was "Structured Solutions" of Tahoe City, California. All were handwritten by what appeared to be the same person and all seemed to be signed by the same person, although none of the signatures were sufficiently legible to permit identification.

DD leafed through the many sheets, vaguely thinking that perhaps the amounts ought to be added up. Then he discovered a black and white photograph of several barely clad women who seemed to be in a hotel room sitting on or around a bed. In examining the picture, he identified Ella Mae, and, upon further scrutiny, he discovered what might have been Ella Mae's ace-in-the-hole.

Just as clearly as Ella Mae, one could see the face and slim body of Drucinda Lacey – the legal assistant to none other than Hugh Keislor, attorney and asshole-at-large. There were other faces in the picture that were more or less familiar to DD, but there was still another one that made it clear this picture was taken before the trial of the matter of Pavlone v LaStrada. The picture included the distinctive face and body of a San Francisco Superior Court deputy clerk, Laura McNeeley. She had committed suicide in the summer of 1979 – only a few weeks before the Pavlone trial had begun. DD was well aware of when Laura had died because he and Joe were long time friends of Laura, whose generous and open-hearted nature never bore the fruit of love by others. Both DD and Joe attended her memorial services and Joe provided a eulogy.

***

CHAPTER FIVE

Mississippi Light

Claudine McNaught had put together a fine dinner of baked ham, yams, and chard – the sort that anyone would expect in a rural southern home. Claudine's tall, slim body did not bear evidence that she had given birth to four boys.

G.A. and Claudine's youngest sat quietly across the table from DD, intensely interested in the adults' dinner conversation about the contents of Ella Mae's envelope. Not only was he significantly younger than his siblings, he was the first who didn't get a "Glen" variation as a name. Oliver had intense, dark brown eyes, and a plump, round face. His presence kept DD from sharing what he knew about the photograph from the envelope, but he was disinclined to share it anyway.

After dinner, the men adjourned to the porch with some fairly good brandy Sonny had brought from Jackson. The two old friends tried to catch up with one another while G.A. checked on the status of crime in Indian County.

Leaning back in the porch swing, taking in the chorus of crickets, night birds, and small town silence, DD looked with amusement at his friend:

"The last time I heard from you was when you decided to go to law school."

"I remember that." Sonny's drawl was faint. He spoke with a measured, rhythmic pace that barely revealed his southern origins. It was a way he discovered to avoid ridicule in the army and get him up the promotion line to a commission. He never said "y'all."

"You wrote me one of those preachy letters about law school and how terrible it was. There was something about how law facilitated the exploitation of the working class, particularly the black working class."

"I do tend to preach, don't I?," DD responded, "but I recall encouraging you to get your degree because of the superb irony of it all. I mean, wouldn't Carl Sweetwater have approved?"

They both broke out in loud, almost hysterical laughter.

Carl Sweetwater was the town marshal of Greendale, Mississippi, back in 1963. He was also the self-appointed chief red neck for miles around, and officially the head of the local Ku Klux Klan. By the time DD and Sonny had arrived in Greendale, Sweetwater and some fellow hooded heroes had taken to "night riding." The purpose of this exercise was to persuade local blacks it was best to stick to the "southern way."

The mission of Sonny, DD and Sonny's cousin, Tyrone Germane, did not get the approval of Marshal Sweetwater and his friends. Unfortunately for them, they gave chase one night to a 1954 Plymouth, thought to be carrying a white civil rights worker and a couple of radical niggers. Unfortunately, too, Sweetwater's big, two-door Pontiac caught up with the Plymouth and ran it into a recently-plowed field.

Before the Marshal and his gang could get out of the Pontiac, Sonny and Tyrone were on them and rendered each, one at a time, unconscious or worse with one or the other door on that very Pontiac. Their shotguns and superior numbers were rendered useless with the paucity of exits.

Sweetwater's enthusiasm for the southern way was cooled somewhat a day or two after he had limped back into Greendale, leaving the Pontiac stuck in that field. While still sporting a bandage around his head and badly bruised eye, the Marshal was interviewed by an agent of the Federal Bureau of Investigation. Over the course of the three hours Sweetwater spent with the agent, he was to learn that it was a federal crime to protect the southern way through force and violence or to arrest someone who resisted that sort of illegal conduct.

Sweetwater tried for years to figure out a way to get back at Sonny Elliott, but in the end Sonny graduated from law school. Sweetwater was shot to death when found in the bedroom of somebody else's wife without his badge on.

More laughter.

More reminiscing, a short discussion about DD's failed marriage, Sonny's successful one, and the vast difference between DD's professional path and that of Sonny.

Finally, Sonny stood up and looked sternly at DD. "Hey, buddy what the hell is this Ella Mae thing all about. I get the feeling you're not coming clean."

DD sighed and also stood up.

"I'm not sure I know. What I know is tough to explain."

DD's confusion was apparent to Sonny. So he took a shot at maybe clearing things up:

"This decedent was on this jury in a multi-million dollar case and that jury dumped you and your client. As a matter of fact, you told me the decedent was the jury foreperson. Now, she's been murdered – and murdered professionally. Before this happens she has prepared an envelope with your name and address on it and which contains copies of all these checks and a photograph. It seems to me she is trying to tell us who killed her. It also seems to me that she believed you would understand the message, or at least you have the information that makes the connection. But, you aren't telling us anything. Because I know you are one of the smartest guys I ever knew or will know, there is something you have to tell me."

"Sonny, I have this life long buddy, Joe Cleary. We share space back in San Francisco and he knows me better than anyone. He has told me a hundred times that I am too much of gambler for my own good. He says that I act on what I feel and don't think about caution. I think I'll heed his advice this time. What seems to be true is just too mind-boggling to accept. I can't say you're wrong about what it looks like. It looks like this woman was maybe bribed for her vote on that jury. I cannot figure out how that could happen. Sure, the lawyer and the defendant in that case are not hindered by any moral commitment that would preclude bribery. But the consequences of being caught are just horrendous. Even if you manage to bribe one person in a civil case, I don't see how you get what you paid for – it takes four votes on a civil jury to defeat the plaintiff. In this instance, the defense got a unanimous verdict. Even if there was a bribe and she somehow managed to deliver the defense verdict, you are forever at risk that the bribee may get religion. Keislor is too smart for that. All that makes little sense, but it really gets chaotic when people get shot in the head. Have you ever come across jury tampering before? "

In the spirit of two lawyers analyzing a set of facts, Sonny offered, "Well, yes. But that was a criminal case. There, to get a 'result' as you call it, all you need is to get one juror to hold out. We've seen this happen with some frequency. I agree this is way different and tough to get a handle on. But Ella Mae obviously thought you would get it. Then there is the oddity that she wasn't more explicit."

That was probably the strangest fact. Why was she so oblique? She didn't strike DD as the sort who would trust a man to figure it out, let alone a white man – an Irish lawyer.

"I'm going to bed," Sonny announced with finality. "I'll talk to you in the morning."

"Wait a minute," DD said urgently, "I can't hang around here. I have to get back to my office."

"C'mon DD, have someone shepherd that big case for awhile. We've got a murder case here and I need your help. You can't possibly need the money."

Sonny was pleading.

"Sit down, Sonny. Let me tell you about the private practice of law." DD was speaking softly and firmly. "I don't have a farthing right now. I have to go back and try to figure out a way to make some money so – come next month – I can pay my secretary, my rent, and my bar bill."

"Bullshit, DD. I've read about your multi-million dollar verdicts. I mean you're becoming legendary."

"Right," DD grinned, "but, as it's known among a small group of people, my spending, giving, and losses are also legendary. I live on the financial edge and have since the day I interviewed my first client."

DD was just as happy Sonny decided against more to drink. But then, his disclosure of impecuniousness tended to put a damper on further discussion. Funny how that works. He did not want to disclose it, but where others might have wanted to keep it a secret rather than risk losing esteem in the eye of an old fiend, DD didn't really care. One of the most interesting characteristics of DD that was repeatedly manifested in his life – he had no respect for money, his or anybody else's.

The next morning, lying in what was G.A's featherbed, DD realized he could hear the basso voice of G.A. on the other side of the wall. He could also smell coffee. Donning his usual sweats and running shoes, he found his way to the kitchen. Claudine was sitting serenely at the table with G.A. and Sonny was standing at the window.

"Mornin', DD."

She and G.A. had taken to DD's nickname after the relative intimacy of the previous evening's dinner.

"Sleep all right?"

"Wonderfully. I haven't been in a featherbed since I was fourteen. I didn't know 'til last night how much I missed it."

"Well, I worried about that. It's kind of a symbol of country poorness 'round here. Arlen wouldn't get rid of the damn thing. Sonny said you wouldn't mind, bein' a country boy yourself."

Claudine rose languidly and poured DD a cup of coffee.

Sonny, also wearing a sweat suit, more elegant than DD's, held his hand up and said, "hold the cup sister. Me and this white boy are gonna do a jogging tour of Magnolia City...unless of course he drank too much last night."

"Drink? You call that drinking?"

DD whacked Sonny on his ample ass and darted through the screen door onto the porch with Sonny right behind him.

The two men jogged up the tree-lined street through cool and fragrant air. The empty streets of the evening before were now peopled with farm workers, their trucks, and tractors. DD set the pace, which was obviously faster than Sonny was accustomed to.

"Y'know DD, Mississippi has not changed in one way."

Sonny was beginning to breathe heavily and droplets of sweat began to run over his dark brown forehead.

"It's still the poorest state in the Union."

They turned into the grass of the park at Magnolia's civic center and zig-zagged through willow and magnolia trees.

"Even so," Sonny continued, by now panting and sweating more, "I talked to Bud Barstow this morning. Got him out of bed. He drank more than both of us last night."

Barstow, DD remembered reading someplace, had been a Mississippi state trooper with a law degree and got himself elected the State's reform attorney general. His program was to reform the local and state police departments and, in particular, eliminate corrupt police officers and corrupt police hiring.

Sonny staggered to a stop, dropping his hands to his knees,

"Hold it, dammit. Jesus, you're in good shape!"

"Handball four times a week, but I hate to jog. This was your idea Mr. Elliott."

DD rarely passed up the chance to needle.

With his breath recovered and walking with DD back to the McNaught home, Sonny continued in earnest:

"We need some help on this. It's not that we don't get our share of murders, but this one is ominous. I came up here because Barstow sees this homicide as way too similar to a couple of other cases where we think a cop is the contract killer. That puts the case smack in the middle of my boss' police reform campaign. "

Claudine ordered the joggers to shower immediately. Once suitable for polite company, the two lawyers sat at the breakfast table with Claudine and G.A., who had just returned from an early morning check at his office. Over fresh watermelon, cantaloupe, cornbread, and coffee, Sonny made his pitch.

"Here's the deal. My office will hire you for some flat fee to work on this case. The State of Mississippi would be just another client of your shop, but with one big difference – we ain't payin' you your San Francisco hourly fee and there is no contingency fee."

DD was spreading a generous slab of butter on his cornbread, saying nothing, but knowing the proposition arose out of the revelations of the night before. His old buddy wanted to do him a favor.

"I have no way of telling what your services would be worth. What I can tell you is what we can afford to spend."

Sonny was arguing the point even though no one else had said anything.

"What we want you to do is, first, unburden yourself, now. I know you've figured out something. Second, you go back to California and put together whatever there is and give us a comprehensive report that can get us someone to indict."

G.A. had pushed his chair back from the table and crossed his legs. Silently, he watched DD's face for reaction, but, as usual DD did not oblige.

"For our part..." Sonny stared at his hands, then grabbed a checkered napkin to wipe them. He cleared his throat. "We'll pay you $15,000 – $5000 every other month for six months, starting with a $5000 check tomorrow morning."

With a slight smile, suppressing a larger one, DD, too, pushed back from the table, catching a long look at G.A.'s stern, unsmiling face with eyes fixed on him.

"I'm not sure what to say," he began slowly, looking at the ceiling and cracking his knuckles as he did. Then, looking back at Sonny, "You know I'd do this without getting paid. If somehow Barstow thinks that my being retained would give him control over what I do, you know that doesn't work. I pretty much do what I think is right – no matter what."

DD was being deliberate. There was a risk of insulting Sonny, and probably G.A., and there was no reason to do that. The money wasn't really very much, but representing the attorney general of the State of Mississippi was a very appealing idea because it was deliciously ironic.

"More coffee anyone?" Claudine offered, to break the now awkward silence.

Holding up his cup for a refill, DD looked at Sonny.

"You said something about this case being important to Barstow's anti-corruption campaign. What does that mean? "

"Well," G.A. said, standing up, "I think you lawyers should talk about this without me and Claudine. I don't want us called upon to testify about this some day."

He began clearing the table. Sonny and DD went to the porch.

"There's a deputy sheriff down in Delta County, LeRoy Praeger, who we suspect is a contract killer," Sonny reported quietly,

"A what?" DD was startled by the revelation.

"We think he kills people for money and, DD, this is as confidential as anything gets."

Sonny looked around to assure himself no one else was listening.

"A pretty well established extortionist was killed in Algiers, Louisiana, last year on a night Praeger had taken off from his regular watch as a deputy. The victim, a scum bag named Rostini, was shot with a small caliber bullet right in the middle of his forehead."

"Sonny, I'm no criminal investigator, but that is one hell of a stretch. There must be more. Do we know whether the bullet from Ella Mae matches the one they got from this guy in Algiers?"

Sonny was prepared. "We do, and they don't. But the New Orleans police got telephone records of another bad guy down there the chief suspect for buying the murder. Two weeks before Rostini takes his last breath, this bad guy calls Praeger's house by dialing an unlisted number and talks for twenty minutes. Two days before, the bad guy calls Praeger's number again, but this time he talks for less than two minutes."

With his arms folded across his chest and appearing slightly annoyed, DD says, "Christ, Sonny, that ain't much. I mean we might – and I mean might – have evidence of a motive to kill Ella Mae. But that "motive" is weak and the people who might have this weak motive are in Vera Cruz and San Francisco, none of whom have any known connections with professional hit men or people who could find them, let alone one in a podunk Mississippi sheriff's department, who has an unlisted telephone number."

Assuming a tutorial posture, Sonny leaned against the porch railing.

"See, DD, cop jobs in this state have, for a long time, been among the best available. They've become old-fashioned patronage – every mother wants her son to be a cop and believes the system ought to forgive and forget about runnin' moonshine or trying to get into Betty Lou's pants over her objection. For the most part, the people who get hired aren't criminals, they just aren't very good cops. We're installing a police academy and trying to get legislation to require every cop and deputy to attend and pass that academy, but there's enormous resistance. There are law enforcement agencies in Mississippi that have frequently arrested and convicted people who were totally innocent. The annual number of deaths of people in law enforcement custody, not attributable to other detainees, is fifty. At the same time, it just doesn't take that much for someone to bribe their way out of prosecution for serious crimes. It's a mess and fixing it goes to shit if we can't nail a guy like Praeger and the people who pay him. "

DD smiled.

"Wait 'til I tell my secretary who our new client is."

He headed for the telephone in the house.

***

CHAPTER SIX

Mississippi Mystery

Jeannie wasn't all that excited about news of the new client, although she was happy to hear about the money coming in. The rent was long ago due – hers and DD's office. She had her own news that portended more substantial money. Buster Levy had called to say that he wanted to talk about settling the Reynaldo case.

"It's about time," DD responded, "but I bet he'll only offer a buck ninety-eight."

"Just call the guy, DD. Luis needs the money, you need the money, and Levy wants to give you some."

Jeannie had heard this from DD before. He really doesn't like to settle cases. He'd prefer to try them. He reluctantly agreed to call Levy.

"Buster, you sweetheart. Jeannie tells me you can't figure out how to gouge your client any more and you want to settle the Reynaldo case."

DD could never resist needling Levy, a nitpicking, sweaty little guy who rushed around throwing insults and threats at plaintiff lawyers, except in court, when his nasty disposition turned to sickening obsequiousness.

"Fuck you, O'Neil,"

He always talked that way on the phone, or just as he was getting on an elevator and DD wasn't.

"I got $350,000 and I seriously suggest you take it. If it were up to me, there wouldn't be a dime. The insurer's examiner has no balls."

DD waited a moment before replying, suspecting that Levy's continued breathing was dependent on his response to this offer.

"Let's see, Buster, you want to pay me and my client $350,000 when we're one month from trial. You know that Luis' medicals are $200,000, his wage loss is $110,000 and he has a permanent disability."

DD knew this one was on the way to being wrapped up.

"O'Neil, you kill me. Your guy has a permanent disability like my wife has a permanent injury. He has headaches once in awhile and my wife has them once a month."

Thinking the devil is making me do this, DD observed, "And if you got a hard-on more often than that, I bet her headaches would be more frequent."

"Are you interested in this or are we going to play dozens?" Levy definitely wanted to get this over with.

"Tell you what Buster, you pay Luis and me $600,000 and we have a deal – if the check is in my hands in ten days."

"Where are you O'Neil? I'll have to call you back if I get ahold of my client."

Yeah, DD thought, the one with no balls.

"I'm with Beth of course."

DD couldn't resist bringing Levy's wife back into the conversation, "so when should I call you? I don't want Beth embarrassed."

Levy sighed. "Make it at four."

"Pep, please."

Five Havanas a day for forty years had left Pep's voice sounding like slurried gravel and his Brooklyn origins seemed like one was listening to the track of a Thirties "B" movie. The best private investigator in the West, Lyle "Pep" Lippman was Joe's close friend and had been working with both DD and Joe since they started in San Francisco.

"Danny boy, where you been? Haven't seen you, even at Tony's"

"I'm in Mississippi, Pep. I'll explain when I get home."

"Danny, didn't you get run out of there some years back? Are you in trouble again?"

"Pep, I need some work done. There's a new client and this isn't exactly a mainstream case."

"Ok, what's the case name?"

Pep was always careful to keep his billing records straight.

Hesitating, DD finally told Pep to call the case "Barstow."

"Whatcha need and when?"

This was an often-used phrase of Lippman. Every time DD heard it he thought of those Flatbush refrigerator salesmen described in some Roth novel with their huge stogies and rhinestone pinkie rings.

"There's an outfit I need a solid line on – basically everything you can get. In particular, I will need the names of the principals and customers. It's called Structured Resolutions, Inc., PO Box 1975, Tahoe City, California. The telephone number is (916) 451-9002."

"What'd they do?"

"I don't know yet. This is pretty open-ended right now. But I need whatever you can get by Thursday night. I am coming in late afternoon, so I'll meet you at the Double Play around 6:30."

"You got it." Lippman said cheerily.

DD felt like he just bought a new Amana, double-door with an ice machine.

"I talked to Buster the shithead." DD reported to Jeannie.

"Well?"

"I told him $600,000 and think they will come across. I have to call him in forty-five minutes. There are some things I need you to do on this Mississippi thing. In the Pavlone case, I had Keislor's opening statement transcribed. Sometimes that includes the last part of the jury *voir dire.* Will you see if you can locate the questioning of Ella Mae White? "

"I already did that."

DD half expected that Jeannie was way ahead of him.

"What do you want to know?"

"Did she say anything in answer to the question about whether she had ever been involved in a lawsuit?"

"Hold on." Jeannie could be heard rustling papers. "Here are her exact words, 'Oh my, no. I'm afraid a lawsuit is not something I would have the courage to try and, of course, I have never hurt anyone, so I have never been sued.' She goes on to say she is not aware of any relative or close friend who has been involved in a lawsuit."

"Who did she say she was working for?"

"Just a minute." Jeannie turned more pages. "Jones and Yamaguchi. She says they develop computer graphics for the printing industry and she's the executive secretary to Norman Yamaguchi."

No lawsuit. No connection to Structured Resolutions. DD thought for a moment, then got back to Jeannie.

"Tell Joe and Rick I need to meet with them Thursday night at the Double Play about 6:30. Tell them about the new client. They'll shit."

DD and Sonny took DD's rental car to G.A.'s office, where DD called Levy on the Reynaldo case. Levy agreed to the $600,000 and agreed to send an unconditional letter confirming that agreement. DD didn't tell Sonny about it.

The house just north of Magnolia looked like someone's fantasy mansion – someone raised poor and black in the heart of Dixie. It sat conspicuously on a low hill, displaying its antebellum columns and portico. It was approached by way of a circular driveway, inside of which was a broad, green lawn and pond decorated by nineteenth century statuary – a couple cherubs under a willow peeing into the water through plump, uncircumsized peckers.

To the right of the house, the paved drive continued as a brick way directly into the three garages, over which appeared to be living quarters. Two garage doors were open and one could see the back of a new Cadillac in one and a Porsche 911 in the other. On both sides of the ornate front door were French windows with dressing that could easily have come off the set of *Gone With the Wind.* Ella Mae had built this house to turn her world on its head.

Inside, there was more of a modern look, although the entryway floor was tiled marble. The staircase did not spiral nor swoop, but its balustrade was at least as ornate as Tara's. To the left side of the entry hall was a large single – not double – door of obvious contemporary design and construction. The yellow barrier tape used by G.A.'s deputies was still across the doorway. DD removed it and he and Sonny walked through.

This was, supposedly, the library. The "books," however, were those decorative volumes one buys by the yard with seeming leather bindings. There were two soft leather love seats facing each other over a large, low glass table. Between the love seats was a high-backed leather chair on which there was a small, dark stain in the middle of the headrest – silent testimony to the place at which Ella Mae's life was ended.

G.A. entered the library from outside where he was once again inspecting the garage area.

"Where was the package with my name on it, G.A?"

The sheriff walked over to a table with an ornate lamp on it and opened its drawer.

"Here. It was the only thing in the drawer except a blank writing tablet and an expensive roller ball pen."

As DD surveyed the room, he realized how stark it was. Two of the walls were French windows and doors that opened to the front or back porticos. But there were no pictures on the other two walls and nothing really that indicated the room had been "lived" in. It resembled a furniture show room, and, perhaps, that is what it really was. Within an arm's reach of the death chair on that same table as the lamp was a telephone.

"I suppose there was no telephone call for help the night she was shot," DD mused out loud.

"That's right."

"What about telephone toll records? Have we secured them? Has anyone looked at them?"

DD had learned early on the value of telephone toll record as evidence.

"The most recent bill was in the mail on the desk in the bedroom; there's a record of calls from last month. The telephone company will give us the last six months, all they have, in a day or two."

Sonny was standing across the room staring into a wall safe behind the faux books. It was empty, as it had been the first time he saw it two days before. Lost in some thought, he finally sighed and turned to DD. "There were two long distance calls, each one to a bank where we found that Ella Mae had money on deposit. People at both banks verified that Ella Mae had called them on routine matters, like the balance in one account and renewing a certificate of deposit for the other. Ordinary stuff."

Hands thrust in his pants pockets and a look of dismay on his face, Sonny also reported, "there was also a call to the Porsche dealer in New Orleans. I checked that out and discovered she was inquiring about a new Porsche."

"So..."

G.A. was standing next to Sonny and facing DD.

"There's really nothing to indicate that Ella Mae thought she was going to die, that she was being threatened or anything out of the ordinary."

He walked over to the windows that opened onto the front of the house and peered out.

"Ya'gotta understand one thing, DD."

The melancholy DD detected his first telephone conversation with G.A. returned.

"Ella Mae was not a happy woman – in spite of this money and things. After she returned home, she would not look at people she was talking to. She would drive by to see her sisters or me, but after the first week she had this house, she never invited any of us over and never accepted invitations from us. For a while, she went to church and made a big donation – so big that Norrie Nash damn near had apoplexy. But everyone figured that was to get our mom re-buried with a fancy tombstone, and to get the blessing of the church to allow her to have a new tombstone in a proper grave for Donald."

DD held his hands up. "Who's Donald?"

"Her son."

DD then remembered the mention in the first telephone conversation.

"How did he die?"

"Meningitis – developed after his head was broken when the fan off an old truck he was fixin' flew off and hit it. That was in 1978, he was sixteen years old."

DD stared at the high backed death chair.

"So, Ella Mae gets this house built, buys a couple of cars, makes big donations to the church, re-buries her mother and son and stays alone."

"Oh, she didn't stay alone, Mr. O'Neil. In fact, that may be the point." Mattie Deare had entered the library with two older women in tow.

"Mattie," the heavier of the two women said sternly, "that ain't got nothin' to do with the terrible death of our sister. I don't want you spoutin' off so's people think badly of Ella Mae – at least worse than they already do."

"Gentlemen," Mattie responded and grinned, "this Aunt Jemima is Olivia McNaught Meadows, and over there is Maude McNaught."

Both women offered a nod toward Sonny and DD, said "Pleased," but looked away and around the room.

"The sisters" as G.A. called them, were older than he and Ella Mae. Maude had left Magnolia with a soldier stationed nearby and lived with him in Chicago for a few years. He left her and she returned home where she had lived as a spinster ever since.

Olivia had never left Magnolia City, except two or three trips to Memphis and twice to New Orleans. She had married a dentist shortly after he moved to town. They had five children, in spite of the fact that Olivia was a whirlwind of local political activity. She was a fast-talking, quick-thinking, aggressive woman who was the driving force behind the election of her brother as the sheriff of Indian County. Now she was greedily eyeing this big house, imagining where she was going to put what when the estate matter was settled. She was, after all, the eldest of the decedent's siblings.

She turned to Mattie. "Y'know, Miss Public Administrator, we got Orland Casey to get this estate thing put together. That means y'all won't really have much to do very soon. It also means we won't have to put up with your vampin' ways much longer."

Mattie smiled, cocked her head, and gave a slight sideways thrust with her hip.

"Miss Olivia, you are just frothing to get your hands on poor Ella Mae's house, ain't you? Anyway, I have enough to do without worryin' about the White estate. But, before you go measuring the place for your new curtains, I think you better have your Mr. Casey look into the whereabouts of one Charles White – the former and probably still legal husband of your beloved but dead sister."

Olivia, maybe in her mid-fifties, had very little gray in her hair, which was drawn back tightly into a bun and fixed in place with a long, plastic hairpin. She looked startled at Mattie's suggestion of a competing heir to Ella Mae's bounty.

"Are you sayin' you know somethin' about Charlie, or are you just bein' your old needlin' self?"

This was clearly a sore point for Olivia.

"Miss Olivia, I suggest you take that up with your lawyer."

Mattie walked out of the room, through a French door and into the new garden at the back of the house.

The subject of inheritance continued to occupy the sisters and, involuntarily, G.A., while Sonny and DD explored the rest of the house. The kitchen looked like something one would see featured in *Sunset Magazine*, but didn't appear used much, nor usable. In a drawer was a neatly paper-clipped bundle of receipts from a local grocer and a dairy that delivered. The kitchen had every imaginable utensil and appliance, some of which DD couldn't identify. There were two complete sets of dinnerware, one probably for formal events that Ella Mae never convened.

DD also took note of an apparent electronic box mounted on the wall at the entrance to the kitchen from the back hall.

There were three small lights on it and what appeared to be a speaker. Remembering that he saw the same type box in the front hall way and the library, DD concluded it was part of an alarm system.

"How does this alarm system work, G.A.?"

The sheriff had escaped Olivia's boundless distress over Mattie's disclosure.

"Well, it's kinda complicated. First, all the doors and windows are wired. If there is any break in the connection after it's been set, these boxes announce that with a chime. Then, Ella Mae, or whomever, can push this button and that telephones my office. This button calls the county fire department. Whichever is activated, the patrol car or the fire engine is on the way. The connection remains open while Ella Mae, through this speaker, explains what is going on. If she says nothing, they come anyway. There is a box like this in every room in the house, including the master bathroom."

"So, when the body was found, was this alarm set?"

G.A sighed. "Yes."

"Who found the body?"

"Well, that takes some explanation. There was a call to my office from someone on the 911 line. That could have been through this system. Our people say there was a communication from either a woman with a deep voice or a man with a 'shallow' one. The message was that there may have been a murder at this address. We have the tape. My deputies were here a few seconds after four minutes from the time the call came in. The lights were on but no one answered the door. We patched through an attempt to call Ella Mae on the telephone, but there was no answer. The deputies broke through the French door there on the north side of the main entrance. When they entered the library they found her in that chair with blood all down her face and front. There was the hole in the forehead."

G.A. choked back a sob as the reality of his sister's murder rushed into his consciousness.

Mattie appeared at the kitchen's back door. "Is there anything I can do to help you gentlemen?"

DD tried to think of something just to keep her around.

"If not, I think I'd better get back downtown." She looked pointedly at DD and continued, "Please feel free to drop by my office if there is anything I can do to help."

DD managed to utter, "I certainly will."

Mattie strode through the kitchen and out the front door. All the men watched her all the way.

G.A. returned to his two sisters in the library. Sonny and DD found a sumptuous couch in what must have been the parlor and sat down – each with a yellow legal pad. Hands on his head, DD stared at the bare opposite wall.

"I want to hear the tape of the caller's voice. There's also the rest of the house to look at."

G.A. rejoined the two lawyers on the way up the staircase and they quietly inspected the second floor. There were three bedrooms. Two of those were pretty standard in terms of size and furnishings, but each had a large canopy bed. One of the canopies was stretched across a waterbed.

In the bedroom that DD guessed was that of Ella Mae, in addition to the large canopied bed, there was a small writing table and a hefty dresser, or "vanity," backed by an ornately bordered mirror. Both pieces were dark cherry wood, richly finished with inlaid leather. The writing table held nothing but a silver cup containing several black roller ball pens.

The closet was a walk-in affair and as large as a lot of bedrooms that DD had been in. There was a chest of drawers, on top of which were elaborately bejeweled boxes that contained jewelry – a lot of it. Neither DD nor Sonny were expert in such things, but the stuff appeared to be genuine and expensive. Inside the top of the largest such box was a brass inscription "E.M. to M.M., with love."

"Any idea about M.M.?"

"Well, there is a towel in the green bathroom next to the master bedroom with the monogram M.M.."

"Malvina?" he shrugged, suggesting 'who knows?'

In the very back of the huge closet was a set of matching leather luggage. None of it seemed to have ever been used. Inside the largest bag was a beat-up cardboard suitcase. It was the sort one uses to escape despair and find hope. In it was only a photograph of a bright-eyed seven- or eight-year-old boy.

Back at G.A's office, the tape of the 911 caller was played several times.

"I think whoever that is was standing away from the speaker in a deliberate effort to disguise his or her voice." Sonny was confident.

DD didn't disagree, but did not know what that meant. Certainly it made no sense for Ella Mae to mislead who was calling. Why would Malvina try to hide her presence? The killer certainly would, but why would the killer even be talking at this point? Was Ella Mae already dead when the call was made?

"Other than what the deputies did, was there any evidence of a break-in anyplace in the house?"

DD was thinking hard, although admittedly, this wasn't his corner of the field.

"No," G.A. responded.

"What about evidence of a strange car in the drive way or footprints?"

Exasperated, G.A. supplied, "No evidence of a different tire track in the driveway or of footprints. This is brick, f'chrissake and it was dry and warm."

Finally, G.A. leaned on his desk with his hands supporting his chin and grimly, softly said, "There is something that bothers me."

He stood up and walked around his desk.

"Ella Mae provided a key to her front door when this alarm system was put in. She didn't want unnecessary breakage in response to an alarm. I hung it right here with all these other keys and lock combinations from around the county."

He opened a large metal door revealing about three-dozen hooks with addresses and keys or notes written on them.

"Here's the hook for Ella Mae's house – there is no key. It was gone when my deputy got the call and went to get it before he left."

Making sure he got it straight, DD asked, "So, conceivably, someone got that key, used it to gain entry into the house. The alarm system was on. It alerted Ella Mae or someone else in the house and the sheriff call button was pushed."

"Yeah."

"Any ideas?" Sonny asked.

"None."

"I'm going to run this by my friend Joe Cleary when I get home. This is his kind of puzzle. I'll call you with what he thinks. In the meantime, I have a stop to make before going back to Memphis."

The Public Administrator's office was in the back hallway of the County building and on the side opposite from the Sheriff's office. The sign on the door read "PUBLIC ADMINISTRATOR, MATHILDA DEARE."

DD was thinking he liked "Mattie" rather than Mathilda, but then maybe his feelings had nothing to do with a name. It was a small, if official, office. A very gray, slight older man with a pronounced limp rose from a desk as DD entered. "May I help you, sir?"

"Yes, I am here to see Ms. Deare. My name is Dan O'Neil."

The old man turned and stepped toward the back when Mattie appeared at the door of what must have been her office.

"Hello, Mr. O'Neil."

 She was smiling.

"I was hoping to see you before you left."

"Oh, why is that?" DD also smiled.

"Hmm, I'm not sure, but I do have something to tell you if you will be involved in figurin' out who did in Ella Mae."

"I am sure I will be."

"The information we have about what was in Ella Mae's estate comes largely from the banks and the contractor who built the house. I knew Ella Mae pretty well since she came back to Magnolia City and I am pretty sure there was some sort of diary. She was very orderly, so I can't imagine what happened to it."

"Why don't you see what you can do about finding whatever it is and then bring it to San Francisco. We can discuss it over a dinner or two."

"I will definitely redouble my efforts."

***

Part Two: Among Friends

Friendship is a commitment of respect and affection that survives crises through loyalty

Ricardo Esquivel, co-counsel and office mate

CHAPTER SEVEN

Stopping for Directions

A consummate moralist, DD was a picture of the ancient conflict between the spirit and the flesh. Catechism, taught by Father Timothy Fears at the insistence of his late mother, snuck through DD's consciousness in his day-to-day, late Twentieth-Century American life like a bad case of heartburn. The irritant was not because of his religiousness but because of his morality. He had long ago forsaken God or any notion of such a being – whether described as a force, a transcendental determinative, a spiritual presence, or little people.

Can the pursuit of Ella Mae's killer result in achieving justice? That became foremost in DD's mind. It could result in nothing and then all this time would be wasted – except for meeting Mattie. DD could not say that his most cherished fantasy was the exposure of Keislor as the vile, bigoted bully that he was. Many already knew that. Get him indicted, help convict him, and send him to prison? Justice may require that. DD chuckled as he poured crappy scotch from the little bottle the airline provided into the plastic cup. It could be fun.

It was nice to be home. Particularly because home was San Francisco.

Rick, DD, and Joe never partnered in the legal sense. They shared space in a small office building on Turk Street about fifty yards from the back door of the Federal District Courts. In various combinations they often worked cases together.

Rick continued to do some criminal law defense – most of that white-collar crime. He had, however, acquired a reputation as a plaintiff's lawyer in medical malpractice cases and he had helped DD try <u>Pavlone</u>. Joe had been otherwise involved when the case started and there was no way to catch up when trial time arrived. Joe was doing a lot of labor work for certain unions. DD seemed to always be in trial or getting ready for trial – head down and charging ahead.

The matters DD and Joe handled through their years together became woven into the tapestry of San Francisco jurisprudence. They were good friends, colleagues, and buddies. The communications between them were easy, casual and, for the most part, clear.

"Jesus, lawyer for the attorney general of fucking Mississippi!"

Rick bared his near-perfect teeth and laughed a genuine, out-loud laugh.

"Shit, this is a dream, isn't it? I mean do we have Keislor by his perverted Prussian balls?"

They were in No. 9 Jones. This was one of the main watering holes for the Butte Twins (DD and Joe). It was a classic beer-and-shot place with a large, horseshoe bar and tables strewn almost randomly around its perimeter. It is also where Jaime ran the tables on one side of the bar.

DD motioned to Jaime for a drink, but not another one for Rick. In an insistent whisper, DD pleaded with Rick– "Jesus, Rick take it easy."

Rick's intoxication gave volume to his thoughts, washing caution through his kidneys.

"We don't need to alert Mrs. McGillicuddy," he said, a reference that came up in banter between DD and Joe that Rick had come to understand. Of course, there is not and never was any Mrs. McGillicuddy, but there might be.

"There are gaps – big ones – and there is a definite gap in the logic," DD said as he drew on his Powers, then screwed up his face to look at Rick through one eye. "It's clear that officials ought to take a look at Hugh the Hun. But there is absolutely no reason to run around saying that the scourge of truth and justice is about to be beheaded."

"Well," Rick loosened his silk Brooks Brothers tie even further, " let me ask you. Is the only 'official' investigation coming from your new client?"

Rick was drunk, but not nodding drunk – his prodigious, if cynical, intellect was relatively unimpaired for this subject.

"The official investigation is not of Keislor. The official investigation deals only with the murder of Ella Mae White. Keislor only comes up by stretching the evidence in that envelope back to her jury service in Pavlone. We can only do that because the envelope was addressed to me. The connection between Keislor and this murder is extremely tenuous and you and I have to keep it real secret."

"Do I get in on some of this fun?"

"Probably, but only informally. You've got criminal law experience and I don't have a lot, and you speak impeccable Spanish. I've got Pep working on some stuff; he's supposed to be here soon, as is Joe."

DD explained the fee arrangement with Sonny Elliott and asked Rick what he wanted to do about getting paid.

"I'll bill you"

They both knew that wouldn't happen.

Ricardo Jose Ruiz Esquivel was a genuine Mexican-American – by breeding, but not by upbring. Orphaned at age four when his farm worker parents were killed, Rick was rescued from the Archdiocese's boys' home in Fresno by William and Ruth Glazier. As is often true for the wealthy, the adoption proceedings were expedited, so that Rick's legal existence as a member of the Glazier household was a matter of record before he was five years old.

William Glazier was one of the wealthiest people in California until the early sixties. By then Ruth had died, Rick, the couple's only child, had completed his second year of college and Glazier had hung on to management of his financial affairs long past the time when he was competent to do so. Just before his death in 1965, Glazier told Rick the truth: he was Mexican by birth and his birth name was Esquivel. It was not a particular surprise because by that time it was becoming clear that Rick's towering stature, strikingly handsome face and black eyes matched none of the apparent traits of either Glazier parent.

Although he never was awarded an undergraduate degree, Rick was accepted to law school. Upon graduation, the San Francisco Democratic party enlisted him to run for a seat in the State Legislature. Having been unsuccessful in that endeavor, he nevertheless did discover the joys of zealous young women working political campaigns. For that reason, he never completely left politics.

Better than a good lawyer, Rick was always able to focus on the business at hand – particularly at a trial. He was doing well enough to make a comfortable living defending people accused of crime, until he realized how much justice could be done representing victims of medical malpractice.

Lyle "Pep" Lippman made his way from the front door, stopping and exchanging greetings with nearly everyone seated at the bar. A delightful small talk artist, Pep was always learning something new and probably, given his trade, useful, simply by asking "What's up?," "How've ya'been?" He was then and seemed always to be chewing on a big Havana, through which he told quick and often obscene stories.

Joe went to the Double Play that day and followed Pep through the front door. He knew some of the crowd at the bar, but not well enough to ask any if they were getting laid regularly, as Pep did.

Denise, a pretty little red headed waitress Joe especially liked, kissed him and told Pep, "Citriani wants to buy you a drink Pep. What'll it be?" Pep looked around the table, "A glass of that fancy Irish stuff O'Neil is drinking." Joe ordered the same.

When everyone had settled with a drink and a little small talk about DD's client was done, Pep pulled out a sheaf of folded papers.

"Structured Resolutions was incorporated ten years ago. Marlin Hanover and David Weisenstock were the incorporators. Marlin had an address of 142 Frederick, here in The City. I don't think he had a lawyer because he described the business of the corporation as, quote, 'developing and administrating the results of consensual resolutions.' close quote – too narrow," Pep authoritatively observed. He looked up at the lawyers at the table – all seemed to think Pep was right.

"What about the bank account?"

DD was impatient.

Like all virtuosos, however, Pep would not be side tracked. "Hanover lists his birth date as December 1, 1949 and gives a social that does not jibe. That number belongs to Lowell Weisenstock – one of my people."

Pep removed the cigar from his mouth long enough to sip some Powers and utter "Hmmm. Weisenstock has the same birth date as Hanover, same place of birth as Hanover – Los Angeles, and the same last name as the only other shareholder of Structured Resolutions – David Weisenstock of Wilshire Boulevard in the very same Los Angeles. I haven't run down David any further, as yet, but I think Lowell and David are related. That means that Hanover is an assumed name and I don't know why that is – yet."

Another sip of whiskey, another "hmmm," and Pep continued.

"Structured Resolutions has a Sierra County business license. The corporation rents a small office on Lake Tahoe Boulevard in Tahoe City, pays its business taxes, has a commercial permit, has no employees except Hanover and owns one 1978 Mercedes 400D, California license number 2GL5656."

A sip of Powers, a drag on the nearly expired Havana, and Lippman turned to a different piece of paper.

"The corporation maintains ten separate checking accounts – one they call 'Southern California Casualty.' All the others have what appear to be code names that I can't figure out. The number on the checks that you called me about is this 'Southern California Casualty'. That account has been opened for about three years, since December of 1979. It has had an average monthly balance of precisely $48,000 every month since then. That means that $48,000 went in every month and every month $48,000 went out."

DD opened the envelope with the copy of the checks he had brought back from Magnolia City. Laying them out on the table, he invited his companions to examine them, explaining what he had found out, but purposefully not mentioning the photograph that accompanied the checks. The four men, careful not to waste any whiskey, segregated the check copies by year and then month. Rick was not helpful in this endeavor and was heard to be giggling.

The amount of the checks varied. But when divided up this way it was clear that the total amount in any given month was $30,000. Upon realizing this, the group, except for Rick, pondered a moment and then DD asked Pep, "What about the other accounts?"

Pep's big finger ran down a sheet in his cigarless hand.

"Can't find out, at least not yet. I have these names but no account numbers."

"What do we know about this 'Southern California Casualty'?"

"Well, it exists. The Secretary of State lists its headquarters at the same address as David Weisenstock on Wilshire in Beverly Hills. It is incorporated, but not publicly held. David is the only shareholder and the State Insurance Agency has never had a complaint or an audit."

DD leaned back in his chair. When Denise came by he ordered fettucine Alfredo and prawns. "Throw some fresh peas on top, will you please?"

Pep ordered the same. Denise looked at Rick,

"You're going to have to eat something. How about some minestrone? GiGi made it."

Closing Denise's hand in his and feigning a swoon, "Denise will you always take care of me? You know I need those kind of assurances."

Taking her hand back, Denise responded, "Fuck you Rick. Do you want the soup?"

Smiling, Rick brightened. "OK. With a glass of milk, please."

Joe begged off a meal and let it be known he was going home.

Over one more drink and while waiting for the meal, DD explained the details of the night of the murder, including the alarm system and the 911 call. Joe made notes and a sketch of what DD was saying.

Pep mused, "We could be talking three people in that house within minutes, if not seconds of the shooting. This roommate – Malvina? – the killer. and the victim. I mean the chimes ring when the circuit is broken. Someone has to decide what is going on and press the sheriff department call button. I don't know the time lapse between the chimes starting and the call button getting activated, but whoever caused the circuit interruption is not likely the person who summoned the sheriff. I think the same thing is true about whoever's voice told the sheriff operator about the murder."

Joe asked, "So why the muted voice in the call to the sheriff?"

"Don't know."

"This roommate was nowhere to be found when the sheriff showed and she hasn't been seen or heard from since. Right?"

Joe left while everyone was still eating, but deep in thought about what DD had said. Pep took Rick home and DD took a cab.

DD's Telegraph Hill flat was a great bachelor pad, only three blocks over the hill from Grant street and the jazz clubs where he could often be found sitting and quietly thumping out rhythms on a back table. Finding it was how he found Melanie, or, maybe more accurately, how she found him.

But she wasn't there any longer and DD was very relieved. Tonight her former presence wasn't even remembered. The face of a woman in Mississippi filled his reverie.

One of the remaining vestiges of his country raising was getting up and getting to work early. An hour and a half alone to deal with the details before anyone else did and before any new problems arose was a routine that DD and, now, Joe fell into and maintained to the day of this telling.

In those days DD and Joe assumed responsibility for the livelihood of three people in the office. Joe's secretary was Pat; DD's was Jeannie, and they shared the expense with Rick of Arty Schmulken.

Arty had attended law school at the same institution as Joe, but he never passed the bar exam. After three tries, he gave up and became a first class legal researcher. Arty was a hard-nosed lawyer and often kept DD's Lone Ranger tendencies in check. Slight in stature, Arty had an annoying habit of clearing his throat every two or three sentences. The affliction was likely related to his two packs a day of Lucky Strikes.

"Without looking at any books, my thought is that there is no cause of action for Judith against LaStrada or Keislor, even if you can prove Keislor or both of them bribed this dead woman."

DD was at his desk with Arty across from him – each drinking coffee and Arty smoking, flicking ashes into a self-made ashtray he carried around the office with him.

"You're right up against the 'final judgment' rule – I mean that is one of the hard-as-stone rules in the law. But, it is fraud. It probably has never happened before and if it did there probably has never been anyone sued for doing it in a civil trial. It will take a while. I'll probably have to cover the entire history of American jurisprudence – maybe English, as well."

Arty made some notes and sipped from a godawful looking ceramic cup which he had also made. "I think it's worth it. We could make some law, but more importantly we could get Judith a bag full of money. In the process we could wipe the floor with Keislor."

DD was making his way to the kitchen, then turned to Arty who was leaving DD's office.

"By the way, you're going to get a pay check. Reynaldo settled." Arty smiled and then snickered, "Levy folded again."

Arty never really ever laughed, never shouted or even spoke loudly – his peak emotion was expressed as a snicker.

"How much?"

"$600,000."

"Dan, that's a hell of a settlement after Levy repeatedly said it wouldn't settle and called you a shyster."

Arty had unabashed admiration for DD.

Singing and comically feigning a dance, Jeannie entered the office singing,

"Weeee're in the money, we're in the money..."

With a crooked smile appreciating Jeannie's humor, DD put on his suit coat.

"Yeah, until we pay the bills. But it's nice. Have you done the disbursement statement for Luis yet?"

"You're a killjoy O'Neil. I thought maybe Arty and I would take the afternoon off while you slave away in the courtroom.

"Better you get into the Pavlone files to see if you can find some of the other jurors."

***

CHAPTER EIGHT

California Crud

More than three years after the original trial, three Pavlone jurors were willing to talk to DD about the deliberations.

"We elected her forewoman because she asked us to. No one else wanted it. Then she explained over and over again that you just didn't provide enough evidence to prove the roof crush is what caused the injury."

Myra Waddington, a small woman who ran the Parkside branch of the public library, twisted her lace handkerchief with thin and spotted hands.

"I knew that someday I would have to face up to being railroaded by that...well, very assertive woman. I just couldn't stand up to her. I am just not very strong. That poor, crippled child should have won the case."

This was the third juror that DD had spoken to and the first white one. Only these three had been willing to talk to him, and none seemed to have much in the way of personal courage. Of the remaining nine, two had disappeared and the others just refused to talk to him. What was becoming very clear, Ella Mae was surprisingly assertive both in terms of becoming forewoman and in terms of defeating DD's case.

"You want this in a written report?" Pep was surprised. This wasn't the usual way DD or Joe worked.

"It's got to go to a State Attorney General. I am told he wants it in writing."

"So give me a day to get that done. I thought you'd like to know that Marlin Hanover is indeed Lowell Weisenstock. My guy went up to Tahoe City yesterday and dropped by the Structured Resolutions office. I had a mug shot from the SFPD and the photo Kenny got of the guy in the office matches."

"Why was there a San Francisco mug shot?"

"It's a pretty prodigious drug arrest record this guy has. Five possession busts in six years. The latest was 1979. There must have been one in LA because one possession charge started with a bust on an LA warrant. Hard stuff – speed, heroin and LSD."

"That's a strange mix, isn't it? Is he a dealer?" DD was taking notes.

"Nope," Pep replied confidently, "he was a user with a suicidal bent. He was in rehab at Vacaville for a year and came out to run Structured Resolutions. The guy's pretty much a ne'er do well. Graduated from UCLA in 1966. He was drafted and made an army grunt...sent off to 'Nam. Having survived that, he was discharged dishonorably for being pretty constantly under the influence. But, Structured Resolutions might be something. With the growing popularity of structuring settlements, and daddy being in the insurance business, Lowell might be on to something. Tough to tell, however. There's no regulatory reporting requirement and this isn't a publicly held company. Who knows?"

"So, who is David Weisenstock?" DD was becoming impatient.

"This guy does real well – financially speaking. He's in multiples of six figures year in and year out. The LA book has him as an insurance consultant, but he doesn't have a broker's license nor is he on any official insurance list. Informal inquiries suggest that the guy does business of some sort with some of America's least liked."

"Least liked?" DD didn't understand Pep's obliqueness sometimes.

"Organized criminals, Danny. You know, the chairmen of crippled children charities at the country club that have people killed for business?"

"Does that connect?"

"'Dunno, just 'dunno."

"There is something else that may well knock your jockeys to your knees."

"What?"

"There's a deed of this small mansion in Brentwood from David to himself and his bride, Darla Willingham."

"That's Darla Reid! That's her former name. That's Keislor's secretary, f'crissake!"

DD was unable to grasp what Pep had just told him.

Pep continued, "They married in Vegas back in 1980. By the way, this guy is now seventy five years old."

Joe was on the telephone when DD came rushing into his office after talking to Pep. He flopped down in Joe's client chair and waited until he finished.

"Do you remember Darla Reid? Keislor's secretary?"

The first time Joe ever encountered her was when she was pimping for lesbian and bi-sexual women. "Yeah. You know I do. What about it?"

"Do you remember that she was Keislor's secretary?"

He did.

DD opened an envelope and pulled out a print of a black and white photograph and laid it in front of Joe.

"Take a close look."

When Joe did, he could make out the faces of the woman that served as Keislor's legal assistant – he didn't remember her name – and Laura McNeeley.

"That's strange company for Laura, but what is the significance of this picture?"

DD leaned over Joe's shoulder and pointed to one of two black women in the picture,

"That's Ella Mae White – forewoman of the Pavlone jury, recently a murder victim."

Startled, Joe asked DD, "When did Laura die?"

"After this picture and before jury selection in Pavlone."

"This is stunning evidence that Keislor's staff was involved with a juror – a key juror – before the trial. Is it evidence that Keislor is somehow involved in the murder of this woman?"

Gazing at the photograph, Joe was thinking out loud. "Where did you get this picture?"

"This was in the envelope with the copy of the checks – the envelope with my name and address on it found in the drawer of a table in Ella Mae's library.

"She was trying to tell the world something and figured you knew what it was. What a strange way to do it. How could she know about our friendship with Laura? Why wasn't she more explicit?"

"This is great stuff, but I wonder if I can get anyone to dig into Keislor based on just this. Dolson, our numb nuts district attorney, certainly wouldn't go any further – particularly because I think he and Keislor's firm are tight. One problem is that the victim is dead in Mississippi and that state's attorney general thinks she was killed by a cop who moonlights as a contract killer. Connecting him to Keislor is near impossible right now, except that now we know,"

DD pointed at Dru Lacey in the photograph still on Joe's desk.

"His legal assistant was playing some kind of game with the decedent before she was selected as a juror. Now, we also know that his ex-secretary is connected to payments made to that same juror."

Joe sat up, "We do?"

DD then related what Pep had told him about the marriage of Darla Reid to David Weinstock, an incorporator of 'Structured Resolutions'.

"Jesus Christ!"

Rick came in. "Brainstorming? God knows this one needs a lot of thought."

He sat down next to DD, who leaned forward, grabbed the photograph and showed it to Rick.

"Jesus Christ! That's that woman Dru and there's Laura." He sunk further into this chair as the content of the picture revealed itself, slowly. "Hey, isn't that Ella Mae White?"

DD confirmed that it was indeed Ella Mae and that Laura had died before the start of the Pavlone trial.

"You know, I specifically remember the both of them – Dru whatsername and Darla – sitting there at counsel table with Hugh while jury selection was going on. No one disclosed they knew this woman White. From the looks of this picture it wasn't a passing acquaintance."

After a moment of looking at the picture, Rick looked up at DD. "This was in that package with the copy of the checks, wasn't it? Jesus Christ!"

Then, DD told Rick about the connection between the checks to the decedent and Darla Reid, but he added. "Think of something to say other than 'Jesus Christ.'"

"By the way..." Joe had almost forgotten an idea he had worked out the night before. "What do you think of this? It has nothing to do with this picture or Darla married to a guy in LA with the same last name as the guy who wrote the checks to Ella Mae."

Standing next to his desk chair, Joe explained, "This is what I think; there had to be three people in the house at the time of the shooting – the decedent, her housemate and the killer. If the housemate was the killer, there is no way to explain the alarm or the statement to the sheriff dispatcher that there had been a murder. If the housemate is not the killer, which I think is clear, then someone else was in the house at the time of the entry. The housemate pushed the sheriff call button but couldn't speak loudly for fear of being discovered by the killer."

DD was nodding affirmatively, but Rick seemed more skeptical. "There's no one there when the deputies arrive in four or five minutes. If this is she, and she's hiding, then the murderer is still there as well. Less than five minutes is not a lot of time to get out of there, down the road and out of sight let alone for two people. They could have been in it together and the voice thing was still a diversion."

"All I can do right now is hypothesize, Rick. You could be perfectly right. However, it seems that if Malvina is in on this with someone, valuables would have been stolen. None were, unless something really valuable was in that safe. But the thesis that has Malvina in on this seems highly unlikely because she could have come and gone without ever bothering about the alarm system."

Rick asked, "Why was the alarm set when the deputies got there?"

"I dunno, not yet. This is a working hypothesis. We can go from there."

DD left to deal with a raft of telephone calls.

With the money coming in from the Reynaldo case, DD felt free to chase the mystery of Ella Mae – chase it at least as far as North Lake Tahoe. Rick was a willing companion.

DD fell in love with Lake Tahoe the first time he saw it back in 1969. While it was not exactly the mountain wilderness of his Montana childhood – vacation homes, casinos, resort facilities – it *is* beautiful. The summer season was well under way, so the upper Truckee was chock full of rafters when DD and Rick pushed the Ford up the canyon from the town of Truckee. The intersection of highway 89 and North Lake Tahoe Boulevard in Tahoe City was chaotic with bevies of near-naked beauties, over-packed family cars, young men in shorts and tennis shoes on skate boards, and an occasional free-standing adult. The lake glimmered in the summer sun, seemingly undisturbed by all the activity and the myriad of boats that skimmed across its azure blue surface.

Another drought year. The mountains were unadorned with the snow that DD knew still capped the Beaverhead. But they were, after all, mountains, and the Sierra Nevada had nothing to be ashamed of.

They found the offices of Structured Resolutions on the north side of the main drag. It was in a small office complex of cedar and pine, up an outside stairway to the second floor. The sign on the door was simple and wholly unpretentious. Looking through the window, DD could see no one and the one room wasn't big enough to miss anyone present. Rick knocked – there wasn't a door bell – and no one answered. He turned the door handle and it opened. The two walked in.

"Hello? Anyone here?" Rick tried, but clearly there was nowhere for anyone to be.

There were two tables in the middle of the room. Each held a computer keyboard and monitor. At a desk overlooking the highway there was what was another keyboard and monitor; the monitor bore images, so the computer was "on." Next to it was half a cup of coffee and half a pastry. DD felt the cup – it was warm.

"You guys lost?"

Through the door came a small balding man neatly dressed in a button-down, short-sleeved shirt, well-creased slacks, and tassled loafers. Startled, DD quickly recovered.

"Are you Marlin Hanover?"

"Are you cops or probation officers?"

"Neither. Are you expecting cops?

"No." Hanover seemed suddenly curious. "It's just that other people generally don't snoop around a guy's desk."

Hanover was an amiable hard case.

DD picked the direct way. "Well, we aren't cops or probations officers. We're just ordinary lawyers from San Francisco and we'd like to talk to you. Do you have a few minutes?"

"Lawyers?" Hanover gestured a "who cares?" and walked to his desk and sat down in the swivel chair. "I deal with lawyers every day. They are always referred to me by people I know. I have no memory of anyone being referred to me recently. Did someone send you?"

Rick insisted, "First, are you Marlin Hanover?"

"Yeah, I am. But you owe me your names before anything more is asked."

"I'm Dan O'Neil and this is Rick Esquivel. We've tracked the affairs of one Ella Mae White to you, or, at least to Structured Resolutions."

DD stopped at that point. Hanover's reaction was no reaction. He just looked at DD as if he expected something relevant to be said.

Still seated, Hanover explained calmly, "Look, even if I knew who this 'Ella Mae White' is, I couldn't tell you anything and really couldn't even tell you that I know anything about her. What I do is carry out the wishes of parties to agreements and in every case those agreements are strictly confidential. You will need a court order to get any information out of me. In the meantime, it is clear that you have no legitimate business here and you are, therefore, trespassing. Please leave or I will forced to call the police."

With that, Hanover rose from his chair, obviously getting irritated.

Rick tried to calm him. "Hey, man, cool down, we're just here to talk. No one knows we came. Just cool it. We just want to know why you or this company were sending this woman $30,000 a month."

Hanover was getting angry and his voice went up in volume and pitch. "You say you're lawyers. You must therefore understand when I say that an agreement is confidential. Only a court can release me from that requirement. So get a court order."

He was unflapped by the revelation these intruders knew the amounts of the checks.

Then DD stepped up to Hanover and, slightly bent over, stuck his face in Hanover's and, through clenched white teeth said, "Look Weisenstock. You call the cops and you'll talk to us with them around. You are going to talk to us one way or the other. We are not leaving."

Weisenstock's acknowledgment of DD's use of his real name was subtle but resigned.

Rick, adapting the role of 'good guy', pled with Weisenstock, "Understand, please, we' re trying to figure out who killed a woman a few days ago in Magnolia City, Mississippi. A woman who had a copy of hundreds of thousands of dollars in checks drawn on the accounts of this company. The cops could well have come with the same mission to talk to you. Would you prefer that?"

In a just audible whisper of resignation, Weisenstock finally uttered, "She copied the checks?"

"She did."

In the same tone, Weisenstock asked, "How did she die?"

Coldly, once again DD leaned toward Weisenstock. "She was shot, right there."

He put his finger in the middle of Weisenstock's forehead.

Weisenstock shuddered visibly. He turned to the window looking toward the lake.

"I really can't tell you anything. I really can't."

Rick, leaning on the big desk, kept to his empathetic tone of comradeship, suggesting that DD was the mean one. "Just tell us why you were writing $30,000 worth of checks every month to this woman in Mississippi."

Weisenstock repeated, "I really can't tell you anything. All I do is carry out other people's agreements. I get instructions and I follow them."

DD had crossed the room, turning toward Weisenstock. "Who gave you instructions on sending money to Ella Mae White?"

Seemingly trapped by the insistence of these intruders, Weisenstock looked directly at DD.

"My dad gives me all of my instructions. If you want more, you have to ask him."

He produced a business card and gave it to Rick.

"If I opened up to you guys, my dad would laugh"

With that, Weisenstock laughed, "Take this up with him. I'm not talking anymore." He then simply walked out the door and down the stairs.

Rick and DD looked at each other a moment. DD finally stated the moment's imperativ.

"We have to keep in touch with this guy and bring in the local gendarmes."

They rushed out the door and to the bottom of the stairs just in time to see Weisenstock go into the MOUNTAIN

AIRE BAR across the highway. As they tried to cross, Rick noted the gray Mercedes with the license number Pep had provided parked in the lot next to the office building. "Weisenstock isn't going very far."

Traffic slowed the pursuers. When they entered the bar, like most things in Tahoe, it was woody, dark and cool. Aside from a few tank-topped, tanned men swilling beer, there was no one else – most particularly there was no Lowell Weisenstock. DD checked the men's room and the booths – no Lowell. Rick pointed to a back door and DD moved quickly through it. The door opened on a stairway leading down to a lakeside mall and marina behind a Safeway store. Weisenstock was nowhere to be seen.

In vain, Rick questioned the fat, grizzled bartender while DD went to the telephone.

"Sonny, we're going to need some help with the local police – and in a hurry."

He gave Sonny a brief summary of what had transpired and asked Rick to go watch the Mercedes.

"It'll be quicker if you give me the telephone number for the local police, DD."

Sonny agreed that he was more likely to get the attention of the local law enforcement, but neither believed there would be a whole lot of energy expended by the Tahoe City police. After all, this was probably the most laid back jurisdiction in the State. DD found the number written on the wall by the phone and gave it to Sonny.

Rick was still watching the Mercedes and, most probably, the slightly clad women that crowded the walkway along the road. He agreed to stay on this duty while DD walked the two blocks to the police station.

A tall, sun-bronzed young man, looking fit and trim in his uniform with shorts, greeted DD as he walked through the station door. Officer Lamb, with the demeanor of an Eagle Scout, had indeed received the call from the Mississippi attorney general's office.

"Mr. O'Neil, I was just on my way out to look for you. It's just as well you came here. Hot today, isn't it?"

DD allowed that it was, and asked if Lamb could give him a hand finding Lowell.

"Sure, be glad to. I know this guy by his assumed name of Hanover. I know his record, too. Everybody on this force knows the guy. Not that he has done anything wrong here; he's pretty quiet. It's just that San Francisco let us know he was coming here and gave us his probation officer's number."

Probation? Weisenstock is on probation from San Francisco? This could work.

Lamb was clearly interested in helping DD and getting some relief from arresting underage drinkers and directing traffic. The teletype rattled, its bell rang, and a message rolled out in police lexicon from the Mississippi attorney general's office. DD felt, for the first time, that he was officially in law enforcement.

Lamb switched on a microphone at the communication desk and informed the other two officers on duty to arrest Hanover if either saw him. DD and Lamb then walked over to where Rick had been posted. Lamb informed DD and Rick that Hanover had four outstanding warrants for parking violations on the Mercedes. He would have it impounded.

"There's really nothing for you to do right now." Lamb didn't want these lawyers mucking around playing cop in his jurisdiction. "I'll let the other jurisdictions around the lake know we want the guy. I think I know where he has been living and I'll check that out. I assure you, we'll have him before the night is out. Where are you staying?"

Through one of his ex-wives, Rick had arranged to stay at a house in Carnelian Bay, just a few miles down the road from Tahoe City. He gave Officer Lamb the telephone number.

Officer Lamb called the Carnelian digs of Rick's second wife about 10 p.m.. DD and Rick had been playing gin and drinking some – with tonic – both liberated from the former Mrs. Esquivel's stock.

"Got him in the CHP holding facility near Forest Glen. He was dirty, so now we have another ground for keeping him close. The DA has to come up from Nevada City, so we can't get him to a judge before 11 a.m.. The judge will set bail at that time. He could be out by 1 or 2 p.m., unless San Francisco wants him held. It's their warrant. If you guy want to talk to him, it had better be tonight"

Lamb was very authoritative.

DD pushed the Ford through the dark mountain chill back to Tahoe City without saying a word. The windows down, Rick sustained a serious disturbance of his usually perfectly-groomed hair, but he was also silent.

DD was thinking. *What the hell am I doing? I just had someone arrested! There's no real indication this poor bastard did anything terribly sinister or, for that matter, truly criminal.*

Officer Lamb explained that Weisenstock, when searched, had less than two ounces of cocaine, found in a tube attached to his key chain.

"Maybe not enough to interest the D.A. in a prosecution, but enough to jerk his probation." Lamb ventured.

When DD and Rick entered the small holding cell, Weisenstock was looking out the window toward the Nevada mountains that ring the east side of the Lake. DD said quietly but firmly, "So, what do you want us to call you?"

Without turning around, he said, just as firmly, "Lowell."

Except for being unshaven, Lowell appeared unruffled for a guy that had been out much of the night and in jail the rest of it. He turned and looked at the two lawyers.

"I'm pretty sure I don't have to talk to you guys and the cops would send you away if I said I wouldn't. The thing is, I feel terribly about Ella Mae and could probably help you, but I want cover to avoid untoward consequences for being a snitch."

"What does that mean?"

"It means that what I tell you has to be kept confidential, at least until I can figure out a way to save my ass. It also

75

means that I want a lawyer. One of your choosing would be fine, as long as he is competent. I am not telling you much until I talk to the lawyer."

"Would you consent to have whatever you say right now recorded?"

DD pulled a small tape recorder from his jacket pocket and showed Lowell.

"Yeah."

"I can get you a lawyer. An experienced lawyer, older than me, and he's nearby. I think you have to appear in Court here."

"Lowell, I'm retained by the attorney general of the State of Mississippi. For a lot of things to happen, I have to share whatever you tell me with them. Otherwise, I am prepared to keep this confidential between us."

DD gestured to indicate Rick and himself. "I just have a problem with this open-ended notion of 'cover' for you. What do you have in mind?"

"The minute stuff starts to pop from my information, they will think it was me. They are going to move quickly to take advantage of my drug history to discredit me. Some of their business associates may even take more drastic action to assure that I won't be around for a trial."

DD thought for a minute. "Does this Structured Resolutions business do much? I mean do you deal with settlements other than this supposed one involving Ella Mae White?"

"Right now, there isn't a lot to do except send checks on a schedule that is in each file in my office safe. There are four cases I'm responsible for right now. There were five, but I was told to stop sending checks to Ella Mae a month ago," Lowell was casually explaining to the men who had been harassing him only a few hours ago.

Rick looked at DD. "Are you sure it was a month ago?"

"Very near. There's a file note to confirm the telephone conversation."

"Who called?" DD was anxious.

"My stepmother, Darla. She works for Dad now."

"Darla Reid? A tall, blond woman?" DD pressed.

"The very same" Lowell confirmed.

Lowell agreed that DD could start the tape recorder, although he made it clear there were certain questions he just wasn't going to answer until he met with a lawyer. For the purposes of the recording, Lowell repeated what he had said about the Structured Resolutions business and about being instructed by Darla to stop sending checks to Ella Mae a month ago.

"Do you think you're in danger because you are talking to us?" Rick turned the page on a new subject for the record.

"Yes, definitely. As soon as you do anything with this information that gets to the principal players, I will be a target." Lowell was resolute.

Rick pressed. "Who are the principal players?"

"I'm not going to answer that question in its entirety until I can consult a lawyer. But the most immediate such people are my father, David, his wife, Darla, Ella Mae – I guess that is past tense, now – and probably Drucinda Lacey."

"Are you saying that Drucinda Lacey is a principal player in Structured Resolutions? How so?"

DD believes in open-ended questions.

"I am not exactly sure. She was the first one I dealt with in setting up the structured settlement of Ella Mae's claim against Norm Yamaguchi. I didn't hear from her after that, but we had been an item before."

Lowell had just opened up new chapters.

"That reminds me," Lowell suddenly inserted into his near monologue, "I insist on paying this lawyer, whoever he is. I know the consequences of someone else paying your lawyer."

"Sure, Lowell. I mean, at $200,000 a year, you can afford it.," Rick observed after an unspoken approval by DD.

Lowell frowned, quizzically. " You said that before. What makes you think I am getting $200,000 a year?"

"We know that account – Structured Resolutions – had $48,000 a month deposited and we know that only $30,000 went to Ella Mae. That leaves $18,000 for, presumably, you," DD explained.

Lowell wasn't sure he believed DD, so he took a deep breath and hesitated, but then relented. "My account records are accurate. When you see them, you will see that on this account, I sent the $30,000 to Ella Mae each month – in varying amounts for each check, but $30,000. I then sent $13,000 to my dad's company in Beverly Hills out of every $48,000 I received. My share was only $5,000. Dad's share was for 'administrative services.'"

"Was there a similar arrangement on these other files in your shop?"

"Well, I really can't give you any details, but roughly that was the deal."

Lowell stopped talking and absentmindedly began stroking the dark stubble of his beard.

Keeping the narrarive on a relevant course, DD asked, "How does Dru become a principal player?"

"Somewhere in there – when I was living in the Haight – Dad met Darla at the Loudon law firm. They were his lawyers."

DD began realizing what a finely woven fabric this was. The full name of the firm was, of course, Loudon, Mueller, and Keislor.

"Anyway, things happened pretty fast from that point. Dad invited me to attend a party the lawyers were throwing to celebrate some big contract Dad just got signed. It had been a year since I had completed rehab and I'd never had a whole lot of interest in women – nothing like my old man. But I ran into this woman at the party – a real beauty in a strange sort of way and she seemed to genuinely like me. Her name was Dru Lacey, and she was connected. The minute she asked me about doing a line, I knew that was what I needed. I did a line and then another and some more. I got sick and then I got sicker."

Some light was showing over the eastern ridge of the Sierra that could be seen through the window of the holding cell. DD was transfixed with the connections that Lowell's pathetic narrative was providing. Rick, however, was asleep on the cot that would have been Lowell's.

"I was pretty much out of it for a few days and Dru became the only woman I'd had since college. Of course, I was so whacked out, I don't think I understood what was really happening at the time. Not long after the party, however, I remember dad telling me he was marrying Darla. Jesus, I remember thinking, a sixty-eight-year-old self-designated stud. I don't know how old Darla was but she fit the bill for a trophy so Dad could have evidence of this self appraisal. Leggy, blond, and slim – she was a hell of a trophy. But it didn't really matter to me. This was his third wife since he and my mom split. They weren't so much wives as they were whores. At least this one had a real job."

"The worst thing was that I had fallen off the wagon again."

DD had never seen any adult with so much deserved self pity. Lowell continued to feign looking out the window. DD could see the morning sunlight reflect off the tears on his cheeks. Clearly, DD was inadvertently playing some other role for Lowell than he planned.

"Ultimately, I had to tell my dad and, of course, I was out of a job. He just smiled, like he always did and was not surprised, or upset. Shit, he expected it to happen."

Hoping there was more connection here than Lowell was suggesting by the course of this whimpering saga, DD asked, "Did you see Dru Lacey again?"

"Oh, yeah. Even with a snoot full of coke, I couldn't perform, and all she was doing was getting the stuff for me. That made things worse. I was spiraling down and down. I wanted out of San Francisco but didn't want to go to LA. Stepmom went to work for Dad at his place on Wilshire. Then, out of the blue, I get a call from her – Darla! She asks if

I would be willing to do some work. Fuck, yes. Is there something I can do that I can't screw up?"

By this time, Rick had stirred, peed, and retrieved a cup of coffee for the three of them from the CHP officer in charge. He asked, "When was this Lowell? Approximately. We know the checks to Ella Mae started in late 1980."

Lowell turned to look at Rick, squinting in concentration.

"Well, it was shortly before that because that was what she was calling to set up. I was still on Frederick in the Haight. My probation officer prohibited me from leaving town. I think the district attorney was trying to revoke my probation."

As if he could see the date on the calendar, Lowell looked at Rick. "It was November of 1980. That's it. Darla explained that a woman in the illustration department of a software development company, Malvina, was claiming that the boss had jumped her and tried to rape her. Apparently, this Malvina was a stone fox."

DD looked at Rick. "How many Malvinas can there be?"

"I remember doing a line with Dru. She said she knew Malvina. She told me something like, 'Don't judge a diamond by the package it comes in.' I have no idea what that meant."

Erstwhile Tahoe City police officer Lamb had come in and out several times during Lowell's soliloquy, scratching his head each time. It no longer mattered to Lowell whether anyone was listening or whether anything he was saying had adverse consequences.

"I had started Structured Resolutions by that time. The San Francisco district attorney agreed to allow me to relocate to Tahoe City, but I still had to report monthly to my probation officer in the City. Dad set me up to carry out these confidential litigation agreements. Dad is an amazing business getter."

Lowell went on for another hour. He never objected to the recording. DD telephoned a long-time friend who had relocated to Nevada City, a few miles west of Tahoe. Arrangements were made for Roy Lindstrom to represent

Lowell in the matters then pending against him, including the probation revocation matter that was expected in San Francisco. Lowell happily agreed to stay in jail for a few days in what was effectively protective custody. He took care of what business he had for Structured Resolutions from a cell in Nevada City.

***

CHAPTER NINE

Meditations

About one hundred yards east of where Shea Creek flows bashfully into the Truckee River, there is a bend where the water is deep, still, and dark on the south side, but shallow, noisy, and white on the north. The experts around there use nymphs and tell everyone that a dry fly just won't work with these browns. Never being one to listen to experts, DD had found this spot several years before and was going to get his line wet with a dry fly on its end, no matter how much Rick protested.

DD had been pulling cutthroats and rainbows out of the Big Hole and the Madison rivers since his pre-teens. Mick had taught him and Joe the art and joy of fly fishing – nearly always using dry flies. Fifteen minutes after he stepped into the Truckee, DD had a fish on and fifteen minutes later he had another. Each was more than a foot long and fat. Each he released back into the stream.

"Why do you do that?" Rick asked from his shaded, sandy spot ashore.

"Don't need 'em. I have plenty to eat. When I don't, I'll keep 'em. In the meantime, they'll spawn more and I might need 'em to eat for a long time."

With the constancy of the rush of the Truckee, DD had drifted into thought. *Weisenstock has provided a direction, if not a complete map. He would be on ice in the Sierra County jail and watched over by Lindstrom while DD took the road he indicated. Maybe more importantly, he could be transferred to the San Francisco jail for an appearance before the grand jury, if he could get someone to go that far.*

"DD..." Rick's voice penetrated DD's river rapture with a plea, "I gotta get back to the City. My ruptured esophagus case goes to trial in two weeks. I can't waste time watching you do your Isaac whatzhisname act."

DD packed his gear into the Ford's trunk. Rick drove down the mountain while DD looked out the window and thought.

"The point is, Luis, if I just give you this $375,000, you are going to get a lot of new friends and relatives. You're going to blow it."

The diminutive Reynaldo sat across from DD in the conference room with an array of papers in front of him, including an insurance company check for $600,000 made out to him and to DD.

"If you put it in a spendthrift trust in a bank, they can invest it for you and you can tell your relatives that you can't get any of it, except what you get from the monthly earnings."

Luis, whose street name was 'Goose', was like most of DD's clients. There was no way they could avoid the pressures of family and friends to invest, loan, or buy for. He would be broke in six months and still partially disabled.

Luis played with his new mustache and stared at the check. He didn't talk all that much, and when he did, the English was "barrio English," although he spoke almost no Spanish.

"Ya'know Dan, you been real good to me. I got this eye fixed as good it's goin' to get – I can almost see out of it – and the hand ain't bad now. Nobody cares about that but you, man, so I trus' you. But can I have $25k now? I want to buy a good truck and take my dad and mom to Reno."

"Luis, take $50,000 now. Just figure that you are to take the rest in monthly payments with a little kicker from time to time. Remember this is tax free."

Luis sat back and looked at DD."Who's this guy – ya'know, the bank guy?" He began signing the papers.

"Kevin Curry," DD provided as he signed each as Luis finished. "Here's his card. Go down to the Hibernia Bank, just down the street. He'll set you up. You trust me; I trust him. He's handling a lot of my clients' money."

Luis' dark eyes twinkled and he smiled. "Hibernia. Ain't that Irish? I learned that from Father Hanley, y'know, at the Mission? I think that the Irish are not like the Mexicans. They trust each other."

"No," DD sighed as he was putting the signed papers together, "they *are* like the Mexicans. Only some of us trust each other. The others take advantage."

On the way back from Tahoe Sunday, DD remembered that he had scheduled a handball game with Larry Harrington in the seemingly endless City Tournament. Harrington was one of the only remaining assistant district attorneys with whom DD had any personal relationship. DD, Joe, and Larry were close – largely because we were arguably the three best handball players in town. DD had decided to use the occasion to enlist Harrington in the cause of unraveling the murder of Ella Mae White.

It was an incongruous friendship. Harrington was from a large, traditional San Francisco Irish family. His dad was a retired police inspector, and three of his four brothers were cops, one of them a captain. The fourth and youngest brother was a fireman. They were all tenors and performed frequently at weddings.

Right on the water at Aquatic Park, near Fisherman's Wharf, the San Francisco Men's Club was a drab, clapboard edifice that had amazingly survived earthquakes and fires over its more than fifty years of existence. It featured a boat launch – rowboats and sculls – over the sandy beach. There were huge rowing boats, a weight room that was damp and dark and four immaculately maintained handball courts.

"This time, I'm going to whip your ass, Danny boy."

Harrington's wide shoulders cast a shadow over DD's efforts to lace his shoes in the locker room and his boast was surely heartfelt. DD had beat Harrington early in the tournament, but then Larry won all of his subsequent matches and worked his way back up the ladder. If he couldn't beat DD today, however, it was over and it would be Joe and DD in a three-match contest for the championship – a championship one or the other had won the last three years.

DD stood up, gently slapped Larry on the shoulder with his gloves and smiled. "Takes more than talk Larry."

On the court, Larry was excited. He jumped around in his warm up, and hit the ball very hard – too hard, all the while watching DD in an apparent and vain attempt to intimidate him. The first game was over in less than ten minutes – 15-5, DD. The second took a little longer and this time Harrington struggled to get eight points. His strength was no match for DD's relentless and clever tactics.

Harrington was sweating and breathing heavily. DD was sweating. They walked up to the locker rooms together.

"Hey, you had a bad day Larry. I think you had the last match on your mind and not this one."

He was conciliatory. "Every time I play you DD, I have a bad day. Six matches in a row, I win. Then you come along."

Following their shower, DD, while buttoning his shirt, walked over to Larry.

"If someone bribes a juror in a civil case," he ventured while Harrington was tying his tie, "would that interest Dolson enough to prosecute?"

"Hey, DD, you know that story. It all depends on who's asking. He sure as shit isn't going to move because you ask. If some high profile, establishment citizen should ask and show there's something in it for Leonard, he'd do it and then give it to me to carry out. But he sure as hell won't be moved if a brawling, left-wing lawyer who kicked his ass in his trial-of-a-career asks."

In his suit and tie, with his scrubbed and handsome face, Larry Harrington didn't look like a vanquished warrior. "What's going on DD? That was not exactly a rhetorical inquiry."

DD leaned on Harrington's jeep.

"Hold on to your hat, Larry, you're not going to believe this. I've been hired by the Mississippi attorney general as counsel to look into a murder culminated there but possibly motivated by events here."

Harrington laughed and threw his gym bag into the back of the jeep.

"DD, you don't do a lot of kidding, but I would tend to believe that is what you're doing here. Mississippi? Jury bribery? You're serious?"

"I am. You have to get back to the office, but let me give you a taste of what I've got. Do you remember that case I tried a few years ago against the Mexican car manufacturer in Rowland's court?"

Harrington thought for a minute. "Right. That's the one where you got your head handed to you by Hugh Keislor."

DD sighed a sigh of pain.

"Correct. Anyway, it turns out that the foreperson on that jury was murdered about two weeks ago in Magnolia City, Mississippi. She had left an envelope with my name on it. The envelope contained copies of nearly four years of checks made out to her that work out to be $30,000 a month. The envelope also contained a black and white photograph of some women in a hotel room. One of them was Laura McNeeley. One was Dru Lacey, Keislor's legal assistant, and one was none other than the decedent, Ella Mae White."

"Larry, you do remember that Laura committed suicide."

"I do. Jesus what a tragic case."

"Larry, Laura was dead and buried before the Pavlone trial. About two months before. "

Harrington thought for a moment. "So, here's the defense lawyer's assistant in a picture with someone who became the jury forewoman. And the picture was taken two months before the trial." Harrington paused again, "So, you would have me conclude that this is evidence the dead woman was bribed? I can't quite get there."

"Add this: Darla – Keislor's secretary – turns out to be married to the guy who set up the payments to the late jury forewoman. Then there is this additional fact: Lacey and Keislor's secretary, Darla Reid, were both in the courtroom, sitting right behind Hugh during jury selection. I am absolutely positive Phil Rowland would remember and so testify."

"Doesn't that just mean that there were two employees of the defense firm who knew the jury forewoman and did not disclose that to Keislor?"

Larry Harrington was a good prosecutor and, as such, not one to idly speculate about someone's criminal culpability. "Clearly that's improper. It might even be some sort of crime, but it is most likely grounds for overturning the verdict or maybe some civil liability."

"How about the money?"

"Yeah, the money. I assume you have concluded there is no other way she could have come up with that kind of money." Larry was getting onto his jeep and looking at his watch.

"Not yet. But that is where I'm going."

" I have to get back. This is more than interesting. I understand there have been complaints about Keislor before. Dolson won't even look at this, however; he and the Loudon partners are very close. The murder certainly gives one pause and I am interested. Connect some dots and keep me informed. A grand jury is not out of the question if you can do that. What about a Mississippi grand jury? They could indict conspirators out here. If they do that, our cops get involved."

As Larry was pulling away big Tom Harrington, Larry's dad, shouted "Larry, wait a minute!"

"I gotta go Dad, I'll see you tonight."

Walking quickly up to DD, Tom Harrington, a big, red-faced, overweight Irish cop, smiled and held out his ham sized hand. "Jesus, DD, y'gotta go to the nationals this year. Nobody is smarter on a handball court than you."

"Well, I always appreciate the flattery Tom, but I have one more match to go and that is against the smartest hand ball player I know. Have you had lunch?"

"No, let's get some lunch. I don't know between you two – you and Cleary. I've never seen you play each other. Who wins more?"

The two walked out on the pier to Scoma's and ordered steamed clams and beer.

"I think it's pretty even over the years. I used to beat him when we were kids because I was just bigger. But he is so quick, I am thankful for any game I can win."

Tom ordered another beer and told the waiter he was buying. DD protested.

"Wait a minute. You're retired, I am supposed to buy."

"Naw. I just won twenty bucks on that handball match. I'll buy."

"You bet against your own kid?"

"I can't afford to bet on him when he's playing you. Besides, I couldn't pass up taking money from that prick deConcini. He doesn't like you, DD."

Art deConcini is the former assistant regional general counsel for the Internal Revenue Service. DD caught him purloining a valuable stamp collection seized from a marijuana dealer in a forfeiture. He ended up doing six months at the United States correctional facility in Pleasanton, lost his license to practice law, and was working as a bookkeeper at his brother's Fisherman's Wharf restaurant. The marijuana dealer whom DD represented in the lawsuit did one year in the same facility. Upon release he was accepted into the University of California graduate program in nuclear physics. He just completed his dissertation and should be awarded his doctorate next winter. DD likes those stories.

"Tom," DD turned to more serious business, "how long did you spend on the fed's organized crime task force for the Department?"

"Two years and some change."

The older man leaned back in his chair wielding a toothpick.

"Not a great experience. The Feds ain't policemen, they're bureaucrats. But what's up?"

"There's a guy I need to get a line on. Pep's working on this with me, but he has run into a blank wall. Supposedly this guy has been doing deals for the mob. We don't even know what kind of deals. Just deals."

Harrington was interested; he sat up. "Name?"

"David Weisenstock." DD spelled it out.

"A Jew," the old cop observed. "Which mob?"

"There's more than one?"

DD seemed surprised.

"Oh yeah. Every ethnic and neighborhood has a mob. Anyone who has been pushed around by the powers that be has a criminal organization of some sort. Some better than others. We Irish, of course, are an exception – like shit." The old man chuckled.

"I'm not sure what it means when I'm told this guy does deals for the mob," said DD. "I guess I better find out more about that. Do you think you can help on this?"

Tom Harrington smiled, and put his big hand on DD's shoulder.

"I am flattered you asked. I'm not sure what I can do, but why don't you tell Pep I'll call him? I still have contacts with most mobs, except the Chinese – those people know how to keep secrets."

***

CHAPTER TEN

Backtracking

"Norman Yamaguchi, please. My name is Dan O'Neil. I'm a lawyer here in town and I have a confidential matter to discuss with Mr. Yamaguchi."

DD expected to have to explain further to the telephone receptionist.

"This is Norm," came the surprising response.

"Mr. Yamaguchi, my name is Dan O'Neil. I am a lawyer here in town. I am working on a matter and your name came up. I would like to come over and talk with you; it is highly confidential."

DD gave it all he had without saying something to frighten the guy off.

"I know who you are, Dan." Yamaguchi's voice was warm and easy. "Apparently, you don't know that my father is Walter Yamaguchi, a former client of yours and Joe Cleary's."

DD laughed out loud over the phone.

"You're Gooch's son? It never entered my mind. I guess I didn't figure a radical Hawaiian trade unionist would have a son who's successful in business.

"Well, Dad's really understanding about that. He was disappointed that I didn't want to be a longshoreman, but Mom persuaded him it was best. He always speaks well of you and Joe. Anyway, can you come over today? I won't be able to meet with you for several days starting tomorrow."

Yamaguchi rose several times to look out the window facing the east side of Twin Peaks. He was uncomfortable as DD gave him the bare outline of the story he had gathered...leaving out what he thought he should.

If the office was any evidence, Yamaguchi did quite well in the business he started only eight years ago. With his partner, Carlyle Jones, a four-foot-ten-inch local computer software genius, Yamaguchi had created a company and a product that seemed to be leading in software development for San Francisco's many printing houses.

As DD related the story, such as it was, from Lowell Weisenstock, Yamaguchi made a note on a pad on his otherwise uncluttered desk.

"I know this is probably embarrassing for you after all these years, and I hate to bear such news to the son of someone I admire so much, but there is a murder involved."

Yamaguchi looked and acted like his father – easy going, congenial and direct.

"I'm not embarrassed," Yamaguchi declared and sat down at the desk. "I'm confused. Dad told me about what you guys did for him and about your run-in with the Teamster boss at Pearl City. You guys are heros around the Yamaguchi house."

He then spoke into an intercom, "Sissy. Could you please get into my personal file cabinet and bring me the file that is marked 'Malvina Montrose' and, from the personnel archives, the file of Ella Mae White."

He offered DD a cigarette from a sleek stainless steel box on his desk. When DD refused, Yamaguchi lit his own with a stainless steel, simulated blowtorch.

"David Weisenstock was, I thought until now, only a claims adjuster for our general liability carrier, about three or so years ago. But from what you say, he was something else. I'm very confused."

"Well, didn't you pay off Malvina on this claim?"

DD was beginning to feel Yamaguchi might not be forthcoming.

A stout young woman with an all-business stride entered the room with two folders in one hand and a writing pad in the other. "Your memory is awesome, Norm."

With obvious admiration, she handed the folders to him and he sat down with them behind the glass desk.

"That's ok, Sissy. You can go back to work."

Yamaguchi began studying one file. He looked at DD,

"I paid a $5,000 deductible directly to Southern California Casualty on November 10, 1979."

Returning to the folder, he read further. "That was apparently in response to a letter from the insurer's lawyer, Hugh Keislor, telling me the matter was settled. This tells me that the policy required me to pay the deductible and I did."

He continued to turn pages, then shook his head and spun his chair to look out the window again. "Fuck, I'll never understand why that bitch was paid so much money. The settlement was structured – so much a month for life – so I never really knew how much was paid out. The limit was, I think, two million."

He sighed and turned back to DD. "I guess I deserved this little embarrassment – my dick led me astray."

"Wait a minute, Norm. How does Keislor get involved? May I see that letter?"

Sure enough, it was from Keislor, with the firm's letterhead and the signature with which DD was so very familiar.

"He was the insurance company lawyer assigned to this case. There's a letter informing me of that from David Weisenstock. I never met the guy."

He handed that letter to DD.

"Please understand," Yamaguchi looked directly at DD, "this woman, Malvina, worked for us about two years. She was some kind of sexy, and dressed – you know – dressed to accentuate that fact. I didn't have much to do with her at first. I mean, I knew she was here; you couldn't miss that. She worked in illustrating on the first floor as a kind of "go-fer'. She wasn't an artist, as far as I know. Once in awhile she would bring me layouts or something they were working on. I was a busy guy putting this stuff together."

This was difficult. Yamaguchi put his hands on his head and stood up, turning the gaze over the cityscape to Twin Peaks.

"One night I was here. Her boss had the whole crew working late downstairs. I worked at that terminal and on that drawing board."

He pointed to the large workstation in the corner of his office.

"She brought in some pizza and a soda. One thing, then another and I'm on the couch between her legs with my pants off."

DD could picture that and Yamaguchi knew he could.

"You know how it is. I felt like shit after my dick shot all its brains. I treated her ok, but, you know, I was married and happily so. I'm not a womanizer. You know how my family is about the family. Christ, what was I thinking of? The answer of course was that I wasn't thinking."

The object of this get together was not to take Norm Yamaguchi's confession.

"Was Ella Mae White your secretary?"

"Shit. I'm sorry. She's been murdered and I am doing this *mea culpa* like a damn fool. Yes, she was. She had worked for a guy I knew in the printing business. A good guy, who died young and his company collapsed. Anyway, she came recommended by people who worked with her. She seemed stiff. Pleasant enough and very bright. I had absolutely no complaints about her work. She was all business and very aggressive on my behalf. I was real unhappy to lose her, particularly when it happened just about two months after this Malvina business."

"Did Ella Mae ever tell you anything about a lawsuit she had pending?"

DD was looking at his old notes from Mississippi.

"No. I'm not sure she would have. We didn't do a lot of chitchat. She seemed real close to Malvina and she might have told her if she had a lawsuit."

"What did she tell you about why she quit?"

"Let's see..." Yamaguchi was trying to remember.

"I recall thinking it didn't seem like a good reason. She had been off on jury duty. It had been quite a while. The whole business about Malvina's claim against me had come up while she was gone. When she returned, she worked for a week, maybe two. One day she came in said she was giving two weeks notice. She said that the trial she was in had disturbed her so she felt she needed to return to Mississippi where she had grown up...Oh, wait a minute. Actually, she didn't give two weeks notice. She called Sissy, who had replaced her during the jury duty absence, and asked her if she wanted the job. She asked me if I liked Sissy. When I said yes, she asked if she could leave right away, and then she did."

DD stood up and held his hand out, "May I see that Malvina file?"

Stamped in large, black letters across the front and back of the file folder was the word "CONFIDENTIAL," but Yamaguchi nonetheless handed it to DD.

"Norm, did you ever get anything from Keislor or Weisenstock or anyone signed by Malvina releasing all her complaints against you in exchange for this payment?"

"I am sure it is there someplace. But I gotta tell you – Malvina never made any complaint to me. She made it to Ella Mae."

DD and Norm each looked through the Malvina file, inspecting each piece of paper. There was no release signed by Malvina Montrose.

After getting Ella Mae's and Malvina's files from Yamaguchi, DD dropped by No. 9 Jones to meet Pep.

"Jeannie told me to tell you to call her right away. I suspect if you don't your ass is grass."

Jaime and Jeannie were principal participants in an ongoing conspiracy to keep DD from making another mistake like Melanie – or otherwise getting lost.

"What's up?"

"You know, O'Neil." Jeannie was feigning irritation. "Sometimes I think I'm working for a ghost. Why can't you just check in once in a while?"

"I told you I was going to work on the Mississippi thing most of the day."

"A phone call. A minute phone call. That way I know whether to get my resume' typed up because my boss is dead or whether I have some time. Is that really too much to ask?"

It's in the female genes. DD had never had any evidence that women get formal training in this, but every one he ever knew used the same language, for the same reasons, and said words in the same sarcastic tone of voice. Every one except Moonshadow.

"So, once again, what's up?" DD was determined to win this game of ignoring.

"Pep will meet you at No. 9. He talked to Tom Harrington. Your buddy from Mississippi – Sonny – called and wants you to call him back no matter what time it is. Finally, and you are not going to believe this, Melanie called. She is back from Hawaii, did not get married, and would like to buy you dinner at Vanessi's tonight. That bitch."

Jeannie had never thought much of Melanie.

"I'm at No. 9 and can see Pep walking through the door right now. I'll call Sonny as soon as I hang up here. You call Melanie and tell her I am otherwise engaged."

"Dan, this is one thing I can't do for you. You have to talk to her even if it is only to tell her you aren't going to talk to her any more. Do it when you're up, and you're up right now."

"I want to stay up, so I am not talking to Melanie. Thanks, Jeannie."

DD hung up and then dialed Jackson, Mississippi.

"Mr. Assistant Attorney General, this here is your lawyer."

Sonny sounded pressed. "DD, I need a report from you as soon as you can get it here. Bud's getting some heat from Ella Mae's sisters' political connections. Olivia is all bent out of shape over us not arresting someone for the awful death of her dear sister."

Funny how death and money bring families closer together.

"Actually, Sonny, I was intending to write a report in the morning. I'll send it by overnight mail. There's a lot to report, but I don't know how far it gets us down the road to an indictment. Is there anything happening at your end?"

"Not really. We've had Praeger under surveillance since you left, but nothing interesting has occurred. We did find out that Malvina is Malvina Montrose and she is or was a local girl from the eastern part of the county. She left here when she was fifteen and didn't come back until she showed up with Ella Mae."

DD was jotting notes. "I just learned she was 'Montrose,' but I didn't know she was from Indian County. I'll put it in my report, but Malvina connects to the money that went to Structured Resolutions. That all somehow connects to the law firm that was on the other side in <u>Pavlone</u>. Knowing all that doesn't make it logical, but I am working on that."

"Danny Boy, Danny Boy...this is almost as much fun as my first blow job." Pep feigned a thoughtful pause..."No, I don't think I can quite say that."

Pep was almost singing, which everyone knows he can't.

"Talked to Tom Harrington – very helpful. He got me to a former task force intelligence officer, Roger Cash – he was more helpful. Turns out that Weisenstock is out of Brooklyn with a long history of paper related busts as a fall guy for the Tamanino crime family. You may remember Benny Tamanino. About ten years ago, it was widely reported that Benny got a sudden hole in the middle of his forehead. This, Cash says, was what happens when your competition thinks you have revealed to the Nevada gaming authorities the true identity of an applicant for a license. The applicant, Carmen 'the Pig' Maretto, had hired Weisenstock to put the application together. When the Nevada officials tripped to Maretto, Weisenstock provided some sort of story that poor Benny did it. After the deed was done to Benny, Maretto realized that

Weisenstock did it. Before Maretto can get to him, Weisenstock, as the smart guy he is, went to the Feds and gave them a map through Maretto's empire."

Pep was really enjoying himself in this story, using all the old movie 'gangsta' inflections."

DD interjected, "Am I right to assume that the Weisenstock you're talking about is 'David'?

"Right." Pep was turning a page in the mass in front of him. "Can I have a drink?"

DD hailed Jaime. In a couple of minutes they were each sitting behind a glass of Powers.

"So, David needs a home and he disappears from Brooklyn only to show up in Beverly Hills. He has hired out to the Grahams and the Browns."

"Hold it." DD held up his hand. "Grahams and Browns? Does that mean David went straight? What is this, a law firm?"

Pep's slurried gravel throat gave up an out loud laugh.

"It's a family business where the principals have changed their names. Graham is Louis Graziani. Brown was formerly known as Lorenzo Bertolucci. So, anyway, no one knows what Weisenstock does for 'G&B', but whatever it is David, Graziani, and Bertolucci have become very rich. The best estimate that Cash came up with for Weisenstock's net worth is eleven million."

"Dollars?"

"Right. Weisenstock may be washing money for G&B. These guys are from a long line of slick customers who basically offered influence with politicians, judges, and bureaucrats. They never went to the can, never got shot at, and had dinner from time to time with J. Edgar Hoover."

DD took a long draw on his whiskey, sat for a moment looking at Pep and said, "So, what've we got?"

DD had never been much interested in mafia stories. Most were born of wild speculation, fed by bigotry, and grew from the families' self promotion. In his experience, the vaunted crime families were low-grade malfeasants and bullies who would usually botch shoplifting in a candy store. The only reason any of them made any money was their complete lack of morality, glazed by sanctimonious Catholicism.

"There are another couple facts that Cash came up with."
Pep motioned to Jaime for another whiskey.

"Remember what I told you about Benny Tamanino? He owned a very successful casualty-line insurance agency in Brooklyn. His general manager was David Weisenstock. For all I know, this was a legitimate outfit – it certainly wrote insurance for some mainline companies."

Jaime brought the Powers – one for each.

Pep continued, "Anyway, aside from doing underwriting, Tamanino's agency did adjusting – you know, investigating, settling and, finally, litigating when necessary. The NYPD tells Cash that there were some strange goings-on regarding some of the claims made. Claimants often ended up dead before the case could be tried or otherwise resolved."

Pep leaned across the table and held up five of his thick, battered fingers.

"Five of them in three years. Judges threw most of the others out of court. Basically, Cash is told, Tamanino's companies paid out almost nothing in claims. Pretty weird in this day and age, don't you think?"

Pep took a sip, looking at DD, waiting for his reaction. DD's chin was in his cupped hand, propped by his right elbow, and he was staring into space. Finally, he managed, "But Tamanino is dead. We don't really know what David Weisenstock is doing – if anything – for the dagos with the Anglicized names. We do know that Tamanino died in a way that is similar to the way Ella Mae bought it. We suspect that Ella Mae's death was somehow related to the Pavlone verdict, but I would not utter that suspicion to anyone but you, Joe, and Rick – it just doesn't connect. What about Malvina Montrose?"

"Almost nothing." Pep sat back in the chair and heaved a big sigh. He relit his cigar and slowly emptied his glass. "She was sent over to Yamaguchi's by a temporary agency that had only recently changed its business from providing high class whores to office workers. That was occasioned by the prosecution of the agency madam for pandering based on the work of the Right Reverend Sargent Jerry O'Shaunessy. I don't know whether Malvina was a before or an after. She has no California driver's license, no credit cards, no credit applications, no voter registration."

DD stopped Pep. "Here's Malvina's personnel file from Yamaguchi. Maybe that will help." He then related everything he had learned from Norm Yamaguchi that afternoon.

Pep examined the file. "So, who appears again? Keislor. Isn't this fun? Oh, here's Ella Mae! My goodness." He stopped leafing through the papers. He stared into space, wiped his thick glasses, contemplated, puffed his cigar and motioned Jaime for yet another.

Looking at DD, Pep spoke slowly. "Do you suppose that somehow Wiesenstock made some deal with Keislor to assure LaStrada a win in <u>Pavlone</u>? How does Yamaguchi's dalliance get to Weisenstock? When was all this, in relation to when Ella Mae was on the jury? How could anyone depend on Ella Mae coming through? Aren't the risks just too big?"

DD shrugged his similar dismay.

"Exactly. I mean there are tracks all over this thing, but none go anywhere. The risks are huge – too huge to take just to win a personal injury case. What does Weisenstock do? Where does Malvina come from – at least since Indian County, Mississippi? How does Ella Mae find Malvina and what the hell is the deal? Is Malvina a switch-hitter? Was Ella Mae a dyke? Does that matter?"

Some minutes passed, along with some more Powers, while both men sat silently, thinking. Somebody punched up a Merle Haggard song on the jukebox; somebody else shouted "Haggard eats shit!" and unplugged the jukebox. Rick came though the swinging doors.

"Lawsuit interruptus. They settled. Jesus, I hate that. I'm cranked up. Stayed up nearly all night doing my opening statement – my brilliant opening statement – and Farnsworth comes in, while my client is standing there and offers $800,000, and it is fucking over."

They had all had this experience but no one complained more than Rick. Of the three, DD probably felt the most deeply. He sees his cases as matters of good versus evil. He prepares each to assure that virtue does prevail; he stages a morality play without apology, without hesitation, and then some sonofabitch offers to compromise. Words like "realistic" and "practical" are used. Phrases, sickening phrases, like, "better a bird in the hand than two in the bush" are repeated every time, or "that's what it's all about, money. Just money."

Pep had a different view; a "practical" approach.

"What's wrong with eight hundred thousand dollars? There just aren't verdicts like that around these days."

"Pep, I know you'll understand if I explain it this way..." Rick feigned exasperation. "Say you end up alone with a beautiful woman that you have long lusted after. Say you have thought about her a hundred times, and here it is. You embrace. Your bodies fully press tightly and fully together. As you kiss, breathlessly, your hands drop and you can trace the full curve of her gorgeous ass. You are there. Then, when she is unbuckling your belt, she looks deeply into your eyes and says 'Is this cash or charge?'"

Pep screwed up his face, looking askance at Rick, "It ain't the same. You're getting your share of that 800 large. That's what you went in there for...wasn't it?"

Recognizing the situation, DD stood up. "Hey, Rick, I'm not getting drunk with you. I've got to have this report to Mississippi tomorrow."

Disappointed, Rick recovered. "Who wants to be drinking with a lawyer for a prosecutor? Besides I'm meeting Helene tonight. What we have in mind wouldn't work for you and me."

They all laughed. Rick was over his post-settlement blues.

"So," Rick switched his focus to DD and Pep, "how much trouble did you guys get into while my attention was elsewhere?"

He was five years older than DD and relished playing senior advisor in professional matters. He couldn't help in matters of personal life because (a) he wasn't qualified and (b) DD wouldn't listen anyway.

DD gave Rick a brief summary of what had happened and gave it his most conservative spin. Pep interjected here and there with editorial and suggestion – all the while making notes.

"I think you have enough to go to Larry Harrington and get some cop help. Keislor should be invited in for a conversation with a senior assistant district attorney. That is bound to shake something loose."

Pep lit another cigar to congratulate himself on this idea.

DD shook his head. "I don't think so. Not yet. I don't want to use up Larry."

Rick heaved a big sigh and looked fiercely at DD.

"Ya'know, DD, I've been thinking about this. At first, I thought you had Keislor by the nuts. But then it occurred to me that's not the way things are; both you and I in particular know that. Guys like us don't get guys like Keislor by the personal nuts. We might squeeze a client of his – which we have not yet done – but we don't get him. Keislor is smart and, occasionally, we are smart, but we are always at a disadvantage. We are not ruthless and, worse, we don't understand just how ruthless he is. We are just a couple of well-meaning slobs compared to him. So, I'm not real enthusiastic about my asshole buddy trying to put the son-of-a-bitch in jail."

DD was taken aback by the intensity of Rick's words and purpose. It was the kind of intensity usually reserved for the courtroom. It was not like Rick to be gun-shy. Certainly Keislor had demonstrated the most calloused kind of behavior during the Pavlone case, so there really was a reason to believe he would continue to do evil things. Why not this scheme? Of course, the answer to that didn't require a lot of thought...this is murder; it is felony fraud – and if it is true, it is personal.

After Pep left with additional assignments and a handful of note-ridden napkins, DD and Rick sat for a final final.

"Rick, I appreciate what you said, but I don't see anyone other than me having the motivation to run this out to the end – and it has to be run out. Certainly, Dolson won't do it."

"Look, DD, I never really thought that anything I said would dissuade you. Don't misunderstand, I think this thing is real dangerous for you. You aren't a cop or a prosecutor and you don't have that kind of protection. You're just a piss-ant plaintiff's lawyer who a lot of people don't like anyway. All you got is me, and I am going to be in this. Of course, you also have Joe. As smart as we think we are, that ain't much in this situation."

DD watched Rick head off to Helene's apartment on Jackson and went the other way to his place. DD never lived high – even when he had some money. His place was a one-bedroom cottage on the lee side of Telegraph Hill. You could get there by climbing a hundred or so wooden steps from near Embarcadero and Battery, or by driving on the very narrow streets at the top, miraculously finding a parking place and then easily descending maybe forty of those wooden stairs. DD almost always climbed.

While he grew up in a starkly-simple leftist home, DD had acquired a taste for good food – perhaps from the frequent forays in Meadorville where some fine restaurants could be found. Certainly, his marriage to Melanie introduced him to gastric delights, as well as what she could whip up in rooms other than the kitchen.

Over a self-prepared grilled halibut steak and out-of-a-box fettucine with Alfredo sauce, DD listened to Zoot Sims and Chet Baker while he jotted notes for his report to Bud Barstow in Mississippi. In doing so, it became clear to him that what was needed here was simply more work.

There are at least three easily proven connections between Ella Mae White and the law firm of Loudon, Mueller and Keislor: (1) Dru Lacey is in a picture with Ella Mae taken before the Pavlone trial, (2) Darla Reid, Keislor's former secretary, is married to the guy who set up the outfit that sends checks to Ella Mae, (3) Keislor shows up as the lawyer hired by Norm Yamaguchi's insurance company – Yamaguchi, who happens to employ Ella Mae. The quality of the evidence is very high. The quality of what conclusions can be drawn from this high quality evidence is nil.

DD then realized there was a fourth connection that was nearly overlooked and also easily proven: Ella Mae was the jury foreperson on the Pavlone trial where Keislor was, of course, the defense lawyer.

"Pep, it's Dan O'Neil."

"Do you realize, Danny Boy, that if I had a sex life you would be interrupting right now? As it turns out, you're just waking me up, so what the fuck do you want at this hour?" Pep was on all the time, even at midnight.

"Max Loudon," DD began unceremoniously, "who was he before he was a partner of Keislor"

There was a pause. "Doesn't the lone ranger ever sleep?"

Another pause. "Bass and Bosnick, that's where he was. Max had been made a partner with his name on the door and everything. Kip Mueller was an unnamed partner and I don't think Keislor had a window. Max wanted to concentrate on doing just insurance defense. Bob did not want to go that route – he was an old time member of corporate boards. Max took Kip and Keislor and started with some foreign companies – getting them into the country and then defending them when they got here. As you know, Keislor speaks several languages. That's all I know and I am going back to sleep."

"One more, Tonto," DD insisted. "How many lawyers at Loudon, Mueller now?"

"Jesus, DD!" Pep was pleading. "If you weren't such a snob and read your own State Bar Journal, you would have learned about three months ago that Loudon is in the top twenty in the state for lawyers and billings – I think that means somewhere around two hundred lawyers and a several million monthly in billings. OK, kemosabe?"

DD decided to call it a day. To seal it with a sweet note, he dropped an old Sara Vaughn vinyl on the turntable, one that she cut when she was about fifteen – Deep Purple.

***

CHAPTER ELEVEN

Confrontation

"This seems enough to get even Leonard Dolson after Keislor." Jeannie just completed typing and copying DD's report to Bud Barstow. Once he ran it by Joe and Rick, it was going to Jackson by overnight mail.

The three of them gathered in DD's office. Joe started with a wet blanket:

"Did I miss something, or is there no direct evidence that Hugh Keislor did anything approaching improper contact with a juror, let alone that he has anything to do with or even knows about the murder of that juror?"

DD shrugged. "Yeah, I know. At least one member of his staff was present during jury selection and with that same juror within weeks of the start of the trial. That's improper. That's not Keislor. It's also not murder."

Clothed in a stylish sweat suit and shod in running shoes, Rick stared at his copy of the report. " Ya'know, when do these things just land in our lap? I mean, why would you expect at this point to have direct evidence? I meant what I said last night. This guy is smart and rich, and smart and rich people don't get caught all that easily."

DD conceded, "No, you're right Rick. There are a lot of things to do. I am not suggesting we are abandoning the trail to Hugh. The strongest evidence is that Ella Mae's murder relates to that trial and her participation in it. I'm ready to face the beast with some questions. I think that's where I'm going."

Joe rose and began putting on his suit coat. "I have an appearance before Sam Conti in a few minutes, but I think you have to honestly answer the question of why the hell you are doing this."

DD stood and gazed out the window into the garden in the building's inner courtyard.

"OK. I want to do this by myself. Probably for all the wrong reasons – glory, revenge, an Irishman's passion for irony, to show off. The fact is that Sonny asked me to do this and I think that is enough."

Rick asked, "Is Dolson still bitter over – what was that woman's name? "

"Jankovic, Andrea Jankovic."

DD and Joe knew who Rick was referring to.

Berle Yankovic, a University of California professor of political science and outspoken devotee of Karl Marx, had been the philosophical backbone of the Bay Area radical movement since the '50s. His daughter, Andrea, at her San Francisco apartment, had shot and killed a former lover – a guy with very weird sexual tastes who was also the son of the wealthiest Republican in Alameda County.

Dolson, then an assistant district attorney, hero of a reactionary police officers' union, and a regular speaker at various right wing gatherings, wanted more than anything to convict Andrea as a stepping stone to greater glories. The trial very nearly ended his career.

DD and Joe were hired for the defense, although neither had a lot of experience at that time. As essential neophytes, Dolson felt he could take advantage of them.

They argued that Andrea had shot Neal Addison in self-defense. He had brought two others with him to partake of her body, whether she wanted it or not. The essential problem in that defense was that the unquestioned weapon of young Addison's death, a Smith & Wesson .38 caliber revolver, had been discharged six times, with five of the bullets striking Addison in a line from near the tip of his right shoulder to the outer edge of his lower left abdomen. It was difficult to make out an argument that the shots were fired in anguished panic. An additional problem lay in Dolson's threat to introduce evidence that Andrea had become an expert in small arms when she trained with the Communist Cuban Youth Brigades as a high school student.

Her defense had spent hours and a lot of money tracking down Addison's companions of that night – they couldn't find them. Dolson was assisted in the trial by a young lawyer who took the district attorney job because it was there. Jim Herbert was treated as a lackey by Dolson throughout.

Early one morning during the trial, Joe received a telephone call at his home from Herbert. He sounded agitated and began, "Joe, I swear to god I didn't know about this until late last night. Dolson knows the location of the two Latinos with Addison – they're both in custody."

Judge Frank Meyer emerged from his chambers with an obvious mission in mind. He mounted the bench and sighed – an angry sigh. The clerk called the Jankovic case.

"The record should note we are in the courtroom out of the presence of the jury," the judge said, glaring directly at Dolson.

THE COURT: I received a telephone call this morning during my early calendar from the District Attorney. He advised me that his office was aware of the location of the two who supposedly accompanied the deceased the night he was shot by the defendant. When I asked where they were, he indicated they are each in a State prison facility. I asked him when he had acquired that knowledge. He told me he learned it last night from Mr. Herbert. He asked me to ascertain from Mr. Herbert how he got this knowledge and when. So, Mr. Herbert?

[DD turned and whispered to Joe, "That SOB is letting Herbert take the heat!"]

[Jim Herbert stood, with Dolson sitting next to him at counsel table.]

MR. HERBERT: Your honor last night at about ten-thirty, while having an after dinner drink with Mr. Dolson, I learned for the first time of the location of the two potential witnesses. Early this morning, I called the defense counsel and the district attorney.

[Herbert stopped momentarily.]

THE COURT: Mr. Herbert, did Mr. Dolson indicate to you how he learned this clearly relevant information and when?

MR. HERBERT: Yes, your honor, he did. He acquired it, he said, when routinely collecting information to respond to Mr. O'Neil's discovery requests.

THE COURT: And when was that?

[Dolson finally stood up.]

MR. DOLSON: About four months ago.

The two witnesses were produced by order of the Court. DD and Joe spoke with them on the record. They both corroborated Andrea's story of self-defense. DD insisted that they testify and that the jury be told of the duplicity of Dolson. The jury acquitted Andrea. Dolson was held in contempt and required to pay a portion of the cost of the trial. Later, he was demoted to misdemeanor prosecutions. Notwithstanding, he was later able to use his political clout to exploit a series of racially motivated murders in the City and get himself elected as District Attorney four years later. He always harbored a particular resentment of DD because DD relentlessly hammered his immoral ambitions in closing argument in the Jankovic case.

After leaving a note for Jeannie, DD caught the Airporter at the corner of Leavenworth and Mason. It is sixty minutes from the San Francisco airport to LAX and the flights leave every hour on the half hour.

A taxi took him to the glass building at the address Pep had given him. It was one of several and was indeed just across the LA city line in Beverly Hills. The requisite lobby security guard directed DD to the eleventh floor – the top floor, it turned out. The sign on the door was small and unassuming:

David Weisenstock – Insurance Consultant

When DD walked in, there was Darla Reid giving instructions to a gum-snapping, busty young woman behind a glass-topped desk. Just behind her was a large, garish painting of what DD guessed was an impression of the Los Angeles skyline.

When she saw him, Darla stopped cold, as if struck with a sudden and sharp pain. She tried but failed for a moment to get some words out.

Finally, "Well..." Her voice strained to conceal her shock. "Mr. Dan O'Neil. I can't believe it, what are you doing here?!"

Darla was a tall, honey blond with her hair drawn tightly in a bun and a gold hoop swinging from each ear. Her facial features were fine and sharp and she wore expertly-applied make up. Her cold grey eyes darted and flashed, suggesting a suspicious person who was intensely alert. Her demeanor, as DD well remembered, was one of supreme confidence and disdain for the unwashed of the world – a group to which she was sure DD belonged.

"Hello Darla. You should call me Dan. After all, you used to, and we did spend several weeks together a few years ago."

DD's tone always had a sarcastic edge around the likes of Darla Reid, but he wasn't much interested in small talk at that moment.

"Sure, Dan. But I am more than a little surprised to see you here. Did you come to see me?"

She had regained her composure and now exhibited a sense of apprehension.

"Actually, I came to see your husband. But you will do for the moment. "

Darla's apparent apprehension became more pronounced.

"How did you know about the marriage and how did you find me?"

The pitch of her otherwise satin smooth contralto rose, betraying the conversion of apprehension to urgent fright.

"I made the acquaintance of Lowell – I guess he's your step son."

DD didn't like ratting out the poor guy, but this thing had to start someplace if anything was going to get done.

She didn't like that bit of news.

"Of course. What – are you back in criminal defense? I mean David tries to take care of the boy but you know druggies...then maybe you don't. What the hell did he tell you that got you here – got you here unannounced? Are you looking for David to pay your fees?"

It was at that point clear to DD that Darla desperately hoped the answer to any of those questions was "yes." but that she knew it wouldn't be and she was nearing panic as she backed away from DD toward a door behind her.

Realizing that Darla could well just disappear behind that door, DD spoke quickly.

"I don't represent Lowell. Whatever his problems with the law, I don't have a lot to do with. I'm really here to get some answers about a woman named Ella Mae White"

DD looked intently at Darla as he floated these words. She was clearly dumbstruck, grinding all the gears of her native cleverness to manage this thunderbolt.

"Are you a cop now, or something? Why are you asking me about this woman?"

DD stepped toward her, catching a glimpse of the young woman at the desk whose rate of chewing and snapping had increased as she watched bug eyed.

"No, Darla I'm not a cop. I'm still the piss-ant plaintiff's lawyer I always was. I'm asking about Ella Mae White because she has been murdered. You remember her, don't you? She was the foreperson of the jury in the Pavlone case."

DD was now standing only a foot from Darla in an intimidating posture.

With eyes wide, Darla took a deep breath and replied, "Look Dan, calm down. I don't know what you're talking about. I hope you're not relying on something poor Lowell told you. Shit, I don't remember all the people on the juries in cases I worked on. Christ, I was only a secretary."

With the cursing, Darla was regaining her cold composure.

"Anyway, I don't have to answer questions and don't intend to. If you don't have insurance business here, you don't have any business. Please leave."

DD backed up a little and lowered his voice again. "Darla, I know a lot about this, so you can't just tell me to go away. Maybe I should share some of what I know. Here's an example: your old boss, Keislor, shows up supposedly as the insurance defense counsel for a decent guy named Yamaguchi. Hugh is defending Yamaguchi in a sexual assault claim brought by someone named Malvina Montrose. The secretary to Yamaguchi is none other than Ella Mae, who is – I guess you could say – 'close' to Malvina. For the next three years Ella Mae and Malvina cohabitate – mostly in Indian County, Mississippi. Ella Mae ends up – just about two weeks ago – dead from a bullet hole in the middle of her forehead. Malvina is nowhere to be found, but what is found is a copy of a bunch of checks written on Lowell's company account – a company your husband set up. Your memory is excellent and you were more than a secretary to Hugh."

DD thought he would try a guess. "There's more but I think you get the point."

She smiled, DD later told Joe, "the bitch smiled at me!"

"Mr. O'Neil, you always have seen the world in conspiratorial terms and brought a fertile if delusional imagination to that viewpoint. It sounds to me like you are laboring under a profound misunderstanding. I know you well enough to know that I am not going to convince you to back off. Here is my lawyer's business card. Talk to him if you want, but get the hell out of here."

"Where's your husband?"

DD wasn't backing off.

"Maybe he'd want to talk to me at this stage rather than force me to talk to the district attorney."

"You're nuts, O'Neil, and what's worse, you're a shitty lawyer. What – are you looking for an excuse?"

She had become like a cornered badger – all but spitting at DD, but wasn't that an interesting comment – "an excuse?" We are getting warm, DD thought as he turned to leave.

DD gave the gum chewer his business card.

"You're forcing my hand, Darla," he said as he opened the office outer door, and then he turned and looked at her, "But, then, I do have a hand."

DD had not looked at the card Darla gave him until he was in the elevator. Son-of-a-bitch!, J.Irving Levy, Counselor at Law, 220 Montgomery Street, San Francisco. Buster! A world of mirrors.

By 4 p.m. DD was on his return flight – landing at SFO at 4:50, some 400 miles later. The world was not only and merely a succession of mirrors, it was getting smaller. At 5:20, he was in his office in the Tenderloin, looking at telephone messages – among them was one that he expected – Hugh Keislor. The return number was direct to Hugh's office.

"Dan, how 're you doing?"

Keislor had a big voice that attempted to communicate sincere concern. It seemed to DD, however, that in reality it sent a message of malevolence. Before DD had a chance to respond to this greeting, Keislor, in quiet tones of reasonableness, went on, "Look, I don't want to beat around the bush. You knew that Darla would call me and so you know why I am calling you. While I don't appreciate you bothering Darla now that she's retired from this firm, I guess, from what she said, you have a justifiable misunderstanding."

A smile crept across DD's face.

"I thought I'd better call to do what I could to set you straight. I mean, there is no reason for you to get into a lot of trouble because of the ruminations of a drug addict."

The smarmy tone, the structure of the presentation, and the veiled threat was exactly what was used on several occasions during Pavlone when Keislor had been caught in some impropriety or the other. Rick called it "creeping crud."

DD's smile had grown wider. "I'm not sure what you mean, Hugh. By drug addict, I guess you're referring to Lowell Weisenstock. You should understand he is not why I went to see Darla."

DD paused, which brought a brief silence. He went on, "Y'gotta understand, Hugh, that there is some real damning evidence that is not likely to be refuted. That evidence is certainly enough for the authorities to look long and hard at you. Hugh, the evidence is that you were the lead defense counsel in a trial in which a murder victim was the foreperson. That same woman was employed by a guy whose insurance company hired you. This foreperson received checks from nearly the end of the Pavlone case for more than three years through an elaborate scheme in which Darla was involved. The murdered woman, in addition, has left me an envelope with material that suggests she was bribed by you."

DD did not mention the photograph or Dru Lacey.

There was silence. Finally, DD felt compelled to check on whether Keislor was still on the other end of the line.

"Hugh?"

"You know O'Neil," Keislor finally spoke, "I have always had a lot of regard for you. I mean, you are a smart guy and not the run-of-the-mill plaintiff lawyer. But this disappoints me and, frankly, gives me a pain in the ass. I can't be responsible for what people do to or for each other. I tried a case and the jury – including Ella Mae White – decided that you didn't carry your burden of proof. Any attempt to make more out of it than that will end up in a terrible wrangle and probably a judgment for slander against you."

Keislor's voice was rising in volume and tone.

"If you want an explanation, I can give it to you with irrefutable evidence to support it. If you just want to run around making claims – I'll just sue you or..."

DD's smile returned. "Or what Hugh?"

At minimum, Keislor was frightened. His mind was racing to assemble a way to defend against this adversary who had always been so tenacious.

"How am I to get this explanation and the evidence, Hugh?"

"How do you want it, Dan?"

"On the record."

"No way. You take your chances with what you think you know, but I am not giving you a free shot at my bare ass."

Keislor was ridiculing DD's suggestion. He regrouped.

"O'Neil, if you push this, you're going to look like a fool, just like you did in Pavlone. You're a smart guy but you don't look beyond what superficially appears. As an example, don't you realize that this Ella Mae hung around with a very shady group of characters?"

A bolt of anger shot into DD's head; this son-of-a-bitch does it every time. He pisses on the character of the victim with stunning audacity – he did it in Pavlone and probably every case.

DD took a deep breath. "You mean like your legal assistant, Dru Lacey?"

She probably wouldn't talk to DD anyway.

"What do you mean – Dru? What has she got to do with this?"

He either doesn't know about the picture or doesn't know that Ella Mae had a copy.

"The murder victim was seeing Dru socially, Hugh, and I think you knew it."

Momentarily chastened, Keislor responded, "Well, I don't know about any such thing. Again, I can't be responsible for what people who work here do on their own time. Y'know Dan, my partner, Kip Mueller, married a woman who was on one of my juries. No one thought anything of that and there was nothing to think."

Not to be denied, DD tipped over Keislor's argument. "I heard about that, Hugh. Kip met the woman he eventually married a year after the trial. Dru was seeing Ella Mae at least three months before the trial and then she sat next to you while we picked a jury."

Another long pause, and Keislor softened his tone and words. "Dan, ok. I'll admit the superficial facts create basis for suspicion – not unreasonably. Maybe what we ought to do is meet – talk face to face."

"Hugh, the only way I will do that is if our meeting is recorded by a certified shorthand reporter and you are represented by counsel."

"What?" Keislor was upset. "What the hell are you doing with this shit?"

He was basically shouting, at this point.

"Your suggestion is outrageous!"

"Hugh. I represent the office of the Attorney General of the State of Mississippi for the purpose of investigating the murder of Ella Mae. I think you should have a lawyer."

DD really enjoyed saying that. He'd never said it before in his life.

Keislor seemed resigned. "Do what you have to do, Dan. Just be prepared for a big fall."

He hung up.

At that point, DD called Joe at home. He related the conversation with Keislor and asked:

"What do you think? Is he run to ground?"

Joe told DD that he was either run to ground or, now that he was alerted, scheming a way to eliminate his pursuer.

Jeannie was earlier than usual the next morning.

"Jesus, DD, I was awake all night thinking about that report you sent to Mississippi. This is serious stuff. Did Hugh Keislor have Ella Mae White killed? I mean, we always said what a bastard he was, but this is hard to believe."

She brought DD a cup of the coffee he had made earlier – a rare occurrence.

He smiled in recognition of the special occasion.

"Of course, if you don't believe it, then how does Dolson? That's the point. I am now convinced Keislor is in the middle of it – bribery and murder. I just don't know how it was done and we're some distance from getting it proven. I saw Darla yesterday and talked to Keislor. She denies everything and basically is calling me crazy. Hugh is trying to convince me that I am looking at this the wrong way. He says it all has a perfectly innocent explanation. He also says what Darla says – I shouldn't believe Lowell because he is a drug addict."

Jeannie sat on the edge of DD's client chair, opposite his desk. "So, you expected him to confess? What did he say when you told him about the picture? "

Casually, DD spoke while he was looking through business cards he had collected. "I didn't tell him. I think I'll keep that for a surprise. I did mention Dru Lacey, however, and that shook him up. He probably can't be sure he's got her under control. It could be he knows about the little affair between Dru and Lowell. If he does, right now that's the only evidence of a connection he thinks I know about. I'm calling Sonny to see how my report was received in Jackson.

***

Part 3: Change of Venue

He can run, but he cannot hide –
even if you must look for six thousand miles.

Sonny Elliot's assessment of Daniel Dermot O'Neil

CHAPTER TWELVE

Flanking Maneuver

DD brought Sonny up to date on his confrontations.

"Your report was thorough and promising, but, as you write, we don't have anything conclusive from your end. The problem is that Bud is now focusing on Praeger. We need to make the connection between him and your friends in 'Frisco. He just isn't inspired about lawyers and the like, unless he can connect Praeger – gotta get the shooter, he says. So, we are getting toll telephone records."

Right. Barstow has a murder and possible statewide cop corruption. He isn't really interested in jury tampering in San Francisco – gotta get Sonny to stop saying "'Frisco."

Sonny continued, "I don't think we have a prayer of getting a warrant for an investigation here. With this line-up of judges, we might just tip off all the bad guys. There's a whole contingent of judges who have been believing cops for years and still others who think Bud is just doing this for glory. All of them think Bud is trying to change things that don't need changing. He's a threat to people who have been in charge around here since the end of Reconstruction."

117

"Sonny, I am by no means a prosecutor, but can't you crank up a grand jury and get around this judge problem?"

"We've talked about it, but it won't work. There is probably one judge we could get assigned for that purpose and expect to get somewhere. But there are two insurmountable problems: (1) all the witnesses that we know of now are in California. The single exception is this Malvina Montrose and we don't have a clue where to find her. Based on what we now have, we would be following the trail from California to find our killer here. (2) If a grand jury cranks up there is just no question that the bad guys would learn about it and skip, lay low, and destroy evidence."

Sonny was exasperated.

The two men were silent for a moment, then DD observed, "That means we're limited to hard digging. Maybe my stunts here over the last couple days will stir up something."

"There is another problem with that DD. Ella Mae withdrew $65,000 in cash just two days before she turned up dead. It's not in the house and we can't find any record of it being re-deposited or invested elsewhere."

"Wasn't she trying to buy a Porsche?"

"There isn't any new Porsche. The problem is that someone could and no doubt would argue her death was part of a robbery and all this jury bribery stuff was just our imagination – or your imagination. The argument would go that we screwed up in hiring you because you have a bone to pick."

"Sonny, that's been a risk since we had breakfast at the McNaught's. But what about Malvina? Did she split with the money? Did Ella Mae give it to her?"

Sonny was in agreement. Something was going on between Ella Mae and Malvina that would suggest an impending split.

Scratching his head, dropping his chin into his free elbow-propped hand, DD could see this had a real chance of working out very badly. He had to make something else – some other approach – work.

"How about finding Malvina? What happens if you or Bud come out here and try to talk Dolson into starting his own grand jury? He would be investigating the bribery itself. Maybe that could be used to convince your judges that the murder requires their attention."

"I suppose a grand jury there could subpoena Keislor and some records," Sonny was ruminating. "Realistically, though, we can't expect much from the guy who has done this. He wouldn't have a problem lying to a grand jury and he sure as hell can't be real worried about his license at this point."

"Okay. I need to do some thinking and I need some legal research. What I think I need from you is a persistent effort to find the money and/or Malvina. Sonny, we need to keep in closer telephone touch."

"You're right. We can't fold at this point. But you're out on a limb there. The portfolio we provided is pretty thin. I think you have to report to your local authorities pretty soon to let them know we're operating in their jurisdiction. Of course, there is the other problem that Keislor knows you're on to him and Darla. I wouldn't overlook the possibility that son-of-a-bitch wouldn't be looking to snuff you."

"I don't think he's that dumb, but I appreciate the concern. Don't you owe me some information on this killer cop from the Delta?"

"Right, I'll talk to Bud about that this morning. Anything else?"

DD cleared his throat and asked, "Have you heard from the Indian County Public Administrator?"

Sonny laughed. "I knew that was going to come up. As a matter of fact, I talked to Mattie yesterday. She said she had run across something that you might find interesting and she was looking to get your contact information. I know she already had that, but it became clear to me that she really wanted to find out if you were otherwise spoken for. Don't get too excited, DD, but the odds are you'll hear from her pretty soon."

DD sat up and looked into the telephone receiver. "Damn it, Sonny. Don't you mess with me!"

"You'll see, my friend. You'll see."

I think I'll stay around the office for a few days. She might call. Damn it, why does the subject of her disturb me so?

DD determined to get back to the case at hand, although he could be seen to be looking off into space occasionally as he made notes on a yellow pad:

1. Why was EMW murdered now? Nearly four years since the Pavlone verdict. What happened in the interim? Was there an event that caused the killing? Motivation unrelated to the Pavlone jury?

2. Was the package for me prepared just before the killing? Was its preparation the reason for the killing? If it was, how come ...not destroyed? Not hard to find.

3. With the apparent purpose of the package to tell me there had been bribery, why so cryptic? Why not be more explicit? Is there something else?

4. Where did the money paid to EMW come from, i.e. how did it get to SR??

5. Why did EMW draw out the $65k? What happened to it?

6. Where is MM? Who is MM? What does she know?

7. Where could Keislor fit into all of this? How could he connect with a cop in Mississippi? Why would he take such a huge risk?

8. With these kind of stakes, why would there be a picture with such obvious relevance? Is there some

sort of lesbian conspiracy? Why? How? Is this a scheme somehow put together by Lacey and Reid??

9. Was EMW's murder just in the course of simple robbery? A spat with MM?

DD copied the one page of questions and gave Rick and Joe each one. He related the conversation with Sonny.

Joe asked, "When was the incident Yamaguchi described where he jumped Malvina? We should start putting together the sequence of events and see what it shows."

Rick agreed. "You know, I'm trying to figure how the hell they do this. How do they decide to bribe a juror in a civil case? As I remember it, this woman was not even on the jury until that little guy...can't remember his name, was found dead in his room."

Jeannie was at the door to DD's office and chimed "Reginald Renfro, that's the name of the guy."

They all sat silently for a moment, then Rick wondered, "You don't suppose that this guy was murdered to make way for Ella Mae. I mean, Jesus, that is just too bizarre. You kill someone to get a result the chances of which are real long?"

"That is unbelievably ruthless, if it is true. But first, let's see what there is to support the notion he was killed," Joe suggested and DD was making a note.

Joe went on, "It is even more complicated than that. Let's assume that Keislor or someone else in that shop told Ella Mae that they would pay her a lot of money to deliver a defense verdict. When would that deal be made? Wouldn't it have to be after she was on the jury? But that picture was taken two months before there was a jury. No one is going to believe contact was made before she was even called – I wouldn't believe that."

"That would mean..." Rick had stood up and began pacing with his hands in his pockets. "the deal was made quickly after Ella Mae was on the jury, even as an alternate."

"Jeannie, when does the Yamaguchi file say the Malvina incident happened?"

"September 1, 1979. That was the Saturday of the Labor Day weekend."

DD looked at Rick. "I worked on my opening statement that weekend and we spent all three days right here getting witnesses ready. Jeannie, didn't I have you check out the jury *voir dire* transcript? That would confirm the dates."

Once Jeannie reported that the transcript confirmed, DD took up a thesis:

"Suppose that Dru finds out that her buddy is on the jury for this big deal trial. She reports this to Hugh and the scheme comes together quickly, bringing Malvina into it. Unless this crowd – whoever it is – has corrupted the jury commissioner's office, getting a friend on the jury was just random fortune. As far as we know right now, it could be that Ella Mae initiated the deal."

"Wait a minute," Rick insisted, "what is this Malvina for? Where does she come from? Why the seduction of Yamaguchi? Jesus, Joe, Ella Mae wasn't even on the jury yet. She was an alternate."

"You're right, Rick," Joe responded. "I can't figure the scheme to trap Yamaguchi. Was something else in progress and that just became a handy way to cover the payments to Ella Mae? Yamaguchi says the two of them – Malvina and Ella Mae – were close. Maybe they were close enough to plan some sort of shakedown of Yamaguchi and this plan came along. Did Weisenstock already have this insurer before this came down? That would be astoundingly fortuitous. It would also line up all the stars in the known universe and that is too improbable to fly for me."

DD stopped writing. "Hey, you guys, what if – hypothetically speaking – Yamaguchi's insurance company in fact never heard of this claim and never in fact did anything about it? That would mean that Weisenstock just appeared once the incident went down and Yamaguchi simply accepted him as an insurance agent. Who checks these kinds of things?"

Rick thought for a moment and then returned to his chair, speaking quietly. "If the money was to bribe Ella Mae for her vote and influence on that jury, LaStrada was the direct beneficiary. Under that theory, it would be La Strada that provided the bread to pay Ella Mae. Can a Mexican corporation hide such payments? As insurance premiums? It seems to me the answer to both questions is 'yes.'"

DD then weighed in. "When an auto maker gets hit with a verdict for a defect – particularly a big verdict – people notice. The press picks it up and every time a vehicle like the first one is in an accident, the question is posed – did the defect cause this injury? That's why General Motors settled as many of the early pickup fire cases it could. The fuel system defect was not recognized by lawyers until I got that verdict here just two years ago. Since then, everything got real expensive for the largest manufacturer in the world. GM only made about 60,000 of the defective pickups and LaStrada has made and sold four times that many worldwide. The budget for claim prevention is likely very, very big. It would be justified by the exposure. So, insurance-type questions arise."

"Yes," Joe concluded, "and if the insurer doesn't have to pay off any claims, there's a compelling incentive to bully or bribe jurors and maybe even commit murder. But that's fantasy logic. The consequences of getting caught are just too dire for anyone with a lick of sense to try it."

DD smiled, "You remember what Mick always said, don't you Joe?"

"Gimme a break, DD. Mick always said a lot of things. Which are you talking about?"

"Arrogance is just a form of ignorance."

Jeannie stuck her head in the door. "Dan. There's someone on the phone identifying herself as the Public Administrator for Indian County Mississippi. She wants to talk to you... says its important."

DD's heart very clearly jumped into his throat. He rudely motioned his office mates out of the room.

In his best, dispassionate voice, he spoke into the handset, "Dan O'Neil."

"Mistah O'Neil, this is Mathilda Deare in Magnolia City. We met just a few days ago when you were here. Do you remember me?"

While it would have been out of character for DD to say it, he thought *you've hardly been out of my mind since we met. Hell yes I remember you!*

"Of course, Ms. Deare. It's good to hear from you. What can I do for you?"

There was a pause, possibly because she too had a thought she dare not express.

"Well, as you know, I was charged with the responsibility of locating and doing an inventory of Ms. White's assets before her apparent heirs retained a lawyer for that purpose. They retained Mr. Casey. He, Mr. Casey, recently handed me a fancy writing tablet that he said was in material I sent over to him – he asked if I knew why it was blank and pages had been torn out. I remembered such a book and didn't think anything of it when I put the papers together for him. But, I didn't notice that there had been pages torn out.

"Mr. Casey suggested that I closely examine the blank page following the torn out section. When I did that, I could make out the imprint of a long-hand entry that seemed to be transferred from the missing sheets. Sheriff McNaught concurs – as does Mr. Elliot in the Attorney General's office."

A little impatient, DD asked, "What does it say or seem to say?"

Mattie's very business-like tone and manner was a little disappointing to DD, but this was, after all, a potentially important subject.

"Well, I hate to do this to you but I have decided to take Mr. Elliot's suggestion and not tell you over the telephone," Mattie went on in the same official tone. "He says that you are the only one he knows who can figure out whether this imprint tells us anything important and if I tell you what I think it says, it might corrupt your reading of it. "

Unsure what to make of this, DD cautiously asked, "Does that mean I have to come back to Magnolia City?"

"Well, I think I can bring it to you."

There was a definite acceleration of DD's heart rate with this suggestion.

"There is a national conference of public administrators in Sacramento week after next. I should attend. Could we get together for a few minutes when I am there?"

Few minutes! I'll make it happen!

"Sure. Just give me the details and I'll arrange to meet you in Sacramento."

"I thought I would take some of my vacation and go out to San Francisco first, then go up to Sacramento. I have always wanted to visit. That way you won't have to trouble with the trip up to Sacramento."

"You're coming here? That would be great. Maybe you'd let me take you to dinner?"

DD was now standing up, speaking carefully into the phone.

"Oh, you wouldn't have to do that. I have to learn to make my way around strange places, I haven't been away from Indian County often and then only to New Orleans or Memphis."

"No, I insist !"

The City Men's Final Match was between DD and Joe. They had scheduled it for that day over the lunch hour at the Y. DD's head was not in the game. Joe did not yet realize that his best friend was in love – possibly for the first time in his life. There was scant knowledge around the shop of his interest in the Indian County, Mississippi, Public Administrator. As skeptical as DD was about women and as protective as he was of those particular emotions, it would not have occurred to Joe that this could be something serious. Women always loved DD – maybe because of his sullen appearance in social contexts or, as in the case of his former wife, because of his lean and muscular body. Nonetheless, he rarely had a serious relationship and never initiated one – serious or not.

After the match – which was short because Joe beat him in two games – Joe became the City Champion again. DD hardly noticed.

Back at the office they returned to the subject of the murder of the former jury foreperson. Between them, a list of questions was developed – a long list – longer than the one DD had made earlier. Jeannie typed it up and DD faxed it to Sonny Elliot in Jackson. Joe was most concerned with DD going too far with this pursuit of Hugh Keislor until there was more solid evidence.

Late that afternoon, DD and Sonny had a long telephone conversation. Sonny recognized much work was needed on the specifics of the murder. He promised to find an answer on the whereabouts of Malvina. The only two cars anyone knew to be associated with Ella Mae and Malvina were in the driveway when Ella Mae's body was found. How did Malvina leave and where was she?

"By the way," Sonny said casually, "our off-the-wall suspect, Praeger, is on vacation. The problem is no one knows where and he ain't home. I know our suspicions about this guy are speculative, but if we're right, he is one dangerous SOB. I teletyped a photo of the guy to your friend Larry Harrington. Praeger might be looking for you if your recent confrontations hit a mark. I will also fax you that additional stuff on him I promised, but not until morning."

Sonny said he would get G.A. McNaught some investigatory help and start canvassing the neighborhood around Ella Mae's house.

"Hey, DD! Did you hear from Ms. Deare? Rumor is she is headed to San Francisco."

DD is given to blushing easily; he did on this occasion.

"Yeah. What do you think of that page with the imprints?"

126

"Christ, I don't know. I'll have it analyzed for a match to Ella Mae's handwriting. The words don't mean anything to me. Of course, we could have sent it by courier or mail. There really is no need for the Public Administrator to trouble herself. Nice of her to undertake the chore, don't you think?"

"You got messages, boss."

Jeannie's disposition was always better when there was money in the bank.

"Rick is at the Double Play, Melanie is pining for you, and Larry Harrington returned your call."

DD stepped into Arty's office. "Can you do a thing in criminal law for me? What is the procedure on interstate crime where most of the perpetrators are in a different state than the one where the crime was committed?"

Arty sat back, pushing away one of several volumes on his cluttered desk. "So, do I assume that there have been crimes by these folks in the state where they are found?"

"Yeah, but we want to bring them into the crime committed in the other state. Could I have something by Monday?"

"Sure..." Arty was writing in his assignment book. "By the way, on the question of whether Judith Pavlone would have a cause of action out of this jury tampering hypothesis, it's fascinating. There are actually two reported cases – one really old and the other semi-old – that say you have a fraud case or tortious interference. I'll write it up for you."

"Hmm. That sounds interesting."

DD picked up the phone on Arty's desk and dialed Larry Harrington.

"Hey, can you meet me at the Double Play for drinks and dinner, or is this go-to-mass night?"

"See you in a half hour."

At the Double Play, DD took a sip of his first whiskey for the evening, as did Rick.

"So, did you and Helene put to rest your depression over the settlement?"

DD wasn't interested in Rick's sex life, but Rick liked to have its prodigiousness acknowledged.

"She's a sweet lady, that Helene. Made sweeter I think when she learned what my fee would be on that case. Of course, I didn't tell her how much that fee goes to the bank. I just sort of reveled in her continued sweetness." Rick was calm and, for the moment anyway, sated. He sat up and flashed his gleaming teeth. "So what has the Lone Ranger been up to since our little session this morning?"

DD filled Rick in on the conversations with Sonny and the list of questions, as well as the fact that a writing tablet was discovered that might prove interesting, but without mentioning Mattie Deare.

"DD, why don't we have more on this possible shooter? I mean, that is something I would think is easy if the guy is a cop"

"We're supposed to get more by fax tomorrow. But that is a piece of this I can't do much about. Sonny is concerned that this guy is a real bad ass and might be looking for me now. I can't see that, at least not yet."

DD gave Rick a copy of the questions he and Joe had worked up.

"I'm meeting Larry Harrington here tonight. He's subbing for Dolson next week. That might be an opportunity to blow some light into the case from this end. I'll need some help from you."

Rick read the list and when he was finished ordered drinks and dice cups from Denise.

GiGi came up to the table. "Jesus I'm glad you guys have enough money to eat here. If you didn't I'd starve."

Harrington's broad-shouldered frame came through the front door, and after a few greetings to some at the bar, he joined Rick and DD and a dice cup. Each rolled. Rick was out with three sixes. "I love to beat the Irish."

"Between the Irish and the Mexicans, Rick, there's not a lot of luck to go around, so we share from time to time."

Larry was shaking the dice cup furiously. It did no good. DD won.

"Shit, you invite me for a drink and then beat me at dice." Harrington was disconsolate. He motioned to Denise, "I pay for these."

"So," Harrington stood up and removed his coat, "what's happening in your big conspiracy case, DD?" He dropped into the chair and leaned against the wall, smiling and sipping.

DD brought Larry and Rick up to date, but again didn't mention Mattie.

"Larry, I need a lot of help. I am running out of ways to get evidence locally – you remember that I don't have law enforcement credentials. Bank records would be helpful – whatever books that Darla has. Telephone records, that sort of thing. "

Larry took a long draw on his scotch and soda.

"You know, Leo Citriani is sitting at the bar. His brother, Tony, is a lieutenant in General Works. If he brought something to me, I could rely on it. To get a subpoena, we'll need affidavits – to do the interview, get the affidavit, and produce a memo will be tough to do in a week. I'll only be acting D.A. for that long. We do have some luck. Jack Richards is the master calendar judge this same week. He's got the balls necessary to authorize a subpoena."

DD leaned across the table. "So, what are you suggesting?"

"DD, we have to find Tony, get him interested enough that he assigns someone or does it himself, starting right now."

Rick quickly grasped the point. "Denise! Could you please get Leo a drink on me? I owe him."

She did. Leo turned from the bar and looked at Rick, holding up the glass in salute and thanks. He then strolled over to the table.

"Hey you guys, what's this? The last time the Mexicans and the Irish got together around here there was a full scale war against the United States. Is that what's going on here?"

Leo Citriani was a short, thick fireman with coarse black hair and a substantial mustache to match. A native San Franciscan raised in the Mission District, he spoke with that strange accent unique to the neighborhood and the generation.

DD was never able to resist. "That was in Texas and Northern Mexico, Leo. At least you know about the event. It's always good to see you. "

"Ok, Danny, now we know why you got divorced." Leo's firehouse bantering skills were finely honed.

"Leo," Harrington spoke directly to the burley fireman, "where's your brother right now? I need some help. Actually, Dan here needs some help."

Leo smiled, looking at DD. "Y'know Dan, I don't think Tony would do anything special for you. You guys are not exactly at the same end of the political spectrum. I mean, he wouldn't give a weekend to help me put in my driveway and I'm his big brother, f'chrissake."

"Leo," Harrington got the floor again, "I think I want him to do it for me. I should talk to him tonight, if possible. I don't want to get Dolson involved just yet."

"So, I don't want to know about it. Larry, for you Tony would do anything, but he's at Kaiser right now. He just had athroscopic surgery on his knee. They're letting him out tonight and he's headed for Cazadero tomorrow and the weekend. As long as you guys aren't putting together a basketball team, he might help."

Leo laughed at his little joke and wrote down Tony's home telephone number.

Harrington took the note and went to the telephone.

"I gotta go." Leo stood up. "Thanks for the drink Rick. Dan, the crack about the politics is just that – everybody pretty much respects you. It's just that you are pretty rough on the cops when they make a little mistake. For my money, they deserve it, but they are my family."

DD smiled at the happy fireman. "You mean little mistakes like beating the shit out of my client because he asked why he was being stopped? Not a little mistake, Leo."

Leo laughed again. "You know what I mean Dan, you know what I mean."

He slapped backs and shook hands down the bar and out into the night.

Harrington returned to the table.

"Well, Tony is willing to help. Kearny is his captain, so that shouldn't be a problem. Now, who is he getting affidavits from?"

DD looked at Rick. "Lowell?"

Rick nodded. "Larry, do you remember Roy Lindstrom?"

Harrington thought for a minute. "Isn't that the guy they thought smuggled a gun into the Black Liberation leader, what's his name? He was a lawyer. That's it. That's all I can call up. I was just a baby lawyer at the time. What about him?"

"It's a long story, but Roy is a good friend of mine. No one could make a case on him for the gun smuggling so they went after him on a variety of other things. Being a radical, he didn't exactly take care of his books correctly, so they got him. He was disbarred but got readmitted about two years ago. He lives in Nevada City. He is representing the guy Tony should get an affidavit from a guy named Lowell Weisenstock."

"So, where's Weisenstock and what will he tell us?"

Rick smiled. "Larry, you are about to have him in your sixth floor accommodations. There's a San Francisco warrant for his arrest for probation violations. It looks like you have a good hand. Right now, he is being processed out of the Nevada County Jail."

DD leaned forward. "Lowell is the only full time employee of the outfit with the bank account those checks to the victim came from. We talked to him a few days ago in Tahoe City. I've a got a tape recording of that conversation. It doesn't say all that much, but clearly he is privy to a lot of information about the checks and the connection to Darla Reid. If you can deal with him on this probation thing, he may share that information."

Harrington sat back and shook his head.

"Talk about interconnections, jesus. DD, this guy Lindstrom is some kind of red. Can I trust him?"

DD dug into his coat pocket and pulled out a business card. "Here, call him. He's more reliable than your Democrats and Republicans. Do you want me to talk to Tony with you?"

"Well, hell yes. I don't want to miss something. You're the only one who knows the facts."

GiGi walked up to the table and hailed Denise.

"Hey, let's get these guys fed before they get drunk."

It was agreed over dinner that Harrington would meet DD at the office on Saturday morning and drive to Cazadero. Rick agreed to draft some subpoena language specifying the information being subpoenaed.

Harrington went home. DD and Rick stopped in at The Ramp to catch a set of Cleve Nunez' Latin jazz. An early night for Rick and a late one for DD.

***

CHAPTER THIRTEEN

Marshaling Forces

"Sonny, we need your official state people to fax a request for help from our DA's office, as soon as possible today. That should help grease the skids, even if we do have a bribery case to investigate."

"Did you get my fax on this guy Praeger?"

"Yes, but I don't understand it. I mean the picture and physical description should be helpful, but what is this about the – what the hell is it? – The Fraternal Order of Mississippi Law Enforcers. Is that the police union?"

"No, there's only one guy in it – the only member and the chief executive officer – Arnold Crossmore. The only legitimate thing they do is sell disability insurance to cops. We don't have a real aggressive state agency that regulates those activities, so we don't know a lot. What we do know, however, is that Praeger and two other cops – all three of which we suspect as being contract killers – have a policy through the FOMLE. It looks like they are the only ones insured in the State of Mississippi – at least they are the only ones who have identified the FOMLE policy in employee forms that we recently required of all cops."

DD leaned back in his chair, cradling the telephone receiver between his ear and shoulder.

"You told me about the grounds for suspecting Praeger. What about these other guys?"

"A little over a year ago, a judge in Cook County, Illinois, was run down in a crosswalk right outside the courthouse. The driver got away clean. The district attorney's investigation turned up a witness that says a guy matching the description of the hit and run driver had been in the judge's courtroom several times that week. It also matches the description of one of these insured by FOMLE. We think he is involved in other crimes with Praeger and this other guy. On this one, they provided him an alibi that he was in Mississippi at the time the judge was done in."

"The connection – other than disability insurance?" DD insisted.

"The judge was sitting without a jury in a trial about injuries and a fire that allegedly resulted from the defective manufacture of a hair dryer. That manufacturer is insured by a company that owns the Fraternal Order of Mississippi Law Enforcers."

"Of course, there have been other complaints against this hair dryer company – right?"

Sonny delivered the salient fact. "All settled early and cheaply out of court."

"This third guy may have made a quick trip to Virginia to hide evidence of a defective truck brake. He was seen and the eyewitness turned up dead – fortunately *after* he gave the description to local police. Nice example of law and order, don't you think?"

A bad movie script. Real bad. Who the hell could come up with this? Sonny's serious. It's overwhelming. There couldn't possibly be a connection to Keislor – it's too insane. Fraternal Order of Mississippi Law Enforcers, f'crissake!

For the second day in a row and probably only the third time in ten years, Jeannie brought DD a cup of coffee. He wasn't going to let this pass for a second time.

"What is going on? Aren't you afraid of losing your card in NOW?"

Jeannie sat on the edge of the client chair, hands folded in her lap, and asked. "Are you in physical danger again? I mean, when this happened the first time, I had just gone to work and really thought it was exciting. I was too stupid to know what it means to have someone trying to kill your boss."

She relaxed into the chair and tried to appear calm, but her bright blue eyes betrayed the kind of concern that most call fear.

"I have great difficulty thinking that I am in physical danger," DD responded. "The evidence, while it is stacking up, just isn't sufficient to justify taking a chance getting caught attempting murder. The prudent course would be just to lay low. For all we know, this guy in Mississippi has taken off and that ends the connection. Of course, I'll try not to be as stupid as I can be, but there is no need to worry about that sort of thing."

Jeannie wasn't convinced. "I think this is different. Keislor is arrogant. He could rely on the big lie gambit – everybody-thinks-I-did-it-but-nobody-believes-I-would-because- everyone-would-think-I-did. Do you understand what I'm saying? This guy thinks everyone else in the world is a fool, so he acts accordingly."

Jeannie was very serious about this.

"You might be an exception to that, so if he deals in some final way with you, he doesn't have a problem left."

Chin in cupped hand, DD leaned on his desk – a light had gone on in his head.

"Maybe that's it. Maybe I ascribe too much rationality to old Hugh and forget about his blinding arrogance. Maybe he really is doing all this 'cuz he just doesn't think anyone is smart enough to catch him."

Exasperated, Jeannie retorted, "I don't want this to go your head O'Neil, but I think he knows you are smart enough, and that's where I get scared."

She then snatched the ringing telephone receiver off the set on DD's desk. "O'Neil Law Office." She paused, then looked at DD.

"It's Mr. Elliot and he sounds pretty excited."

She handed the receiver to DD.

"DD, we got some luck. The truck driver who lives down the road from Ella Mae's house just returned from a long haul. We talked to him. First of all, there is no car registered to Ella Mae or Malvina that we don't know about. The ones we do know about are in the garage. So, this truck driver tells us that he was leaving early on the day of the murder – June 16 – to make his run. This was about 6 a.m.. He saw a dark-colored sedan of Japanese manufacture pulling into Ella Mae's driveway. There was only a driver and no passenger. That driver, this guy swears, was Malvina. This guy says he had eyes for Malvina and had plenty of chance to become familiar when he helped her and Ella Mae start the Cadillac one day. He's very confident. He also says he was surprised to see her because he was aware that she had not been around for more than a week before that. He doesn't know what happened after she drove into the place because he left for San Diego and stops in between."

"Malvina was there that day?!"

So, Joe's theory is starting to look pretty good. If she wasn't the killer, she likely knows who is.

"Well, this seems to tell us how Malvina left the house and maybe the area. I'm checking car rental agencies. There aren't any in Magnolia City. The closest is Memphis, then Jackson, and then New Orleans. I mean it could be that she was just down the road and bought another car. We're re-checking registrations." Sonny was excited to finally have something to offer the investigation.

"What does this do to your Praeger theory? I mean, Ella Mae wasn't shot until the late afternoon. Malvina was presumably there all day. Did they reconcile, then argue, and Malvina did the shooting? Was the argument over the $65,000?"

Sonny interrupted, "If there was an argument."

"Right. With Malvina there, it does explain how the alarm system was dealt with. She could get in and out and simply reset it before it was tripped."

"DD, if she can get in and out without tripping the alarm, how come it was tripped?"

It had become clear to DD that nothing in this matter was going to be easy – certainly what appears to be true, won't be.

"Are you telling me we can't confirm that Malvina had been gone for days? What about the sisters? Somebody must have been around in the days before this happened."

"You're right and I forgot. The kid who delivers groceries says he had not seen Malvina on the last two deliveries. She was the one who always tipped him. That would make it about eight days before the shooting."

With a big sigh, DD's frustration became audible. "What the hell does it mean, anyway? What about Praeger, where is he?"

Now it was Sonny's turn to sigh. "Ya'know, we can't stay real close to this guy without tipping him and others. We have a guy who is more or less reliable down there, but he's dumber than a box of rocks. He called last night to say that Praeger was on vacation and had not been seen since Monday. In other words, we don't know where he is. We're looking for his car in the New Orleans airport and the Memphis airport. I'll let you know."

"Sonny, I have to tell you that I really don't see a lot of support for the notion that this guy Praeger killed Ella Mae. It seems logical, however, that we do what we can to find him if for no other reason than eliminate him as a suspect. "

Summer Saturdays in San Francisco rarely start out clear and sunny. This one was no exception. The fog chilled the City all the way to "Tenderloin Heights." DD suggested that he drive, but Harrington declared emphatically, "You scare the hell out of me when you drive, DD, and this is a winding, two lane road."

The fog on the Golden Gate swirled around the roadway and obscured the famous towers and suspension cables. When Harrington pushed his wife's Pontiac station wagon through the Waldo Tunnel, the clouds suddenly disappeared, revealing a stunning blue sky and sun.

About sixty miles north of San Francisco, the Russian River flows lazily west through vineyards and thick stands of redwoods to Jenner at the Pacific shore. As long ago as the Twenties, well before the building of the Golden Gate Bridge, this was a resort area for well-off San Franciscans escaping the summer fog. Since then and the building of the Golden Gate, the wealthy found more exclusive areas and the San Francisco working class filled the vacated river beaches and enchanting hills. A lot of cops, firemen, longshoremen, and City bureaucrats brought the City's diversity to the Redwood forests and Russian River's sandy shores in western Sonoma County.

Old man Citriani bought early in Cazadero canyon west of Gurneville...he and his brother, Gino, a small time hood who ran sports tickets on the waterfront and in the City's warehouses. The Harringtons were in the Irish enclave back down the highway, closer to Gurneville. There, Larry's fireman grandfather built a house himself, just next to the creek.

Tony Citriani was a taller, slimmer version of his older brother. Quick witted, easy going, Tony was a St. Ignatius High School athlete who blew his knee out in his first football practice at Notre Dame. He came home, sulked awhile, managed to complete a few classes at City College, and applied for the police department. He thereafter dedicated himself to catching the "bad guys," but he did it with widely appreciated integrity and intellect.

DD did not know Citriani well and had never worked with him. All he knew about what Tony might think of him was what Tony's brother said two days before.

"Hey, come on in, guys."

He showed little sign of the surgery except a limp. A cane in the corner of the front room on the big family-vacation house bore witness, as well.

"Hey, want something? There's some beer and Chardonnay in the fridge. I'm not supposed to be moving around much, so help yourself."

Larry looked around. "Isn't Maria around?"

He always looked forward to seeing her. In her late forties, he described her as a "luscious creature."

"Naw, she's at the beach with the grandkids. She'll be back soon."

DD and Larry each got a beer and sat down in the appropriately mismatched, overstuffed chairs on the opposite side of the big, stone fireplace.

"So, how's the knee?" Larry was solicitous.

With feigned cheeriness, Tony smiled. "Well, it looks like I am going out on disability. Not happy about it, but I don't want to draw full pay and sit all the time. Shit happens. So, what's the big deal that gets a couple of good for nothin' lawyers away from sailboats and golf on a beautiful day?"

"We need some help on a very complex matter and figured you were the guy – probably the only guy. But, Tony, are you able to get up and around for some work this weekend?"

"O'Neil, you're blowin' smoke up my ass, but right now I can use it. At fifty-two years old, I'm too young to retire. I figured I'd make captain before I tossed it in. Right now, I'm a little down, but I am not out. What are we talkin' about?"

Larry weighed in. "We've got a murder in Mississippi, Tony. The victim is a woman who was on one of Dan's civil juries about three years ago – in the City. There's reason to suspect that her demise has something to do with that trial and maybe she was bribed by some locals. Those locals include a big time, Montgomery Street lawyer. We want to get some affidavits real quick to support a warrant for subpoenas. That's what we want you to do."

Harrington went on to provide details and, where necessary, DD filled in. Tony Citriani sat motionless, except for an occasional adjustment of his leg with the bad knee propped on the ottoman. DD retrieved a couple more beers from the refrigerator, this time one for Tony Citriani.

"Mississippi? Jeesus, I love it." Tony smiled at DD. "So, will I have to go there? I don't know that I can sit on a plane for long with this knee."

"No, I don't think so," Larry put Tony at rest. "We're taking this one step at a time."

"The really good news is that at least the first affidavit will be of a guy who is, or will be, come Monday, on the Sixth floor. So, you won't be traveling at all, except to 850 Bryant Street."

DD opened a file folder he had brought in from the car.

139

"Here's a memo I wrote setting out pretty much everything we know right now. You should look at it, digest what you need for the interview of Weisenstock, and give it back to me."

"Well, I'll have to make some excuse for how come I'm back at the job when I am supposed to be out for awhile," Tony mused.

"That's easy" Larry offered, "I'm acting DA next week. I'll just call Kearny and ask for you."

Just then, two small children burst through the front door.

"Gran'Papa!" the younger shouted, "T.J caught a fish!"

Sure enough, the older boy produced from a canvas creel a small shad.

"Great," Tony managed, realizing the importance of the moment. "Your first fish. Where's Nona?"

At that moment, the very same "luscious"' woman walked through the front door wearing a bright beach skirt over her bathing suit. Petite and curvaceous, black hair sportingly bobbed, and with shining black eyes, she lived up to Larry's billing.

"Tell you what Ton'. That's not much fish for all the work it took."

She bussed Larry's cheek in a familiar hug and introduced herself confidently to DD with a big smile.

DD and Larry then excused themselves and arranged to meet Tony at the Hall at 8 a.m. Monday morning. On the way back to the City, Larry quietly said to DD, "You know, this is the first time we've worked together on anything. You're a serious guy...not just on the handball court. I guess I now understand why you have the reputation of a bull dog."

DD smiled, politely, and nodded.

There's something to this, but I don't understand it. Doesn't everybody decide what is right and then do it? If not, then what's the point?

"I'm pretty sure your guy will be there Monday morning for Tony's interview. Won't the lawyer be a hangup?"

140

DD responded, "No, I'll call Roy tonight. He's expecting it and I am sure he is planning on spending a few days in The City on this. He can flop with me if necessary, but I expect he has more attractive companionship in mind. By the way, Tony will need a copy of this."

DD pulled out the photograph of Ella Mae, Dru Lacey, and Laura McNeeley and handed it to Harrington.

"Oh. I had forgotten about this. Damning, I think."

Harrington looked at it for a long time.

"Where is this taken? Is that a bed? It looks like a funny bed. This is enough for Tony to pay Ms. Lacey a visit. Don't you think so?"

"DD, I need to put some distance between you and this investigation. I don't think I need an affidavit from you. You can't be with Citriani when he interviews Lowell. You're just going to have to trust we'll get from the guy what you think we should."

"You're right." DD said. "I can always find something else
to do."

If he remembered correctly, there was a visitor from Magnolia City with whom he hoped to spend some time.

Seemingly going about his usual Saturday routine at the office, opening mail, checking the calendar, DD was mainly preoccupied with the expectation of a call from the Indian County Public Administrator, and, about 3:00 p.m. he was not disappointed.

"I was afraid y'all would be off for the weekend."

Her voice was smooth and languid, without the edge he had encountered in Magnolia. It brought clearly to mind the lovely face and body, although the truth was the images had not been far from his mind since he first encountered her.

"Naw, I usually work Saturdays. So, where are you? Can we meet?"

Suppressing a near squeal, Mattie reported, "I'm at the Mark Hopkins Hotel on Nob Hill. Can you imagine? It really is a bit much, but god what a beautiful town."

Staying as cool as possible, DD agreed. "Yeah, we like it. I don't know why most people go to the Mark on their first visit; must be the advertising, or something."

"It's the view! I mean, I'm just sitting here looking at the water – what is that body of water, by the way?"

"That's San Francisco Bay, and if you're looking north and see a bridge, that's the Golden Gate."

"Anyway, I am looking at this wonderful view and the people. My god, the people!"

"Right. Not exactly main street Magnolia City, are they?"

She laughed a light riff, observing DD's humor.

"I want to do some shopping. The guy downstairs – how do you say that? The con-see-urge – gave me some directions and recommendation. Then you can take me to dinner."

She paused. "That's what you had in mind wasn't it?"

Her uncertainties sprung back into her consciousness.

Without drawing breath, DD happily snapped, "Absolutely. What time do you think? People around here eat about 7:30; how about I pick you up at 6:30?"

He was beginning to realize that was hours away. He would have volunteered to go shopping but, jesus, he hated shopping.

"Now, you remember," she cooed, "nothin' fancy. I'm a little town girl from the south and I'm not sure I can handle this elegant city."

"Not to worry. This is a friendly town and visiting dignitaries are pretty much immune to its dangers. Meet me in the front of the Mark where the cars pull in. I'm driving an old green Ford."

Except for a couple of tumbles in the hay with Christine Wright – Helene's blond sister – DD had dated sparingly after his breakup with Melanie. To hear Rick tell it, Christine was not as sweet as her sister, and DD observed she came to sexual matters as a routine. The Indian County Public Administrator didn't appear to be like that, but, DD reluctantly remembered, such things are a lot like the search for the Holy Grail.

DD was right; Roy Lindstrom had made other arrangements for the weekend. He was happily ensconced in the five-bedroom Berkeley house of his law school classmate – that is, the five-bedroom Berkeley House of his now-divorced former client, Andrea Jankovic. He would be meeting Tony Citriani with his client on Monday morning at the Hall of Justice.

Notwithstanding his thick-tongued anticipation of what the evening might hold, DD worked on his opposition to a defense motion to dismiss his case against a collection company and its lawyers. *She didn't even mention the page of imprints from Ella Mae's notebook! It couldn't be, could it, that she found other things more important? Probably just the discovery of one of the World's most spectacular cities...probably.*

He made reservations at the Cypress Club – he wanted to impress.

Someone had clued Mattie into the weather – it was summer in San Francisco, so it was breezy and cool. Had he been a timid man he would have skulked out of the Mark's courtyard when he saw her. She stood there on the front stoop in a short black dress with her shoulders covered by an electric blue and violet, what...wrap? Gold chains hung from each ear, framing her exquisite face. Dwarfed by the towering doorman, she waved when she saw the Ford pull into the courtyard. The doorman was disappointed.

DD bounded out. The doorman looked protectively at him and opened the passenger door. Mattie hopped in without hesitation, with a broad, gleaming smile to set off the little black dress.

"I was thinking about being a little late," she happily announced, "but I couldn't do that. It's really cold here!"

DD chuckled, "I was thinking the same thing. It ain't Mississippi."

The doorman cleared their way out of the courtyard and they were on their way down California Street. In just a few minutes, DD pulled up to the curb in front of the Cypress Club and handed the Ford off to the valet. When Mattie stepped out of the Ford, DD noticed – she's barelegged.

When they were seated – temporarily at the bar – coherence returned, slowly, but it did return.

"My god, what a gorgeous place! Do you come here often?"

The hostess had taken her wrap, revealing her soft beige, clear shoulders, around which the spaghetti straps of the dress were strung. The vision momentarily distracted DD, but he managed, "The truth is that I've only been here a couple of times. It is a few levels up the elegance scale from the places I frequent. Given the way you're dressed, I'm glad we came here."

"Dressed! I'm hardly dressed at all. That guy, she mimicked, 'con-see-urge' – Gary was his name. He sent me to Joseph Magnin's – which I never heard of before – where his sister works. Man, she had all kinds of ideas and you're lookin' at most of them!"

There was nothing left to do for DD but to say, "You are lovely. Very lovely."

With that, he dared not try another word without first having a drink.

"Mattie, I'm sorry, but I don't even know if you drink. Do you?"

She laughed delightfully,

"Well, I've had some backyard gin and once I had a mint julep. What do you recommend?"

He looked at the bartender. "An Old Fashioned, light. Powers on the rocks for me."

They sat awkwardly silent while awaiting the drinks. DD was thinking he was going to be careful not to drink too much – something he had been doing of late. When the drinks arrived, he explained, "This is bourbon, which I understand all you southerners like. If you don't, we'll get something else.

Before you try it, however...he raised his glass and she did likewise... "To the Magnolia City-San Francisco connection."

They clinked the glasses and drank.

"Hmm! I think I like this. It's warming and I need some of that right now."

She sipped again, her twinkling, onyx-like eyes looking at him. "I decided this wasn't the time to talk about Ella Mae and her notebook. Could we do that tomorrow?"

Through his now unbroken smile, DD assured her, "Good idea."

She raised her finger casually. "Oh, before my toast, I want to warn you, Mr. O'Neil. If your intentions run along the lines of plying me with drink, my daddy taught me how to keep my wits about me, backyard gin or not. So, don't make any plans."

She giggled, just a little, and raised her glass:

"To this incredibly beautiful city! I'm enchanted."

They clinked again and sipped.

"I know I should be past calling you 'Mr. O'Neil,' but I don't feel right calling you DD."

She had obviously thought about this for some time.

"So, call me Dan; a lot of people do."

Not satisfied, she leaned back, smiling. "I guess it's really because I don't know why you are called DD."

"It's not all that exciting. My middle name is Dermot. When I was a small child, I was told 'You are Daniel Dermot O'Neil.' All I got out of that was 'DD' – that's what I called myself, what my family called me, and then a wider circle of friends. When I got to San Francisco, I introduced myself that way – not knowing any better. It just stuck."

Mattie was disappointed.

"If we're to be friends, am I supposed to call you DD?"

"Naw. You can call me anything except 'Mr. O'Neil.'"

The sumptuous setting of the Cypress Club with its vaguely *Arabesque* decor was made more sumptuous with the cool sounds of Buddy Blakely's trio. Spotting DD, the musicians each waved at him. The Indian County Public

Administrator was duly impressed and the couple prattled on through the early evening – each gingerly exploring the other.

Having ordered something she had never heard of, then experiencing her first taste, Mattie said, "My, that's the best fish I ever tasted. What is it again?"

"There's not a lot of petrale sole in the Gulf Of Mexico, so it isn't surprising you'd not heard of it before. I like it. The sauce is caper, butter, wine and a little fresh lemon juice."

Holy crimeny! The guy is a gourmet! This is a red book scene.

The magic and the delicious food and drink reached its end and the time for leaving and decisions came. A short visit at the pier – some kind of jazz joint – led to 'I'm tired,' to 'me, too,' to finding the Ford, and rolling into the Mark's courtyard. The most efficient and accommodating doorman, stuck his head into the driver's window and said, "Are we staying the night, or may I find a spot for the car for a few hours?"

Of sufficient maturity to appreciate this as humor, Mattie and DD laughed – they laughed out loud. The doorman opened her side and she stepped out gracefully, then moved toward DD, who, too, was out of the car. She gently pushed his hands away as they reached for her, and from her toes, kissed him lightly.

"DD," she whispered, "this has all the earmarks of being something important. We gotta go slow."

A little surprised, DD pulled her wrap around her tightly, and kissed her – not so lightly.

"I think you're right. I'll walk you to the elevator. I'm not gentleman enough to go slow in front of your door."

"So..." she was leaning against the wall between the elevator doors, "we have to deal with this business. Tomorrow is Sunday. Can we get together? "

"You bet. Would you like to take a ride? Or, maybe just get a brunch near my place in North Beach?

"Ya'know, I never had a brunch before."

"How about I pick you up at 10?"

"No. Just tell me where and I'll take a taxi."

Ten it was, at Rosa's. He thought of nothing but her in the meantime.

***

CHAPTER FOURTEEN

Interrupted Messages

The phone's ring was anxious. It was 3:30 a.m., only an hour after DD had fallen asleep with sweet visions in his head.

"DD?"

It was Mattie.

"I'm so sorry to disturb you, but Arlen just called me from back home. He said Malvina called him in some kind of panic. I called the number she left and I've been talking to her since. DD – aren't you looking for her?"

Stepping out of the mighty fantasy about Mattie that he had been in and stumbling into this reality was a difficult thing to do quickly.

"Where is she?"

"In New York City. I have her telephone number and the address for the Western Union Office she wants money sent to. I'm sorry I didn't tell anyone before, but she had called before I left home. She wanted me to go to the house to retrieve a package and send it to her. Now I know that package has $65,000 in it."

Having gathered himself, DD raised his voice slightly,

"Mattie, slow down. Is there some sort of emergency with Malvina?" *Why did she call Mattie and then call her office?*

Taking a deep breath, Mattie paused and then continued slowly, "I think so. She said someone was after her and she didn't have the money to get away. I told her to call the police and she screamed at me that she couldn't do that. No, I don't know why. I had Arlen wire her some money – two thousand dollars was all we could get together. Obviously, I hadn't gone to the house to get the package."

"Who's Arlen?"

"Oh, you met him. He's my assistant. Malvina has a lot of problems, but she has never been one to panic, so I'm taking this seriously. Maybe you better do something."

How does she know Malvina doesn't panic?

Mattie gave DD the location information Malvina had provided. DD decided he was going to bring Sonny into this and hopefully the New York police department.

"Doesn't Malvina have family she can call or even friends?"

DD asked.

"DD, I *am* family. I'll explain that later. But she mumbled that she did call a friend here, in San Francisco, but could only leave a message on the machine. The friend's name is Dru."

Immediately, DD realized what was happening.

"Mattie, I have to hang up and call Sonny in Jackson. You stay put and I'll call you back."

It was a little before 7 a.m. in Jackson. Sonny Elliot was just moving around when he picked up the phone. DD explained the call from Mattie.

"There's $65,000 in the house right now? How the hell did we miss that?"

"Jesus, Sonny, that's hardly the point."

DD was trying to direct his friend to the immediate relevancies.

"Malvina is a key to all of this and she is very likely in danger. Do you know where your killer cop is right now?"

"No," Sonny conceded.

"Ten-to-one he's in Manhattan. You need to introduce this case to the New York City police department – immediately."

"I can do better. My best special forces buddy is in the District Attorney's office. Where are you going to be?"

"Here for a while. Call me here when you get any news. Then I'll go pick up Mattie."

Sleep was out of the question. DD took a quick shower with the phone within reach. A half hour passed. Mattie

149

called. She had calmed down but her voice still revealed her anxiousness.

"What are you thinking, DD? Is there something I need to know?"

"Right now, Mattie, I am waiting to hear from Sonny. Once I do I'll come get you and we can get all of this out."

Mollified for the moment, Mattie got off the phone.

Sonny had made it to his office. He found Val Kaslewski's home number and was able to talk to him before he went to church. Kaslewski would get a police unit out to the address with the phone number and call Sonny back.

"If you're ready, I'll pick you up. We can get breakfast and go to my office. I don't see we'll make the brunch."

"I'm ready. I'll bring the notebook. Did you sleep?"

"I'll be there in fifteen minutes. Meet me in the courtyard. "

The sun had broken through the summer morning fog as DD pulled into the Mark Hopkins courtyard. Mattie stood at the hotel's door with a different doorman. She was carrying a jean jacket and wearing blue jeans and a red and white cotton blouse – looking every bit the country girl.

Her face lit up when she spotted DD and his battered Ford.

"Hi!"

There was no sign of the sleepless night, nor the anxiety of the early morning just passed.

"Look at that sky! Let's go to breakfast. Do they do that well here, too?"

At a corner table in Sears, just up the street from Union Square, Mattie surprisingly ordered biscuits and gravy, so DD followed suit.

"OK, now," DD started with a determined tone and look, "why did Malvina call you? What do you mean you're family? What's the connection?"

Mattie smiled slightly, dropping her eyes, seemingly occupied with re-folding her napkin.

"I told G.A. that I was going to tell you this because I want you to know and I know you'll understand. He didn't think I should."

Impatient, DD replied, "Enough with the preliminaries; what is it that you think I'll understand?"

"Malvina is my sister – more accurately, my half sister. We have different mothers but the same father. She's a little older than me and her mama was Bella. They – Bella and Malvina – left Magnolia City when I was about five years old. My mama – Manda – told me that Bella had a boyfriend that messed with Malvina, so that's why she left town. That and Daddy wasn't too happy about the boyfriend."

DD must have looked stunned, because Mattie paused her narrative to suggest that he eat his biscuits and gravy before the heat disappeared.

"Malvina is your half sister?" He hadn't caught up quite yet.

"I had seen her only once since we were infants by the time she showed up back in Indian County with Ella Mae. That was at Daddy's funeral about ten years ago. I had just finished college but hadn't been any place in my life except Memphis. She ran my head full of how great her life was – you know, fancy clothes, nightlife, being taken care of. Maybe in her eyes I was a country bumpkin, but I was old enough to recognize a whore when I saw one. She was trying to recruit me."

DD's mouth was open in amazement, so he put some gravy-smeared biscuit in it. Washing that with coffee, he managed, "So, um, who was your father?"

"Oh, I forgot that part. Cornelius Jackson Deare. He owned the saw mill in Indian County, the lumber yard, and a few hundred acres of cotton...and he was white."

Virtually nothing that DD ever knew about Indian County and Mississippi had included such a possibility, but Mattie had more to teach.

"Daddy never married, but he sired four children – each by a different black woman. All of us were legitimized. None of us were ignored so long as we were living with him. He fed us, treated us well, and sent us all to college, except Malvina. He also built each of us a house, including Malvina. She sold hers, but the rest of us still live in ours."

Accurately sensing that her breakfast partner was not fully appreciating what she was saying, Mattie explained, "Ya'see, DD, Daddy was of the mind that the backwardness of Mississippi was caused by racial separation and hatred. He thought the best way to remedy that problem was propagating people who were of both races. He set out to do it all himself."

Thus wiping away the cloud of DD's ignorance, Mattie briskly folded her napkin and picked up the bill.

They emerged into the breezy street.

"This sounds like an unpublished work of William Faulkner. So, you have two other siblings?"

"That may be, but it is true. By the way, how come you can park in this 'no parking' zone and not get a ticket?"

"Faulkner's stories were essentially true, as well. This must happen all the time in Mississippi."

"My grandfather was, I am told, a personal friend of the writer. That would be my daddy's daddy. Anyway the other two are brothers: Mathew – he's the most popular doctor in Magnolia City – and Michael – he runs daddy's old businesses. They are both older than me. None of us could park in a 'no parking' zone in Magnolia City and not get a ticket."

Very nearly befuddled, DD drove them to Turk Street and his designated parking spot in the basement. Not a word passed between them, all the way to DD's office.

"Sonny? Do we know anything yet?"

"Is Mattie there?" Sonny's response seemed muted.

"Yes. We're in my office."

"I don't know how to tell you this and how you are going to tell Mattie. We were too late DD. They found a body that I am presuming is Malvina – overdose of heroin. She had been dead for no more than an hour. Mattie's money wire was never picked up. Jesus, I'm sorry about this. G.A. told me the Deare story, so I expect this is going to be hard on Mattie."

DD looked at Mattie. With that look, she guessed what the message was. Her eyes welled and she walked to look out the window.

Sonny had told DD there was a suspect, but that it was likely not Praeger because witnesses described the person who was around the apartment and last seen leaving it just before the police discovered the body. It was a woman. Sonny's assistant district attorney friend was pushing the department to investigate further.

"Sonny, I am now sure that this was a killing and that it is connected to the Pavlone trial, as well as the death of Ella Mae. Do you remember my explaining how Ella Mae got on the jury? There was another juror that ended up dead. Ella Mae took his place. He died from an overdose of heroin – two shots."

"Jesus! Then they recruited a woman. I guess there are plenty in New York for something like this. She would have been more likely to trust a woman. We found Praeger's car in the Memphis airport parking lot. It's been there since last Tuesday. He could have gone anywhere from Memphis, including San Francisco or New York. I sent a description and what pictures we have of Praeger to my buddy Kaslewski in New York. I didn't send the one to New York until very early this morning, so if the guy came and went since Tuesday, that was a waste of time. "

DD hung up and turned to Mattie, still peering into Ramon's garden in the courtyard.

"Daddy always said Malvina would turn out all right. She had a bad start, but she would come home ok." Grabbing a tissue from the box on DD's desk, she turned to look at him, still weeping. "Damned if she didn't come home. Who's to say she wasn't ok. She loved Ella Mae and I guess Ella Mae loved her. No one else ever loved either of them."

"When did Malvina first call you about this package?"

Mattie had been carrying a small briefcase. She opened it and pulled out her calendar. Thumbing though it, she looked up at DD with the answer: "Wednesday. Last Wednesday."

"Is that when she told you that she had called this person 'Dru' here?"

"Yes."

Praeger's car was left at the Memphis airport parking lot on Tuesday. Presumably, Malvina had already alerted Dru to her location. Praeger was on his way. Dru didn't call Malvina back and didn't send her any money because to do either would have left a trail marker like a flashing light.

"When you called me, you said you had been talking to Malvina for nearly an hour. What was that all about?"

"Well, understand DD, near the end there was lot of crying and blubbering about us being sisters and not really knowing anything about each other. But she was explaining that she knew Ella Mae was dead; she didn't say right away how she knew. She also knew something about you and this case where Ella Mae was on the jury out here. I guess they were living together out here, but it wasn't a good place for Malvina to be – too many temptations, she said."

"She told you someone was after her? What exactly did she say?"

"She told me that in the first conversation, but at that time, she wasn't sure. Then, last night, she was in great fear, nearly out of control, and was positive she had to run."

"Where would she run?"

"Here, to San Francisco, to Dru, I guess."

"Did she say that?"

"No, she said she was going to San Francisco. That was part of the figuring out much money she needed – I think it was $400 for a plane ticket. She did mention this Dru a couple of times, saying she could hide out with her."

"Why would someone be after her? "

"I guess because she has Ella Mae's diary."

Mattie said it nonchalantly – as if everyone knew there was a diary and that Malvina had it. Of course, no one knew there was a diary, or if there was one, that Malvina had it. How all that came about was yet to be figured out.

"How do you know she had Ella Mae's diary?" DD anxiously posed the question, surprising Mattie a bit.

"Malvina told me last night. She – Malvina – had torn it out of the note book thinking she could use it – I guess – to black mail someone. I mean, this is all I could figure from what she was saying. Apparently, they – she and Ella Mae – had a break-up. Malvina came back, but Ella Mae didn't think she would stay and didn't think she meant it when she said she would be with her forever."

Mattie had sat down in the client chair opposite DD's desk.

"Are we getting to the diary?"

Mattie was a little annoyed, but continued, "Ella Mae had taken money out of the bank to give to Malvina. When Malvina said she didn't want it, because she was going to stay, Ella Mae told her it would be in a hiding place for Malvina if she changed her mind. Ella Mae did not want to keep Malvina from leaving just because she needed money."

"That's one less mystery. We now know what the money was for. So, where was the hiding place?"

"In the umbrella stand beside the front door. At least that's where the 'package' was that Malvina wanted me to retrieve."

DD thought for a moment. "Y'know, Joe Cleary suggested that someone was in the house at the same time as the killer because of the faint voice on the alarm system recorder. If that someone was Malvina, she couldn't get to the umbrella stand because the killer was there or nearby. Somehow, she could get to the library, grab the diary portion of the tablet and escape. But why did she tear the pages out? Why didn't the killer find the diary at the time he shot Ella Mae? Wait a minute, did Malvina tell you about the shooting?"

"Not exactly." Mattie knew this was the crux of the matter. "She was speaking very quickly and softly, as if to avoid being heard by someone nearby. She said she was upstairs in her room when she realized the alarm chime was ringing. Then she heard talking downstairs that sounded like Ella Mae and a man. She emphasized that the voices were coming from the library and the male voice was ordering Ella Mae to give him something. It was then she realized that this man had unknowingly activated the alarm. She said she had a pretty good idea what this stranger was demanding. No, she never told me what that was. When she heard a muffled gunshot, she went to the hall alarm box and pressed the sheriff button and told them she thought there had been a killing or something like that. She got to the library, grabbed the diary pages and ran out the back door."

"That's it?"

"That's it. She never told me why she ripped out the pages. She didn't say whether she saw the guy who was in the house, and never explained exactly how she got to New York."

They sat there silently for several minutes, and finally DD made the lame observation, "And now she's dead. Where do we go from here?"

"Well," Mattie went to her briefcase, "do you want to look at the note book imprint that I carried all the way from Indian County?"

"May as well; I may never get to see the real thing."

DD retrieved a large magnifying glass from his desk and laid it over the first page of the notebook. The imprint from the missing page could plainly be seen and appeared the same as other handwriting of Ella Mae on the envelope containing the check copies. Making out the words was another matter.

Peering through the magnifier, DD audibly reported what he thought he saw: "I had other – 'c' something, maybe six or seven letters – about the Armando crowd."

He looked up at Mattie. "I'll be damned. Armando's. If I am not mistaken, that's like a pickup center for lesbian prostitutes, at least it was about eight years ago."

He continued, still trying to read the imprint, "Malvina was too – something, maybe five letters – to them. If she leaves me, they get her, I go to O'Neil." He stopped. "That's it. The last part is real clear, as if she were bearing down on the pen."

Mattie had come over to look over DD's shoulder while he was studying the imprint. Softly, she said, "I didn't know what this 'Armando's' was about. Now that I do, I'd venture a guess that people there wanted to use Malvina, and Ella Mae wasn't about to let her go. She was prepared to go to you, if that happened. I would guess that was the issue when Malvina had split from Ella Mae and I would guess somehow these 'Armando' people knew of this threat and decided not to risk it any longer."

Not willing to move lest the touch of Mattie's breast on his arm would go away, DD simply provided, "You are probably right."

At that moment the whole subject of their combined attention suddenly changed, but only for that moment. Mattie stood up, cleared her throat, and asked, "Does this help? Does it get us anywhere?"

Refocusing, DD similarly cleared his throat. "I think it confirms that Ella Mae's death was motivated by a fear that the scheme, whatever it was, would be uncovered."

Mattie wandered over to the window, again.

"I didn't really know Ella Mae. I was far too young to understand much of anything by the time I learned that she had abandoned her son, Donald. I never heard anyone say much about her, except that she would be all right – she was bright, but no one really judged her for leaving that boy behind – no one but her brother, G.A. Daddy wrote to Malvina often, although he never talked to me about it. I heard from my momma that Malvina never wrote to him, except to ask for money. Eventually, he told her she could sell her house if she really needed money that bad."

"Mattie, does G.A. know all of this? He's not only the victim's brother; he's the sheriff."

157

"I told him what I knew just before I left to come here. Of course, I didn't know what I learned last night. G.A. is pretty hung up over what we all have known somehow for awhile – Ella Mae was homosexual. So, he just doesn't talk about it. We're a pretty naive lot there in Magnolia City, so when Ella Mae came home with Malvina – whom we all knew had been a prostitute – there was a good deal of confusion around. Confusion and judgment, tongue clucking and the like."

"Your only sister came home more than three years ago; didn't you talk to her in that time?"

"I did. She seemed to be an intelligent woman. There was no hint that she was homosexual, in the sense that she denied or hid her femininity. She always dressed to the nines and always made herself sexy. But she hated men. She really hated men and she told me all the ugly reasons why – starting when she was about seven years old. That's why I wrote that note to her when I sent the money – the note she never saw."

"Note? What did you write?"

Mattie looked softly at DD. "I told her there were good men working on her side of this. I meant you."

DD was about to melt completely under Mattie's gaze when the telephone rang. It was the inside line.

"DD! They got him. They got Praeger. He is in the custody of the NYPD. Jesus but I was wondering whether we would ever get any luck in this damned thing and we got real lucky."

DD was startled, "They got Praeger? Are they sure? What happened?"

Sonny laughed. "The details are best left for Kaslewski to tell you, but this is what I understand. Remember that we thought the deed was done by a woman? Well, the cop who put together the bulletin wasn't so sure, and for the hell of it suggested that this was a guy in drag. So, when a security guy at Penn Station who read this bulletin gets a report from a citizen that a woman went into the men's head, he decides to check it out and finds this guy in a stall taking off panty hose, a stuffed bra, a skirt and a blouse. Get this, though, he kept the panties on. He's a freagin' pervert! It turns out to be our boy. His resistance is a little weak, since he's standing there in the stall wearing lace panties and carrying a shopping bag with used panty hose and bra."

"Who disguises himself down to his underwear? How do we know this is our guy?"

"The police ID, including picture, are in his boy pants folded neatly in a small travel case."

"Sonny, there's a diary. Handwritten pages torn out of a notebook. Did they find that?"

"A diary? Ella Mae's? Fantastic – didn't you just know there had to be? But the NYPD didn't say anything about that."

"So, now what?"

"This is enough for me to get a subpoena to search his house and his police locker. I am going to collect as much as possible as quickly as possible. But we – Bud and I – want you to go New York as a special assistant Attorney General. You're the one that knows the motive stuff and Kaslewski is real interested in that."

"Sonny, I've told you this before, I am way out of my element in this. I have never been a prosecutor and wouldn't know what works and what doesn't in getting a guy to plea."

Sonny cut him off, "You have got to do this, DD. You're the only one with facts that will persuade this freak to come clean"

"When?"

"Tuesday at the latest. The longer the wait, the more time he has to rally his nasty friends. You check into the Abby Hotel on West 43rd. We pay for everything. Vladimir Kaslewski will meet you at the downtown precinct."

"Whoa! I have stuff to do here, not the least of which is to deal with the San Francisco police interview of Lowell Weisenstock tomorrow."

"I'll talk to Harrington. You don't have to leave until tomorrow night. You can take a red-eye."

DD explained what he knew about Praeger to Mattie, who repeatedly shook her head in disbelief. He also explained that Sonny wanted him in New York and why he was going.

"Mattie, I am afraid my fate in life is to do what is front of me to do. There doesn't ever seem to be a time when I can do what I really want to do. Not even as much as I want to stay with you now."

They discussed it at length over seafood cannelloni at Castagna's.

She smiled broadly. "So, you're suggesting that we abandon the 'go slow' pledge because you are leaving for New York and I am due to leave San Francisco tomorrow. That sounds entirely too loaded with disaster for whatever can be ...to paraphrase you...'in front of us.'"

DD conceded, "You're right. So, why not stay here. You're going to be important to Larry's pitch for a grand jury. Besides, I am seriously wary about what faces you back in Indian County. Right now, you're a link between Dru Lacey and Malvina's murder. If they get wind of you being home and vulnerable, you could be in danger."

She went silent for several minutes. "How long will you be gone?"

"Can't be more than a couple days."

"I cannot stay all that time at the Mark Hopkins. Neither my office or me, personally, have that kind of budget. Besides, it does tend to give me heartburn."

"I have no question that we can put you up in a decent place for much less and there is also no question that the City and County of San Francisco will pay that tab because you are a material witness. It seems to me that would be a much better way to spend taxpayer money than how they usually spend it."

"So, you'll be back shortly. I guess I can skip the national public administrators' conference. Be sure you're back here that quick, though."

Smiling, she stood and looked deeply at him. "That just may qualify for, the time being, as 'going slow.'"

160

DD's heart jumped. He dropped Mattie at the Mark, from which she started making arrangements by telephone to have her half-sister's body returned to Magnolia City.

At his office, DD made his travel arrangements and gathered Rick Esquivel and Joe Cleary, telling them what had happened. Each wanted to meet Mattie, so Dianna Cleary was pressed into having a dinner party that evening.

DD moved Mattie into a small hotel on Bush Street, the Orchard.

"This is delightful. It's far more comfortable for me than the Mark."

Notwithstanding all the pledges of gilded, if temporary, abstinence, there was a kiss, possibly more, before leaving for the Cleary house in Noe Valley.

Most of the dinner conversation was of the introductory variety – each finding out about the other, each explaining. Dianna was a gracious hostess, making Mattie feel comfortable in such – for her – a strange place. The talking never strayed far from the project and the cause of Ella Mae White's demise.

When it became clear that Mattie didn't have a lot of the important answers, Joe observed, as was his wont, "It just isn't going to be that easy. Pieces, small pieces need to be assembled for any kind of a picture. Most of all..."

Rick sat back and laughed, mimicking Joe, "Don't make assumptions !"

Unflapped, Joe simply continued, "That's right. That is particularly true here. This thing is fraught with traps – each of them capable of inflicting serious if not mortal injury."

Mattie was bewildered. "You mean you gentlemen have had this conversation before?"

DD leaned forward. "Well, sort of. It's kind of like our mantra. Joe is the most disciplined in that regard. I'm a charger and often get bruised but, as you can see, not yet killed – figuratively or otherwise – except for the Pavlone case. I assumed that my opposition would not bribe a juror."

Joe interrupted, "And now you are assuming he did. That could be the killer assumption."

"This is crazy." Mattie looked at everyone at the table, "Are you seriously saying this law firm bribed Ella Mae and then shot her and now killed Malvina?"

Joe explained, "It is very hard to believe, that's true. In figuring stuff like this out, you gather evidence and make conclusions in baby steps. With the evidence that exists right now, it seems reasonable to accept that this woman Drucinda Lacey had a relatively intimate relationship with Ms. White well before she was on that jury. This relationship was not disclosed when Ms. White was about to be selected as an alternate – nor at any time. Of itself, we have unlawful conduct by Ms. Lacey. Given what happened later, we may indeed have some sort of bribery of Ms. White. Why, nearly four years after the trial and the apparent willingness to continue to pay money to Ms. White, was she murdered? We don't know that. The answer, it seems to me, is the key to any action against Hugh Keislor. There's a lot more to this that I haven't mentioned, but I just wanted you to understand how, at least, I'm thinking."

Mattie sat quietly for a moment. "But what about Malvina? Why is she dead? Why was someone after her? Who was it?"

DD put his hand on Mattie's. "Let's hold those questions for when I get back from New York. I may be meeting her murderer."

**

CHAPTER FIFTEEN

Introduction to Evil

At the door of Mattie's Orchard Hotel room, DD mustered all of the self-restraint he could, but a long embrace nearly destroyed the effort.

She looked up at him and explained, "I want to be here when you return with the information on Malvina's killing. Maybe I want to be here anyway, I'm not saying. But I don't think anyone back in Magnolia City knows where I am except G.A. and Arlen. Neither one of those gentlemen are going to give me up – accidentally or otherwise. So, I don't think I am in danger from those bad guys."

He kissed her hand. "You forget, Mattie, you told Malvina where you were in that telephone call. Who knows who she told?"

"Oh, that's right. And she had been in touch with this woman Dru. But it's unlikely, given the timing of her death. Anyway, no one knows where I'm staying, and I'll be around your friends until you get back. I'm going to lunch with Dianna tomorrow."

DD turned to leave. "By the way, who's Clyde?"

"Clyde? Did I mention him? Well," she smiled coyly, "he's a nice guy back in Magnolia City whom I've been dating recently. Nothing, absolutely nothing serious."

"Did you just giggle?"

Starting early the next morning, DD began drafting his affidavit to support Harrington's application for record subpoenas. *This is going to bring out the wolves. Not sure that there is really anything in this that Keislor or Darla had not already guessed. Neither is there much here that is admissible evidence.*

There really isn't anything wrong with circumstantial evidence and it is often much better than so-called direct evidence. In the matter of the death of Ella Mae White, everything thus far was not only circumstantial, but doesn't get to Keislor, circumstantially or otherwise. *The issue right now is whether there is reasonable cause to look at these records, i.e. whether there is any rational basis to believe a crime has been committed -that's easy. There must also be a rational basis to believe the records will lead to the person or persons who committed that crime. But what crime – the murder in Mississippi, bribery of a juror? Who? At least it's not entirely irrational. Remember, dummy, you're not a prosecutor.*

"You want me to make some coffee?" Rick was leaning against the doorjamb, clad in his weekend cotton shirt, blue jeans and top-siders.

"Yeah, that sounds good. I'm almost done with this affidavit; I need you to look at it."

Rick sat down in the client chair while the coffee brewed. "That's a hell of a woman. You gonna screw this up too?"

Typing the balance of the affidavit, DD's face reflected that he was peeved at Rick's comment. "Don't tell me you're giving me advice on romance? At least I've only been married once."

"I can't help it if the wrong kind of women are attracted to me. Except for Melanie, you did have one hell of a shot with Liz Downey, a very high-quality woman. So, I'm just curious about this new very high-quality woman. Can you handle it, or do you stick your head up your cowboy ass and pass?"

Ignoring his concerned buddy, DD turned from the typewriter and handed him the document he just typed. "See what you think..."

Rick took the paper and retreated to the kitchen while reading it. He returned with two cups of black coffee in one hand, a finger in each.

"There's not a lot of hard stuff here, except the premise of Lacey being at jury selection no less than a couple months following whatever this is with a juror. You can provide the

164

hard connection between the trial, the juror, and her message for you. I've seen less move a judge to authorize a search. You didn't mention the imprint from the notebook. Isn't that a connection to Darla and still another Loudon firm tie?"

"I don't want to give that up as yet. They couldn't know about it. I don't know that Praeger has or knows about Ella Mae's diary. It just doesn't add enough to take a chance at this point."

"Ok, I agree. Tony is meeting with Lowell in the morning, right? That will fill some gaps and the shit and you will be flying by the afternoon. "

Rick handed the affidavit back to DD. When Jeannie came in she notarized his signature, copied it, and sent it over to Larry Harrington at the Hall of Justice.

DD had packed before leaving for the office that morning. The plane left at 3 p.m.. Rick would take him to SFO. In the meantime, Tony Cipriani was interviewing Lowell Weisenstock outside the jail, at an interview room at Northern Station, just three blocks from DD's office. By noon, neither Cipriani or Harrington had called. DD was getting anxious about hearing nothing when Mattie walked in.

She walked around his desk and, before he could get to his feet, she kissed him – once on the forehead and once one the lips. "I'm sorry if that seems forward but I couldn't help myself. How about I buy you some lunch before you fly away?"

Happy to see her, DD nonetheless stood, lifting the telephone receiver simultaneously. "Just a second..."

He dialed. "Larry! What's going on?"

"They are typing up the statement right now. Lindstrom has proven to be cooperative but difficult. He's going over this thing line by line by comma, but it looks like we got everything we could expect from Weisenstock. His stepmom has been giving him orders regarding Ella Mae. But there are others he deals with and I don't know if these are like the Ella Mae thing. They could be legit. That may or may not matter right now, but we have enough to get an order for the Loudon firm telephone records, the telephone and at least some account records from Southern California Casualty, and the personal telephone records of Drucinda Lacey."

DD was elated. "So all this is going down while I am in New York. Damn, I want to see those things."

"DD, if you think Keislor and his associates are going to sit still and let us waltz in and pick up these records, you are smoking something unlawful. It will be at least a week before we get an order, let alone records. You'll be here when anything happens."

"Can you send me a copy of Lowell's statement to my hotel in Manhattan?"

"Sure," Larry promised.

"That reminds me. Did you know that this woman Darla Reid has a record? Under the name of Willingham, she was busted for pandering eight years ago at a place called Armando's. Your old flame, Liz Downey, was one of the arresting officers."

"Yeah, I just realized that. Small world."

He looked at Mattie, "Ok, buy me lunch. See ya Larry."

Commercial flying was becoming more and more a part of DD's practice, but little did he realize while winging his way to New York on this occasion how much he would be traveling in the future. As it was, the five-hour trip was uncomfortable for its confinement.

Sonny's package on Praeger had arrived just as DD and Rick were leaving the office for the airport. Now, just over eastern Nevada, DD opened it. The photograph of Praeger surprised DD a little. A good-looking guy, a year younger than DD and just about the same size. Born in Winter Lake, Florida, in 1942 and awarded an honorable discharge from the Marine Corps in 1974. Otherwise there was nothing remarkable in his service record, except that he had married an Okinawan woman and there is no further mention of her in the file. He was hired by the Delta County sheriff's office in 1976. Again, nothing notable in that record, except that he had run the County's pistol range for three years about the time that Ella Mae was making her deal to be bribed in the Pavlone case. No discipline, no commendations, no promotions.

However, there was an internal sheriff memorandum from a lieutenant in the department. Apparently, someone anonymously reported that Praeger had a bank account in a New Orleans bank and a safe deposit box in the same bank. Upon discreet inquiry, the lieutenant learned that the account had more money in it than one would expect of someone making what Praeger was paid. Nothing more was included in the report – no follow up, no explanation from Praeger.

There was a faint copy of a handwritten letter with a message from Sonny on a yellow post-it: "This is interesting!" The letter was dated April of 1978 and addressed to the then Sheriff of Delta County asking for leave to work a private security job in New Orleans for a meeting of the "National Product Liability Insurer's Association." Could we put Keislor or Weisentock the elder at this meeting?

This guy has no depth! Apparently the only reason he got the job is that his grandfather was a military buddy of the sheriff in 1952. He had no prior experience. In the Marine Corps, he did not serve in any battle zone, but he did have a number of marksmanship awards. He didn't seem to belong to any clubs or churches and there is no report on his wife or any children.

In this second folder was Praeger's application for the deputy job. In it, he reports he had a brother who died young from scarlet fever. While he indicated a high school diploma, Praeger's neat, block printing revealed poor grammar and spelling. Not unlike Rick.

It was 11:30 p.m. by the time DD checked into his modest mid-town hotel, the Abby-Victoria. He immediately walked over to Kelly's pub and ordered a Powers, eventually eating some cold soft-shell and fries.

It was surprisingly comfortable for a mid-summer New York morning. DD rose early and walked over to Times Square where he caught a taxi to NYPD mid-town south precinct. The desk sergeant immediately inside the main door directed DD to the third floor. There he found one of those places which is in perpetual motion, and stopped a hurrying uniform to ask how he could find Val Kaslewski. The intense brown eyes, nearly obscured by long black hair, paused and looked at DD for a moment, then replied in a thick New York brogue.

"Hey, I know this guy for five yeahs and never knew how to say his name. What, ahh you his relative?"

In dismay, DD shook his head, no.

The young cop said, "We just call him 'Kas'; I'll get 'im."

Kas, more than six feet tall – very big, maybe three hundred pounds – brushed his long, blond hair out of his eyes and flashed a bright, toothy smile at DD.

"O'Neil! Mississippi Attorney General, right?"

DD was already self conscious about his status and not about to mislead anyone, "That's not exactly correct, I..."

Kas was not interested. He put his big arm around DD's shoulder and guided him down the hall while he explained, "This is a real wierdo we got for you, O'Neil. I guess Sonny told you about the lace women's panties. The turnkey told him to put on his own underwear before they locked him up with some of our home grown. I mean, jesus christ?"

Kas roared a guttural laugh that DD wasn't sure was justified.

DD valiantly tried to explain what he started, but the din of the hallway was too much to overcome, and by the time they made it to the fourth floor cells, it didn't seem worth a try.

"We gotta get this guy out of here at some point, but right now we can keep him safe. Cops aren't usually safe as inmates. It's only a matter of time 'til someone figures it out. Sonny says our guy has some story – or might have some story. Have you thought about this? I mean we got this guy dead to rights. He's going down for murder. We don't get these kind of cases very often."

DD had the impression Kas wasn't going to wait long for an answer to any of these questions.

Kas suddenly stopped and thrust open a door into an office. Two men stood at the window on the opposite side of the room, each appearing about DD's age and each obviously a plain clothes cop. Kas threw the papers he was carrying on the desk in the middle of the room,

"This here's Dan O'Neil from Mississippi come to shed some light on this weird cop you guys collared."

The taller, better dressed of the two stepped forward with his hand out. "I'm Vic Luca, this here's Martin Simon. The weird cop is upstairs. Wanna see him, or is there something we need to talk about now?"

DD shrugged and the four stepped into the hall, and walked to the elevator bearing large black letters "HOLDING. FOURTH FLOOR."

Simon explained in a thick Brooklyn accent, "We wanna keep this guy here as long as we can. Any place else will be a little dangerous because he's a cop. I don't know he'll be any better off back in your jurisdiction. If we can figure a federal rap, maybe that's the way to go. You should keep that in mind."

"Other than what you found on him when he was busted, what do we have?" DD inquired.

As the elevator door opened on a barred cage, the three flashed their credentials for the turnkey and he opened the door admitting them to a short hallway.

Responding to DD's question, Luca explained, "Eyeball people. Reliable. Great lineup – very clean and no wavering. Ya gotta understand, they saw a guy – not a woman – the day before and that's who they id'd in the line up. When we put a wig on him and the others, they still nailed him. But they described a 'sort of' big woman' around the place and on the day in question he's spotted in front of the victim's door less than two hours before we think she bought it. What's her name?"

"Malvina ...Malvina Montrose," DD supplied.

"So," Simon picks up the story, "Malvina talks to this woman at the door and lets her in. Then another eyeball sees the woman leave, less than two hours later. No one sees Malvina alive again."

The overweight turnkey led the four men down the hall lined with doors with small, wire-and-glass windows.

Simon says, "This is one for my memoirs. You heard about the panties, right?"

DD nods affirmatively.

"Do you know this guy shaved his legs? Is he into his role,

or what?"

Kas chuckled. "So, the guy's a little eccentric."

The turnkey stopped.

"He's in here with the PD, so knock."

Kas knocked on the interrogation room door,

"Linda, it's Kas; can we come in now?"

"Just a minute Kas," a woman's voice from inside responded.

In a whisper, Kas explains to DD, "Praeger wouldn't talk without a lawyer. In the best tradition of due process, we got him one. I'm miffed, 'though. They sent over Linda Tocci – she's a little vigorous in these matters."

The door opened. Linda Tocci stepped out. She appeared in her early forties, a little sloppily dressed, possibly pretty. Her mousy brown hair needed attention, having been repeatedly mussed by her putting her eyeglasses on the top of her head. The straight skirt of her linen suit revealed a trim figure, as well as the bottom of her slip. As she stepped into the hall, she was looking around. She hesitated when her eyes landed on DD, and quickly looked away at Kas.

"This guy might have a better chance if he tried to escape. Jesus, a white Mississippi cop in a New York jail – or any lockup." Ms. Tocci seemed to have no New York accent and DD wondered for a moment why that was.

Kas engaged her. "Linda, with the case we got, I guess he may as well run for it. He is definitely going away for a long time – someplace. It's goin' to be murder in the first degree."

Looking away from Kas and back at DD, "He's got other problems, Kas. This the AG from Mississippi?"

Shaken from spectator status, DD managed, "Oh, I'm Dan O'Neil." He shook Ms. Tocci's unconcerned hand.

"No drawl. I'm disappointed. I love that Mississippi drawl."

She looked away and again started with Kas. "As I said, this guy's got other problems. Those problems are probably the reason Mr. O'Neil has come all the way from Jackson. I'm not saying what those problems are, or even officially telling you they exist. But, if we're going to work something out, we're looking at something that keeps him out of New York as well as Mississippi."

Ms. Tocci was very analytical, wholly efficient and cold – very cold.

Kas leaned his big body against the wall. "New York maybe; Mississippi unlikely." He looked at DD. "What do you think O'Neil?"

Not at all sure what the other two lawyers were talking about, DD charged ahead: "Listen to me. I am not from Mississippi. I'm from San Francisco."

Kas looked at Luca and Luca looked at Simon as if to ask: "Did we pick up the wrong guy on the way up here?"

"I do represent the Mississippi attorney general and you should have a letter from him giving me his authority in this situation. But you have to understand, I am no prosecutor and never have been. I'm a private lawyer doing civil cases and haven't handled a criminal case in over five years."

Looking relieved, Kas took the clue. "Well, you do see that anyone representing this weirdo cop is going to be concerned about his sentencing and where the sentence would be carried out? Forty per cent of the population of any New York prison is black and I would bet all of those have a clear image of what a white Mississippi cop has done. I would not bet on his chances of living through the first month he is locked up."

Incredulity had spread across the faces of the public defender and the detectives,

"You're not a prosecutor; you're a real lawyer?" Luca was the first to utter anything.

Simon then chimed in, "But you try cases, right? You have tried a criminal case, haven't you?"

DD wasn't sure how much he had to pre-qualify himself for these people, but maybe to make everyone – including himself – feel better, he told them, "Yeah, I try a lot of cases – complex ones. I have tried twenty criminal cases – all but two were felonies. I never did a lot of plea bargaining in those days. There were seventeen acquittals."

Ms. Tocci warmed. "That's a hell of a record Mr. O'Neil. Either you are real good or the prosecutors in San Francisco aren't worth a shit."

Luca chuckled. "Or the cops aren't worth a shit."

"But you are prepared to make a deal here and now, aren't you?" Kas had to know.

"That depends on what this guy is willing to give up, but, generally, yes. Look, Kas, we're not going to get anywhere with him unless we have a way of hiding him out where he isn't so vulnerable."

Heaving himself off the wall, Kas assured DD, "Yeah, I think we can work that out, but there is no way that people who kill people get off in this State. There will have to be some serious time – particularly because you think this guy killed no less than two people."

"Mississippi needs this guy to serve time, as well. So, let's get started, I am anxious to meet him."

As they were entering the interrogation room, Val said, "So, you're from San Francisco, My sister lives in Los Angeles, Victoria Baltestrari, know her?"

Everybody in New York thinks California is a village and everybody knows everybody else.

"No, actually. Los Angeles is about 400 miles from where I live and several million people."

Praeger was sitting in a bare-walled room at a large table with six chairs around it. There was a plastic cup of water in front of him. He had a deep bruise above his right eye and he was shackled – hands and feet.

Kas and DD introduced themselves to him; he had already met the detectives. About DD's size, he appeared to be fit, alert, and intelligent – maybe just cunning, but seemingly intelligent.

Kas followed the initial introduction. "Mr. O'Neil here represents your home state of Mississippi."

Praeger managed a handshake with DD, revealing a surprisingly calloused hand and muscular forearm bearing the tattoo of a dagger. "So, you're the guy from Frisco."

Praeger smiled as he let his antagonists know he knew a lot. He was signaling there was much to deal for. "Doesn't Barstow have his own troops? Can you really help here? Do the people in Frisco know you're here?"

Poker-faced, DD simply said, "I don't know what the people in San Francisco know. Barstow wants me here because I am from San Francisco. If I can't help, you'll likely be sent to prison here. If that happens, it is my understanding you won't live long enough to serve any time in Mississippi."

Jesus! This guy knows who I am and that Barstow has sent me. He probably knows that Barstow is on to him. Does he have the diary? Has he prepared to run? I probably should be looking for a stash that will finance his getaway.

"As far as you are concerned, I'm it. If you have anything to say, maybe I can help with arrangements. If you don't have anything to say, I'm on the next plane home."

"Well, I'll be. Maybe I don't have nothin' to say."

Praeger tried faking a dumb cracker pose and lexicon.

"And if I don't, then this is a short day for y'all. I learnt in my career that eyewitnesses are not all that reliable. Y'gotta have more than that. I was scopin' out this apartment house looking for someone to play with. Could say I'm a little kinky, but that doesn't make me a killer, now does it?"

Kas had put one foot on a chair, sighed, and then leaned across the table looking huge,

"We put people like you away every day on less evidence. We're not interested in spending a lot of time to entertain you. We got you in the building and in front of it two days before the killing. We got you in women's clothes that meet the description of a 'woman' visiting the deceased the afternoon she is found dead. We got heroin in the bra that was in your shoulder bag when you were arrested. You, Mr. Praeger, are going to fall."

Praeger's steely exterior was moved, just a little bit. There was silence for a moment and Kas sat down. DD took that as a cue.

"Do you think anyone is going to buy the claim that it was just coincidence that you met up with a woman from the same state as you while you were out looking for weird thrills in a town with, what, eight million people? A woman who left Mississippi just a few days before you? As Mr. Kaslewski here says, you fall. You go to prison and those you worked for in this deal will walk and ultimately die a natural death. Between New York and Mississippi, you will spend the rest of your life locked up, unless, of course, Mississippi chooses to execute you."

There was no doubt that Praeger had expected this approach, but with its presentation, he was perceptibly shaken – the smirk had disappeared. "Y'all can't make me on anything in Mississippi. I got friends there and they ain't so quick to jump to conclusions."

He sat back, waiting to see what they had from Mississippi.

Quietly and with a stone face, DD began, "I don't yet know how you got into it, but some people in California wanted Ella Mae White dead. You got your hands on a utility company truck and found your way to the road behind Ella Mae's mansion. There, you were seen walking toward that

174

mansion, through the woods, with that very same black shoulder bag you were carrying when you were busted in the Penn Station men's toilet. There is, then, the matter of access to Ella Mae's house. It turns out that the Sheriff of Indian County keeps the keys from all the automatic alarm premises in the county. Ella Mae had given him one. These keys are all stored in the same place and well marked. You, Mr. Praeger, were in the Indian County Sheriff's office two days before the killing of Ms. White. Your proffered reason for this visit was to pick up a prisoner and take him back to your county. That prisoner you picked up in Indian County never showed up in Delta County. I think that is how you got into Ella Mae's place. "

DD then turned to Kas. "Can we talk for a minute outside?"

The lawyers and the two detectives went to the hallway.

"I need to call Jackson. They should have something from the search of Praeger's residence – I think I am going to need it."

Luca pointed to a public phone hanging on the wall just outside the interrogation room. Kas returned to talk to Praeger and Tocci.

"We faxed a report and inventory to Kas about twenty minutes ago." Sonny was excited. "DD, this guy's name isn't Praeger. That's the name of a guy he was in the Marines with. The real Praeger died within months after his discharge. This guy's name is Michael John Bolton. When we ran that, we find he was dishonorably discharged from the Marines after conviction for attempted murder! He tried to garrot his company commander."

DD could only shake his head. "Sonny, I got this guy in an interrogation room at a Manhattan precinct. He's got a lawyer and she and he are ready to deal. It seems to me it's a matter of what he is stuck with. What else do you have?"

"Probably the beginning of the unwinding. Bolton is the nephew of Clem Cadbury, the former sheriff of Delta County. He is now an insurance underwriter for...can you guess?"

"The Fraternal Order of Mississippi Law Enforcers."
DD let it out like a deep breath.

"You're a smart guy, Danny O'Neil. There's more in
the fax."

DD hung up when he saw a uniformed police officer exit
the elevator in an apparent hurry, carrying what appeared to
be several pages of faxed sheets.

"I'm Dan O'Neil; are those for me?"

After assuring himself that DD was indeed the intended
recipient, the young officer handed over what DD guessed to
be about twenty pages. As he read it, DD handed Luca and
Simon each page for their enlightenment.

Inside the interrogation room, Kas was explaining to the
suspect: "The way this works, Praeger, is that we can make no
deals for some sentence that is less than you deserve unless
and until we know that we can get something from you that
would..." the big prosecutor paused for effect... "definitely
help nail these other people – not maybe but definitely. In
terms of what we can do, if your information is really very,
very good and you agree to testify, I can see a prosecutor's
recommendation to accept a plea for murder two with a
conspiracy count. That would cut your sentence in New York
to ten years. Now, if your information is even better than that,
maybe we can prevail on Mississippi to help place you where
you have a chance of living out your sentence."

Linda Tocci, sitting to Praeger's right, seemed occupied
with some papers she was reading. When Kaslewski finished
his "explanation" she smiled slightly, and leaned forward,
pushing her glasses up into her mussed hair.

"Without a motive, Kas, you can't get murder one and
you sure as hell can't get a conspiracy conviction. Right now,
it looks like this conspiracy notion is a pipe dream of people
looking to close difficult cases."

DD entered the room at this point and stood by the door
listening to Ms. Tocci do her best to straighten out Kaslewski.

She stood, as if to stretch, then held up the papers she had
been reading.

176

"What you have, according to this report, is something saying that the decedent said that decedent was going to call someone that may or may not be involved in a bribery case in San Francisco. There's nothing to connect my client with that person in San Francisco; you have no one to say that the person was called by the decedent or that Mr. Praeger here talked to that person. You sure as hell don't have any direct evidence that Mr. Praeger killed this woman – disguised or not. If you don't have motive then your circumstantial evidence leaves you with a cross dresser making contact with a heroin using lesbian former whore."

Praeger sat back and smiled at his lawyer.

DD smiled at Praeger *qua* Bolton, and Bolton stopped smiling.

"Ms. Tocci," he began quietly, "I guess what you just told us would be persuasive if that arrest report was all there was on this fellow sitting next to you. But it isn't all there is. "

Looking directly at Bolton, "We can start with the fact, can't we, that you are not LeRoy Praeger? Rather, you are Michael John Bolton, dishonorably discharged from the United States Marines following your conviction for attempted murder."

Bolton sighed; Ms. Tocci shook her head.

"You are positively identified as the person who entered and left the decedent's apartment an hour or two before she was found dead. The NYPD thinks the eyewitness is quite believable. But the credibility of this eyewitness becomes absolutely golden when considered in light of some other salient facts. Ms. Tocci's observations about motive are apt, I think. But we are not without evidence of motive. I have a fax from the Mississippi Attorney General's office that reports the results of a search – a search with a warrant – of your home in Rice. Among other things recovered was a leather-covered notebook which contains various telephone numbers. Two in particular caught the eye of the assistant attorney general – one follows the handwritten words 'Uncle Clem.' That telephone number is the same as the Fraternal Order of

Mississippi Law Enforcers, so we believe that 'Uncle Clem' is Clem Cadbury – your uncle."

Bolton was no longer looking at DD, but at his hands.

DD turned to Ms. Tocci. "The Mississippi Attorney General has reason to believe that FOMLE has been facilitating the hire of Mississippi cops to murder people."

Kaslewski's eyes widened and both Simon and Luca sat down to hear how DD was going to connect Bolton to such an elaborate plot.

"This leather notebook also contains another telephone number and name, to wit: 'Drucinda' with a San Francisco number that I recognize to be the law firm of Loudon, Mueller and Keislor where Drucinda Lacey is employed."

DD again turned to Ms. Tocci to explain. "This woman was working with the lawyer who represented the defense in the case where I was the plaintiff's lawyer and a murder victim in Magnolia City was the foreperson of the jury."

Ms. Tocci looked incredulous, so DD went on, "We have a description of someone who was walking on a little-used path behind the house where this woman was killed on the afternoon of the murder. That description fits Mr. Bolton."

"Don't you think that is a mighty stretch Mr. O'Neil" The assistant public defender was doing her job. "A guy who might look like...my client...two thousand miles away? I mean what can that have to do with," again having trouble deciding what to call Bolton, "...my client."

"Your client, Ms. Tocci, knows exactly what the connection is. At this point, you should confer so he can decide how much further he wants me to go before this great big district attorney sitting next to me decides there is no reason at all to deal with him. I understand that New York prosecutors have a lot of things to do."

She looked at Bolton. "Do you want to confer?"

Bolton shook his head, "No."

"It might help to know that the items I have described were found under the flooring of your residence, a house, I believe. And there is more: a .22 caliber pistol and four different, interchangeable barrels in a metal container meant to store a socket-wrench set. A safety deposit key, which is thought to be for a safe deposit box at the Riverside Bank of New Orleans. By the way, a warrant served on that same bank revealed an account in the name of LeRoy Praeger with a current balance of $43,000.

"The under-the-floor stash also included uniforms for three different police or sheriff departments – including one for the New Orleans police department. There were various items of women's makeup and clothing, including a few items of negligee. There were five women's wigs."

All pretense of control and disdain had gone from Bolton's face. He was staring at the top of the table. His lawyer was making an occasional note.

DD continued: "Remember we're really just getting started with this investigation of you, so this ain't bad, is it?"

"It's still serendipity, Mr. O'Neil, but why are we going through this? What are you offering, Kas?"

Linda Tocci was becoming concerned that if DD continued, there would be little to negotiate over.

Before Kas could respond, DD pressed the matter.

"We're not talking about what we're offering until Mr. Bolton here tells us what he knows and does so under oath with a commitment to testify. Serendipity? This guy," pointing at Bolton, "is placed in Mississippi on the day and near the place of the murder of the New York victim's long time companion. You can't seriously believe that anyone will fail to conclude from this evidence that there is a connection. There are a number of motives to kill Malvina (a) she may be one of two people who knew the scheme to bribe the Mississippi victim back in San Francisco – the other was already dead. (b) she had the diary and wouldn't give it up without being killed."

DD gave no hint of not believing that theory. Bolton was visibly shaken. DD sat back.

"You do know about the diary, don't you Mr. Bolton?"

Bolton didn't respond. He looked confused.

"What makes you think I would know about a diary?"

Jesus, he doesn't know! Where is it?

"Bolton, Sargent Luca is over there taking notes of what you are saying. There is, in addition, a tape recording being made of what we are all saying. Do you want it a matter of record that you know about the diary or that you don't know?"

Bolton thought for a moment, then leaned back on his chair and against the wall.

"I don't know about any diary."

Why doesn't he know? Why did he chase Malvina all the way from Magnolia City to New York? He must have thought she had it?

"Ms. Tocci, I hardly think this is serendipity. I think we have this guy for two murders, and that reminds me – just over four years ago, in a flea bag hotel in the San Francisco Tenderloin, another juror in the <u>Pavlone</u> case was found dead shortly after his selection – dead from an overdose of heroin – two injections. One in the thigh and the other in the neck, from behind. So, do we have you on three murders?"

Ms. Tocci stood up. "Maybe you gentlemen should excuse us."

"You should know, Ms. Tocci that the Mississippi Attorney General is having the .22 barrels tested and compared to slugs pulled out of other victims. I think there will be more murders than three."

DD was menacing.

In the hallway, each officer lit a cigarette. Kas leaned against the wall.

"Good work, O'Neil."

He turned and knocked on the interrogation room door. "Yo, Linda! Why don't we just go to lunch? We'll be back here about 1:30. Ok?"

She opened the door and looked at Kas as if to say he was a cad for leaving her alone with this serial murderer.

***

CHAPTER SIXTEEN

Closing In

DD took the lunch break as a chance to call the office. It was nearly 10 a.m. in San Francisco.

"Jeannie, what is going on?"

"What are you talking about? You're in the middle of the action, Mr. O'Neil. You tell me."

"Ok. I will. Just tell me if Mattie is all right."

"She's fine. She had some papers sent from her office and she is working at your desk. Of course, Rick is hovering like the buzzard he is."

"Why don't you open the speaker phone in my office and get Mattie and our Lothario on the line with you so I only have to say this once."

One could hear Jeannie herding and bodies stirring and then Mattie's voice,

"Dan! Are you coming home?"

"I think so. At least by tomorrow afternoon."

Rick rang in, "DD, are we any closer to saving the American working class?"

"I think so, Rick. I really think so."

DD provided a brief synopsis of what had happened with Bolton.

"Rick, we have to get Larry Harrington going on the subpoena for phone records of the Loudon firm."

Rick laughed. "Well, as you might imagine, they are screaming to beat hell about the subpoenas Larry served. They will be on the criminal master calendar *ex parte* calendar this afternoon. I think that means Judge Benjamin. Shouldn't I put together a declaration on what you've told me about the Mississippi discoveries and your conversations with...what's his real name?"

"Bolton," DD supplied. "Can't you just tell Larry and when he argues, can't he just say he is 'reliably informed'? I am concerned about getting on the record anything that says I told you something because that might mean they could successfully inquire about just about anything I told you. Not a good idea."

"I'll try that, but you know how upset these guys are. I have suggested that the judge appoint some kind of master to review the phone records and report calls made to or from certain numbers. This is only to get around the firm's claims of confidential communications." Rick was seeking DD's opinion on his idea.

"If it comes to that, I suppose that will do for now. There will be items we miss, but I think if a master is involved, the order ought to require that the records remain available. They may become important as the thing develops. Listen, I've got to get back in there. Mattie?"

"I'm okay, Dan. Just get home."

With the imperative from Mattie, DD hung up and returned to the interrogation room.

Tocci worked out a detailed arrangement with Kas for Bolton. The big sticking point was where Bolton could serve his time with a reasonable expectation of living to testify. He would stand convicted in New York and sentenced to a minimum of seven years, but would have to work out his sentence in Mississippi and possibly California. No one mentioned the probable murder in Louisiana and that would hang fire for some time to come.

The recorder went on and Bolton began talking about 2:30 p.m. – not stopping until 11 p.m. that night. He confirmed that he had been brought to Mississippi by his uncle Clem Cadbury, who at the time was Sheriff of Delta County.

It was Cadbury and Arnold Crossmore who recruited him to do side jobs. They introduced Bolton to two men at a lawyer conference in New Orleans, maybe four years ago. Actually, he did not learn the names of these guys but only to answer their questions and forget them. One was a "big" guy with black hair combed straight back. The other was a tall thin fellow with grey hair and wearing what appeared to be diamond cufflinks. The big guy did all the talking. Clearly, Bolton thought, he was being interviewed.

The side jobs were murders. With another small town cop, he helped do the judge in Chicago and was notified by "Uncle Clem" of the target and details. When he nearly got caught and thought he was identified, Uncle Clem had him call a number in San Francisco and ask for Dru. When he did that, she devised a plan to get him back to Delta County and to make it appear he had never left.

"This woman Dru is a genius. A true genius." Bolton chortled his praise.

His bank account in New Orleans under the name of Praeger was periodically credited with part of the payment for each side job. No large sums were deposited and no large sums were withdrawn. Instead, about every two weeks there was a deposit of the same amount of money – usually $5,000. Occasionally, Uncle Clem would tell him he earned a bonus. That would be anywhere from $500 to $1,000. For his part, Bolton withdrew only modest amounts every month – usually no more than $4,000. He didn't know the details of the deposits; that is, he didn't know where the money came from or how it got to his account.

The hit on the black woman in Magnolia City was the first one in Mississippi for him. He had heard that others were assigned Mississippi jobs, but declined to name these "others." He had also heard that one of these "others" was assigned to assassinate Attorney General Clarence "Bud" Barstow.

Uncle Clem and Crossmore met Bolton at a bar in Arkansas about two months ago. They explained the assignment to murder Ella Mae White. Bolton shared that he was surprised at the assignment because just about anyone could be paid a lot less to kill some old "nigger woman." He learned that Ella Mae required special attention and that he would have to find something and bring it to them – a diary.

Being careful not to be taking special time off his job as a deputy, Bolton had to wait for two weeks before he attended to this new assignment. His uncle was no longer the Sheriff, but nonetheless called him several times to urge him to move because the target may do something to endanger their clients. He watched the house for a week. There appeared to be no one living with the target and she had few visitors – two or three tradespeople and the grocery delivery boy.

He arranged to be sent to Magnolia City to pick up a prisoner from the Indian County sheriff. While there, with information supplied by Uncle Clem, he found and purloined the key to the back door of his target's house. Bolton went on proudly to chronicle the clever way he acquired the temporary use of a water company truck that took him to the street below White's house, on the other side of some thick woods. From there he entered the house through the back door, using the key he had stolen. After entering the house, he found his target in what he called the front room, sitting in a high-backed chair reading.

She was startled and let out a muffled yell when he raised his pistol. With the muzzle pointing directly at her, he demanded she tell him where the diary was. She said something like "Bullshit." At that moment, he heard what he believed to be the chime of the alarm system, and thought he heard footfalls upstairs. Deciding he would have to look for the diary anyway, he shot Ella Mae in the forehead.

"Was the muzzle silenced?" Luca asked.

"Well, yes and no. It could be heard in a quiet place and it was quiet there."

He then described running upstairs and frantically looking through all the rooms. As he raced downstairs, he heard a car start up in the driveway and speed away. He charged through the front door, but all he could see was a small, black sedan heading off down the road at a high speed. There was no way he could give chase. So he went back into the house where he began looking for the diary. He concluded that whoever that was driving away had torn the diary pages from a notebook sitting in the drawer in the table beside where the corpse of Ella Mae White sat serenely.

"Did you reset the alarm?" DD quietly interrupted Bolton otherwise compelling narrative.

"Yes."

"Why?"

"I don't know. Maybe just being tidy. Maybe just to throw off the investigation. The fact is, I didn't know how the system worked going in."

Luca then asked: "What about fingerprints? Did you wear gloves?"

"Latex medicals."

"Go ahead," Kas directed.

He ran out the back and through the woods to the utility truck. He couldn't leave it there, so he drove downtown and parked it near the water company yard. He walked to his car and headed off down the road to the interstate.

He stopped before he got to the interstate and called Uncle Clem using a public phone. Cadbury told him to go home. Don't panic. Don't speed. Just go home. Cadbury explained that "we" had a major problem. That diary would put the clients at risk and whoever took it probably saw Bolton. Cadbury promised to call Bolton at home, later.

In a rare revelation of personal fear, Bolton went on to explain that he realized he was out front. If anyone gets caught, it will be him. He had to figure out how to find this person who took the diary, so he called the brilliant Ms. Dru and called her collect. Her reaction was angry.

"Don't call me at this number unless you are directed to. Never call me collect. Go home. I'll call you in the morning about 9:30, your time."

When she called, she again told him never to call that number and never collect to any number he might have. She wanted to know about the phone he had used. She told him that the person in the house was probably Malvina Montrose, a dyke living with the woman he just shot. She told him to sit tight and do nothing out of the ordinary; she expected she might hear from this woman within a few days.

A couple days later, Uncle Clem called. He told Bolton that this woman, Malvina, was in New York and gave him an address in Manhattan.

"He also told me she was probably looking out for someone to be after her. I had to be real careful in this approach. I learned she was a former junkie. That was the break. They always go back under stress – that's my experience. Anyway, Uncle Clem said he was having $5,000 deposited for expenses and I was to get to New York and clean this up as soon as possible. I was also to find this diary. It had to be a clean job. It had to appear accidental."

"Do you remember what day it was that your Uncle Clem telephoned?"

DD knew the telephone records of FOMLE had been subpoenaed.

"It was always the same time, Friday evening between 7 and 8 or Tuesday morning between 10 and 11. Tuesday was my usual day off from the department. I just had to be at the telephone at those times."

Once again, Kas kept the group on track. "Tell us about taking this woman Malvina down."

He explained that he couldn't approach her in the street. He was afraid she'd freak and make a lot of noise.

"Dru had assured me she would avoid calling the police, and I got the feeling she and Dru had talked. So, once I cased the place, I let her see me. She wasn't going to bring in the police; she might give me something to go on if she thought I was after her. Then, I just put on the disguise I had with me and knocked on her door. I told her I was from Dru and that Dru had sent me to give her something. She seemed very relieved. I persuaded her I was a friend and that Dru wanted her to completely relax. I showed her the junk and she at first resisted any notion of it. Finally, I cooked it up and let her inject herself in her thigh. Good-looking woman. I told her I was a cross dressing queer and she laughed. She told me she felt better than she had felt in a long time. I asked her about this diary that she had mentioned. She said she hadn't remembered telling me anything about that. Then she laughed. She told me she had been in the house when the guy killed her long time companion and had grabbed the diary on the way out the door. She had to tear it out of the notebook so she could conceal it in the back of her panties where maybe she could get away with it if caught. Then, she started to cry."

When Bolton pressed Malvina about the whereabouts of the diary she just said "It's safe." Then she dosed off.

"I loaded the syringe and injected her in the neck, just below her skull"

This is one cold motherfucker...

Returning to San Francisco aboard a red-eye flight, DD made an outline and a list of things to be done.

Harrington will be able to get a grand jury case together against Dru Lacey. Will she turn on Keislor? The telephone records will have to corroborate Bolton. Clearly, Dru is out front here – why? What happened to the diary and, if we find it, we'll need to authenticate it. Is it a dying declaration and admissible? Chain of custody? Handwriting? Who were the guys Bolton met in Memphis? One may be Keislor – as close as we've come. Photograph? Who's the other guy? The elder Weisenstock – best bet. Photograph?

DD had told Tocci and Bolton that he wasn't sure where they could stash Bolton pending Mississippi proceedings. In any event, he would be as safe as they could make him. The problem was that Bolton wasn't giving up any of the other people in this Mississippi "murdering cops for rent" scheme. Bolton asked that DD try Cadbury and Crossmore before coming back to him on that. *Strange sense of moral obligation.*

This remains a slippery conspiracy. What is it? Who are they? A young woman legal assistant in San Francisco could not be the leader of this sort of thing, no matter how clever she is. Why would it be Keislor? It would seem to be enough of a task just to do the "legal" work. It has something to do with insurance – nationally.

Ricardo Jose Ruiz Esquivel is easily picked from a crowd – his tall good looks and Californio countenance just sticks out. DD spotted him immediately upon exiting the jetway and then, of course, there was Mattie standing beside him. Rick's presence was suddenly forgotten and DD stepped up and threw his arms around her. She kissed him and kissed him passionately. What seemed to Rick to be several minutes passed before they hinted at disengaging, so he had to speak:

"Look, you guys, this lip-locking right here in public is a little awkward. Um, do you want me to call a cab or are you still riding home with me?"

DD smiled at Rick and said, "We're with you partner. But just drop me off at the Orchard. I'll find my way home."

All three laughed.

The reticence was gone. Going slow was forgotten. They embraced, kissed, tasted, stroked, and entered that place where two people become alone and where they cannot comprehend the rest of the universe.

When he awoke, it was light. She stepped out of the bathroom naked and utterly beautiful. All he could do was smile. She moved lightly and then sat on the side of the bed.

"My god. I've never experienced anything close to that. I never even knew it was possible." She did – she giggled a little. He sighed.

"You must be exhausted. I mean that was not only an artful performance, it was physical and you just flying clear across the country."

The tones were quiet – intimate.

"Uhmm." he agreed.

She fingered his thick auburn hair and the caressed his freckled shoulders.

"You're darker than me – in spots."

188

They laughed. Finally, he managed, "What is that scar on your back?"

Mattie blanched, slightly. "It's from a burn. It is why I don't wear a conventional brassiere. My former husband stuck a hot steam iron on my back and held me down until the flesh burned away to the bone"

DD sat up. "What the hell was that about?"

"I was just twenty. My daddy didn't want me to marry so young, but I had earned my bachelor's degree early. And Brad was such a promising guy. He was an instructor in history at Ole Miss; he had graduated with honors and seemed solid enough. I think he was the first black faculty member since Reconstruction."

"Well, how long had you been married when this happened?"

"Just four months. I had just been admitted to the graduate program in Government."

She stood up and stretched. When she did, DD very nearly forgot the conversation. She turned to look at him softly and continued, "I don't know whether it is our culture, inherent in maleness, or what, but I have come to conclude jealousy is a more powerful motive for evil deeds than we have ever understood. Brad resented my admission. His station as my professional superior was crucial to him, so crucial he was going to cripple me in a violent reaction to the news of my admission."

"Jesus, Mattie. He could have killed you. What did you do? What came of it?"

"I couldn't do anything. The pain was so great I passed out. Our neighbor heard me scream and apparently came charging into the room. When she saw me, she immediately went to the phone and called the Jackson police. Brad made up some fool story that no one believed. He came to hospital after I was sufficiently off of morphine to talk. He brought flowers and apologized over and over again. He asked me to forgive him and I told him I wouldn't. He slapped me right there in the hospital room. When I was released, I moved back to Daddy's house. His lawyer filed the divorce papers two days later. Daddy told Brad to leave town and Brad did. I haven't seen him since – that was ten years ago."

"Any children?"

Mattie kissed him on the chest. "Not yet."

She smiled up at him.

"Yeah," DD conceded. "I'm hungry."

"I am not going out in public with you unless you shower. You sweat all night long like no one I've ever seen. You sweat all over me."

"I'm sorry; I guess I got a little worked up."

"It's ok. I loved it, but I already showered. So you get going."

It was the first time that Mattie had ever had dim sum and Pearl City was DD's favorite. He helped her order and she just kept ordering.

"I feel like I'm in a foreign country!"

"Well, in very real sense, you are. The Chinese have been here at least as long as the Irish, but they haven't completely assimilated. It's happening but it's been more than a hundred years. It's a fascinating culture, but I don't really know how it stacks up against the Chinese in China."

Seemingly satisfied, Mattie sat back with her herb tea and looked at DD. "Ok. You don't have any scars I can see, but from what I hear, your marriage had some of the same features as mine."

"You've been talking to Jeannie. Oh, and Dianna."

"You're surrounded Mr. O'Neil. Which reminds me, what is a 'Butte Break'?"

He smiled. "Some people say it is boyish rudeness, like a secret society. In a sense it is. Joe Cleary and I are pretty close. When we need to talk about something that we don't want to share necessarily with anyone else, we take a Butte Break and just talk about it between ourselves. It has helped me tremendously over the years because I have this tendency to act before thinking. Yes, we even exclude wives."

She thought for a minute. "OK, so tell me about this divorce from ... what's her name?"

"Melanie Langley. I guess she's pretty much your age. Beautiful woman who'd make PLAYBOY centerfold, if they would pay her enough. I met her at an anti-war planning meeting and later when she was working for her parents renting the cottages on Telegraph Hill. In fact, it was when I made the deal on my current digs. Anyway, I had broken up with a woman I didn't think I should break up with, but I did it and it had been a few months. Melanie had been a hippie while a student at UC Santa Cruz. In the beginning she seemed to be pretty politically compatible with me, and that is rare.

"Anyway, she seemed sophisticated and big-hearted and we got along well. I never thought about marriage; she asked me. Actually, she had started planning the wedding before I knew what was going on. Joe and Dianna had developed a family and a lifestyle I very much admired and wanted. So I didn't do a lot of thinking about it and we got married.

"Nothing ever went right. Melanie's father is Robert Gordon Langley. He is the Chairman of the Board of Pan American Trust and Casualty and one of the richest men in the country, if not the world. Melanie lived in an apartment in The City in a building that her father owns. Her parents lived, and she grew up in, Marin County – just across the Golden Gate Bridge. These are not people whose lifestyle resembles anything I had ever experienced.

"I guess I better explain that part.

"My dad is Mick O'Neil, a blacksmith in Silver Bow County, Montana, and an Irish immigrant. Mick did well enough financially to raise me without really wanting and helped send me to college and law school. But, my father is the former Chairman of the Socialist Party of the USA. I was raised a socialist, an atheist, and generally opposite to the rearing of Melanie. I wear my red credentials on my sleeve. If this lasts between us, it will require that you at least tolerate this personality disorder, as Melanie characterized it."

A flicker of light went off in Mattie's eyes, and she asked: "Is this socialism what led you to meet and befriend Sonny Elliot?"

DD nodded affirmatively.

"He has told me a little about your political lecturing, but I really didn't appreciate it. Now, I am beginning to. Please tell me how this led to your divorce."

"I had a client – a young black guy. His dad was a longshoreman, and an old-time communist party member. His mom was white and Jewish and she was also a former member of the Communist Party. Randall Young, the son, was a musician who had been arrested one night on the way home from a gig – the gig was in The City and he lived in Richmond. The arrest was made by a suburban cop. The cop beat Randall up pretty badly, resulting in moderate brain damage that affected his playing – he played a tenor sax. I sued the suburb on his behalf."

DD paid the Pearl City bill and they walked out onto Clay Street in the middle of China Town.

"Let's walk while you tell me this story," she was pleading with him.

"The afternoon before Randall was busted, an inmate of the maximum security wing of San Quentin prison – Gerald Mann – had supposedly obtained a gun and tried to shoot his way out. The first news was that this guy's lawyer, someone named Roy Lindstrom, had slipped the gun to Mann. Lindstrom disappeared. My client, Randall, had told me that he saw Lindstrom in the club he was playing the night he was beat up by the cop.

When I first represented Randall, in a moment of marital intimacy I mentioned to Melanie that Randall may have assisted Lindstrom in his escape. Five or so months later, during the deposition of Randall in this case against the suburb, out of the blue, with absolutely no clue, no hint of a connection, the lawyer for the insurance company that insured the suburb asked Randall if he had assisted Lindstrom in his

192

escape that night. My wife had betrayed my confidence and betrayed Randall."

They had paused and sat on a bench in Portsmouth Square.

She asked, "How do you know that Melanie did that?"

"She doesn't deny it. She told her father what I told her. Her father's insurance company covers that suburb I was suing."

Neither felt like saying anything for several minutes.

"You know, DD, I have to get back to Indian County, soon. I'm an elected official and my employers will complain if I am not there."

"Yeah..."

DD hailed a taxi at Kearny and California.

"I think I don't want to part with you. If I don't, then I have to deal with this geography thing, don't I?"

"You're not saying, are you DD, that you are making the decision, as opposed to 'we?'"

"No. More like thinking out loud."

In the office, everyone looked at the couple knowingly when they came through the door. Jesus. Rick told everyone! Jeannie had a silly grin.

"Here are your telephone messages, Dan. Your chief legal researcher is waiting to see you. Mr. Elliot has called three times. I'm afraid I couldn't tell him the whereabouts of the special assistant attorney general."

"Thanks, Jeannie. Where's Rick?"

"Oh, I forgot. He's drafting the order issued by Judge Benjamin yesterday on the telephone records of the Loudon firm."

Mattie went to DD's office to resume working on her public administrator files. DD went to Rick's office.

"I didn't tell you last night – it seemed your mind was on something else – but Benjamin granted a kind of provisional order along the lines I had suggested. Jesus, Hugh was there and equating the subpoena with pissing in the Holy Grail. So now, what we have to do is decide what telephone numbers we want the master to look for and report to us."

"Here are the only ones that I can think of; we'll have to get the actual numbers from Pep. I got Bolton's and FOMLE's from Sonny." DD jotted a list : Bolton, FOMLE, Cadbury, Crossmore, Weisenstock in LA (business and home), Lowell in Tahoe, Ella Mae's, and Dru Lacey's home. "Do we know we have all the Loudon numbers? Does Dru have a special number that she uses?"

"We're not going to know that, DD, until we get somebody under oath before the grand jury. I'll get this over to Larry. I guess he takes it from there."

DD returned to Jeannie's desk to pick up his telephone messages as Mattie stepped out of his office. With a look of wide-eyed confusion, she spoke softly,

"I just talked to Arlen. He said I have a package that was posted in New York. I told him to open it. He says that inside was a pair of women's bikini type underpants and several pages with handwritten notes."

"The diary!"

"That's my guess. What do we do? I told Arlen not to say anything to anyone except G.A. McNaught."

"Good thinking, Mattie. Let's call Sonny."

Sonny agreed to contact G.A. to have him retrieve the diary. After Mississippi technicians had a chance to examine it, it would be sent to DD in San Francisco. Sonny had also received a return on the telephone records of FOMLE and Bolton. A copy was on its way to the San Francisco D.A. and to DD's office by priority mail.

"I agree that Mattie probably has to come back, but now that these subpoenas have been served, a lot of bad people are getting desperate. I think G.A. will have to provide some protection for her and you, DD, will have to persuade her to cooperate. Her cussedness is legendary up in Magnolia City."

"What about indictments of Cadbury and Crossmore?" DD was anxious for some action.

"Well, I've got a grand jury and it looks real solid. The judge isn't the greatest, but I am pretty sure he isn't on the payroll of the FOMLE group. Bolton won't part with the identity of his fellow killer cops, and until he does, he's coming home to spend time as a material witness. We should get an indictment by Monday or Tuesday at the latest. I'd like something that will preclude bail. That will depend on what Bolton is prepared to tell us. He'll be here tomorrow. We've got a lot of manpower watching who we think are the bad guys. They are probably trying to figure a way to waste Bolton before he testifies."

"Sonny, can I tell Mattie that you recommend she stay away until Bolton testifies? That would get her to Memphis on Sunday. Maybe you will have enough to round up some of those suspects by that time."

"Sure. That is probably the best idea. Remember, we don't know what the San Francisco conspirators know about her. So, just keep a look out."

"Of course."

Mattie willingly agreed to stay two more days. She made her arrangements and moved into the cottage on Telegraph Hill. DD cooked a couple of meals when Mattie confessed that toast was the best she could do, unless it was precooked and frozen. There was an awkward avoidance of any reference to their future.

On Thursday morning, the parcel from Sonny was delivered. DD immediately began to go over the toll calls made from the FOMLE, Cadbury, Crossmore, and Bolton telephones. There was a surprising number of calls, but only one Bay Area number had been called from each of the phones.

DD called Larry Harrington. He, too, had been studying the records from Mississippi. He promised to get the address that went with the one Bay Area number. He and DD agreed this was a key to the center of the conspiracy.

Suddenly, DD told Jeannie, "I'm going home for a minute. I'll be back in a half hour."

When DD returned, he went to Joe's office and told him, "We need a Butte Break, right away."

"Funny, I was thinking the same thing."

Jeannie and Pat were alerted. Both men were behind Joe's closed office door.

***

Part 4: A Startling Surprise

Be alert, be careful, be ready,
and life still comes up with kick-ass surprises.

an observation of Pep Lippman

CHAPTER SEVENTEEN
Butte Break

"You go first," DD insisted.

Joe leaned back in his chair, loosened his neck tie and threw his feet up on his desk.

"I understand that you brought Roy Lindstrom into this Mississippi thing."

"Yeah." DD had anticipated Joe's concern.

"I understand and wholly support your reasons. Roy needs the work and he's really a good lawyer. But, your opposition in this thing includes the most ruthless sonofabitch in town. If he gets wind of you and Roy, you and I will end up doing another couple rounds of explanation and suspicion. We did that once and neither one of us had any fun."

"I know. I should have talked to you about it before I called Roy. It just seemed like a perfect opportunity. We needed someone near Sierra County and it was Roy."

"Do you plan any more contact with Roy before the case is over?"

"He's representing Lowell Weisenstock, who is implicating his mother-in-law, Keislor's old secretary, and her husband. The records we have from the Loudon firm reveal dozens of calls over six months to Southern California Casualty – Weisenstock's company. I guess that makes some legitimate sense, given the Loudon firm business. Anyway, as things sit, there will be a connection from Lowell to his dad and an indictment of Darla. That keeps Roy in the picture."

Neither spoke for several minutes. Each was remembering the horrible onslaught of accusations, threats, and media attention ten years ago that accompanied the disappearance of Lindstrom following the attempted armed escape of Gerald Mann and the consequent blood bath just inside the walls of San Quentin. Joe was president of the Bay Area Chapter of the National Lawyers Guild at the time. The Guild was accused by various and sundry law enforcement organizations, as well as a Federal judge, of arranging the disappearance of Lindstrom. DD got in the face of the judge in a hearing covered by the press in an attempt to bring some sanity to the issue of what Lindstrom had done. The attempt, though eloquent, was interpreted in the local press as indicative of DD's involvement with Lindstrom.

Leonard Dolson, then assistant district attorney, tried to convene a grand jury to indict both Joe and DD for obstruction of justice when they each denied knowing anything about Lindstrom's whereabouts. The indictment never happened, but it left deep wounds in both Joe and DD.

"There are a number of clichés that occur to me, but you know them and what the problem is. Roy's in the clear but not us. Hang on. I expect this to come up. Then, I can't but wonder what your ex will do when it does."

"Now that you mention it, so do I."

"So, what's on your mind?"

DD leaned forward and laid an old spiral address book on Joe's desk. "This was an appointment/address book that Melanie and I had when we were maritally one. In this page of emergency numbers, you will note this over-the-top feminine hand? That's Melanie's. She has three numbers there for emergencies – this one, with her designation 'Dad special, 398-1928' appears in the record of calls made by the

Mississippi members of this conspiracy – Cadbury and Crossmore. It appears that Crossmore has called that number at least once a month for the last six months – that's all the records we can get. Cadbury called once in May and twice in the last two weeks. Bolton has never called that number from his house phone."

Joe whistled. "So, one of the wealthiest men in the country gets calls from Mississippi evil doers who were involved in the killing of your jury foreperson and her roommate. And he can be found at the same telephone number as Dru Lacey, employed by the law firm that defended the lawsuit where the late jury foreperson sat. Jesus Christ!"

"That's what it looks like, but it's not all that clear. First, Dru has her own telephone number, here on Nob Hill. That other number goes with an address in Sausalito. Second, we know that Langley spends most of his time in New York and has this palace with Mrs. Langley in Kentfield. How could anyone know to reach him or her at this Sausalito number?"

"Can I look at the records Sonny got from the Mississippi bad guys? You know I like puzzles like this." Joe had stood and was staring into Ramon's garden.

"Also, do we move on this to subpoena the toll records on this telephone? Or, does that tip everyone off too soon? Do we take the risk of getting the records through Pep? Do we know who this phone is assigned to?"

DD stood beside him.

"I'm trying to get my mind around the idea that my former father-in-law is somehow mixed up in a wide-ranging murder scheme. But, I don't know whose name is on this number and what I have is about six years old. Jesus, he's the biggest financial supporter of Grace Cathedral Charities!"

"I'd go slow on concluding Robert Gordon Langley was involved in a murder scheme. I mean, his daughter knew this number six years ago. I don't think he would have given it to her if that was what was going on. Maybe six years ago nothing was going on and since then it became a love nest for him and Dru. She is a very attractive, if weird, woman. So, before you tell anyone about this connection, let's get more information."

"You're right. There are a lot of Mrs. McGillicuddys around."

Larry Harrington and one of his associates met with DD on Turk Street. DD introduced Mattie and they discussed the diary. Harrington had a draft indictment he wanted to present to the grand jury in the morning. DD agreed but said nothing about the Sausalito telephone number.

As he was leaving the office, Jeannie announced a call from a reporter at the *Examiner*. DD took the call – it was Ed Slater, an old friend.

"So, you're now a prosecutor. The world is becoming a strange place, indeed."

Never one to miss a chance, DD replied, "I know, Eddie. I mean, there's a rumor around that you finally took an English class."

"Are you going to confirm that you are working as a special assistant to the Mississippi Attorney General? I mean there is a certain sweet irony about that DD and I really want to write it."

"OK. I confirm."

"So, does that mean that you are involved somehow in this nasty business of the subpoena of telephone records from Loudon, Mueller and Keislor?"

"Eddie, that's a grand jury matter. Even if I was inclined to answer that impossibly loaded question, I couldn't."

"C'mon DD! You're always such a sanctimonious ass. Loosen up and slip me something here. Is Hugh Keislor going to be indicted? Wouldn't that just delight you, given your history with the guy? And I'm told your old buddy Roy Lindstrom is representing somebody, a witness in this grand jury investigation. I mean, shit, Dan. This is a story and I want it."

"Eddie! Write this down. No comment. Don't screw with me on this. If you sit on this, it will be a bigger story later. Right now, all you can do is fuck it up. There'll be some information down the line you might be entitled to, but not if you get greedy on this little shit right now."

"DD, you're such a pain in the ass. How the hell am I going to make my child support payments?"

"See ya Eddie!"

DD grabbed Mattie, who had been working diligently on her office papers. "We gotta go. We're fixing dinner tonight for Joe and Dianna and probably Rick."

"We are? I have to clean up the cottage. It's not suitable for visitors right now."

He laughed. "You mean the bits of clothing here and there around the place?"

"Yeah. That's what I mean. What are we going to feed people?"

"Let's do that first."

DD parked the Ford in the members-only parking lot of the San Francisco Men's Club.

"This is nice," Mattie exclaimed. "Are you a member here?"

Not looking at her, DD responded, "No."

They walked the three blocks to Fisherman's Wharf. DD bought seven pounds of Willapa clams, two pounds of butter, and two rounds of sourdough French bread. They stopped at a Chinese market on the way to the car and bought four bottles of chardonnay and the makings for a big, green salad.

While Mattie picked up the various bits of clothing scattered about the little cottage, DD chopped onions and parsley, which he dropped into a large pot, made the salad, and consumed a glass of Powers. They both changed, although that nearly got more complicated. The guests arrived promptly at 6:30.

The conversation was light – principally about Joe and Dianna's kids, Kelly and Tom. The east side windows were open and the Bay breeze stroked the gathering.

"Ok," Mattie finally said, looking at DD, "What was that confab this afternoon that someone called a 'Butte Break'? I mean, shouldn't I know?"

Dianna stood and started clearing the table of dishes, Rick stood, as well. "I'll help."

"Mattie," DD spoke resolutely, "there's a real good chance that you and I will spend the rest of our lives together. That's just an objective observation, by the way. As close as we may become, there will always be Butte Breaks, so long as Joe and I are alive. The best thing about them is that no one else knows what goes on in them. The reason for that is all the things people do and say to each other often carry hidden motives and are protected by notions of politeness or sensitivity about another's feelings. When Joe and I go into a Break, we don't have those problems and the results have always been good for both of us."

She cocked her head defiantly and looked at DD.

"So, I am to butt out? It will always be a secret from me?"

DD kissed her on the nose and said, "Yeah."

As Joe and Dianna were leaving a little later, Dianna hugged Mattie and whispered, "It's ok."

The next morning, after about an hour with the telephone toll records from Mississippi, Joe emerged from his office and declared another Butte Break. DD went into Joe's office

"They have a contact schedule," Joe said. "This number is called only on a certain day of the week and within certain hours. It looks like it is twice a week – Tuesday morning between 8 and 9 a.m. and Friday, between 5 and 6 in the evening. I think we need to convert for Central Time. Bolton told us that and I didn't catch on. Pretty simple. It's risky. Something could come up at other times. But it minimizes exposure. So, do we have Larry issue a subpoena for the records on the Sausalito number?" DD's mind was racing.

"I think we take the chance with Pep. I don't want to be standing up in court and saying that Robert Gordon Langley is a principal in a nationwide murder scheme without more than we have. Maybe we have Pep stake out the Sausalito pad with a camera on the days and at the hours we think they are open for business. We really don't know who is at the other end of that telephone when the Mississippi crowd calls it. We could use some harder stuff if we are going to confront Dru when she is arrested."

The dangerous route was typically DD's choice.

"You have to warn Larry somehow, without tipping off the Pep possibility. Screwing around there tapping telephones could crash an entire prosecution. Could the cops get an order to allow a tap? Maybe. Let's just float that suggestion with Larry. I think you should also talk to Rick about it."

"OK. But make sure I'm there for the conversation with Rick. I bet Larry is with the grand jury right now."

The Acting District Attorney, with Rick in the hallway, had indeed been at the grand jury courtroom in at the Hall of Justice. Both came through the door at Turk Street with the pace and countenance of victorious warriors.

"It's done!" Rick announced with sufficient volume for everyone in the office to hear. "Drucinda P. Lacey is indicted for First degree murder and conspiracy to commit same. Our prosecutor is doing his job for a change."

DD looked at Larry. "Was there any problem?"

"No. I have to get the warrant together. You guys keep quiet until we have her cuffed. I'm asking Tony Citriani to do the collar."

"Hey. Wait a minute. Both you guys – we have to talk in my office," DD insisted. Of course this really peeved Pat and Jeannie.

"Sit down; Joe and I have something to discuss with you."

"Larry," Joe started, "what does it take to get a wire tap authorized?"

He was taking the illicit tap by Pep out of play.

"You mean in this case?" Larry clarified. "Well, I don't have anything to give a judge, but we can't have this indictment go public if that is what we're going to do."

The Butte boys explained the results of the analysis of the Mississippi records.

"Robert Gordon Langley? Are you kidding? No fucking way! Isn't he in the *Fortune* magazine top ten? No fucking way?"

It was decided that Larry would have the SFPD secretly inquire into the tenancy of the Sausalito address. He would consider the whole notion of a wiretap. To do it, however, he would have to have DD's declaration under penalty of perjury and that would eventually, before trial, make the press. It may compromise the prosecution.

"You mean because I got this number from my ex-wife and it is for her father."

Hesitantly, Larry added, "And, my friend, because Roy Lindstrom is involved. I'll call you in a few minutes. Keep this absolutely under your hat – including the indictment of Ms. Lacey. Get your staff to keep it quiet as well."

DD met Joe at Tony's for lunch after his appearance before Judge Conti.

"The tap warrant is served on the telephone company. The customer doesn't get notice. What you want out of the deal is a recording that will assist in identifying the answerer. Y'know, Langley doesn't have to be there and if he isn't, all we have is evidence against Dru if she answers. I suppose that couldn't hurt, but we aren't likely to get anything on Langley from such a call."

"We may need to make the call during the critical time ourselves."

"Why?" Joe asked.

"All that a police tap can do is record a conversation. If no one calls, there's nothing to record."

Inspector Mike Heaney and Lt. Tony Citriani were parked on Pelican Court, a short, dead-end street just up the hill from 93 Richardson Bay. There were three flats at that address – one on each floor of the '60s structure that overlooked Richardson Bay and the Sausalito marina. Down the hill and maybe 100 hundred yards away, Pep Lippman sat in his car with his massive telescopic lens mounted on his 35 millimeter camera, loaded with very high speed film. It was 4:30 p.m., Pacific Daylight Time, Friday.

The police detectives had two photographs clipped to the dashboard – one a copy of the photograph DD had found in the package left by Ella Mae, the other a *Fortune* magazine portrait of Robert Gordon Langley. When Pep learned of this, he irritably told Larry Harrington that it was a mistake to provide photographs on the assumption that is who will be in the flat. That is one reason he was there and prepared to take pictures of everyone going in the front door of any of the flats in the building.

Public records revealed the title to the building was, as everyone had suspected, held by Robert and Beatrice Langley – free and clear. They had purchased the property in 1977 and paid all cash.

Pep watched the police up the hill and thought what he always thought:

Who couldn't notice a police stake out; may as well put in neon – flashing neon.

At about 4:50 p.m., with the sun just sinking over the hills, Dru Lacey appeared driving her spanking new yellow Volkswagen Golf. She parked in the open garage just next to the flats and let herself into the middle one – the one under surveillance. Pep could see stirrings in the police car. He snapped off four exposures before Dru disappeared through the door. Excluding the possibility that someone had entered the flat before Pep or the police team arrived, it seemed that Dru was alone in that flat.

Suddenly, however, the figure of a man appeared in the front window of that same flat, pulling a cord to open the blinds. "Shit!" Pep thought. He snapped, but couldn't be sure he got anything useful.

There was a warrant-authorized tap on the telephone line of the number that had appeared in the records sent from Mississippi and that had matched DD's ex-father-in-law's emergency number. That tap was patched from the listening post two blocks away to a receiver in the car occupied by Heaney and Citriani. DD's simple remedy to identify the occupants of the flat was abandoned lest they be alerted. Nonetheless, the phone rang and the results immediately broadcast to the police car.

A woman's voice answered with an innocent "Hello."

An instant passed and then another woman's voice could be heard,

"What do we know about Praeger?"

The first woman, thought to be Dru Lacey, answered, "I was hoping you could tell me. If there is anything going on at the Hall, the lid is on it."

The caller's voice commanded, "Give up the schedule and stay away from the flat. No more contacts until we know more and then I'll do it. Talk to no one, except me."

The call was disconnected.

A half hour passed. The front of the flats was in shadow. Dru Lacey could be seen leaving in her yellow Volkswagen – alone. Pep stayed until 10PM. It had been dark for almost an hour. No lights came on in the targeted flat, but lights were turned on in both of the other units. Pep left. The police had left at 7:30 p.m.. No one was seen leaving that flat after Dru had left.

***

CHAPTER EIGHTEEN

Mystery – Deep and Slippery

The Turk Street conference room was a busy place on Saturday morning. Pep had set up a slide projector and the office screen, around which were gathered Larry Harrington, Tony Citriani, Joe, DD, and Rick. The slides were from Pep's photographic efforts the night before in Sausalito.

The depictions of Dru Lacey entering the flat were clearest, as they were shot before the shadows deepened. A woman and a child entered the lower flat only a minute or two before Dru arrived. The depiction was sufficient for all to conclude that both were Asian. Around 5:05 p.m., a large Caucasian male wearing a suit and carrying bags climbed the exterior stairs to the upper flat and appeared to be in a hurry. The shadows dimmed the fidelity of the picture taken at the bottom of the stairs, but the one shot at the top caught about one-quarter of his right profile.

"Wait a minute!" Harrington demanded. "Pep, can we see that shot of the guy headed into the top flat?"

Pep obliged.

"I think I know who that is," Larry announced.

"I think I do, too." Rick looked at Larry. "It looks like the former assistant district attorney Dick Baldachre.

Harrington agreed.

"Why would he be there?"

Studying the photograph, Joe muttered, "I can't really tell from that picture. I mean, he's got the big muscles and general demeanor of Dick, but I can't be sure."

Larry Harrington shook his head, "I have no doubt, but what does it mean?"

"There's a stairwell in the back where each flat has a landing for garbage and the like. If someone were in the top flat, he could easily enter either of the other two without being seen from the front. Let's take a look at this shot of the guy in the subject flat opening the blinds."

"I can't tell from that," Rick allowed. Harrington agreed.

Everyone studied the slide on the screen. No one could agree it was Baldachre; it did depict a Caucasian male, but only a small portion of his face and the fact that he was wearing a tie.

Pep shut the projector down. Rick stood up. "If he lives there, I can find out in a telephone call." He left the conference room.

"What does it mean if what we see is Baldachre? Is he part of the plot?" DD was searching – desperately searching.

"I suppose," Joe continued, "it could be wholly coincidence that Baldachre is in this apartment. He could live there and know absolutely nothing, but jesus what a coincidence!"

Rick reentered the conference room. "That's where he lives. We can go further to confirm, but according to his ex-wife, that is where he moved when they split."

Pep smiled knowingly. "You called his ex-wife?"

Matter-of-factly, Rick explained, "Yeah, we got to know each other pretty well here a few years ago."

"So, we're nowhere. From what we know about Dru, he could just be providing her entertainment a couple times a week. As for Robert Gordon Langley, that note by his daughter is what, six years old? Maybe he was using this place at the time."

"Well," Tony Citriani interjected, "let's listen to the tape of the phone call. These guys – more accurately – these women suspect we're on to them."

Rick played a copy of the tape on the office player. Each listened intently. Both Rick and DD nodded to each other.

"The voice is disguised somehow. It doesn't seem real. She's talking through something."

Pep straightened up. "She's talking through a microphone plugged into a synthesizer. I've done it myself. Very clever. Dru didn't have any problem knowing who she was talking to. Very clever."

Except for the possible involvement of Dick Baldachre, there were no other surprises coming out of the stakeout in Sausalito. The permutations possible to explain Baldachre's presence at the same flat as Dru, while not infinite, are certainly large in number. Then, maybe he wasn't even in Dru's flat.

"All we know is that there was a guy there that nobody saw go in. But nobody saw him come out. Both of those results have a lot to do with the fact that no one was there earlier and later."

Joe was doing a tutorial. "I don't think we can conclude he's involved here."

Everyone sat silent for several minutes. Finally, Harrington stood.

"We're driving ourselves nuts trying to figure it all out at once and I don't think that's going to happen. Dru Lacey is indicted, Darla Reid Weisenstock should be, we need to ask Bolton to look at some photographs to see who else we indict. There isn't anything here to justify going back to the grand jury on Keislor. Oh, Rick! What's the story on the diary?"

Rick sighed, "Most of it is not legible because it got wet. I am not able to say why that is so and I'm not going to speculate. The Mississippi state crime laboratory test came up with urine. What can be read probably needs the collaboration of the Butte Boys and Mattie. This appears to be some sort of reconstruction of the past. The only dates I can make out are references to something in the past – such as the death of Donald. Dru and Darla are very clearly referred to, several times. She wrote about her love for Malvina and that she and Malvina set up "Norm." There is a faded page that contains all the critical information about the jury service and, if one reads carefully, it appears one could say that she talked about the jury summons and Dru approached her with the proposition. The elder Weisenstock is not mentioned and neither is Keislor, but she does say she knows there are others involved in this, what she calls 'business,'"

DD asked, "What about the 'Armando' crowd I thought she wrote about in the imprint?"

"That's pretty clear in the last page. By the way, these pages are numbered. Makes it easier to follow."

Larry interjected, "Is any of this admissible?"

DD responded, "As I suspected and Arty has confirmed, it might be if we can establish it is Ella Mae's handwriting, she thought she was about to die, and we can't get the information into evidence any other way."

Rick weighed in again, "She does talk about dying – actually, quite a bit. Apparently, she and Malvina had been talking a lot about Ella Mae's guilty conscience. From what I can make out, Malvina was a longtime friend of Dru and Darla, maybe in the whoring business. Anyway, Ella Mae and Malvina were having problems. Ella Mae is saying in this diary that the money didn't really help Malvina stay and everything else was barren. I would guess, and can't find a lot of support for it in this diary, that Malvina was going to split and Ella Mae was going to send DD what she ended up leaving him in the envelope. Maybe she was writing the diary to send along, but didn't get it finished before Bolton shot her. Anyway, it is clear that she fully expected someone to kill her when Malvina told Dru what was happening."

Larry stood and looked at Tony Citriani. "Why don't you get Mike and go pick up Ms. Lacey. I'm tired of jawing this thing. As it stands, we get to hold her for the rest of the weekend. This is a murder indictment."

DD briefly described what had happened as he drove Mattie to the airport.

"I'm going to cry all the way to Memphis. That poor woman hung on to the hope of something she seemed never to have had. Jesus, she never got there and she sold her soul trying."

DD very much appreciated the tenderness of Mattie's outlook here. "Did she always know she was homosexual?"

"I don't know, DD. I don't know why some people are and most people aren't. There are whole chunks of her life that I know nothing about. If she had experiences similar to Malvina – and that seems to be a large possibility, given the fate of black women at the hands of most men – then it was hatred that built it. I don't know that is the reason other people prefer their own gender. But in the end, it doesn't matter. She loved Malvina and Malvina just couldn't be loved."

She stood on the walkway at the departure level with her small bag, still crying,

"You know you can't park here. It says that right there on the sign by the front of your car."

DD unloaded the bag she brought with her and the one she bought to fill with after-acquired, San Francisco items, and headed through the terminal doors to the ticket counter. On the way, he acknowledged her observation, "Yeah."

"What are we going to do?" he asked his companion with the tears streaming down her face. "I don't want you to leave. I can't stand the idea. I need to deal with this. If you don't stop crying, I'm going to start."

She laughed and they hugged a long hug. "Let me get home. Let me think without you being there. I can't do this either, but we have to."

"G.A. is going to meet you at the end of the jet way in Memphis. He'll take you home and we'll have someone guard your place for a while. Just don't fight it. We still don't know who's in this thing, but I guarantee you – they are not nice."

There was a last hug. As Mattie turned to board, she asked, "Tell me what happens when you talk to Dru."

Leonard Dolson, the officially-elected District Attorney for the County of San Francisco, had been expected back in the office by Monday. When DD returned to his office after leaving Mattie at the airport, Larry Harrington had just walked in.

"He's taking a few days off. He asked me if everything could run without him. I don't lie to my boss, so I told him it could. He wanted me to find out why Max Loudon was calling him. I told him I would. So, he won't be back until Thursday." Larry was ecstatic.

Barely acknowledging Harrington's good news, DD asked, "Did you pick her up?"

"Yep. She immediately called Walter "the Rocket" Bennington."

Bennington was a well-known criminal defense lawyer seemingly specializing in high-profile cases. It often appeared that his particular strength was in building a sympathetic case in the media, well in advance of trial. Rick had often commented that the media gambit usually followed an intense period of negotiations with the prosecutors. If that proved fruitless, he'd drop a dime and turn up the heat with the press. Usually, he would actually bring in someone with real trial skills to handle the case if it went that far. His nickname, "the Rocket," was pinned on him because of the extraordinary speed with which he would disappear from a case that was about to go to trial.

"This will be interesting. How about the Sausalito flat? Did we find anything?"

"Actually that's going on right now. We're also searching Ms. Lacey's apartment. It will be a bit before anything comes down from forensics."

The telephone rang. It was the inside line. Rick picked it up.

"You guys want to get a drink with Joe and Pep? They were just at Kelly's track meet."

Larry nodded affirmatively as did DD. They met at Tony's.

They sat at the corner table in the bar.

Joe started. "Pep and I were talking. Bolton can identify two guys that may be the chief bad guys; can we show him some pictures?"

"Where is he, by the way?"

Larry pulled an envelope from his jacket pocket and read the memo it held. "As we speak, he is still in the Tombs in

212

New York. Officers of the Mississippi state police will be retrieving him for transport to Magnolia City bright and early Monday morning. He has already been indicted and will be arraigned on Tuesday. He will be housed in the Indian County jail until such time as Sonny is through with him and will go from there to an undisclosed lockup."

Larry handed the memo from Sonny to DD.

"They got Cadbury but they haven't got Crossmore. Apparently, Arnold got wind of the indictment and skipped. Uncle Clem ain't talking. Sonny says they'll execute a search warrant on FOMLE offices, as well as Crossmore's residence tomorrow morning. Oh, look at this! Sonny also got indictments of Dru and Darla."

It was decided that Pep would attempt to find photographs of Keislor and, if possible, of the other Loudon firm principals. DD remembered photographs of the elder Weisenstock in his office in Beverly Hills. The problem would be how to get them. To avoid the single picture line up problem, Larry agreed to assemble some photographs of assistant district attorneys meeting Bolton's rough description of the people he met in Memphis.

As the gathering broke up, Joe looked at DD and asked, "So who is the woman on the phone?"

DD frowned. "Not a clue. Maybe it is just a shill for the big boss. Didn't sound like it, did it? All I can think is that it's Darla."

Joe shook his head. "Anyone this clever isn't going to be found easily. Face it. We may be looking for another woman."

Sonny reached DD in the office at 8 a.m., Monday.

"Crossmore cleaned out the FOMLE office. It looks like he did it with a toothbrush and vacuum cleaner. We should have had a stakeout on this guy. You try to believe that an indictment can be kept secret.

Anyway, his house was something else. We are still taking inventory of the weapons we found there. Mostly guns, mostly illegal. There were the makings for several different types of bombs, including C-4 plastique. Wire with battery and handles. Jesus, what a collection ! But we did find some stuff on point. In the wood-burning stove we found a scorched, but readable business card of none other than David Weisenstock, Senior Underwriter for Southern California Casualty. Sifting the same ashes we found what are clearly blank checks for a bank account in Birmingham with Crossmore's name on it. We froze that account with a call to the sheriff."

"Sonny, will Cadbury talk?"

"Well, he's scared to death right now. He appears older than the 47 years that has been reported. If he talks, he's likely to be a target of Bolton's 'others'. There won't be a cop in this state that won't want a piece of him for the damage done to law enforcement. I don't know. Right now, all we have is Bolton and the telephone records to tie him into this scheme – and this business card. What about Weisenstock's office? Can we see what treasures it holds?"

"There are a lot of courts in LA and a lot of lawyers. It takes a little longer than Magnolia City to get a warrant. I'm pretty sure we'll have one by tomorrow. Darla will be arrested today. That should generate some pressure."

The Los Angeles County Sheriff detective who arrested Darla apparently did so discreetly. Whether it was Darla's charm, good looks, or the detective's good sense, he allowed her to write a note to her husband before leaving the office. The detective called Tony Citriani.

It turned out that by tracing the social security card found in her handbag it was discovered that Darla was originally Darlene Lindsay of Orange, New Jersey. She is fifty-one years old – a rather well preserved fifty-one. From there, it was easily determined that she is no stranger to being arrested. At age nineteen she was convicted of burglary in Maryland. She served no time, but a year later was arrested for prostitution twice in New York City and jumped bail. These arrests are notable as the first time she used the name "Darla."

Citriani made arrangements to have Darla retrieved from the LA County jail. By Wednesday afternoon she was securely ensconced in the San Francisco County Jail and represented by the nationally-famous Ruby Baxter. For the moment, Ruby wouldn't let anyone near her new client.

Having completed undergraduate school at Berkeley at age 19, Ruby Baxter entered the prestigious University law school at Boalt Hall. When she finished there number one in her class, she became one of the first women to be admitted to the California State Bar. Notwithstanding, she couldn't get a job. So she opened her own office and began doing criminal defense work – the very first woman to do that in California.

Ruby married at least three times and never changed her name. She was, legend has it, a beautiful young woman with a definite flair for the dramatic, but also with a razor-sharp wit and encyclopedic knowledge of the law. At age sixty-three, Ruby's beauty was relegated to legend as she had had one or two too many martinis and way too many pasta dishes at Fior d'talia. She walked with a cane and wore broad-brimmed, wildly adorned hats – and the jewelry; there was a lot of jewelry, thought to be exacted from each husband and lover as a price of her favors.

Darla was arraigned on Thursday morning on charges of conspiracy to commit murders, criminal fraud and jury tampering. The murders were specifically Ella Mae White, Malvina Montrose, and Reginald Renfro. Ruby had the matter on the afternoon calendar for bail and Larry Harrington appeared for the prosecution before Judge Benjamin.

"Ms. Baxter, please!" The judge was pleading for Ruby to let up. She had spoken vigorously for nearly twenty minutes trying to get a low bail set. "Your client is charged with participating in a plan to kill three people, f'cryin' out loud. She has a long criminal record and she has not resided in San Francisco for three years. She has every reason to run. She has the wherewithal to run. I appreciate the art of your presentation but the prosecution's request for no bail is much more persuasive. Bail is denied. Next case!"

Pep, DD, and Larry left the Courtroom with higher spirits than when they went in.

"I can't believe that I'm actually happy about a no bail order."

"Well, Ruby had to lay it all out in hopes of getting a bail set. They obviously don't care about how much money would be required, so long as it would get Darla sprung. We learned a lot, didn't we?"

Neither DD nor Pep had had any clue about how extensive Darla's criminal record was. The whole legal secretary thing was the result of a probation requirement that she get a legitimate trade. Pimping, prostitution, child pornography, burglary and now murder, fraud, and jury tampering.

"Ya'know," Pep ventured as they left the Hall of Justice, "Keislor must have known about Darla's past when the Loudon firm hired her. You don't suppose that Darla's particular skills were used to land that job?"

"She was Darla Willingham less than six years ago. Light on her feet, that woman."

Mattie had been delivered safely to her home in Magnolia City and returned to her post as the County's Public Administrator. While irritated about the bodyguard, she did heed DD's advice about not fighting it – at least for now. Then a very sobering event occurred.

The man DD had interviewed in New York and who was accused of killing Ella Mae had been transferred to the Indian County jail only a day after Mattie had returned. The following morning, Bolton was being transported to the courthouse in an armored Sheriff's van when two men attacked the van with automatic weapons. Deputies following the van managed to fight off the attackers and shot one – seemingly inflicting a mortal wound. Two additional armed men came from nowhere, filling the area with automatic weapons fire to grab the injured attacker, throw him into a car, and speed off. Three deputies suffered non-fatal gunshot wounds. The chase lasted for more than an hour when the attackers simply disappeared among the dirt roads west of town.

Bolton was delivered to the court by way of an underground drive closed at each end by a steel gate. When he emerged from the van, he said to G.A., "There are more 'others' than I thought. Maybe I ought to talk to Uncle Clem."

Bolton was arraigned on two counts of murder and the court was informed that a plea agreement was in the offing, depending on Bolton's willingness to identify other members of the conspiracy in Mississippi.

Sonny responded to Bolton's request to see his uncle and had Cadbury delivered to the courthouse in a laundry delivery truck. Public defenders were summoned and appeared for each man. Sonny sat quietly.

"Uncle Clem, you heard what happened?"

When Cadbury allowed that he did, Bolton went on,

"You and I are dead meat, unless we make a deal. I'm in for quite a spell on the New York thing alone, so unless I want to die in the lockup, I gotta make some sort of deal here and get someplace relatively safe. What the hell you gonna do? You're not well. They'll smell you out and carve you up. So, make 'em send you elsewhere."

Cadbury sat stonefaced, looking at his youngest sister's son. "I can hire lawyers. I got a shot of beating this thing if you keep your mouth shut."

At this point both of the public defenders interjected, admonishing their clients to remain silent.

"Uncle Clem, I already told them. They already found your money. They got your phone records and that got that woman Dru's records. It's not going to get better for you with lawyers. You'll just end up broke."

Sonny then spoke up. "You know, Mr. Cadbury, we will find these people, whether you help or not. We'll also find Arnold Crossmore. All that is a matter of time. You stay here and await trial, you're a target – actually a sitting duck. You make your deal, we get your case wrapped up and you will be moved only to return to testify."

One of the Public Defenders asked, "What are you offering?"

Grimly, Sonny answered, "He'll spend a minimum of seven years in prison outside the state of Mississippi ... if he behaves himself."

Cadbury began to sob.

"Jesus, I been a cop all my life. What will my family think; my friends?"

Bolton looked at his uncle in disgust. "What the fuck are you talking about?"

In the end, Cadbury and Bolton identified four men working in different Mississippi law enforcement agencies and one employed as a Drug Enforcement Agent of the Federal Government who had been assigned and carried out murders throughout the country. All of the assignments came at the behest of Dru Lacey. All of the information and the assignments were made by telephone. To Sonny's great disappointment, Cadbury did not know the men to whom he had introduced Bolton in New Orleans. He asked, but Crossmore told him he didn't want to know. All he knew was that he received $7000 by way of a deposit into his Birmingham, Alabama bank account basically once a month. He had no idea where the money came from.

The body of Arnold Crossmore was found floating in the Mississippi River, under an old landing at Greendale. He had been shot twice in the head. It was Thursday evening. Arrest warrants were issued for the apprehension of the men named by Cadbury and Bolton, search warrants were issued for their residences. Bud Barstow's crusade was getting results.

The events in Magnolia City had humbled Mattie. She accepted the protection of the Indian County sheriff's office and appreciated them with every nightly telephone call from DD.

"The Rocket called a few minutes ago," Larry Harrington reported to DD. "He's on his way and I got to get something from him before Leonard returns tomorrow."

218

"Should I be there?" DD was anxious.

"No. Let's see what he has to say. I'll call you. By the way, they're sending stuff from Weisenstock's office by courier. Citriani tells me it is a treasure trove of Mob records and schemes. He can't tell what connects to our little conspiracy, but he is bringing some pictures of Weisenstock for Bolton to look at."

Walter Bennington confessed to Larry Harrington that his not-yet client wasn't going to talk to anyone about a plea deal. Drucinda Lacey was insisting that the matter go to trial, if necessary, but the prosecution wouldn't have a case. She wanted him, Bennington, to get a press drumbeat going that this prosecution was being masterminded by a known radical who not only harbored a fugitive responsible for the death of law enforcement officers, but who, leading up to her arrest, seized on flimsy evidence from a drug addict to excuse his own poor performance in a personal injury trial. Bennington insisted that his own personal code of honor prevented him doing any such thing and that he would resign from the case. Other lawyers would have to protect Ms. Lacey's rights.

It could be said that "the Rocket" was being sanctimonious, but that might be an unfair characterization. True, he was flagrantly betraying his client's confidences, but one supposes that was not troubling to Bennington. It's been observed more than once of late that DD's character was respected among the bench and bar, with few detractors. The strident red-baiting of Ms. Lacey rang hollow for Walter Bennington.

The flat in which the telephone was located that received calls from Cadbury and Crossmore was not in anyone's name. Indeed, there was no record of a lease. A subpoena of the bank which managed the property (along with other property of the Langleys) yielded a record of a lease for the top flat (Richard Baldachre) and the bottom flat (Mr. And Mrs. Tai Ngyuen).

The middle flat was sparsely appointed with expensive furniture. Nearly fifteen ounces of cocaine was found simply lying on a piece of waxed paper in a kitchen drawer. The kitchen seemed adequately equipped for preparing a meal for several and was stocked for someone with gourmet tastes. Liquor – in particular various flavors of schnapps – was in generous supply and stored in a tasteful cabinet of probable Italian manufacture.

DD and Rick accompanied Tony Citriani, Mike Heany, four SFPD lab techs, and Larry Harrington to Sausalito. There were two bedrooms. The one in front, with no particular view, was not used as a bedroom. For one thing, there was no bed in it. There was a desk, on which was a telephone and a large calendar. Saturdays and Tuesdays for each of the previous six months were marked with different colored pencils – the marks were all "X's." Indeed, there were large poster markers in the drawer of the desk – yellow, red, green, blue, and black.

The other was clearly a bedroom with a large, lavishly covered bed. The nightstand contained what Rick announced were "sex toys," the practical use of most not even Rick could figure out. The closet and the drawers contained only women's clothing. Indeed, the only item of male attire in the place was a large, silk dressing gown. Strangely, the drawer of the nightstand on the other side of the bed contained one dozen yet-to-be-used condoms.

Scratching his head, DD muttered, "What the hell is this place?"

A latex-gloved laboratory technician emerged from the bedroom closet. "Do you understand that two women used this place?"

"Why do you say that?" Larry asked.

"Shoes. There are two sizes of shoes. One is about a 5, the other is a 9."

"What about the other clothes?" Rick was on the way into the bedroom.

"Same thing." The tech followed Rick. "Look, here's a negligee for someone very small and one for someone about medium."

Rick and DD looked at each other.

"Well," Rick concluded, "we always knew that Dru and Darla swung both ways, we just didn't know it was with each other."

Larry directed the techs to make sure to box up all the contents of the place and to get prints from anywhere. "Photographs, gentlemen – photographs."

DD glanced out the front window and there he was in his profane glory – Dick Baldachre coming out of the garage and up the stairs.

DD pointed Baldachre out to Rick and Larry.

"Let's stay quiet for a bit and see what happens."

Baldachre's heavy footfalls thumped first here and then there from above. Then they could be heard descending the stairs at the back of the flat. Using a key, Baldachre entered the rear door of the middle flat carrying two bottles of white wine. He very nearly fainted when he saw DD and Rick standing in the kitchen.

"What the fuck?"

"Easy Dick," Rick warned. "These are SFPD." He pointed to Citriani and Heaney. "I'll bet they want to ask you questions about what you are doing here."

"What's going on; is somebody dead?" Baldachre had become essentially unglued.

Tony Citriani stepped forward flashing his badge, "We get to ask the questions, Mr. Baldachre. Let's start with what you are doing here."

"Tony. This is me, Dick! We worked prosecutions of bad guys together for years. I'm not a perp."

Baldachre betrayed more than dismay at the attitude of his old workmate.

"Ok. Dick – what are you doing in this flat and how come you have a key?"

Baldachre thought for a moment.

"I am using Ms. Lacey's refrigerator to keep my wine cool. My refrigerator is not working right now. I have a key because as Ms. Lacey is not often here; I watch the place for her."

Upon a little investigation and because of Baldachre's eager cooperation, it developed that indeed his refrigerator was not working. There was plenty of wine in what was understood to be Dru's flat. Baldachre's little story had a superficial credibility. Further questioning revealed that he had been carrying on an affair with the pretty Ms. Lacey, but he protested that he did not know why she maintained this flat when she lived in another in the City. No one present believed that story. When the nature of the police presence there was explained to Baldachre, he became ill and lost whatever it was he had at lunch and possibly earlier that day.

"So, Dick..."

DD had waited until Baldachre was done with his immediate problem. "Is it that you suspected something like that, or that you are an active participant in a murder conspiracy?"

With his composure more or less restored, Baldachre squared his muscular shoulders and looked at DD. "You're Dan O'Neil, aren't you?"

DD allowed as to how he was and that he was affiliated with Joe Cleary. This prompted Baldachre to refuse to answer any questions until he had counsel. Citriani and Heaney then took Baldachre into custody, promising to let his old buddy Larry Harrington decide his fate.

The lab techs remained after the detectives left with Baldachre in handcuffs. For the moment, Citriani and Heaney decided to book Baldachre for possession of cocaine for sale. Baldachre had called someone concerning being counsel.

Rick and DD stepped through the now open back door of Baldachre's flat. It was clearly more lived in than the one below. Rick Baldachre was a slob – the kitchen reeked from days of dirty dishes and pots and pans. On the floor next to the very large bed were two used condoms that appeared to be of the same brand and make as the ones in the nightstand in the bedroom below. Laundry had accumulated in a bag in the bedroom closet – an impressive volume.

Citriani had superficially searched the flat. A black brief case was not opened, but was taken by Citriani back to the Hall for a decision as to whether it could be searched.

DD went through the old mail stacked on a table just inside the door. It included the magazine of the product liability defense association. It also included bank statements from a small bank Rick recognized as being located in Santa Rosa – fifty miles north of Sausalito. DD called Larry Harrington to tell him to find out what Baldachre had been doing since leaving the District Attorney's office. He also suggested Larry subpoena the telephone toll records of Baldachre's telephone.

Larry told DD that he had just heard from Ruby Baxter. "She wanted to know what role you were playing in the prosecution of Darla. I think she's going to call you, DD."

Rick drove back to The City across the Golden Gate. DD let thoughts flow in his head. *We know that Ella Mae was murdered by a contract killer because she was about to spill the beans on her being bribed in Pavlone. Cutting through all the side issues involving Malvina and Donald, we know that Dru Lacey was in contact with the killer as well as the killer's 'handlers.' We know the same Ms. Lacey knew Ella Mae with significant intimacy as much as two months before the Pavlone trial began. Lowell gives us the participation of Darla in laundering the money. Of course, Darla was the secretary to Keislor in Pavlone. It's tough to see clearly that she is a co-conspirator in the murder scheme. Jesus, I wish I was going home to Mattie.*

"A drink?" Rick interrupted DD's reverie.

"Okay. Let's go to Tony's. Something with veal sounds pretty good right now. I can walk up and get my car at the office."

It was nearly 5:30 when DD and Rick pulled into the parking lot next to Tony's. The ocean breeze was kicking up and the low clouds were swirling in typical summer fashion. Harry the cashier had a telephone message for DD.

"Ruby! This is quite an honor. Have you ever called me before? I mean anything but 'whippersnapper'?"

She laughed.

"My client wants me to talk to you Dan. She is convinced you are the motor behind this prosecution, as well as the one in Mississippi."

Ruby was working on something that required audible sipping. "Have you had anything to drink yet?" she asked. She sounded strangely hopeful.

"Not yet. Why?"

"Well, I thought I'd have Trent drive me down to Tony's. I haven't been there in a long time. Can you wait? I'm just up the hill."

Truly, DD was flattered that Ruby Baxter would come down to the Tenderloin to have a drink with him. "I'll see you in a few minutes."

She kissed Rick on the lips.

"If I were just a tad younger, Ricardo, you would be mine."

Looking at DD, "Don't you think he's beautiful, Dan?"

"I'm going to defer to you, Ruby. I usually love 'em for their mind."

She laughed and Windy brought drinks. As DD had suspected, Ruby drank martinis. She was a character from an old *film noire*. A female Sydney Greenstreet. They settled into a booth. Ruby removed her hat and Windy found a safe place for it.

"Pretty wild case, isn't it Dan? I heard that 'the rocket' is already out. That's ok by me. Walter isn't real bright and he can't drink worth a shit. But, Jesus, what a case."

"Ruby, if you're looking for a plea agreement, I'm afraid I'm not authorized."

She stirred the last half of her martini with the olive-laden toothpick,

"You know, Dan – I guess your friends call you DD, is that right? Can I? It is more or less sexy. Actually, you're too dangerous to be sexy – at least to me."

"Call me DD."

"Darla can give you a lot, but not everything. We are talking about a plea agreement, so this is all confidential. Do you understand and agree?" Ruby knew and insisted on her business.

"Ruby, you have to understand that I'm completely a neophyte in this plea bargaining. You can't be subtle. I'd probably miss it. Tell me what you think Darla can offer in terms of testimony so I can make some sort of recommendation to the official prosecutors."

"Jesus, you are direct, aren't you. The first problem is whether the marital privilege precludes her from testifying against her husband, David."

DD and Rick looked at each other as if to ask 'Do you know?'

DD spoke first. "All I am going to deal with right now, Ruby, is that you are saying she can implicate her husband in the conspiracy. That, we obviously have already done. To be sure, no one has concentrated on him yet. I know what his son will provide. But this is a matter of interest and we'll have to look in some books about that issue. But maybe you ought to suggest the character of this evidence, so I can discuss it with, as an example, my client, the State of Mississippi."

Ruby chuckled and held up her empty martini glass for Windy to see.

"David is an old time mob functionary of variable loyalties over the years. His current and longest affiliation is with the insurance and property firm of Graham and Brown. These guys are in their eighties now, but Darla's husband seems to be a major mover and shaker."

"Ruby, we know about Graham and Brown and who they are and were. Can Darla testify they are behind this 'claim adjustment-by-murder' scheme? Is David the king pin?"

DD was trying to cut to the core.

"I don't want to mislead you guys, but Darla can only go so far. She doesn't go to the top of this thing and can't say who actually decides who dies and why. She can testify about money, but with only hints of where it comes from. You also have to know that she thinks – and I agree – that her life is very much in danger."

"Y'know, Ruby," Rick flashed his dazzling smile and put his big hand on one of her bejewelled wrists, "you are making it tough on my buddy here. He's too polite and awestruck to point out that you really aren't telling us anything. I am afraid that Daniel Dermot here will need some detail to decide what he is going to recommend to his clients and friends."

She chuckled again and looked up.

"Can we get some dice cups here?"

Three rolls and Ruby lost. "Some gentlemen you are."

They ordered dinner, during which Ruby recounted – in often colorful terms – other times and other hosts at Tony's. She obtusely inquired of DD's background and accomplishments and finally, dinner cleared from the table and a glass of port in front of her...

"Darla's fifty years old. She has managed to stay out of the slam for a long time and learned to love the good life. She is intent on avoiding any time and willing to risk death to do it. Is that plain enough? Just don't expect too much. Cops and prosecutors – even substitutes – still will have to work for this one."

Acknowledging the truth of her lecture, DD still went directly at Ruby.

"How about Hugh Keislor? Will she give us him?"

"I am no longer good at being coy, Mr. O'Neil. I can only tell you that I will not disclose anything on that subject with you. At the appropriate time, you will have to ask her."

Over the better part of the next hour, Ruby described in more or less specific terms what Darla could testify about. Ella Mae was recruited by Dru Lacey as someone with a great need. She was introduced by Malvina, who had been an associate of Dru and Darla in their little side business of getting deciders laid for the Loudon firm.

Dru particularly enjoyed the company of other women and used her penchants in that regard to advance her fortunes and concomitantly those of the Loudon firm. Laura McNeeley was a case in point. Apparently, Dru had identified her as someone in need and got her in the same way she got Ella Mae in.

Malvina and Ella Mae had already hatched a scheme to extort money from their employer. Malvina confided in Dru and, once it was discovered that Ella Mae was on this jury, the scheme quickly developed that the "guaranty" could provide a cleaner and far more lucrative way than the straight blackmail of Norm Yamaguchi they had planned.

Ruby didn't completely understand the guaranty, but as she described what Darla may testify about, it became clear to DD. *This isn't something that started with the* Pavlone *case or even with Dru and Darla. It had been going on in one way or another for centuries. It is simply an extension – an expansion – of the whole notion of liability insurance. Supposedly legitimate insurance companies have always looked for a way to avoid providing the insured the "benefit." Somebody finally went to the extreme. Here, large, legitimate businesses ponied-up huge premiums to protect them against losses from legitimate lawsuits. The insurance company would act to assure that the client's tormentors did not succeed. The client was guaranteed a result. Best of all, the whole scheme went on unseen as 'business as usual' risk avoidance.*

Rick had remained silent for much of this exposition by Ruby, but, shaking his head, said, "I'm sorry Ruby, but this case is full of enough improbabilities. You're asking us to believe that all this maneuvering depended only on Ella Mae bringing the jury along. Can't buy it, dear."

"Rick, you're a terrible cynic for such a handsome man. But, I think you are right. As Darla will explain."

"So, Ruby, where does the money come from to pay Ella Mae, Bolton, Cadbury etc.?"

A burning question, DD thought.

"Darla knows and will tell you. All I can tell you is that the source of the money is obviously the 'client.' Money is channeled along a kind of Alice-through-the-looking-glass pathway. It is handled and re-handled and massaged and is intended to look like an insurance company paying indemnity. It is, in most instances, Southern California Casualty or one of its alter egos that handles the pay out. The problem is that Darla can't tell you who is at the top, who directs this show or how. Dru Lacey might know that, but Darla doesn't."

Rick sat forward looking intently at Ruby.

"So, what we have to do is figure out who was the beneficiary of the guaranty and get the details of how the money changed hands."

"Hey," Ruby protested, "I do criminal defense work. I don't understand all that other shit. In fact, it gives me a headache."

DD agreed to carry the message to Harrington and to Sonny Elliot. Ruby could provide nothing about Baldachre and again referred to Dru Lacey. Ruby stepped out of Tony's onto Taylor Street and the dutiful Trent was waiting with the Lincoln's back door open.

DD looked at Rick. "More mysteries than solutions."

"My plane to Dallas is in the morning – 9 a.m.," Rick said. "I'll be in Veracruz by tomorrow night."

***

CHAPTER NINETEEN

Following the Money

Harrington and Sonny Elliot had the same reply when DD broached the subject of Darla's potential plea agreement:

"We need to know more about what she did."

Ruby was a little perturbed when DD apprised her of the prosecutors' position. Nonetheless, she agreed to meet with him and Larry Harrington that afternoon. For his part, Harrington wanted something on the record from Darla before he went off to get an indictment against David Weisenstock.

"Dolson is going to be looking for me in the morning and I am going to get a whole load of shit for this, so I have to have more from Darla than she has been willing to give up – including where Keislor fits into this."

Documents unearthed in the files of Cadbury's bank in Birmingham and Bolton's bank in New Orleans revealed that money deposited in the accounts of each was wired from the funds of the Fraternal Order of State Law Enforcers with a New York City address. Vic Luca and Martin Simon of the NYPD found the address to be a commercial mailbox. The clerk of the store reported that the mailbox had no action, that is, nothing ever came in for that box number. The rent on the box was paid annually and apparently in cash. The bank record of the accounts from which the money was drawn for the wire transfers ultimately revealed the name of "International Underwriters and Reinsurers."

"I.U.R." had a rather more prominent address than the Fraternal Order – Wall Street.

The information thus gathered sent Pep back to now-retired agent Roger Cash from the Federal task force on organized crime. Pep later reported that Cash had laughed out loud when Pep told him about 'International Underwriters and Reinsurers'.

"I had no idea that old horse was still around. That's the rubric the Tamanino mob used for their city-wide extortion racket. Tamanino had something on the law firm that ran the estate that owned this Wall Street address, and leveraged that to an office with a Wall Street address. Jesus, they're still around?"

Pep furiously made notes of his extended conversation with Cash. I.U.R. actually took on deals to insure risks that smaller, mob-related insurers couldn't handle. They employed practices similar to the bookies, even using some of the same language. When Tamanino turned up dead it is believed, but not proven, that Graziani and Bertolucci somehow took over the I.U.R.. This was before Graham and Brown emerged on the scene. Tamanino's operation was so sophisticated he actually got a New York State license as an insurance broker and wrote legitimate insurance policies for legitimate companies. Graham and Brown ended up with the whole thing.

Pep was sitting on the deck with a spectacular view of the Pacific Ocean from Cash's modest retirement home in Carpenteria, California. Cash was intently reading the Grand Jury testimony of Lowell Weisenstock and an outline of the proposed statement of Darla Reid Weisenstock.

"So, the authorities got Darla. What you want is the chain to the top, right? Obviously, I.U.R. is still in business. This ain't the old days; they have to be under some umbrella – everyone in the casualty and liability business is. There are only five of them: Travelers, Pan American, Intercontinental, Global, Aetna, and Industrial.

"Finding out who is at the top of any of these is easy, but, I think, unproductive. I mean, these guys carry on their own brand of larceny, but it just doesn't figure they'd be involved in the kind of messy shit you're talking about. Maybe down the chain – some entrepreneurial underling, regional manager or the like – but these outfits have tens of thousands of employees."

Pep probed. "Robert Gordon Langley, the Chairman at Pan American, does that ring any bells?"

"Well, sure. He's always in the pretty news, with his pretty wife and daughter, and beautiful home in San Francisco. Other than that, no. Should it mean something else?"

Pep stood up and studied the bright scene before him. "I don't know. Could you find out if anyone has suspected him of any racketeering type activities?"

Cash excused himself and went inside. In a few minutes, he returned.

"Langley has been around some pretty interesting guys in the last ten years or so – including the Angloed wops," Cash reported on his return to the deck.

Pep asked, "Angloed wops?"

"Graham and Brown. Jesus don't quote me on that but the head of the department coined that little identifier."

"Roger," Pep pressed, "that's pretty close to our situation. Can we get more?"

"It's on its way. We should get it by Monday. Can I send it to you?"

"Please."

When he got back to San Francisco, Pep met DD for lunch at the Double Play.

"My thinking is that the insurance company here is a screen to permit large sums of money to be received and to be disbursed. No one suspects anything when a company parts with a large sum to an insurance company, and then that insurance company buys a structured payment scheme from another insurance company. Weisenstock, the elder, is the traffic director. He finds the situation and then somebody – again my guess – probably Dru and Darla, make the pitch. That no doubt takes place on a pillow in a downtown hotel room."

"Is this just any insurance company or is it a specific one?" DD wasn't sure he bought into this idea.

"That, I don't yet know. Right now I am looking at just one, Pan American Trust & Casualty."

"What? My former father-in-law's company? Why?"

"All I presently know is that Federal organized crime intelligence people tell me Robert Gordon Langley has been seen with Graham and Brown. There is a very strong connect, as you know, between those guys and David Weisenstock."

DD sat back. "Well, that ain't much."

Pep nodded in agreement as he attacked his sand dabs.

"Rick might have something going in Vera Cruz. He is meeting with LaStrada's Mexican lawyer for lunch. We should know more soon. It may well be that these payments were made in Europe and not in Mexico. We're waiting."

Pep paused eating long enough to swallow some wine. "A lot of things are up in the air. This case hasn't really had a pause. By the way, do you have any idea when I'm going to get paid by Mississippi?"

Surprised, DD asked, "Have you been paid at all?"

"Zero."

"What's the total?"

"Eighteen hundred, give or take."

"I'll pay you and when they pay you, you can repay me. OK?"

"I love clients with money."

They both laughed.

DD was on the phone that night, as all other nights, with Mattie for an hour. Then, feigning something he had forgotten to tell her, he called her again. Principally they talked about the twists and turns of the case, especially the frightening shoot-out in the streets of Magnolia City. Finally, they got to the point of what was going to happen and each acknowledged that something has to change – she comes to California or he goes to Mississippi. It was decided that at the very minimum, DD would bring the photographs to show Bolton and Cadbury. That would give them a chance to talk more in depth.

DD flew into Birmingham out of Dallas and rented a car. From there he followed Sonny's directions to a small army post in western Alabama where Bolton and Cadbury were being held. For the first time, DD got the chilling sense of imminent and real danger. Serious people were taking the threats seriously and doing serious things to avoid a serious consequence. It was a grim little Army outpost that once housed segregated black troops in the second world war.

Sonny greeted DD on the immaculately-kept lawn in front of the building holding the offices of the provost marshal. Shaking hands and then hugging, neither spoke a word for a few minutes; both managed a chuckle.

"This is nice. I bet Bolton is happy."

"I guess he is, except for the food. I keep telling him it's a lot better than what he would be getting in a Mississippi prison."

Bolton was stashed in the old stockade. It had not housed anyone for more than twenty years, but it was nonetheless clean and operational. Importantly it had steel sheeting in all the walls and a large, steel door in the front and in the back.

Reluctantly, DD shook Bolton's hand. He seemed content and settled in. Bolton had shaved his head that day and looked more bizarre than ever as a consequence. Cadbury was brought from the opposite side of the stockade and joined DD and Bolton in a secure conference room. He looked worse. His face was greying, his hands were shaking, and he was nervously chain smoking. He looked at Sonny and said, "Did you tell him? Does the nephew know about what happened today?"

Cadbury was in a complete panic.

DD turned to Sonny. "Seems someone blew up Clem's home last night. Big charge. Blew it to smithereens. The house that Bolton rented was set fire night-before-last. Pretty clear they are connected and clearer still their motive is to stop these guys from talking about this murder-for-hire racket."

DD looked at Bolton and Cadbury. "Seems it is also clear they don't know where you are."

"Fuck no, they don't know where we are. They're just demonstrating what they will do when we surface – like in Court." Cadbury was not going to be mollified.

DD asked Sonny, "We didn't get all the bad guys when we got those shooters the other day?"

"We got some local assholes. These were the guys who were cops and doing side jobs. The houses were torched, we think, by out-of-town talent. That's why we still have Mattie under guard. That, and the fact that she received a note suggesting she join you in San Francisco and never testify."

"Got the note?"

"At my office. You know this suggestion she go to San Francisco is also a suggestion they know about her and you. We know they want your ass, and maybe they are thinking they get that by staying close to Mattie."

DD gave the photographs to Sonny and G.A., who had shown up about twenty minutes after DD arrived. Twenty photographs of white men roughly similar to those described by Bolton in his New York revelations were spread out in front of Bolton and Cadbury on a large table. The group included assistant San Francisco district attorneys (including Dick Baldachre), Butte Boy Joe Cleary, and their banker, Kevin Curry.

Immediately, both men picked out the photograph of David Weisenstock. It took several minutes for either of them to find someone they thought was the other man introduced in New Orleans that night. Then they each selected a picture they both decided was the second man – the one with the straight black hair and who did all the talking – Dick Baldachre.

Asked again to look at a photograph of Hugh Keislor, neither man recognized him.

"But, this guy doesn't have straight black hair..."

"Sorry, Mr. O'Neil. But that is the guy. I don't know, but maybe he was wearing a disguise – a good one, but a disguise."

Bolton was certain and so was Cadbury.

Leaving the army post, G.A. looked at DD and asked, "Was this a surprise, DD?"

"Yeah, G.A., a surprise. I was certain he would identify someone else – the lawyer in the case against me when your sister was the juror. I certainly didn't expect this guy to be so high up in the organization. Jesus, Dick Baldachre isn't very smart and doesn't have crime-family connections that I know of. I guess I should have known better. Assumptions are very dangerous things."

G.A. took off his official hat preparatory to getting in his car.

"Here's the deal Dan. We think that there are people after you and they know you will be headed straight for Mattie. Won't you?"

DD smiled guiltily.

"Then what I am going to do is move Mattie, right now. She has an idea this is coming. While we drive from here, a couple of my boys and one of Bud Barstow's will be driving her to Memphis. We got you a nice place on Beale street. You like blues?"

"I certainly do. I don't know about Mattie."

G.A. got into his car and looked up at DD. "I don't know either."

In the old city portion of Vera Cruz, Rick had settled into a posada worthy of a California don. He would meet Raphael d' Arroyo, local counsel for *Internacionale* and La Strada for a lunch at 2:00 – it was eleven in the morning, Vera Cruz time – seven, San Francisco time. Rick had spoken to Arty, who had been reviewing the terms of *Internacionale's* manufacturing arrangement in Mexico. Among other things, La Strada had to maintain certain levels of worker injury insurance and liability insurance. A standard feature of such deals in Mexico, it was rarely enforced by Mexican authorities beyond requiring written evidence that insurance had been procured. Worker injury insurance was provided by a Mexican company with relatively modest liability limits. Liability – including product liability – was covered by a European insurance consortium that included Pan American Trust and Casualty. d'Arroyo had

235

negotiated for *Internacionale* with the Mexican authorities and had dealt with the insurance company representatives to assure compliance with the insurance terms of the Mexican arrangement.

In high Spanish, Rick and d'Arroyo got down to the business at hand over a local beer before lunch.

"My position here, Mr. Esquivel, is a little awkward. The Mexican manufacturer of the car, LaStrada, is a separate corporation, incorporated here in the Republic of Mexico. My fees are paid by that corporation and my letter of retention grants me only the authority to represent that corporation. On the other hand, 51% of the Mexican corporation stock is owned by *Internacionale,* with the balance being held by various Mexican companies and citizens. So, while I don't feel I have the duty of loyalty to *Internacionale* that I would ordinarily have to a client, I am not exactly without some obligation to be mindful of potential problems for disclosing information I get from *Internacionale.*"

Finding Mexican beer hard not to like, Rick ordered another, smiled, and looked at d'Arroyo. "My friend, does that mean you can tell me what money, if any, was paid for claims alleging injuries as a result of a design defect in the La Strada?"

d'Arroyo, too, smiled. "I appreciate your directness, sir. I believe I can tell you what money was paid related to such claims but I can't say it was paid to claimants. I can disclose this to you because I have been required by the executive of my client to compile a list of such payments and reimbursements for disclosure to *Internacionale,* which is not my client. Thus, I am sure you can see, my client has specifically waived any claim of confidentiality on that subject."

"You have such a list?" Rick immediately inquired.

d'Arroyo reached into his richly ornamented leather case and handed Rick a packet of several pages. "Yes. Here it is."

Rick examined the pages. The document was a compendium of claims made in the United States for injuries alleged to have been caused by the design defect he and DD had argued in the Pavlone case – indeed, Pavlone was listed. There were twelve such cases, each described in Spanish.

"How did this document come into existence? Who composed it? Why was it done?"

Rick had not imagined getting this sort of information.

"Hector Domingues is the chief executive for LaStrada-Mexico. He is the person who directs me and who speaks for my client. Mr. Domingues telephoned me one day, and asked that I meet with him and a representative of the European insurance consortium – a Mr. David Weisenstock – concerning claims being made against the company in the United States for injuries caused by the design of the roof on the La Strada."

Rick interrupted, "When was this, my friend?"

"I believe this document was completed about three weeks after that meeting. You can see the date of completion in the bottom right hand corner of the last page."

Rick looked; it said "June 30, 1979."

"So, you are the author?"

"Well, myself and my staff. It is a report to Mr. Domingues based on a review of information provided by Weisenstock and confirmed by my office. The gentleman spoke at great length about the cost of defending the company in light of these claims. He implied that the fault for this situation was entirely ours – in Mexico. Mr. Domingues angrily denied that, pointing out that the engineering for this product came from Europe and that both European partners had engineering representatives on our staff from the beginning."

Studying the memorandum, Rick asked, "Did he speak of some monetary amount the company was exposed to?"

"The lawyer did."

"Weisenstock wasn't alone?" Rick didn't expect him to be.

"No," d'Arroyo replied firmly. "I noted the name of the other individual." He referred to some handwritten notes. "A lawyer from California. Max Loudon"

Truly surprised, Rick asked, "What did these guys tell you and Mr. Domingues?"

"That the cost of the defense would be extremely high in this California case, but it would be worth it if it discouraged all other claimants from insisting on large recoveries. Weisenstock said he could guarantee the most dangerous case – your Pavlone matter – would result in a win for our company.

The meeting lasted more than two hours. Weisenstock had explained that Mexico had to share in the cost of the defense of this product – inasmuch as Mexico was showing a profit for the first time in years. Additional premiums would mean an increase in the liability limits.

It had been a long time since a Mexican affiliate of an American or European company had made money. Mr. Domingues was proud of this and insisted that Mexico had no blame in the situation. The lawyer, Senor Loudon, had insisted that under American law, the Mexican corporation would be held responsible, along with *Internacionale.* "I wasn't so sure that was true, but had to concede that the two engineers from Europe were on our staff."

"So, how did it end?"

"The issue remained unresolved, even following meetings with executives from Europe. Then at the end of August, we received word that our European partners were putting up money for this defense. Then they insisted that we do so as well.

We refused to relent and paid only our agreed $3 million premium. It was, in our view, a problem of our European partners – not ours. This became a contentious issue, pending resolution when Mr. Domingues met with the highest executive for the insurance consortium in St. Tropez, France, on the first weekend in September."

Nearly breathless, Rick asked, "And who was this executive?"

Sensing he was disappointing Rick, d'Arroyo dropped his eyes and admitted, "I don't know."

"Does Domingues know and will he tell me?"

"I don't know if he knows, but if he does, I am positive he won't tell you. We ultimately paid the consortium demand for $13 million following Mr. Domingues' return from St. Tropez."

"How did Mexico justify this $13 million?"

"It was paid in two installments and as far as anyone knows outside me and Mr. Domingues, it was paid as additional insurance premiums."

"What was Mr. Domingues' explanation for that?"

"We never spoke about it again."

The men ate lunch, exchanging only pleasantries and personal background. d'Arroyo paid the check and insisted on doing so. He shook Rick's hand.

"Mr. Esquivel, I want you to know that I am delighted you came and much relieved to have a chance to talk about this situation."

***

CHAPTER TWENTY

Obdurate Pursuit

It took Leonard Dolson until nearly 11 AM to get around to speaking to his chief trial assistant and stand-in, but when he did he was red-faced furious.

"So, you've launched – in my absence, you've launched – this massive prosecution proposing to indict not only a former assistant district attorney, but a prominent member of the private bar. This bold effort is based entirely on the urging of a known radical – probably a communist – and bar room brawler. Have you lost your fucking mind!?"

Harrington, a full head taller than his blustering boss, had anticipated Dolson. Folding his arms on his big chest and assuming a resolute posture, Larry Harrington replied quietly, "Leonard, I received information from a citizen that serious crimes have been committed in this jurisdiction. O'Neil may be the things you mention – I don't happen to think so – but he is widely respected in this town for truth telling and Hugh Keislor isn't. As for Baldachre, Jesus, you fired him yourself."

Since his election, Dolson had resolutely and cleverly avoided controversy – decisions were either easy or they were shuffled off to someone else to make. Here, things had gone too far; he couldn't get out of it. If he called off the prosecution, the press would skewer him and there wouldn't be a second term. If he took his effective chief trial deputy off the case, he'd get the same result. The danger in letting this go on was the loss of the patronage of Max Loudon and Dolson's own future with that firm.

The ensuing exchange was voiced through clenched teeth, but it wasn't loud. Both men finally exhausted the points to be made and a silence fell on the room. Harrington had turned to leave, when Dolson asked, "Do you have Baldachre?"

"Yes. At minimum for possession for sale, but very likely on the 187 conspiracy, based on a photo ID by the shooter in

Mississippi. By the way, there's a stack of letters from the Mississippi attorney general in your mail. A response from you would seem required."

Dolson looked at the mail stack and began to sort through it when he looked up at Harrington. "What about Hugh; have you got him?"

"No. Shit all around him but none we can find on him. We're not done, yet. His ex-secretary will testify and maybe his ex-research assistant."

Harrington left Dolson's office and gathered his notes for his meeting with Ruby Baxter and her client, Darla Reid Weisenstock. Dolson picked up his telephone and dialed.

"Max Loudon please. This is the San Francisco District Attorney."

"Len, welcome back. Len, you can't believe what has been happening in your absence. Wait 'til I tell you."

"Max, I've been reading about it for the last three hours. Meet me at the club; get a small room. Make it for 11:45."

This was not at all the demeanor of Loudon's old, pliant classmate, Len Dolson. Max Loudon would do the District Attorney's bidding – a reversal of roles.

DD's sexual experience had begun early in life – most notably at age 13 on an old couch in Susan Meikel's parent's basement – and occurred often enough since. He realized long ago that sex was a central part of his existence. But none compared with his time with Mattie – either in San Francisco or now, at the Heritage in Memphis. Nothing had proved so satisfying and yet he remained insatiable. He assiduously avoided confronting the meaning of this phenomenon.

The Heritage was not all that far from the clubs on Beale and both DD and Mattie wanted to walk, but the bodyguards from Mississippi refused to allow it. DD's protests nearly got him and Mattie jailed, but they relented and rode to Beale Street. While Mattie claimed to know nothing about the blues, she squealed in delight when DD suggested they drop in to catch Spud Hardwick. His smooth – almost stride – piano rhythms countered his gravel-throated voice as he delivered the true stuff of today's heartache with hope for tomorrow.

Red beans and ribs followed and, then, inevitably, the whispers turned to the status of the pursuit of Ella Mae's murderers. Mattie's deep brown eyes peered across the table at DD asking, "So, this woman Dru isn't talking. The discussions with the other woman – Darla? – are going slowly. Bolton and his uncle have identified someone who has already been arrested as involved. So, we're making progress, right?"

DD leaned back, quietly feasting on his view of Mattie's unfettered breasts.

"I think so. It is just taking a lot of time and seriously challenges what one always thought was the way things are. Who's heading this thing? Who gave the order to kill Ella Mae or even Malvina? I'm not ruling anything out at this point, but I just don't think it is Dru Lacey, whom I believe is just over 30 years old. There's nothing that directly ties Keislor and there is only slimmest connection to Robert Gordon Langley, my former father-in-law. So, we're following the money. More accurately, Rick is following the money – he's on his way home from Mexico right now."

"DD, why go on?" Now Mattie was leaning back with her arms folded. "Really, you were hired by Mississippi to help them break up their corrupt police problem and that seems to be done. If there are bad guys still in Mississippi, you tell me that Sonny thinks they are from out of state. So, Bolton and his uncle can just testify to what they know and it will be over – as far as Mississippi is concerned. I mean, that is your client. It's even better. You can get that insurance fellow prosecuted, as well as his wife and that woman Lacey. Isn't that enough?"

DD smiled. "No. Mattie, we have people who have really messed with others – including ending their lives – who will continue doing it and must be held responsible. More than anything, there is Judith. She has been deprived of a more tolerable life.

Then there is the truly evil lawyer, Hugh Keislor. He's raking in money and will apparently escape criminal prosecution simply because he was clever enough to avoid being implicated. He's looking the other way and will profit from it."

She sighed. "How long are we going to need a bodyguard? When will we know it's over and we can get on with deciding what we're going to do? Criminy, DD, the San Francisco District Attorney wants to end this and he might, leaving you high and dry."

She was showing signs of stress that DD had not previously seen.

"Look, Mattie, I understand, and I'm sorry. I have to do this. I don't care what Leonard Dolson does, but I am not letting go of this. Somebody has to bring the chief bad guys down – it will be me, even it is only me, but I need your help doing it."

She sighed again, then smiled. "Ok. What do you want me to do?"

He smiled. "First, finish your coffee. Then let's run back to the Heritage and work on that question."

Eight years as an assistant district attorney. Two years as the new, "can do" associate of one of San Francisco's biggest private law firms, Dick Baldachre was now an inmate of the San Francisco County Jail and couldn't get a lawyer. Never had he thought Leonard Dolson – gutless political hack that he was – would actually pursue a vendetta against him. This, to Baldachre, was clearly a vendetta.

He had carefully built a reputation for ruthlessness and cunning while on the District Attorney staff. But that didn't immunize him from Dolson's rage when he publicly blamed Dolson for the loss of the very high profile murder prosecution. Dolson fired Baldachre after he told the press that the acquittal of Ahmed Ferrell was the result of Dolson withholding evidence of Ferrell's violent past. Of course, Dolson did no such thing, but his own history of withholding evidence in another celebrated San Francisco case was raised in every press story on the subject for a week.

What the hell were O'Neil and Esquivel doing at the apartment? These guys are different sorts than Dolson. Baldachre requested telephone time and called a number he never thought he would have to call.

"This is urgent. I need to speak with Mr. Bennington. My name's Rick Baldachre."

In a wood-paneled small conference room of the California Athletic Club, Leonard Dolson leaned across the marble-topped cocktail table. In hushed but firm tones, he spoke.

"Jesus, Max. There's really nothing I can do right now and maybe never. A member of your staff and a former member are done – sizzled. It's murder Max, it is felony fraud, it is a mass of serious and, as far as I can see, well-supported charges that implicate your business. The current urgent question is whether one or the other of these women fries your partner, Hugh Keislor. Did I point out this is multiple murders?"

Dolson was clearly beside himself.

Loudon's well-coiffed personage exuded calm control. He placed his hand on Dolson's and in the same hushed, but not-so-urgent tones, "Len. Len, relax. We understand. You are desperately needed to avoid serious damage to the firm. We can do this. We just can't panic."

Exasperated, Dolson sucked nearly half the scotch from his glass.

"Damn it Max, I understand about panic. But you should understand we have this near-maniac involved in this prosecution – you know him, Dan O'Neil!"

Loudon frowned. "What the hell is he doing in this? I mean he's a plaintiff's lawyer isn't he?"

"He is, but he was a criminal defense lawyer ten years ago. Do you remember the Jankovic case?"

"You mean the red professor from Berkeley? "

"His daughter was indicted for murdering her boyfriend."

"Oh. And you were the prosecutor. Yes, I do remember. So, this guy O'Neil was the criminal defense lawyer along with his partner, Joe Cleary. So you think this guy is real good, but what the hell can he do here – he's not a prosecutor?"

"Max, for reasons I don't understand, the State of Mississippi has hired O'Neil – even made him deputy or something – to chase down the murderer of this woman in Mississippi. He's a leftwing nut and relentless. We are not going to cover this thing up. If Hugh is dirty, O'Neil will get him and I don't dare try to stop him."

In the warm afternoon sunshine in the courtyard of the Heritage Hotel in Memphis, DD and Mattie met with G.A. and Sonny over iced tea.

"Would Mattie be better off with me in San Francisco than to remain here?" DD inquired.

"Dan," the big voice of G.A. was directed at DD with some force, "we're perfectly capable of taking care of Mattie. You are the target, we think. She is an incidental target and probably seen as the means to get to you. Your friend Larry Harrington called yesterday to say that they think there has been someone tailing you for some time. He is having an investigator named 'Pep' try to get a picture."

"Here's my thinking, guys. I don't question your ability to protect Mattie, but this shit has to end before somebody goes nuts and somebody else gets hurt. So, why can't we give them a concentrated target. Sure, they'll know where we are but if they are after us, we'll know where to find them."

Mattie spoke up. "Whoa, DD. That means you're making us bait. Doesn't it?"

"I suppose, Mattie, but you want this ended and so do I. It's all I can think of."

G.A. spooned some sugar into his iced tea.

"I don't think that's a bad idea, Sonny. I know Mr. Barstow wants to control this show, I just don't think we're going to catch any of these bad guys doin' the arson and bombin' unless we change course. The more I think about it, the more I think we should also move Bolton and Cadbury to San Francisco for the time being."

After several minutes of silence, Sonny finally said, "Ok. I'll talk to Harrington and to Bud. I'm persuaded." He stood to find a telephone.

"Wait a minute! I'm not persuaded. Among other things, I hold public office and I have duties which keep getting interrupted by you all and your justice chasing." Mattie was not sanguine about these plans. "Damn it, DD, this is starting to look like THE DECISION is being made by default. That is not the way it is supposed to be."

"Mattie, I'm trying to deal with ending the intimidation factor as soon as possible. That's what you told me you wanted. I don't think it ends if I announce to the world I quit. Rightly or wrongly, they'll find out that is unlikely and will redouble their efforts to get at me or you."

Calming down, but still steaming a little, Mattie, folded arms and, with cocked hip, asked, "Can we get someone to substitute for me in probate court and work with me on files if I am in San Francisco?"

"Mattie, we'll do everything possible. We don't want to lose you as Public Administrator."

G.A. put his arm around her.

Few words passed between them on the flight to San Francisco. It was their first argument and both knew it wouldn't be their last. As the plane leveled off just above the Bay, Mattie asked, "You think I could work at the cottage? Working at your office is a little awkward, don't you think?"

"Doesn't that defeat the purpose of focusing the would-be assassins? We'll get you some space all to yourself on Turk Street."

Indeed, Pep did get a photograph of someone he and Tony Citriani think had been tailing DD. A young, nondescript white man with an athletic appearance and varying clothes – sweats, work clothes, suit and tie, slacks and jacket. No one knew who he was, but he certainly was diligent. He couldn't get close to the cottage without assuring he'd be spotted, so he left DD every night at the bottom of the stairway. *Who sent him? Why? Whoever it is has taken a risk of discovery and certainly has missed catching DD unaware if their goal was to kill him.* Pep's nephew stayed on the tail and Pep went to work identifying him.

Right after arriving at the office, DD telephoned Larry Harrington. Arrangements were made to transfer Bolton and Cadbury to California – most likely the Marin County jail. DD and Mattie would have full time police protection.

"If you can believe it, Rocket Bennington has given notice of his appearance for Baldachre."

"He can't do that, can he?" was DD's immediate reply.

"No, he can't and I'm waiting for his call back to tell him that. He'll probably call you."

Sure enough, about a half hour later, Walter Bennington was on the phone for DD:

"Why do I have a conflict of interest problem in representing Dick Baldachre?"

"Think about it Walter. You met with Dru Lacey and listened to her story. Whatever she told you is clearly confidential. If you represent Baldachre in the same prosecution, he has the right to your undivided loyalty, including your knowledge of what Dru told you – but you can't ethically tell him. Therefore, you can't represent Baldachre."

Disappointed, Bennington snapped, "So I screwed myself out of this big case because I wouldn't attack you. Jesus, there's press everywhere on this. These ethics rules are really something, huh, Dan?"

"Sorry, Walter."

Before leaving the Athletic Club, Max Loudon had sat for a moment at the table where he and Dolson had spoken.

He ordered another scotch and slowly drank it. Then he asked for a telephone and spoke with his secretary.

"Tell Hugh to cancel his plans for tomorrow morning and meet me in my office at ten. Tell him it is real important. Right now, I'm going home."

Upon hearing the demands of his senior partner for a meet the next morning, Hugh Keislor became uncharacteristically anxious. He knew that Darla was likely to provide information to the prosecution, and she might even implicate him. He was unprepared for exactly what to do if that what was on the mind of Max.

The next morning, Keislor settled into Loudon's posh client chair. The room reflected – as no other in the firm's sumptuous quarters – the extraordinary wealth of the partnership. "Extraordinary" in terms of the accumulation of money and national clients, but "extraordinary" as well in terms of the shortness of time it took to accumulate that money and those clients. Large original European oils hung just behind Loudon's Italianate desk. The carpets permitted no sound of footfall as Loudon made his way behind Keislor to take his big leather chair on the opposite side of the desk.

Electing to appear ignorant of crises and terribly busy with the firm's business, Keislor said "What's up?"

Loudon had closed the door and remained wordless since sitting down. He appeared as he always appeared, calm and cool.

"Can we isolate this thing to Dru and Darla?"

Loudon looked directly at Keislor with a fixed and powerfully compelling stare.

"Shit, Max, I don't know. It looks to me like that is all there is inside this firm. I mean, as far as I know, no one else is involved – if they are. Did Dolson tell you that Dru and Darla had confessed? Unless they have, we shouldn't be jumping to conclusions."

Keislor was gathering confidence.

Elbows on his desk and chin in his extended thumbs, Max Loudon sighed.

"Hugh, a very shaken district attorney told me – just yesterday – he expects Darla Reid – your former secretary, whom you have been shtooping for years – to implicate you in a multi-murder scheme. So we're not talking about Dru and Darla anymore. It's your ass that is at risk. Hugh, are you able to say that you didn't know that this dead woman was bribed to influence the verdict in that case?"

Keislor swallowed hard, brushed some unseen something off his pant leg, lowered his eyes and answered the question, "Of course I didn't know. I don't really believe it as I sit here now. Jesus, I tried a great defense case. The design didn't paralyze that young woman; her drunken boyfriend's crazy driving paralyzed her."

Loudon stood and strolled over to one of his prized paintings, seeming to examine it closely,

"Yes, I remember that case. I was there when your arrogant German engineer expert was on the stand and O'Neil took him apart, equation by equation. When Herr whatzisname got off that stand, I was sure we had lost. I didn't see the rest of the trial, but it clearly appeared to me that all the work and risk I put in to assure a verdict was for naught. It now appears that your confidence at the time had nothing to do with the strength of your case or any weakness in the plaintiff's. You either arranged the bribery or you authorized it, didn't you Hugh?"

Keislor gasped. The man with whom he had gambled his career and who had cleared the way for him to show his skills was accusing him of bribery.

"Max, f'crissake, you don't believe that do you?"

"Hugh, I don't know. But it is real hard not to believe the evidence that I've seen. What are you claiming, that all this was going on and you just didn't know about it? That will be a tough sell, Hugh, and I don't think you're good enough to sell it."

"Max, you brought this client into the firm. I mean, if I should have seen something, wouldn't you have been in a similar position?" Keislor sounded like a kid pleading someone else ate the cookies.

"Well, maybe you're right Hugh. Maybe you're right. But murder? That never entered my mind."

"DD, I met with Ruby and Darla yesterday afternoon. Darla won't come forth with much unless you are there. Ruby didn't explain why, but I suspect they think you're the one that needs persuading." Harrington was a little peeved again, but this time largely because things were happening very fast and he could not figure out why Dolson was doing nothing – if he was doing nothing.

A meeting was set for the next morning with Ruby and Darla at the San Bruno jail. In the meantime, DD picked up Rick at the airport – that is to say, DD and his bodyguards picked up Rick. Rick briefly described what he got from La Strada's lawyer, Raphael d'Arroyo. By this time, Rick had compared notes with Arty and supported d'Arroyo's thesis that the Mexican incarnation of LaStrada was probably sufficiently separate to allow him and Domingues to disclose the list he had in his pocket.

On the walls of Leonard Dolson's large office were hung framed newspaper articles trumpeting his prosecutorial victories, letters from mostly retired judges congratulating him on his election and on his Welsh terrier, Jerry.

Dolson sat uneasily. He was overwhelmed with a sense of foreboding – a sense he felt intensely the last time he faced Daniel Dermot O'Neil in Court. If he did anything to interfere with the prosecution that Harrington initiated, he would again suffer the ignominy of being exposed as a traitor and craven public office hack. There would be no second term and there wouldn't be a cushy, highly rewarded position with the firm of Loudon, Mueller and Keislor. But, if he couldn't head off the prosecution, there very well may not be a firm if he managed to get through a second term.

I always knew it would be Hugh. His vanity, his personal conceit, and unbridled ambition made him vulnerable. This woman! Christ, everyone in town knew he was laying her. He wanted them to know. She'll bury him.

Larry Harrington walked easily down the hall toward Dolson's office in response to Dolson's call. He had resolved to get past Dolson's whining and blustering. The cases were coming together and there is very little of substance that Dolson could do about it. Even if he lost his mind and fired Harrington, the entire staff would revolt.

"I'm going to stay out of this," Dolson told him. "You're going to handle the press. You can't have any other assistants – I can't spare them. As far as the press is concerned, I am supportive of you but busy doing other things. I have utter trust in you – that's what you tell them and anyone else that asks. You're making a terrible mistake in pursuing all these powerful people, in the end they hire lawyers and buy witnesses and twist the law to gain a verdict of acquittal and if not a verdict, then a reversal on appeal. It's a lot of public money and effort for very little. But I won't stand in your way."

Harrington was nearly floored. Recovering quickly, he said bravely, "I need Angie to help."

"You've got O'Neil and his gang; you don't need Ms. Bettini."

"Those guys are great but they have staffs to support and full dockets themselves. They are not prosecutors. Angelina is quick. She knows this conspiracy stuff and she is one hell of a prosecutor. I can't explain to the press that we're relying on private counsel to do this huge case."

Relenting, Dolson, asked, "What cases does she have now?"

"None. McGuire folded yesterday afternoon."

Bitterly reluctant, Dolson said, "OK."

***

CHAPTER TWENTY-ONE

The Gathering

"Ruby, I'm going to be meeting with Darla's husband as soon as we wrap up here. Actually, he's just across the yard. As far as this question of marital privilege, I don't think it arises where the spouse pleads guilty. I have a feeling that David will do just that. They tell me he has a stage-four tumor on his lung. If he's lucky, he'll make it for more than eight months. He isn't going to spend that time in a penitentiary."

Bejeweled and powdered, Ruby Baxter crossed her arms atop her substantial bosom and looked askance at DD and Larry.

"I don't think Darla is without feeling for her husband. Granted – it's not the sort of feeling one would normally expect of a woman for her husband. Still, I think we can avoid getting to the subject of David's health or even David for a while. When we get there, you tell me what you want to ask and I'll discuss it with her."

Without makeup and in a straight jail dress, Darla wasn't quite the seductress of her reputation, but still an attractive woman. In this setting she gave DD the impression of a trapped badger, figuratively baring her teeth and hissing. She began calmly and precisely, "I was sent by the probation department to the firm of Loudon, Mueller and Keislor to learn a job. I began by sorting and delivering mail to then just seven partners. They had just organized and needed people."

"Why were you on probation?"

"I was a whore, Mr. O'Neil. An expensive whore, but still a whore and the San Francisco vice squad set me up with an undercover guy. While I am sure he would have rather fucked than arrest me, duty called and he arrested me. That was the fifth time. I also had arrests, if not convictions, for pimping."

She smiled and wiggled suggestively.

"I was just a bad girl, like I always was."

Ruby sat up. "Darla, darling, you are not going to lay Mr. O'Neil. You are going to explain to him what you did – what you know, and hope like hell it persuades him to recommend a lesser sentence for you. So, get off the sexy siren trip!"

Having been dragged into relevance, Darla began talking seriously. Her memory proved prodigious. Her consciousness of the need for corroboration anticipated the lawyers' questions and solidified much of the prosecution case.

Malvina had been in Darla's stable for sometime before she met Drucinda Lacey. Malvina was a "veteran whore," whereas Dru had turned an occasional trick for school money or thrills since she was 17. Darla met Lacey when the probation department sent her to the Loudon firm.. Dru was already employed as a legal researcher, having attended three years at law school before failing the "moral turpitude" requirements of the California State Bar.

Shortly after meeting Malvina, Darla decided that doing for women what she and Malvina had been doing for men was a more profitable and less physically risky business. Both actually preferred that sort of sex, so she began to open up contacts for such business. The main contact became Armando's near the Embarcadero. It had begun to pay off when she was nearly shot by a little would-be whore's babysitter while making an arrangement at Armando's. The bust didn't lead to a conviction but a subsequent one did and that led to the probation.

With Darla on probation and lying low, Malvina was looking at street walking or something straight to stay alive and to feed a heroin habit. About that time, she ran into a woman from her hometown and they got a thing going. That woman, Ella Mae, was typical of those Darla often recruited because she was seriously lonely. But she was not typical in the sense that she was smart and could be very commanding. She was obviously and deeply in love with Malvina.

Ella Mae had a job in a printing business. She wouldn't put up with Malvina's heroin use and, frankly, neither would

Darla. It was Ella Mae, however, who got Malvina off the junk. Once that was done, Malvina really blossomed – a beautiful woman by any standard.

"Then Ella Mae's boss goes under and she is called by Norm Yamaguchi, who wants her to go to work for him. When she told me, I realized I knew the guy. He was on my rolodex for future reference because one night he called my 'service'. When I show at the airport hotel, he tells me he changed his mind, pays my fee, and sends me on my way. I kept track of guys like that because they are so vulnerable. Who knows what they could be good for in the future?"

By this time, Darla had been at the Loudon firm for two years. She had gone to paralegal school and done well and she was regularly having sex with a firm partner, Hugh Keislor.

"That didn't take long. Among other things, I don't think Hugh had ever had a blow-job before. Then, of course, he believed that I had no way to resist him – him being such a hunk and everything. Guys like him are easier to deal with than most. They are so full of themselves that all the good things that happen to them can be traced to their good looks, vigor, or intelligence. The bad things are always somebody else's fault. A woman's role is limited to the bed, the desk top, or whatever is handy, and we are so grateful."

Darla then described how Ella Mae got Malvina a job at Yamaguchi's shop. The three of them hatched a scheme whereby Malvina would trap Yamaguchi and Malvina would threaten a sex harassment lawsuit. They needed Darla to help them orchestrate that. She was sure that Yamaguchi could be had, based on her prior experience with him.

"What prompted this photograph?"

DD thrust the picture of the scantily clad women in front of Darla.

"Jesus, I had no idea that fucking thing got out of my apartment. It was stupid. We're all high and having a good time. I took the picture."

She explained she was working for Keislor and Dru was assigned to him for this big case against a Mexican car manufacturer.

Max called her and Dru into his office. He explained this was a real big one; at least one of the plaintiff expert witnesses needed to be compromised.

"He gave us a list with particulars and suggested that one or the other of us get with the plaintiff's reconstructionist, Kurt Meinor. Time was short but we got the guy out of Slim's gym and did a merry wives thing. The pictures were actually on the same roll as the one of our little girls' party."

Matters were complicated by the fact that Ella Mae absolutely wouldn't go along if the money from the Yamaguchi extortion was given to Malvina. She felt that if Malvina got the money she would disappear and start using junk again. Surprisingly, Malvina agreed that Ella Mae should handle the money.

Then, Ella Mae received a jury summons. It was only six weeks to the scheduled start of the Pavlone case. Dru and Darla sat around Dru's apartment and "nearly fried our brains" trying to figure a way to capitalize if Ella Mae was in fact seated on that jury.

Harrington stirred at this point. It had been suggested that a member of the court staff, possibly working in the Jury Commissioner's office, was involved.

"At that point, exactly what was it that you knew about Ella Mae's chances of getting on the jury?"

"Dru had some familiarity with this process – more than me. It appeared to us that Ella Mae was only one of over one hundred fifty jurors called to duty in the civil courts that Monday . There were other cases to be called for trial that day. Pavlone was only one. If she were called, it was still unlikely she would sit. We thought the chance was just too delicious to pass up. "

"OK, so what did you do?"

"We already had Meinor, but that was risky because if Meinor didn't come through, all we could do was let his wife see the pictures. There was also the chance that a jury would ignore Meinor's opinion change. Getting Ella Mae on that jury gave us a far better chance."

Shaking his head, Harrington put up his hands to signal a pause:

"Wait a minute. Was this first time you got into this extortion business to influence a trial result?"

"No. We'd been doing this insurance for nearly two years before this Mexican car thing came up."

DD leaned forward. "I don't understand what insurance had to do with it."

"At the beginning, I didn't either. Then I got a couple of assignments and it became clear to me. I'll tell you about one. A guy suffered a serious head injury when the defect in a construction crane caused a cable to break. David had someone lean on a witness, an expert witness, and he dropped out of the case just before trial. It was way too late for the plaintiff to find someone else. About the same time, Hugh brought a motion to suppress evidence of other incidents."

"David had the business of the manufacturer's insurer to 'adjust' the case and hire the defense lawyers. He met with people from the manufacturer and the insurer a couple months before the scheduled trial. Both were very concerned about this defect, and the insurer was telling the manufacturer that there may be a coverage problem."

DD sat up. "You mean the insurer was saying that claims from this defect may not be insured under their policy?"

"That's exactly right. I'm not sure of what he told these people, but in the end the primary insurer and the manufacturer put up an additional 'premium' of two and a half million dollars.

I used a kind of Crimson Pirate tactic. You know, my car breaking down on a lonely road where the judge was traveling. I was able to get the judge to a place where I could show him things he had never experienced before. David got the pictures and someone, whom I don't know, discussed them with the judge. The judge granted Hugh's motion to exclude the evidence of other incidents and otherwise steered the jury to a defense verdict. I don't know if it would have worked if the judge wasn't a Methodist."

Harrington asked, "What were you paid for that?"

"Fifteen thousand."

"Did Hugh get involved in any of these conversations with David, the manufacturer, and the insurer?"

"I don't know. I wasn't there and no one told me Hugh was."

"Is there any indication that Hugh knew you had approached the judge?"

"No."

"Do you believe he did?"

Darla sat back, stretched her slender arms and looked at the ceiling a moment.

"I may as well tell you what I think and what I know on this subject."

For awhile after Darla first went to work at the Loudon firm, she would have one kind of sex or another with Hugh about once a week. She considered it kind of job security. Hugh's particular brand of self-regard allowed him to convince himself Darla was in love with him, so he told her all manner of things that would otherwise be confidential. Never did he disclose to her that he was a participant in the scheme she had become involved in

"...and I just don't believe that Hugh's vanity would allow him to do it. But, really, someone would have to be a damn fool not to know this was going on when case after case resulted in a defense verdict. No other defense lawyer was having that experience."

"When," DD began, "did this little scheme get serious and people get murdered? I mean, there have been instances of trying to use sex to blackmail trial participants before. Killing people seems...innovative."

"I don't really know. I think it happened long before I ever came along. There were all manner of bribes, threats, and sex, of course. I've heard stories from David that his partners had, in the past, paid someone to kill somebody in the interest of the business. "

"So, David is the kingpin in this operation?" Harrington asked.

Darla took a moment and looked directly into Harrington's eyes, and firmly said, "No."

"Then who is?"

"I don't know."

Harrington's voice volume increased. "What do you mean you don't know? Are you gaming us? How the hell do you go as far as you've gone in this thing and not know who runs it?"

Sensing the danger here, Ruby jumped in, "Mr. Harrington, take it easy. Just keep questioning. Obviously, you are getting a lot that you didn't have and that you need for whatever prosecutions you conduct."

Without waiting for another question, Darla answered, "That was information that was very carefully kept from me and, I am pretty sure, David."

Incredulous, Harrington pressed, "Didn't you ever talk to this guy – this 'kingpin'?"

"It isn't a guy. It's a woman."

Darla knew this was a bombshell for those in attendance, so she was very firm – very definite.

DD chimed in, "You've talked to her, but you don't know who she is? Have you seen her?"

"I have talked to her. I haven't seen her. The conversation was on the telephone."

DD pursued, "Was there more than one telephone conversation?"

"No."

"So, when was this conversation"

"About three weeks ago."

DD and Harrington looked at one another, then Harrington repeated, "Three weeks ago? You've been involved for about five years and the only time you've talked to this head woman is three weeks ago? Why?"

Ruby couldn't stand it."'Why?' what, Mr. Harrington? The question, like others here, is impossibly compound and I don't want my client guessing which part she should be answering."

Chagrined, Harrington rephrased, "What was the reason for this conversation three weeks ago?"

Ruby nodded approval.

"She wanted details of what Mr. O'Neil had said to me when he showed up at our offices in Los Angeles. She wanted to know everything I knew about Mr. O'Neil's participation in the investigation of this woman's death."

"This woman?"

"Ella Mae White."

There was a relatively long silence. Then DD asked, "Where were you when you talked to this woman?"

"At our offices on Wilshire. I don't know who made the call – her or David. I was in my office when David came in and told me to pick up. You will have to ask him who called whom."

DD returned to the interrupted and more pertinent line.

"Did Hugh know that you and Dru knew Ella Mae before the Pavlone jury selection?"

"Dru and I both told him that we thought Ella Mae would be a very good juror for the defense. He didn't ask us for reasons, but getting an apparently strong-minded black woman on the jury would not be something he would do in the usual course."

By this time, Darla had told David about Ella Mae. He became very excited and after a day or so, called Darla and told her he thought there might be a way to take advantage. He wanted more detail on each of the jurors that were sitting. She and Dru then got on the telephone with David and went through a description of each juror. A day or so later one juror was found dead and Ella Mae was put on the main jury.

"That guy's name was Reggie Renfro. Do you know how he came to be so conveniently dead?" Harrington's prosecutorially indignant blood was boiling.

"Only what Dru told me that morning before court. She told me that Mr. Renfro would not likely be appearing for his jury duty."

"Did she kill him?"

"I don't think so. It was about this time that Dru began to know more about what was going on than I did. David thinks she arranged to have Renfro done in. It was pretty clever. Until recently, no one knew the guy was a homicide. It was chalked up as an accidental overdose."

Darla suspected something was going to happen the day before. Dru had begun talking to Ella Mae on the telephone about what an opportunity this was. She asked me what I thought David could arrange in terms of money to persuade Ella Mae. Clearly there had to be cover for whatever was paid. That is the reason for going ahead with the Yamaguchi plan. The deal was set before Malvina ever got Yamaguchi up her skirt.

As agreed before, there was the <u>Pavlone</u> chance, money was to be paid Ella Mae. There just had to be enough smoke to make it tough to figure out.

"I carried the papers to Hugh on the sex harassment claim. I drafted the letter supposedly from a lawyer here in town and forged his signature. No one ever told Yamaguchi's insurer – we just bypassed that little problem."

She went on to explain that ultimately Ella Mae had to be eliminated because she was keeping a diary and threatening to go to DD with it. Darla presumed she was suffering some sort of guilt, but also Malvina had begun disappearing for days and they fought.

"The word got back to me that Ella Mae had said the money was not solving anything. That's when we discussed it with Dru. David said he would have to go up the line and a decision would have to be made. The next thing I knew was when David told me to stop sending checks for Ella Mae and to tell Lowell that the 'trust' had ended."

"How did you know that Ella Mae was keeping a diary and all this was going on with Malvina?"

"Dru kept in touch with Malvina. They were playmates."

"Oh." DD connected a dot or two. "In Sausalito?"

"You know about that? I thought so. Yeah, with Dick and maybe others, except on Saturday morning and Tuesdays."

Harrington and DD looked knowingly at each other, "Dick Baldachre?"

Darla nodded. "The same. What a schmuck. David took him to New Orleans for the product defense lawyers conference a few years ago. He told him they were interviewing some investigators and he had to convince the candidates how tough he was. I guess that is when David met Bolton and hired him."

"Did Dick do anything else for this little enterprise?'

"Not really. He scored all the coke for us from some poor bastard he had put away a few years ago. He did one case that David sent him to make a client happy – a reckless driving defense. Dick damn near blew it, so David didn't get him involved anymore. He may have done other things, but you'll have to get that from Dru – she had him by the nuts."

DD made some notes, and looked at Darla. "You mentioned David's "partners." Who are you talking about?"

Ruby put her hand on Darla's. "Honey if you only know this from what David told you during your marriage – told you when no one else was around – then you may not have to say so now. David can be presumed, at this point, to want to preserve his marital communication privilege."

"I understand, Ruby, but Max Loudon was present when David told me his former partners were Brown and Graham – two old time Mafia guys. He used other names, as well, but I don't remember those."

"Can you tell us whether Loudon already knew these guys – Brown and Graham?"

"He didn't say that, but that was my impression. David had raised the issue of his partners in a meeting at David's Beverly Hills office. Loudon had heard of the shooting of Ella Mae and asked for an immediate sit-down. He was anxious to terminate his association with David because he had never thought the arrangement would go so far as to include murder. David allowed as to how Loudon always knew he was connected and had never complained when his own staff were fucking witnesses, judges, and prospective clients. Max repeatedly told David that he wanted out and David told Max that there was no way out – his new partners wouldn't let him out alive."

Looking up from taking notes, DD asked, "When was this Darla?"

She smiled. "About a week before you showed up at my doorstep."

"So," Harrington spoke rhetorically, "Ella Mae had been dead only a few days. Did Max get his information from David or from Dru?"

"I don't know. I was not in the murder loop. Dru had developed communication with guys in Mississippi that I would describe as 'hit' men. In fact, I think Ella Mae's actual shooter talked to Dru."

"Darla, do you know where the money came from to pay Ella Mae?"

"Actually, from a legitimate annuity company."

"You mean you were able to buy an annuity on Ella Mae from an insurance company?"

DD did not expect this.

"Sure. All they care about is that the money is paid, they get their fees and cuts and invest it. Lowell was perfect to administer the annuity. Something like this had been going on for some while by the time I came along. David told me it always worked to wash money. The money for the annuity came from a variety of sources. In this case, from the manufacturer and the primary insurer. It was initially paid to IUR. They paid us, and we paid the Mississippi people, or me or Dru."

"So, who is IUR?"

"It was owned by Brown and Graham and some other connected people I don't know. David told me they have had this operation for fifty years. Then, just before this <u>Pavlone</u> deal, I understand it changed hands."

DD was insistent. "Who? Wasn't David operating this?"

"Well, no. Someone else does, but I don't know who. My best guess, and I don't know that much, is that it is someone real smart, no criminal record, and from the insurance industry."

"Would that be Max Loudon?"

"I don't think so. He was too far away from the decision-making. His interests were strictly to get the legal business, although he was aware that most of the shit that was going on was not on the up-and-up."

"Is Dru more of a player in this than Loudon?"

" I think so. She's meaner and she has a young body that she loves to use. She's also very smart. Max kept looking the other way and Dru kept wanting to get involved. He was more than willing to let her do it. "

DD stood up. "I take it you don't expect Dru to give us any information."

Darla chuckled, "If she does it probably will be a smoke screen. It won't be reliable."

"You're different, Darla?"

She stood and looked intently at DD. "The only asset I've got left is getting too old to have value. I have to make a deal. Pissing you off is a scary proposition for me. I saw enough of you in the <u>Pavlone</u> trial to know that I don't want you on the other side again."

The meeting with Darla and Ruby consumed nearly three and a half hours. In the end she provided chapter and verse against her husband, Dru Lacey, and Max Loudon. Harrington outlined the complaint against David Weisenstock and assistant district attorney Angelina Bettini presented the case to the grand jury. The indictment was issued the next morning. In the meantime, discussions began with David Weisenstock.

Regis Klienman, long time counsel for Brown and Graham, had appeared for David when he was arrested, in an attempt to get him released pending trial based on his poor health. The Los Angeles judge to whom this application was made deferred to San Francisco and ordered David transferred there. Klienman persuaded Ryan Beard to undertake David's representation. Ryan made clear his long and close relationship with DD, Joe, and Rick – a relationship that Kleinman hoped would smooth the way to a plea agreement for his ailing client.

In his second meeting with David, Beard's obvious competence had gained David's confidence.

"Ya'know, Ryan, I am not in such good shape – physically, that is. They say this thing is growing in my lung and spreading. There's a real good chance that they won't get me to trial. But I don't want to die in a stinking lockup and this is a stinking lockup. What do you think we can do?"

"David, do you want to tell the story in exchange for a sentence?"

"No, Ryan, I don't. I don't want to die in a lockup. If I can spin out something to avoid that, I'd do it."

"If you have some kind of notion that you can feed these guys a line of shit and walk, you have to forget it. I don't think any prosecutors would do that. Most particularly, I know these guys won't. They are smart and they'll simply walk away from you if you bullshit them. Remember, we already know your wife has pretty much told the story. They can get you without you saying squat."

A tall, at one time handsome, man, Weisenstock stood. "Yeah, but Ryan. I can't give them the top in this thing. I don't know who that is. Shit, the Wops aren't the top and would croak if they were arrested. I'll give them Loudon, that's easy enough. What, they want the fool Keislor? If they want him, I'll figure a way to give him up, but the truth is he never took part in anything I'm aware of that violated the criminal law."

Beard relit his ever-present pipe. "What does the doc say about how long you have to live?"

"Eight months – maybe nine."

Speaking quietly, as he almost always did, Beard wanted clarification. "So you want to get out of here before you die and expect the prosecutions here and in Mississippi and probably New York to agree that you'll testify against people who haven't yet been indicted but not against the people who actually master-minded this murder scheme?"

"Yeah."

Beard blew some smoke and then tapped the bowl of his pipe. He smiled and looked intently at his client. "It ain't gonna happen David. It just ain't gonna happen."

"My wife is cutting a deal isn't she?"

"But your wife is going to do some time in prison, David. And please, take my advice. Don't try to fool these guys. It could destroy any chance you might have for a quiet place to die."

The prosecutors – including DD and Rick – sat looking toward the windows on the grass yard of the City and County's jail in San Bruno. Ryan Beard and David Weisenstock sat on the other side of that table.

Ryan explained, "David is going to die before he can serve any meaningful time under a plea deal or sentencing after conviction. The only incentive he has to answer any of your questions is to be able to spend his last days in some place other than a jail or prison."

Indeed, Weisenstock looked near death. His skin was grey. His eyes red. His hands shook and his voice wavered. He seemed unable to hold his head up. Incorrigibly vain most of his life, according to Lowell and Darla, he had no swagger now. DD was convinced he was a man in full realization that his end was very near.

"We'll need to confirm that with our own medical guy's opinion, Ryan."

Beard nodded affirmatively.

Harrington turned to David. "Nothing can be done, no matter what you have to say, to keep you out of prison – period. We have enough to convict you. The only thing I may be able to do is to have you incarcerated in a prison hospital. As I understand it, the state of Mississippi has such a hospital that is outside the State prison walls. I don't have much control over what happens in Mississippi, but I can ask if you agree to testify. If that isn't good enough to get you to do that, then let's save our time and do something else this afternoon."

The old man managed a smile. "You're a tough guy. No feeling for an old man? Someday you're going to be old, you know."

Harrington wasted no time. "Mr. Weisenstock, someday I'm going to be old, but when that happens I will not be sitting where you are being asked to explain a lifetime of murder, fraud, and corruption."

He shoved his yellow pads and other papers back into his briefcase and stood – as if to leave.

Rick and DD did the same, but Rick hesitated and asked Weisenstock, "You want a priest?"

Again, the old man laughed. "I'm a Jew, f'chrissake! I don't think we get absolution. Anyway, what kind of religion would let a guy like me off?"

"So," DD thought he would try, "why not tell us what you know. What the hell difference does it make to you? Your wife is already on her way to the slam. So is your son. Maybe the only thing decent you do in your life would be to tell us about this operation. Maybe we can stop it before it kills someone else."

Weisenstock grabbed a cigarette and, with one hand, lit it expertly with a paper match. He sat silently for a few minutes. Beard's eyes widened a bit behind the smoke from his pipe.

Finally, Weisenstock spoke. "So, you record my statement. I sit around until the trial of someone. I then get a suit on and go to court – maybe a meal, a non-jail meal. One of my Armani suits, a silk shirt with French cuffs, my favorite diamond cuff links, the Gucci loafers – shit, I'd even shine 'em myself. How about that?"

DD, Rick, and Harrington looked at one another. Beard smiled, cleaned the tobacco out of his pipe into the ashtray.

Then, Weisenstock spoke more hopefully, "Could we have one of those court reporters with the little machine. A woman. A good looking woman?"

Before Harrington could recover from these demands, Weisenstock thought of something else. "I want to do my time in Sing Sing. I wanna die as near as possible to where I was born."

"I don't know about Sing Sing, Weisenstock," Harrington responded, "but the rest we can and will do – if you tell us the truth."

So at about 2:30 p.m., David Weisentock began to answer questions about what he knew concerning the deaths of Ella Mae, Malvina, and Reggie Renfro, and the boys in Mississippi. Tall, black haired, blue eyed, and comely Judith Slattery was the court reporter.

David had a tendency to wander off the subject and go into the old times in New York. As fascinating as that story was – and possibly helpful to current Mob prosecutors – DD tried to keep him on the main issue of Ella Mae's death and the Pavlone trial. David's association with Benjiamano Tamanino started when David was just out of high school. He ran numbers in a little open neighborhood near Four Corners in Brooklyn. Benny brought him inside to keep books and supervise collections for a small protection racket Benny had opened across the East River on the lower East Side of Manhattan. It was there that Weisenstock hit on the insurance gambit.

Within a few years of selling the idea to Tamanino, David had secured a front to hold a New York State license to sell insurance, collected premiums from Tamanino's old protection victims and washed "tons, I'm tellin' you, tons of cash, besides making some." He did business every weekday with legitimate liability carriers in what he called, "laying off some of those bets."

He explained at length and more than once that the beauty of the insurance scheme was that it was virtually free of law enforcement interference. Businesses were insured against loss. When an unfortunate loss occurred, David was there to make sure the "customer" was paid off with legitimate insurance company money – some of which David claimed as "administrative fees." No one complained.

Through his association with legitimate insurance company adjusters and underwriters in the '70s, he learned how some kinds of claims threatened the existence of manufacturing companies or, at least, cost a great deal of money. Insurers were getting out of the field of covering product liability. On a whim, he asked an insurance executive from San Francisco whether it would be worth it to get into the business of covering these product design claims if you could control the result of the claims. David was excited all over again,

"This guy says, hundreds of millions. But it can't be done. These companies have screwed up and there are enough smart lawyers out there to figure it out."

DD's interest was piqued at this point. "Who was this 'Insurance Exec from San Francisco'?"

"I guess the deal is I gotta tell you."

David stood, lit a cigarette and looked out the window,

"Robert Gordon Langley – Pan American Casualty. Classy guy. Very smart."

"When was this, David?"

"Probably 1975 or 1976. I try not to keep those kind of records."

David then got wind of a small electric cookware manufacturer in Philadelphia that was getting sued for toxic coating on fry pans they were making. The place was owned by a large family that included the wife of a Tamanino button man in Jersey. The family had a lot of money and the old man had planned to leave the company to his sons. If these lawsuits went on – no company.

David suggested that he might be able to help depending on how much the ownership was willing to pay. As far as Langley was concerned, David was an up-an-up insurance adjuster, so when David called him to ask for an underwriting report on the fry pan company, he referred David to the top underwriters in Pan American.

There was one chemical engineer in Wilmington who had figured out that the pans were covered with toxins and that it was a design error. A close friend of his, a public health physician from Johns Hopkins University had diagnosed two pan users as suffering fatal levels of the toxins from the subject pans. Both of these cases were filed by the same plaintiff lawyer in Philadelphia. Checking around, David found out the lawyer had very little money and had borrowed from friends to pay the engineer and the physician expert witness fees.

"I did a little leg work and talked to some people and – bingo. This engineer and the doc – they had a thing going for years. Now, I understand that it is just nobody's business what people do between the sheets at night, but each of those guys are married. The engineer was consulting with Dow and of course the doc was on the faculty and a high-placed administrator with the University."

"At this point, what role was Robert Langley playing in this deal?"

Matter-of-factly, Weisenstock looked at Rick. "None, really. Our relationship was strictly professional – friendly professional. I had very little to do with him directly for a long time. But there is one thing; I called him and asked him for the name of a broad-minded defense lawyer in San Francisco. He gave the name of Max Loudon. I needed some help with this deal from somebody who was a long way from Philly."

DD sat up with this news. "Did you get that help from Loudon?"

Weisenstock had flown to San Francisco and met with Loudon – first at his office and then at the athletic club. He led Loudon to believe that he was simply handling a case for an insurer as an independent adjuster. He massaged Loudon's ego by suggesting he was highly recommended among a wide variety of insurers.

Loudon explained the legal limits of approaching the expert witnesses but thought it could be done. He didn't think the experts would be enthusiastic about their case once they realized what it could mean in terms of disclosing their sexual relationship to the public. By the time David left for New York, he understood that the case against the fry pan company would have to go to trial, but that the plaintiff experts would have to adjust their courtroom testimony. He also had made a good and valuable friend in Max Loudon.

On the stand at the trial of the design defect in the fry pan covering, the chemical engineer volunteered, without a question asked, that the toxins in the covering would not ordinarily be released except at temperatures exceeding 600 degrees, Fahrenheit. That, he continued, would almost never happen unless a pan were left on a burner and unattended for twenty minutes. This was never part of his opinion before he met with David Weisenstock.

The doctor had a similar change of heart, explaining that upon a re-examination of the medical records of each of the decedents, he discovered they had high blood alcohol levels. He pointed out those places in the record he had on the stand and the plaintiff lawyer was never able to get anywhere claiming that the original records had no such references. The court directed a verdict for the defense. David claimed he was paid two million by the primary insurer and the manufacturer.

As Weisenstock concluded this tale, silence fell over the room. The ease with which this was done, the vulnerabilities of the justice system in the face of this sort of evil, were realizations that served as a bolt of lightning to the three lawyers.

"Did Loudon know that you blackmailed the plaintiffs' witnesses in that case?" Harrington wanted to hang his boss' classmate with this.

"I didn't tell him. After I got paid, I sent Max a crystal decanter and glasses for his office. Set me back about three large. I wonder what he thought that was for?"

"But you worked with him several times didn't you?"

"Well, a couple times, but Darla was the main contact, even before we got married. We liked to work with that law firm – they were pretty cooperative and that Keislor, what a great sonofabitch. He'd dump on his own mama – if he's got one."

"Wait a minute!" Harrington was a little irritated by what he saw as David avoiding the Loudon question. "Was Max Loudon a conscious participant in this guarantee business?"

"Yeah, actually, he was. He was instrumental in helping me tip over the La Strada car people in Vera Cuz. Of course, we always arranged to pay the firm outrageous legal fees – way above market, and the girls performed as necessary, and Hugh the animal performed. So there wasn't a lot of palaver necessary."

DD looked at Harrington and Rick and asked, "Do you guys think that is enough to get Loudon indicted? I mean Dolson will probably do anything to protect him."

Harrington responded, "This pompous, sanctimonious asshole has held the DA's office hostage for the last four years. I think that Citriani and Heany ought to just arrest him."

DD turned to Weisenstock. "David, let's get to the Pavlone case and the killing of Ella Mae White."

Weisenstock explained that the approach gained some momentum by the late '70s and a lot of inquiries came his way. Nearly all were from mainline liability carriers looking for some of David's luck or whatever it was. They would submit the information to David and David would submit it to the person who was above him.

"You mean Graham and Brown?"

David laughed. "No. Those old goombas wouldn't know what to do with that much paper. I mean I'm grateful to 'em – they gave me my start, got me out of the mess with Tamanino by dropping him in the Hudson and, from time to time, connected us with somebody we might use. They came up with the Fraternal Order in Mississippi – I don't know the prior connection, but it turned out to be real handy. No, they weren't sharp enough to make the decisions and run this deal."

Rick had become impatient. "Who the hell was it then?"

David lit another cigarette. "We got a deal, right? I mean I ain't asking for that much."

Harrington looked askance at Weisenstock. "What are you saying? Are you welching?"

"No, I'm not but I want to make sure that Armani is pressed and I look like people expect me to look when I take the stand. The truth of the matter is that I don't know who it is. I never met her. I've only talked to her on the telephone. She's too fucking smart for me. Christ knows I've tried to find out, but when I did she knew it and told me she'd have my nuts cut off with a dull chisel if I ever did anything like that again."

***

CHAPTER TWENTY-TWO

A Reckoning

Weisenstock rapidly went through the details of the scheme that resulted in the bribery of Ella Mae White. He didn't know Yamaguchi's insurer but knew that coverage for such things as nailing the help was always resisted by insurers. He didn't want the actual insurer looking at this with his own adjusting personnel. There was enough money to be made from the manufacturer and its insurer, so Yamaguchi's liability carrier was never notified.

"She" liked the whole deal. She said to hold on for a couple hours and she would call back. When she did, she told David to do nothing. She would handle it. That had happened before, so David just cooled his heels.

She came up with this Mexican-based German engineer. The guy turns out to be deathly afraid of his wife. He is also deathly afraid that his role in designing the car's roof structure would be exposed in a trial and if the company lost the case it would cost hundreds of millions. He would be blamed. His passionate pleas to have the European parent companies retain Weisenstock to "adjust" the Pavlone matter apparently prevailed. "When they heard the deal, it became just another insurance premium."

"How much?" Harrington asked.

David smiled; he looked out the window. "Thirty-five million."

"So," Harrington began to realize the size of this gambit, "all your money came from insurance companies?"

Relaxed and affable, David Weisenstock explained to the near dumbstruck district attorney, "No. She told me to take Max and go to Vera Cruz and talk to Domingues. The British insurers wanted some help with the premium. Remember, I did nothing about any deal but what I didn't get HER approval. She is one sharp cookie. We had a lot of deals that were straight, legitimate insurance settlements. That's why I had to get Darla and even my son in to deal with the paper. But the serious money arrived with the guaranty."

"Did you decide that Ella Mae ought to die?"

"No. I never made that kind of decision. She did. She had some other source of information and, from time to time, asked me to check it out. But if someone was going to get hurt, I was simply told it would happen."

Weisenstock went on to say that Max Loudon probably knew less than he did about whether something was going to happen to someone. David was sure Loudon didn't want to know and Keislor played dumb the whole time. Darla was a soldier.

David married her and she married him to keep an eye on each other and hopefully for the loyalty it might create. Her payment for the Pavlone deal was a community property interest "plus a little bank account that I set up for her as a loving husband."

Drucinda had some other role that David never figured out, but she was definitely more knowledgeable about the heavy action than he or Darla.

The assistant district attorney and his colleagues walked slowly across the moonlit yard inside the jail. No one said anything.

Ms. Slattery had gathered her notes and packed them neatly into her stenotype case. She walked ahead, then stopped. "Am I in some kind of danger here? I mean would someone do something violent to get these notes?"

Rick took the case and Ms. Slattery's hand. "I'll bring 'em up to your office in the morning. How's that?"

Jeannie was grim on the telephone. "DD, Tony Citriani just called looking for Larry. They found Max Loudon dead in his office. Apparently a suicide. There's a note. The District Attorney is there. "

"Where's Mattie?"

"At the cottage, I think. The bodyguards have doubled in number around here. Shit, there's hardly any room to sit. The entry hall is full of reporters and television cameras. Would you get here so I can go home?"

Dolson was seated in the client chair opposite Loudon's body with its mouth open and drooling into the blood already pooled on the polished walnut desktop. The note was in front of Dolson as he slumped in the soft chair. In his despair he didn't realize that Larry and DD had entered the room.

As well coiffed as Max always was, as apparently in control and calm – his scratchy hand written note had the appearance of panic and abject fear.

> *As I write this, I know what I am contemplating is an act of cowardice. I am not, it turns out, a courageous man. If I were, I would not have succumbed to a desire for power and wealth that this filthy scheme brought me. Having proven bereft of character at the beginning, I redoubled my cravenness by refusing to face the consequences of what I helped to nurture and bring to evil fruition. My sins are mine and the shame is on me – if I don't end my life, I'll squirm and ultimately rationalize what cannot and should not be rationalized. I seek therefore to hide in the dark. The eternal dark, thereby sealing the entirety of my existence in the pall of cowardice.*

DD read the note. "Max just didn't understand, did he?"

Larry took the note and also read it, "You mean that it really wasn't all about him? Shit, you'd think he'd tell us something we could use."

Dolson stood and pulled a sheaf of papers out of his inside pocket. He handed them to Harrington. "He compiled this list of accounts – his own. The last page is a summary of the firm's net worth." Dolson left.

"It says here that Loudon had personal assets of more than ten million. The firm has a net worth of thirty million.

Lot of money. I wonder if it all came through this scheme. Do you think there's anything here?"

DD examined the sheets. "If there is, I can't see it right now. He doesn't give a clue to what is supposed to happen to all this money. This does appear to be his own personal accounting. Note that there are some entries here that bear looking at."

Larry nodded. "You go on back to the office. I'll look around here for a while. Call me in the morning." He sat down in the client chair as the coroner's staff loaded the body in a bag and onto a gurney.

DD walked out into the San Francisco evening and hailed a taxi to take him to Turk Street. Once there, he pushed his way through the dozen or so reporters that remained in the entry hall, refusing to answer any questions, and went immediately to Joe's office. Rick was leaving.

"Right now, Rick, the death of Max Loudon just about eliminates someone else to question. He didn't leave us anything."

There was still Drucinda, "but we seem to be catching a lot of people except the most responsible."

DD explained to Joe what had happened with David Weisenstock's statement, Darla's startling revelations, and Max Loudon's suicide note.

Joe asked, "So who is monitoring all this blood and bomb stuff and the guy who is following you and Mattie? I mean it looks like everyone nearby is accounted for."

"Actually, I hadn't thought about it. Pep was running down this guy who Tony caught following us. Do we know any more about that?" DD was unnerved at having not considered this.

The slurried gravel sound of Pep's voice came rattling through the office from the front door, "Doesn't anyone drink around here any more? What kind of an Irish lawyer place is this, anyway? By god, I remember the days when a man could count on Irish barristers being around to share a libation.

Especially, most especially, when the loyal private investigator has news – not great news, but news."

Jeannie and Pat announced they were leaving and told Pep where Joe and DD were.

"Drink?" DD asked.

"Sure." Joe responded.

DD called Mattie before he left. She explained that a San Francisco plainclothes cop was at the top of the Filbert Street stairs and another was at the bottom. She felt safe. Pep and the lawyers waded through the crowded entrance to Turk Street and down to No. 9 Jones.

"Brandon Hislip – that's his name. He's a 24-year-old law student at Golden Gate – part time, apparently. He isn't all that forthcoming, but he is scared and started telling Tony that he didn't know anything. All he did was take some pictures of DD and, I am pretty sure, Mattie. Then he said he wanted to see a lawyer – his own lawyer.

"So, eventually, this afternoon, Tony Romano shows up. Citriani – lotta 'Tonys' around – tells Romano what is going on and says he thinks Harrington isn't interested in prosecuting this kid. Ms. Bettini, working with Larry on this, tells Romano that Citriani is correct, but there is no margin for bullshit. She tells Romano they want everything and unless there is something else on this guy, maybe he walks without a blemish. Romano just called me to tell me to tell you, young Hislip is prepared to do an aria. So, Angelina and I will tune him in tomorrow morning."

"I want one more drink and I'll buy this round."

Joe signaled Jaime.

Brandon Hislip's application to Golden Gate was his second attempt to get into law school. In his first, a year after he graduated from the University of Hawaii, he was deemed dishonest and was disqualified for his failure to mention an arrest for trying to lift jewelry from a woman he had met on the beach at Kihei. That application, made to the University of San Francisco, similarly failed to disclose juvenile misadventures such as being charged in a sweep of a

277

pornographic film studio in Honolulu where he starred in at least one – more or less – standard copulative cellophane essay.

Pep could make no connection between young Hislip and the aging Mafia insurance dons. Pep suggested that his time was probably best spent, for the moment, chasing down Hislip and letting his friend and former FBI agent, Roger Cash, run down what he called the "Angloed wops."

The next morning, Citriani was happy to have Pep in the room for the questioning of young Hislip. Pep and Tony Romano were good friends and had worked together several times.

"If you're persuaded that Brandon is telling the truth, then we can go on the record in exchange for a very definite deal. This kid has a chance and he hasn't done anything to warrant time. The people who hired him might well have committed heinous felonies, but clearly he is not culpable for those. Tell me now that you are insisting on time, and I'll save the afternoon for something else."

The deal was cut, contingent on Citriani and Pep being "persuaded."

"Never met the person. Never saw the person. Don't know the gender, the race, the age or anything other than that person is very scary for all that he or she knows."

Hislip received word he was hired by way of an envelope in his mailbox at the Golden Gate student center. There were three or four typed pages together with three one hundred dollar bills. The letter instructed that he destroy it upon committing it to memory. The three hundred dollars was earnest money, according to the letter. There was a photograph of Daniel Dermot O'Neil and details about where he lived and worked and what sort of car he drove, together with the car's license number.

"I was to follow the guy and note everywhere he went and describe to whom he talked. The letter assured me this was legal but required that I not get caught because the employer did not want to be discovered. I could subcontract with anyone that I felt reliable and it was up to me how much to pay them. I was required to write a report every night on what happened with this guy O'Neil that day. I could not get close to him when he went up or down those stairs to his house, but I otherwise I was right on top of him. "

Pep asked, "What about when he left town? Did you follow him?"

"Right. He went to the airport and got on an American Airlines flight to Dallas. If that happened, I was to call this telephone number and leave a message. On that occasion that is what I did."

"What is that number?"

Pep was anticipating an important lead to the mystery head of this cabal.

Hislip handed Pep a small piece of paper. The telephone number was that of the Sausalito apartment. Citriani called Heany and Tim headed out for Sausalito while Hislip was being interviewed.

"What did you do with the reports? I assume they were written?"

"Yeah. Well, I just went about three blocks from the school where there is a post office with mailboxes. I deposited the reports in an envelope in the mail addressed to this mailbox."

Hislip provided the mail box number and Citriani made note. He received questions in response to the reports and received further instructions in the way he had received the original instructions. When he reported that he had seen O'Neil with a woman, his employer enquired about her and what impressions that Hislip had.

"I just reported that the woman was very pretty and that I had seen her going up the stairs with O'Neil to his house on several occasions. That's when I got some high speed 35mm film along with my pay and my instructions. I was directed to get as many photographs of this woman as possible. So, I did."

The day before Hislip was arrested by Citriani was supposed to be regular payday. Hislip went to his school mailbox and found the usual envelope, but this time there was only cash for the hours he had reported and nothing else. That was two days before his arrest. He has heard nothing since and believes the deal is over. He is positive his employer knew he was going to be arrested.

Angie Bettini agreed to a guilty plea for criminal trespass and three years probation. She would not agree to give Hislip a pass on his record before the State Bar. It was up to the State Bar to decide whether Hislip's adventure was relevant to his suitability for licensing. Hislip's statement was taken by a stenotypist, printed and signed.

Mattie appeared on Turk Street as DD was jotting notes and drifting off into the tangled, seemingly pathless jungle in which he found himself. She was in jeans, a light sweater, and DD's Forty-Niner windbreaker.

"Hi." She smiled the way DD loved and needed right then. "So, who's the bad guy? Tell the cops to get him, and we can get on with our lives. OK?"

Postponing for now the search for the pathway out, he just stopped and appreciated her by first just looking and then embracing and, in this context, finally kissing.

"No, not yet. I think I'm supposed to know what to do next, because now we have a lot. But, I don't know."

Joe stepped into DD's office with Rick right behind him.

"So the kingpin remains elusive? Is this the woman who Weisenstock talked about?"

"Shit, I don't know."

Over burritos at La Cubre, DD and Mattie got to the point. "My home is in Magnolia City. My job is there and that isn't going to change unless and until we decide the big issue."

Stepping reluctantly out of his preoccupation, his eyes brightened.

"I don't know if that's true – that the danger is over. These guys certainly could do something else." – he nodded at the two policemen sitting in a squad car outside the restaurant

–"but I don't know that Harrington is going to let them until we get this ringleader or ringleaders wrapped up."

Challenging her lover – just enough to convey her seriousness – Mattie quietly asked, "Are you going to be able to do that?"

DD sighed and understood she was serious.

"I'm sitting here thinking I must have missed something. There is some way to do this, but I can't get my mind around it. This woman and maybe others are really cunning – ruthless and cunning. I want to take a crack at talking to Dru Lacey. Depending on how that goes, I'll try to persuade Larry to let the security go."

Mattie smiled and her eyes flashed lovingly. "OK. But I'm doing what I have to do – even going back to Magnolia City on Monday – five days from now, unless..."

She raised her voice slightly for emphasis.

"Unless I'm persuaded to stay longer."

DD smiled as well; he knew she wasn't angry, but he also knew she was serious.

It was not yet midnight and the telephone rang. DD grabbed the receiver. "Yes?"

Larry Harrington announced himself and with grim tones told DD, "Dru Lacey somehow got bail yesterday and Angie didn't tell me. Someone put up a cashier's check and sprung her about six o'clock last night. They found her dead in her apartment about an hour ago. A neighbor heard a scream and called the police. A .22 slug right in the middle of her forehead. Jesus Christ!"

DD looked at Mattie lying beside him. She had figured out the news was not good.

"Any suspects?"

"We got suspects up the yang, we just don't know who they are." Harrington was fairly shouting.

"Nobody saw anyone go or leave the apartment. There's just this report of a, quote, terrible scream, at about 10 p.m.. When the uniforms arrived, the door was ajar and there was little Dru lying face up on her living room sofa, mostly naked and bleeding slightly from a small hole in her forehead."

"Bail. How come she got bail? Who paid it?" DD was waking up.

"I don't know DD but I'll be finding out. Go back to sleep. We'll talk in the morning."

He hung up.

DD lay quietly, breathing pensively. Mattie kissed him on the chest and rose, donning her short robe. In the kitchen, she prepared some herbal tea for two. She knew, at some point, he would talk to her about the telephone call.

So, who gets prosecuted? The connection to the evil one – Dru – is gone. Do we press Darla and David for more on this woman? At least that. She's very elusive – diabolically so. I know I can figure this out, but will it be in time?

***

CHAPTER TWENTY-THREE

And Then There Was One

It turned out that Lacey's lawyer managed an *ex parte* motion for bail and got it before Judge Mary Strattford – well known to be opposed to "no bail" arraignments, such as was in place here. Dru's attorneys bolstered their constitutional arguments with well-developed background evidence about how Drucinda would not be a flight risk. Most of that evidence was in a declaration under penalty of perjury provided by High Keislor. Judge Strattford granted the motion over Angie Bettinis strenuous objections. The attorney delivered the cashier's check for $1 million. Dru was released. There is not a shred of evidence of where that money came from.

"So," Joe began. "The 'she-devil' got her accomplice before her accomplice could spill some beans. Because of Weisenstock, we know that this evil woman was behind the attempt to extort from Domingues and La Strada. But we still don't know who she is!"

Rick and DD looked at each other and then at Joe. Rick said what they both were thinking.

"Yes, we do."

Joe stood up. "What? How? Who?"

DD swallowed and then spoke softly, "Joe, it's Melanie."

Several minutes passed with the three of them avoiding looking at one another. Finally, Joe asked, "How do you know? I trust you are correct, but how did you get there?"

"There's been an irritating buzz in my head for some time. Jeannie has been telling me for weeks that Melanie is calling me. I never take her calls – she kept calling. The kid – what's his name, Hislip? – says his handler's really interested in Mattie and gets pictures of her. Darla says the head of this outfit is a woman and she is very smart and knows something about insurance. She also says that this boss breaks her own security rule to ask Darla directly details about me and my questioning of Darla."

Rick then added, "The Sausalito apartment had no tenant listed in the Langley files. The only person who could get away with control of that place without a lease is Melanie. The only known occupants of that apartment were either in jail – Baldachre, Darla and David Weisenstock – or dead. That would be Dru and Malvina. The logical leaseholder is Melanie. It seems to me she's the logical suspect for the death of Dru."

"So, DD," Joe turned to DD, "Is Melanie ruthless enough to kill people or have them killed?"

"Yeah, I'm afraid she is."

"Is this enough to have her arrested?"

"Let's ask Larry. He needs to know about this anyway."

DD explained the revelations to Harrington in a telephone call. It was decided to seek a warrant to have Melanie arrested. So far as DD knew, Melanie was living in her parents' apartment house on Russian Hill. Citriani and Healy were dispatched there to arrest her. DD sat back to wait and hesitated about telling Mattie.

"Boss, there's mail you haven't looked at all week." Jeannie was unaware of the most recent development in the case of the Ella May White murder. "In particular, there's a letter in there from your ex. It's been there since yesterday."

DD hurriedly shuffled his mail to find an envelope addressed in that over-the-top feminine cursive that was unmistakably Melanie's. He pulled a handwritten letter from the envelope:

My dear Dan:

By now you have figured it out and I so much wanted you not to. You understand, I had no choice but to do what came naturally to me in making an economic life of my own. That poor woman White and the others who died had miserable little lives, so ending them was really a public service – something you know always interested me.

Of course, your <u>Pavlone</u> case was the first big one for me. This scheme is an old one and was going long before I came along. It was saving our investment and our skins that brought me into management of the matter – to do the planning and issue the orders. You always told me how clever I was – this whole thing certainly proves that.

That woman, Dan! How could you do that to me and all the good sex we had? She's black, isn't she? A high yella, for Christ sake! God, I should have had her killed, corrupting my man that way. Aren't you sorry now for letting me get away?

I made a terrible mistake forgetting just how persistent you can be.

So, by the time you read this all trace of me will have disappeared – including me. No, I'm not killing myself – HA! I am simply leaving. Starting a new life and establishing a new identity. I know you'll try to find me, but I am prepared for that – if it's a choice between me and you or your picanniny lover, she will be the first to go. Maybe that will slow you down.

Love you,

Melanie

***

285

Part 5: Wisdom

*If you're going to start a thing, you ought to finish it,
if for no other reason than to justify starting it.*

Mick O'Neil's fatherly advice

CHAPTER TWENTY-FOUR
Justice From Granite

"My first inkling that Melanie was somehow involved came when Darla revealed that her boss was a woman, then when she speculated it was someone real smart with no criminal record and with a lot of knowledge about the insurance industry. I can't say that was a conscious inkling, but, in retrospect, that's what it was."

Mattie sat down at the keyboard and played "Mean to Me," slowly, without joy.

"So is this over? I mean can we get down to deciding about us?"

DD smiled at her. "It's mostly over and what's to decide? Aren't we in love? Aren't you here and aren't we happy together?"

Mattie frowned, turned on the piano bench and looked at him. "I'm trying to think of a song that says my man misses the point – at least when it comes to me. DD, this is a fantasy world we have going here. If we are in love and want to spend the rest of our respective lives together, there are some serious realities we need to face and deal with. As an example, marriage. Shouldn't we do that and seal the deal? But that isn't even first. How do you feel about becoming a lawyer in my native Mississippi – maybe opening a practice with your buddy Sonny Elliot?"

Dumbfounded, DD could only muster, "Well, you love it here. Why would we go back to Magnolia City?"

By this time, Mattie was standing and her hip was cocked in the way she had of signaling challenge.

"I do love it here, but I was born in Magnolia City, and I have a house there and a prominent position, and a lot of people there love me. Here, you have a cottage. I don't know anyone outside your circle, and no one knows me. So, there are a bunch of reasons for me going back to Magnolia City."

Alarmed by the vigor of her argument and frightened by its apparent merit, DD gathered himself. "But Mattie, I can get a house here. You can meet new friends here. I have a law practice which I have built over the last several years. Starting over again someplace I barely know would be extraordinarily difficult. The ability to provide for a family is really dependent on that. Besides, I have to finish this Pavlone business."

"Finish!? What's to finish?"

"I think I'm going to bring a lawsuit against Keislor and that firm, against *Internacionale* and against Pan American Casualty. We're going to try to recover the money that Judith Pavlone should have recovered in the first place."

Mattie's shoulders dropped, her eyes teared, and she grabbed DD by the shirt. "DD, there'll never be a time will there? You are just not going to seriously deal with our love, our future together, or my dreams and goals. Your pursuit of justice – I guess that's what it is – counts first; everything else is second. I know you love me, but that fact apparently pales before the relentless demands of this justice shit!"

Mattie was angry. She was hurt.

Now, DD was hurt. He wasn't angry; he was surprised. She walked out the door, but returned within seconds, slamming the door and in an obvious tantrum.

"That goddamn cop is still out there!"

A Butte Break was convened the next morning in DD's office.

"I've read Arty's memo. It looks pretty good, but DD, I don't think you should try the case. You are a subject. You may be a witness. There are a ton of reasons that someone else should lead this. My worry is that your objectivity would go in the toilet." Joe was firm.

"Mattie is leaving, Joe. I'm not sure I can stand that."

"I'm sorry, DD. She's a hell of a woman. Is there anything you can do?"

"Move to Magnolia City."

DD's dismay was painful to see.

"That's not it, DD. She's a strong person. She has a lot of pride. Those facts have to be served. You just keep going down this road like you have the only game around. You have to work at this, DD. We're not going to suffer like we did over Liz Downey."

"Will you try the case?"

"Will you let me? We have always worked well together but you have a lot of stuff in this one – you're ex-wife is the chief bad guy; you're losing the woman you love over it; your own pride is hurt over getting so fooled in the Pavlone trial. Will you be able to shed that stuff and let me do the case?"

"What would I be doing while you ran the litigation of my life?"

"How about trying to figure out how you keep the woman you love? Plus, there'll be a lot of tasks for you as this thing gets to trial. There are other cases like the one against Ford and this one against General Motors. Those are your thing."

"You think she'd go to Montana to see Mick?"

"Yeah. That might be a good idea. Ask her like you really are giving her the choice of not going. I'll draft a complaint before the end of the week and pin down juristiction and venue."

He shouldn't have done it on the telephone, but he did.

"No, I'm not going to Montana now. It's just another Daniel Dermot O'Neil deal where Mattie Deare is some appendage of Daniel Dermot. Damn it, DD, think about this!"

"Are you coming to the office this morning?"

"Yes. I plan to be there in about twenty minutes. Do you want to talk then?"

"I do."

With red eyes and lower lip thrust out, Mattie was displaying her hurt and her anger. She dropped in DD's client chair with an air of petulance. He was showing a little anger himself,

"At the last count I have been in Magnolia on three occasions since we met. On one of those I met your brothers and an uncle. My father's birthday is coming up and I just thought he should meet the woman I love. I had no clue that I was threatening your identity by suggesting a few days of early autumn in Western Montana."

She sighed, walked around the desk and kissed him – first on the forehead, then on the mouth and she sank into his lap.

"I feel I am being silly," she began. "And I can't quite figure out what it is that bothers me. So, here's what I propose. I pack and go to Magnolia City, where I take up thinking about us where I left off back when the bad guys were trying to kill us."

DD frowned. "What led to this conclusion?"

"It's true I admire this 'justice' thing you are looking for, and really would not want to get in the way of that. But, it's also true that I can't handle being ignored or not having my way. When I think about it, I am inhibiting your pursuit of something that you started long before I entered your life. So, let's see how a separation works – me in Mississippi and you here. We can use the telephone, and you can visit me, and I can come here as our individual responsibilities permit. How's that?"

DD sighed a long sigh. "Well, that would definitely give me an incentive to get it done quickly."

"I would hope so"

A kiss, maybe two. He knew he didn't deserve her, but he also knew he wasn't going to lose her.

Pep and San Francisco's finest – as well as the FBI – expended every effort to find Melanie Langley. Harrington got an indictment against her and a fugitive warrant was issued.

Rick had concluded that Dru's pre-fatal scream was her reaction to seeing the gun and that Melanie was the one with the gun. Dru's negligee on her otherwise naked body suggested she expected something else that evening. There were no prints in her apartment other than her own and the cleaning woman's. No one saw any stranger around at the time. The only possible anomaly was the presence, just outside the door to Dru's apartment, of a small quantity of talcum on the carpet – the sort used to facilitate the use of latex gloves.

The Langley home in Kentfield sits well off the main road behind twenty foot, blooming hedges and yards of green grass. It is not the largest house in the neighborhood, but it is very much the most elegant. Robert Langley had inherited a sizable fortune from his father, "Cudge." The elder Langley was the darling of the San Francisco employing class in the late twenties and through the '30s, and, conversely, the enemy of the budding trade unions, particularly on the San Francisco waterfront. "Cudge" got the moniker as a young college student at Stanford, when he mercilessly beat a hobo to death with a club. He wasn't arrested. He wasn't prosecuted.

DD had called ahead, so that the big iron gate was opened as he approached in the Ford. Beatrice – Bea – was in her seventies. Herself a child of a wealthy family from South Carolina, she remained very handsome and never tried to lose her southern drawl – seemingly trying to play and re-play Scarlet O'Hara.

"Dan. I never thought I'd see you again."

Bea never resented DD for dumping her only child – she seemed to understand what a difficult woman Melanie was. Bea nonetheless outwardly cussed DD – particularly in the presence of her husband.

"Well, Bea, I guess it's just as much a surprise to me to be here. I'll bet you can guess what has brought me."

She invited him in and through the house to the veranda at the back, overlooking the creek that ran through meadow and woods.

"I'm having a toddy, as you might have guessed. You may recall that I don't care all that much where the sun is on the yardarm. I've ordered up some Irish for you; please help yourself. You haven't quit have you? So much has changed since we last talked."

She sat easily with her back to the early September sun. DD poured himself a glass of Irish whiskey over some ice cubes.

"Yes, we got a note, as I expect you did. Sad, really, our losing our only child this way. She wasn't very specific but I gather she got herself involved in fraud, maybe worse."

DD sipped his whiskey. "Worse."

"Well, I expect Bobby knows more than I do, but I don't suppose he'll ever be able to talk about it."

"Where is he, by the way."

"In The City, at the club – the yacht club. You know he had a stroke, don't you?"

"No, I didn't."

"We managed to keep it out of the papers. It's really quite embarrassing. He really can't talk without slobbering and moves painstakingly slow. Christ, I don't imagine we'll ever go to or have another party. Poor Chuck, he's stuck with Bobby nearly all day every day. You remember Chuck, don't you? He's Melanie's cousin – the son of Cudge's illegitimate daughter."

*I haven't seen Melanie's letter to her parents, but mom
has concluded that her baby daughter is involved in fraud and
"worse" but her primary concern is that her husband drools.
There's a genetic consistency of some kind here.*

"Can Robert talk?"

"Sort of. One needs more patience than I have to
understand him. Of course, when he tries, he just drools more.
Do you want to ask him something?"

"Bea, I want to know where Melanie is and the San
Francisco Police Department will soon be here with that same
interest. "

She freshened her toddy.

"Oh my. I'm afraid I don't know and can't even guess. I
haven't seen her in more than a year. She went off to marry
that thug in Hawaii and I would not witness that foolishness.
She had her own business and her own property and just didn't
feel the need to visit her poor old mother."

Robert Langley's *persona* was depicted in magazine and
newspaper photographs for years. He was always a handsome,
well-dressed man from an *Esquire* ad page. His beautiful wife
and daughter were always somewhere near him as if
themselves part of his tasteful and elegant attire.

He could no longer speak coherently. All that DD could
manage from his attempts to talk was "Go fuck yourself."
Even at that, under-achieving Chuck had to interpret. Bea was
right – he slobbered a lot.

The accounts with the State of Mississippi were settled,
and the pursuit of the civil case against whomever the Butte
Boys and Rick could find began at full tilt almost
immediately. Joe and Arty were huddled for several hours and
when they emerged, a "shit-together" was called.

"We have a lot of material that tells us what justice
requires, but what we'll try here is truly without much
precedent. When we swing, we want to hit something. If we
swing and miss, there'll be an inertia that will threaten the

whole case. I don't want to be suing somebody just to see if we can get some money out of them. 'See if it sticks' is not a legitimate reason for us to sue someone."

DD, Rick, Pep, Arty, and Joe laid out an investigatory program designed to fill the gaps between what had been learned and what was needed to join parties in lawsuits. Pep was asked to pursue the connections between Robert Langley and his daughter and the "enterprise." They began to call themselves the forces of good and the defendants, "the enterprise" or "the forces of evil."

DD managed a couple of trips to Magnolia City and, aside from a few hours with Sonny Elliot, spent most of his time with Mattie at her house. Relaxed time, that is. The relationship matured in these visits, and Mattie's brothers were ecstatic over their little sister's man.

California law on fraud and conspiracy were preferred bases for the lawsuit. Even if the federal anti-racketeering statute would clearly fit, no one wanted this one to be assigned to Federal Court. Everyone agreed that if they could get past a motion for summary judgment and get to a jury, the case would result in a sizable verdict.

"Summary judgment" is a procedural device used in one form or another throughout American jurisprudence. The idea is that if the law does not provide relief (damages, injunction, reimbursement, fine, imprisonment) on undisputed facts, then the lawsuit should be dismissed. A trial, after all, is held only to determine facts, not law.

***

CHAPTER TWENTY-FIVE

Planning the Blows

Judith Pavlone had gained weight as a consequence of her limited ability to burn calories. It always pained DD to see her in the wheelchair, struggling to sit up and maintain her attention. While her charm and amiable personality seemed to have survived the agonies of paralysis, a fatigue was detectable.

"Oh, God. You want to do this again?' she asked. "You suffered the last time as much as I did. You didn't show it, but I know it's true. Explain, please."

She was Judith – more concerned with others than herself and always game.

DD explained what they had in mind. Judith squealed when he told her the plan was to sue Keislor, as well as the insurance company. She was completely intrigued with the story of murder and bribery, although she had been informed with some regularity over the several weeks since DD got the call from Magnolia City. Still, she hesitated. The painful part would be the need to prove that but for the bribery of Ella Mae White, Judith would have won. That means all the evidence from the original trial would be presented – it would be a case-within-a-case.

"You know Dan. I'm in a routine now. Since my last accident in the van, I've had a driver provided by the disability insurer. It has made life a lot easier, and I really don't miss driving. What more could I want from a lawsuit? Well, there is more help around the house. Modifications of the house. Less hassle when I need medication for bladder infections and the like. A new van. Oh, and my niece's tuition." She was thinking out loud.

"If you're up to it, I'm game. I want to be there when that evil man takes the stand. It's ok if Joe tries the case. He's almost as good as you. Will Rick be there? He's such a doll."

At Turk Street, Pep arrived with the usual commotion and an oral report.

"Robert Langley is the primary investor/owner of Pan American Trust and Casualty and has been since 1948 at age 28 when his father died. Old Cudge played with some pretty rough guys when he was head of the San Francisco Employers Association – rough in the sense they would pull all manner of stunts – legal or illegal – to discourage unionization in an association enterprise. Cudge was madder than hell when some of these employers made claims on his insurance company for damage caused by strikes. He set about to do something about it. One of his solutions was to destroy the unions."

Joe interrupted, "Pep, get us back to Robert Langley and his daughter. We'll do the deep history some other time."

Chagrined, Pep consulted his notes. "Robert, in his role as chief executive of Pan American, acquired our now familiar International Underwriters and Reinsurers. The New York insurance people have a filing that shows the old man bought IUR from Graham and Brown – six years ago. So, our boy David Weisenstock did not exactly come clean about how well he knew Robert Langley. But, it is even more interesting to discover that the president of IUR is – you guessed, didn't you? – Melanie Roberta Langley."

Joe's mouth was agape. He turned to DD, who went to the heart of the matter.

"So, did we look for her there? Wherever IUR is?"

"Your friends in New York definitely did that. In fact they were there yesterday. A 3,600-square-foot office on Wall Street, people all around, and no one can tell us anything about how it became completely empty. She didn't even get her security and cleaning deposit back from the building manager."

Joe insisted, "She had to have a bank account. What about that?"

"Wiped out with cashier's checks last week. That was about the time Ms. Lacey took the bullet. Sorry guys; this ain't going to be easy."

Pep lit a new cigar. "Didn't Sonny describe the office of FOMLE – you know when that guy Crossmore disappeared – as cleaned out like a vacuum cleaner had been used? Apparently, that's how this Wall Street office looked."

Over the next several days, Rick and DD drafted discovery requests addressed to Pan American and Robert Langley. Those were served in due course and the team started on requests addressed to the law firm of Loudon, Mueller and Keislor, as well as Keislor individually. Those were followed by discovery demands to *Internacionale* and its insurer, Bidwell of London. The two foreign defendants had to be served pursuant to international convention requirements that meant, as an example, the complaint and requests to *Internacionale* had to be translated into the German and Italian languages and served on the respective embassies.

The "forces of good" planned to attack the 'forces of evil' in discovery by digging out the evidence first from Pan American and Langley, then the Loudon law firm and finally the foreign defendants. They waited for an attempt by the foreign defendants to remove the case from the San Francisco superior court to Federal Court. Treaty provisions would likely make that fruitless, but it was a standard gambit of foreign companies. The attempt never came, but lawyers representing *Internacionale* and Bidwell did pay a visit to the forces of good.

A senior partner from one of the largest law firms in the United States, accompanied by a phalanx of young, fierce-looking men and women, met with Joe in the Turk Street conference room. Joe deliberately made them wait a few minutes before joining them, and when he did he was in an open collar golf shirt and shorts.

"We think this is going to trial," The senior partner began sonorously. "We don't want to be there when it does. We don't think you can sue our insurer for simply accepting the reports of its contract examiner – Mr. Weisenstock – but we recognize that a judge may think differently and deny a motion for summary judgment. Herr Bettinger is most likely going to reveal enough for you to stick *Internacionale* with knowledge of the scheme and its ultimate goal of defeating Ms. Pavlone's case. We think it will be most difficult for you to prove your 'case-within-a-case,' that is, that Ms. Pavlone would have recovered but for this business about Ms. White's bribery. However, we don't want to ask a jury to decide we knowingly went along with a scheme such as this, but that it made no difference to the outcome."

Joe smiled. "You guys don't get paid all that money because you're stupid, do you?"

The senior partner smiled back. "And if we were stupid, think how difficult your job would be."

Joe nodded. "What do you have in mind?"

"Paying you and your client a lot of money in return for a dismissal and release."

The phalanx were obviously concerned about Joe's reaction to this as all their eyes were intently fixed on him.

"How much?"

The eyes shifted back to the senior partner.

"Two million."

"Other conditions?"

"Well, the usual 'no admission' clause and a clause that says this payment is not for punitive damages. We would want the punitive damage allegation dismissed before the settlement was consummated."

Joe was clearly not sanguine about this offer. The eyes of the phalanx became even more intent.

"How about cooperation in the presentation of evidence?"

"How about it?"

"Domingues will testify, no matter whether we settle with you. I want Bettinger as the designer of the roof to basically confess on the stand that it was defective, but also to what

297

Keislor did in preparation of the defense case during original trial."

"I can't tell Bettinger what to say. Whether you get Keislor can't depend on what Bettinger says – he didn't even testify at the first trial."

"We know he didn't. He was never identified as the designer of this roof. We didn't know he existed until we talked to Domingues. That means that Keislor lied about who did it to keep a vulnerable witness off the stand. I want Bettinger here and I want to talk to him without notice to the other forces of evil. I want him to take the stand and tell the truth. I also want *Internacionale* to waive any claim of lawyer-client privilege as to Keislor and produce all the written correspondence between him and the company regarding the Pavlone case."

"Mr. Cleary, Two million dollars is a lot of money. *Internacionale* and Bidwell want the peace that much money should buy them. 'Peace' here means when the money is paid, we are gone, period. I don't want anything hanging on or continuing to connect these companies with this mess."

"Mr. Senior Partner, I understand what your clients want. It is simply that they can't have it, because what they wanted six years ago was to escape liability to a young quadriplegic woman when they knew they were responsible to her. While we are talking about this, sir, you should also know that the plaintiff will not in any settlement agreement with any defendant in this case agree to any clause that suggests that the settling defendant is not liable. Neither will we agree to dismiss the punitive damage claim, nor will we agree to characterize any money paid as not being for punitive damages."

At this point the eyes of the phalanx exchanged looks with each other, and some rolled. There were murmurs among the heads with the eyes. The senior partner, returning to his sonorousness, "Uh, is there anything else? I want to be sure I have everything when I talk to my clients."

"Yes," Joe said quickly, "two million is not enough. We will consider four million, subject to approval from my client."

All the eyes of the phalanx were looking at their respective hands. The Senior Partner stood. "Can we get back together in the morning? I am not sure I can reach my clients at this time."

Joe also stood. "I'm playing handball in the morning but I can be here by 11 a.m.; how's that?"

Disconsolate, the Senior Partner and his phalanx filed out of the conference room and then onto Turk Street and bright sunshine, amid drunks, drug addicts, and street whores. Joe watched briefly through the front door and thought *those guys will give the neighborhood a bad name.*

The next morning, Joe played in a pick up doubles match at the YMCA. No pressure. Nothing at stake except the exercise. He could easily display his speed and gamesmanship with plenty of laughs and gaffs. He showered and dressed in plenty of time to meet the Senior Partner, who was early.

"Who won?"

"It doesn't matter."

Joe had donned a suit and a tie, suitable for his afternoon appearance in Court. The Senior Partner was without his phalanx. Joe guessed they were preparing for the same appearance this afternoon before the civil law and motion judge, Noah Benjamin. His disdain for the Senior Partner was more apparent than he would have wished. He never was as good at hiding his emotions as the other Butte Boy.

"My clients are disturbed by your demand that the agreement not include a 'no admission' clause, but my guess is that you don't much care about what disturbs my client. Our CEO, D'Lesandro, may be willing to cooperate as you have suggested, but he doesn't want to sit for a deposition. He knows nothing. It seems to me you can do without this little added indignity."

Joe hung his coat on the conference room coat rack and went to the kitchen for a cup of coffee. Wordlessly, he offered a cup to the Senior Partner, who declined.

"So, we get the documents. Bettinger comes here to talk to me and, if I choose, he testifies. Four million, a straight release agreement – you don't have to confess, but don't ask me to agree that you don't have or don't admit to liability, and don't characterize the payment. If you can tell us where to find Melanie Langley, we'll take three and a half."

The Senior Partner pondered a moment.

"How about this: you put one million of that four in some sort of escrow account – it can earn what you can earn with it. Keep it available for, say, three years. Then if we find this woman for you, you give us that one million back"

Joe smiled. "I'll recommend it."

The deal was consummated. The litigation dragged on. Depositions were taken, documents demanded and produced. Motions to dismiss and for summary judgment were made and denied. Strangely, the defense requested very little by way of discovery from the plaintiff, so it did not know before trial of the deal struck with *Internacionale* and Bidwell. DD sat for his deposition. Keislor was present and feverishly wrote questions out for his counsel. Of course, many of those had to do with Melanie and DD's friend Roy Lindstrom.

Joe and Rick were prevented from taking the deposition of Robert Langley when the Court denied their motion to compel it. A physician for Langley appeared and testified that he was physically and mentally unfit to be deposed. Upon an examination by plaintiff's own doctors, it was agreed that Robert would not and could not testify.

Lionel Woodman, a very distinguished insurance defense attorney from Los Angeles represented the Loudan law firm. Tyler Ruud served as counsel for Keislor. Ruud was a corporate litigator in San Jose and made a reputation for aggressive advocacy representing Silicon Valley venture capitalists. All together, there were eight lawyers on the side of the forces of evil.

At about 6:30 p.m., just over a week before the commencement of trial, Joe, Rick, DD, and Pep were at Turk Street when Dianna called. She had been watching local TV and the commentator said that Ruud would appear; she was unsure of the context. Rick turned on the office TV and after a few moments there was Tyler Ruud.

The interviewer was heard to say, "So, this current litigation over the bribery of a juror three years ago will bring up the famous prison shootings by the notorious prison radical Gerald Mann?"

Ruud: "Most certainly. Primarily because the plaintiff's lead lawyer and his partner were directly involved with helping their friend, Lindstrom, escape arrest after the friend gave Mann the gun."

"And who are you talking about, specifically?"

"Joseph Cleary and Daniel O'Neil."

A file tape then ran of the news story ten years before about the San Quentin shootings leading to the death of Mann and several others, including several prison guards.

Joe turned the television off. "Shit."

DD said, "They're going to subpoena Roy. We should call him."

Rick was outraged. "Why the hell would these producers raise this now? Isn't Ruud out of line?"

"Are you kidding me?" DD stood and put on his jacket. "This asshole Ruud is representing the greatest asshole, Keislor. This isn't the least bit surprising and, I suspect, is only the opening shot. Let's get a drink."

Joe got his jacket, and, on the way out the door, disagreed with DD. "They aren't going to subpoena Roy. They're going to poison the jury pool and maybe force us to do something stupid."

Jaime was about to clock out, but brought Joe the telephone.

"Roy?"

"Hey, Joe. I already heard about Ruud's TV appearance. It's getting cold up here, so I don't think anybody is going to happily come looking for me with a subpoena."

"Roy, we want to talk about maybe you volunteering to appear for a deposition if the Court orders it. As it stands, Ruud can go on and on saying whatever he wants about you and us, but we need an official record as soon as we can get it. We've got friends in the news business, too. Maybe we can force Ruud to notice your deposition. They can shit or get off the pot at that point. What do you think?"

"Joe, you guys know your case. But you're right, Keislor can't want the truth out because it won't help him. If you try to avoid my testimony, they'll characterize that as sinister. So, ok. Depose me."

Joe went home. DD and Rick went to Roland's, a jazz club on Fillmore. It was Thursday night. Bobbie and Larry were appearing with George Lane sitting in on drums. Lane was the head of Channel 18 news – the most popular news operation in the City. He was also a native of Butte, having left it ten years before Joe and DD.

A couple glasses, a brief conversation between sets, the business was done, but Rick and DD stayed on. DD played the only song he knew on the piano ("No Money Blues") and Rick (a very accomplished singer) joined Bobbie in a duet of "Stars Fell on Alabama." They left before any further damage was done.

A week later, Joe sat in the Channel 18 studio for taping to be aired on the following Sunday afternoon. It happened that the public affairs program of the station had been featuring "the status of the courts." Using that general subject, George Lane outlined an interview of Joe as an active plaintiff's trial lawyer. Following some general questions, the answers to which demonstrated that Joe was a knowledgeable and even-handed expert on the topic, the interviewer asked about the comments of Ruud about the Gerald Mann incident and the coming trial.

"I don't know where Mr. Ruud gets his information, but I would think that a man of his experience would know better than to raise such a topic and make such accusations without reliable information. That unfortunate tragedy took place a long time ago and it was conclusively established that neither Dan O'Neil nor myself had anything to do with Roy Lindstrom's disappearance following the shooting. It has also been conclusively established that Roy Lindstrom did not provide the gun that precipitated the shoot-out."

The interviewer, on cue, asked: "Be that as it may, Mr. Cleary, what does this have to do with the case that you are about to try?"

"Good point. It has nothing to do with it. I am afraid that it looks like Mr. Ruud is trying to influence the prospective jurors before they are called. So, I am told by Mr. Lindstrom that if Mr. Ruud wants to ask him questions under oath, he'll make himself available for that purpose. Frankly, I doubt that Mr. Ruud will take advantage of Mr. Lindstrom's offer. He does not seem to be much interested in the truth."

The newspapers in The City and even in New York became interested in the case, so that Joe and Ruud were interviewed. Long, more or less analytic, stories appeared in the *Examiner,* the *Chronicle*, the *Los Angeles Times* and the *New York Times*. An editorial sharply criticizing the plaintiff's team for bringing the lawsuit appeared in two successive days of the *Wall Street Journal* – which didn't send anyone to interview Joe, DD, or Rick.

A lot of media attention was being generated – so much so that Joe was worrying about the potential effect on a jury. Not wanting to reveal the gambit of the *Internacionale* and Bidwell settlement, Joe's mantra became, "Come around and listen to the evidence. That's why we try these things."

Turk Street began to look very much like the staging area for a large army in a large war. Joe brought in enough Samoan friends to man the front door to physically control the press and others who might interfere. Four law students were hired to summarize testimony that had been gathered in the course of the grand jury investigations, sworn statements, and depositions, as well as transcripts from the original trial. DD pored over the documents obtained from *Internacionale* and from La Strada.

Jeannie, Pat, and Pep gave DD a ribbon and wire halo mounted on a stick fastened to the back of his shirt because he refrained from clobbering Keislor. During the course of his deposition, Keislor suggested DD had married Melanie for her father's money. When he found out there would be no money for him, he left Melanie. Actually, DD concluded from that that Hugh was feeling terribly vulnerable – and, of course, he had no idea how vulnerable.

Joe went to Judge Benjamin with a motion asking the judge to order Ruud to take Roy's deposition or never mention the Gerald Mann thing again – in court or in the press. The press picked this up and Ruud had no choice. In less than two hours, Ruud ran out of questions for Lindstrom and learned only what Joe had already made public. The only thing he could establish was that DD and Joe were friends of Lindstrom. Judge Benjamin then ordered Ruud never to mention the Mann matter publicly or in Court.

Jimmy O'Hearn, Jury Commissioner, telephoned Turk Street at 5:05 p.m., Thursday. In his nasaled south-of-Market twang, he asked, "You guys ready to go? Monday morning in the P.J.'s department. Time for motions is over. It looks like you'll be assigned."

O'Hearn's call got everyone's heart beating quickly.

"We have three defendants left – Pan American, Keislor, and the firm. There are three departments open. The odds are not good that we'll make it through challenges and get a judge."

Ever the pessimist, Rick slouched in the conference room chair.

"Well, we gotta be ready, anyway."

Joe stood and shouted to Pat from the conference room door, "Call Judith. She needs as much time to prepare as we can give her. Tell her we need her Monday just to meet the jury and the judge. She won't be testifying right away."

Rick was concerned. "Jesus, Joe. Judith is pretty persuasive. Don't you think we should put her on first?"

Joe answered, "I don't want to appear to be jerking heart strings here. We want to start with hard evidence."

"He's going to put Keislor on the stand as the Plaintiff's first witness – aren't you, Joe?" DD was smiling, ear-to-ear.

Joe and DD hugged and laughed.

Rick didn't like the idea. "You gotta be kidding. It's one thing to pull that stunt when you have some dumb ass engineer, or a street cop. This guy is an experienced trial lawyer. That kind of witness can tear you up. Are you sure?"

"I think Darla was right." DD was recalling her statement and deposition. "She talks about Keislor's view of himself. He thinks he's too smart. He also thinks we're smart, so he is likely convinced that we won't call him first."

Joe added, "I just think that with him on the stand first, we identify a force of evil for the jury, as well as get some fundamental points in. It's a lot easier to get evidence in when the witness is a defendant who also happens to be a lawyer."

The San Francisco Superior Court runs on a master calendar system. Although the Court is divided into two general parts – civil and criminal – the system allows all courts to be available for criminal cases and, theoretically, a criminal court can try a civil case. The Superior Court is the California trial court where cases are initiated and, if necessary, tried. A "trial" is the process of determining the basic facts in a case and to apply the law to those facts.

A presiding judge assigns cases on a more or less first-come-first-serve basis to available judges. Assignments – again more or less – are random. In the period that is the subject of this story, the San Francisco Superior Court was the venue for hundreds of asbestos claims. That not only presented unusual administrative nightmares, it also meant that other civil litigants would be more delayed because of the crowded docket. A case such as the second Pavlone matter might get to trial before others because of its projected length, i.e. a judge may be available for the entire predicted period of the trial.

Actually getting a case out to trial was itself a matter of brinksmanship and luck. Once the wait and the motions were over, the next problem was getting past the peremptory judicial challenge available to all litigants. Any party may challenge any judge for no reason whatsoever. The catch is that a party may do that only once. The party must also exercise the challenge under oath and before actually appearing before the objectionable, assigned judge. Presiding Judges don't like peremptory challenges, so any technical error by a party will be used to deny the challenge.

"So, who's up?" DD handed Joe the list he and Rick had figured out.

Looking at it, Joe thought out loud: "Newman, Riordan and Sabatini. Not bad. Defendants won't like any of them. I think we're dead."

"Maybe not."

Rick walked into Joe's office all decked out in his trial day best.

"Rita McMurray is coming open this morning. That gives us four and Delia Harris will be available *pro tem* tomorrow. It will depend on whether people in front of us will get the good guys and how smart our defense is in the use of the challenges."

***

CHAPTER TWENTY-SIX

Trial

Monday morning in the department of the Presiding Judge is the convening of legal energy and foreboding of monumental proportions. The din of voices – casual, anxious, angry – is overwhelming. Everyone is dressed in their trial duds – suits, ties, skirts, heels, shined shoes, done hair. DD was a spectator, something he had never been. Joe's adrenaline was rushing through his body and, strangely, it left him calm – taut and alert – but calm.

Jimmy O'Hearn has a balding red head with large freckles on every square inch of skin that he exposed. Not a big guy, but a very experienced one.

"Ladies and Gentlemen. Find a seat. Say your last words until addressed by me or the court. If you intend to challenge any assigned judge, you must have your affidavits ready, read it into the record, make sure it is signed, and hand it to Marie. Remember, if you haven't made your motion for a continuance, you may not make one now unless somebody died over the weekend – like the plaintiff, the defendant, or key witness. In that event, be prepared to prove it."

Marie, the clerk, announced Judge Noah Benjamin, and he took the bench quickly – all business.

"Lot's to do ladies and gentlemen. We have four and maybe five courts; many of you will be assigned." He nodded to O'Hearn.

Jimmy called the first case on the trial calendar. The lawyers rose and announced that it had been settled. Pavlone was called.

Joe regarded this moment as one of the most thrilling in the trade:

"Joe Cleary, your honor. Ready for the plaintiff."

There had been some mumbling among the defense team about asking for a continuance. Having been dissuaded by the announcement of Jimmy O'Hearn, no motion was made. They announced they were ready.

"Excuse me your honor, I'm Lionel Woodman of the firm of Shelby, Sutcliff, and Woodman of Los Angeles. I am sorry to say that I am not aware of this court's view of the rule of peremptory challenges. That is to say, I am representing the Defendant firm of Loudon, Mueller and Keislor. Mr. Keislor is separately represented. Will Mr. Keislor get one challenge and the firm another?"

For some inexplicable reason, Woodman let his question stand at that. So Judge Benjamin simply said "No."

Looking at a large printed sheet, Judge Benjamin then intoned, "The Pavlone matter is assigned to department 49, Judge John Newman."

Immediately, Ruud popped up and announced that Keislor would challenge the assignment to Newman. Jimmy O'Hearn stood and addressed the Court,

"Your honor, may I pick up Mr. Ruud's affidavit for the record?"

"Go ahead. In the meantime, Mr. Ruud please be sworn by the clerk."

Ruud was sworn and he recited the magic words, that Judge Newman was known to him and/or his client and that he in good faith believed that Judge Newman was biased against him and/or his client. In this instance, there was probably truth to the statement because John Newman had held Keislor in contempt of court in another case for refusing to turn over documents in discovery that the judge had ordered turned over.

Another case was assigned to Judge Newman and Pavlone was called again. Judge Benjamin announced that Judge Jack Riordan would be unavailable to preside over a case that was expected to take six weeks to try. "I am therefore assigning this matter to Judge Sidney Sabatini in Department 52."

Joe's heart was in his throat. Sabatini was a well-known legal scholar, teaching constitutional law at the University of

San Francisco law school. Joe had served with him on a panel to analyze the constitutional issues raised by the proposed civil procedure rules of the Court. Sabatini trusted Joe, and most people in the trial bar knew it. Surely, the remaining defendants would challenge him. They didn't.

Rick called Turk Street from the hall phone while Joe picked up the file cart to transport the voluminous court files to Department 52.

"Jeannie? We got a Court and we got a judge. Sabatini. Tell the witnesses and Judith. It's showtime."

The law clerks brought the Turk Street files over in hand trucks. Exhibits for the opening statement had been prepared and wrapped. It all had an air not unlike a Cecil B. DeMille production.

Counsel assembled in the judge's chambers for the initial briefing. Sidney Sabatini was one of the most senior members of the San Francisco trial bench. He was the rare academic who had fairly extensive experience in private practice as a trial lawyer because he never taught full time. As a young man, he had helped frame the argument for the plaintiffs in the Japanese Internment cases, thereby establishing his reputation in Constitutional cases. This was a fact he could never understand, because his clients lost the cases on internment.

A wiry, black-haired man of about 65 years, Sabatini always wore short sleeved shirts under his judicial robes and often during court, while considering some issue, he would place his hands on his face, revealing his slender forearms covered with black hair. Born of a well-off Portuguese family in Rio de Janero, Brazil, the judge emigrated as a teen with his mother, who had been effectively deported upon the complaint of his father. He grew up in Fremont – East San Francisco Bay – opening his practice in the late forties.

"I've read the newspaper reports and caught some television coverage of this case, gentlemen. The coverage is so vague and generalized, I don't think our jury pool has been tainted. Make a motion, if you wish. I'm only suggesting that

309

right now I don't see that as a problem. However, I do intend to issue a gag order. There will be a lot of heat generated in a trial like this and I do not want to give you guys an excuse to vent your spleen with the press."

"Do you intend some restrictions on the press as well?" Woodman asked.

"Yes." Judge Sabatini sifted through some papers in front him and pulled one out.

"When the panel for the jury comes in, I need those seats. The press will have to relinquish them. There will be no TV cameras or lights or even radio recording equipment in the court room or in the hallway until further order of this court. I am suggesting, but not requiring, that the media pool their personnel to ease crowding. If that doesn't happen and the press disturbs the running of the trial or fails to yield to parties and other participants' seats, then I'll be more assertive on this issue. I am informing the press that you and your clients are under a gag order so that they should refrain from trying to interview you. Is there anything else I should do?"

The judge was sitting in his short-sleeved shirt, leaning back in his chair behind his desk, turning from his media order and reading off what was apparently a checklist he had composed after learning he was assigned this case.

"As Mr. Cleary can tell you, I don't like conferences at the bench with the jury just sitting there. First of all, I don't think jurors are idiots. Secrets should not be kept from them. When they are told to disregard something they've heard, I believe they will. Secondly, these people come in here and give a part of their life to this system. It doesn't work without them. We just aren't going to waste their time sitting around while we lawyers hassle over legal points which are probably meaningless anyway. Third, we will run full tilt from 9:30 a.m. to 4:30 p.m., 45 minutes for lunch, Monday through Thursday. If you have a motion or anything else that can't be handled in breaks outside the presence of the jury on that schedule, we'll deal with them at 2:30 p.m. on Friday, after my Friday calendar. So, except in extreme circumstances, don't ask for a conference at the bench while the jury is present. Any questions?"

Ruud asked, "Your honor, as you know, my client, Hugh Keislor, is a practicing attorney. As such, he cannot spend his time here in Court every day..."

The judge cut him off and turned to Joe.

"Did you serve notice that he was to be present?"

"Yes. We served that notice for all defendants individually and for their lead executives."

The judge turned to Ruud. "What do you want me to do? Notices to appear can't be willy-nilly ignored."

Appearing affable, Ruud replied, "Of course, your honor, but it seems fair that Mr. Cleary give us notice of which of the defendants he intends to call and when."

Judge Sabatini sat forward. "I don't think so. We're going to have an order that requires each party to disclose who they are going to call twenty-four hours in advance, but that order will not apply to parties. Other than parties, if you fail to disclose, you can't call the witness and run the risk of me forcing you to rest if you don't have a witness. I routinely issue an order that prohibits prospective witnesses from being in the courtroom. It is counsel's responsibility to enforce that order. We have a sign for the courtroom door, but if a prospective witness gets in during testimony, that witness will not testify. Parties are excepted. So, let's go pick the jury. The candidates are on the way."

Joe emerged from chambers to find his trial mate, briefcase, boxes, and exhibits all set up and ready to go. It occurred to him that this is the point in this trial that DD and Rick were in the first trial, when the conspiracy was working feverishly at their dastardly scheme. The prospective jurors began filing in, led by Jimmy O'Hearn. Joe smiled and thought to himself, *what a collection of humanity!*

Jury selection was tedious and predictably long. The length of the trial brought on many claims of hardship from the jury pool. The City and County at the time paid jurors $12 a day. There was no general practice of employers keeping jurors at full salary while serving, except public employers and the utilities such as the gas company, the telephone company and the electric company. Retired people usually had no problem with serving, so that the jurors for the longer trials are predominantly made up of civil servants, utility company employees, and retirees – all more conservative than the general population. It took a day and a half to get a jury. Opening statements were to begin the next day.

There were two major demonstrative exhibits for the plaintiff that served Joe's one-hour-long opening statement. The first became known as "dot-to-dot." It was a large foam board illustration visually connecting each of the defendants together and to elements of the claims that Judith was making. As the evidence came in through the witnesses and the documents, the penciled lines would be traced with felt pen in ink.

The second was the timeline. This listed the events the evidence was expected to show in chronological order. Chronologies often are powerful evidence of conspiracy and, of themselves, proof that each event occurred. With the "dot-to-dot," it served well to make Joe's opening very clear. The jury was riveted.

It was noon when Joe finished and the Judge broke for lunch. The defense would do their respective opening that afternoon. Ruud waited until the jury cleared the room and Joe was standing at counsel table alone.

"Good opening, Mr. Cleary. You and I know you can't prove that stuff, but it certainly is impressive. So, now let's talk some sense and discuss resolving this case."

At that point Lionel Woodman joined the conversation.

"Tyler, if you think I can't prove what I said, you are going have a terrible time during this trial. And if that's the premise for your suggestion, that we resolve this by settlement, there really isn't anything to talk about."

Ruud chuckled. "You're a tough guy, aren't you Cleary? So what do you want?"

"Whether I'm tough is a question you'll have to answer after the trial. What are you offering?"

"We think you got more from *Internacionale* and Bidwell than the case is worth. Quads always bring a lot of money – if you hit. I don't know how you think you can prove that Ms. Pavlone would have prevailed if Ella Mae White had not been bribed. Even if you get to that point, you can't get Keislor for anything other than being a dummy. Anyway, I am pretty sure I can get a million dollars between my people and Woodman's client. That gives you a cool five million – enough to take care of Ms. Pavlone's problems for the rest of her life."

Joe put his foot up on the counsel chair and smiled at Ruud and Woodman.

"I am not going to argue the merits with you guys. I came here to make my case before the judge and the jury. I won't waste my time and energy explaining what you should already know. Anyway, that isn't enough money, but you should know that money won't be the issue for settlement."

Ruud was surprised. "What do you mean?"

"I mean that if there is an agreement on money there will also be an agreement that does not permit your clients to claim they did nothing wrong – the non-admission clause will not be agreed to. Neither will there be any language in the settlement agreement that characterizes money paid as anything but punitive damages."

Ruud laughed out loud. "You're kidding me! Are you saying that whatever amount of money is offered, these are conditions?"

"I am."

"Fuck you Cleary. That is not going to happen."

"Thanks for the thought, Tyler."

The defendants' opening statements contained no surprises, except a very cryptic reference by Ruud to "serious credibility problems of the plaintiff's principal witness, which will be revealed in the course of the evidence." Joe, Rick, and DD concluded at the break that this was a reference to either

Darla or David Weisenstock or both. It was useless to worry about it. It was time to start the evidence.

THE COURT: Your first witness Mr. Cleary?

MR. CLEARY: The first witness for the plaintiff, your honor, is the Defendant Hugh Keislor. He is being called, your honor, pursuant to Evidence Code section 776.

[Keislor's eyes betrayed his surprise and possibly fear. He had discussed this possibility with his lawyers, but all had decided Cleary would not try to take on so formidable a courtroom tactician as Keislor – particularly early in the case. Keislor, his lawyers, and their assistants had pored over the deposition transcripts in an attempt to discern whether there was anything Keislor had said or which was attributed to him that would tempt the plaintiff to call him as a hostile witness. They could find nothing. Joe had counted on that.]

[Keislor smiled broadly as he stepped into the pit in front of the judge and held up his hand to be sworn. As big as he was, he moved deftly and quickly into the witness chair. He looked directly at Joe and it was apparent to all that the battle was on.]

QUESTION: Mr. Keislor, you are a named partner in the law firm of Loudon, Mueller and Keislor – is that correct?

ANSWER: Yes.

QUESTION: You would describe your role in that firm as its chief trial lawyer, wouldn't you?

ANSWER: [Remembering that he had said that during the deposition] Yes.

QUESTION: That firm employed Darla Willingham Reid as a secretary, didn't it?

314

ANSWER: Yes.

QUESTION: The same Ms. Reid left the firm's employ about four years ago when she married David Weisenstock – correct?

ANSWER: That's my understanding.

QUESTION: Why can't you just answer the question by a simple "yes"?

ANSWER: Well, I can say yes to the obvious, that is, that she left our employ about four years ago.

QUESTION: So the marriage is your "understanding"? But you attended the wedding reception, didn't you?

ANSWER: Yes.

QUESTION: So, you don't have any doubt, do you, that Ms. Reid married Mr. Weisenstock?

ANSWER: No, I don't have any doubt.

[Joe had served notice that he wasn't going to let Keislor slide on any point.]

QUESTION: Wasn't Mr. Weisenstock in the insurance business?

ANSWER: Yes.

QUESTION: He did a lot of business with your firm, didn't he?

ANSWER: That depends on how you define "a lot."

[With barely a second's hesitation, Joe turned to counsel table and picked up a copy of the transcript of Keislor's deposition taken months before.]

MR. CLEARY: Your honor may I approach the witness? I want to hand him this transcript of his deposition.

COURT: Yes. What page or pages will you be referring to Mr. Cleary?

MR. CLEARY: Page 114, your honor, beginning at line 10.

QUESTION: Mr. Keislor, you do recall that you have previously given testimony under oath in response to questions I asked at a deposition?

ANSWER: Yes. [Keislor turned to face Joe squarely – sitting up and uncrossing his legs.]

QUESTION: Does the transcript I've handed you appear to be a true copy of the verbatim report of your deposition testimony?

ANSWER: [Keislor almost smirked.] I couldn't possibly tell that without reading every page and comparing it to the one that I signed. [He sat back, satisfied that he had stymied Joe.]

[Joe turned to the judge without any hint of being stymied.]

MR. CLEARY: Your honor, pursuant to the rules of this Court, our office deposited with the clerk the original deposition transcripts taken by us in this matter – in particular one signed by Mr. Keislor. It is in a sealed envelope. Could we break that one open and show it to him. I think it will save time."

[Shirley Chen, the court's clerk, had anticipated Joe. She handed the judge a large sealed envelope and a letter opener.]

[Ceremoniously, Judge Sabatini opened the envelope, removed the transcript and handed it to Keislor, who sheepishly took it. His meaningless resistance was over.]

COURT: Let the record show that I have handed the witness a transcript that indicates it is the deposition of the witness and it is labeled "Original." The last page inside the cover bears what appears to be an original signature. Mr. Keislor, is that your signature?

ANSWER: Yes.

COURT: Is there any question, sir, that this is a verbatim transcript of the questions put to you and the answers you gave at the deposition?

ANSWER: No, your honor.

COURT: Mr. Cleary, please continue.

QUESTION: Looking at page 114 of that transcript, starting at line 10 – please read it to yourself.

ANSWER: [Keislor read it, or pretended to and then looked up]

QUESTION: For the record, Mr. Keislor, did you read that portion referred to?

ANSWER: Yes.

QUESTION: Isn't it true, Mr. Keislor, that you said under oath that your firm averaged $23 million in business annually with Mr. Weisenstock?

ANSWER: Yes.

QUESTION: Isn't it also true, sir, that when you gave that earlier testimony you described the volume of the business with Mr. Weisenstock as "a lot"?

ANSWER: Yes.

QUESTION: Is there anything that has come to your attention since that deposition that would change your mind?

ANSWER: No.

QUESTION: So, your firm did a lot of business with Mr. Weisenstock, correct?

ANSWER: Yes.

[This seemingly minor point was chosen as a point of resistance by Keislor because his trial experience dictated that he take control of the courtroom as soon as possible, or, at least, derail any momentum his opposition might be gaining. Joe was aware that Keislor would attempt to interfere with his presentation early in the examination. Joe won the small issue, but also demonstrated to Keislor he was not going to let Keislor take control or even get in the way of his presentation. The authority in the case quickly became Joe and the one who was wasting time was Keislor – that's what Joe wanted the jury to conclude. Of course, it also demonstrated that Joe thought Keislor was a fool and could prove it.]

QUESTION: Please describe what this business was that your firm did with Weisenstock.

ANSWER: He was kind of a special insurance adjuster. He would undertake to investigate and adjust a claim against an insured of an insurance company. I guess you could say he was a freelance insurance adjuster. He didn't work for just one company. If a claim could not be resolved informally and litigation appeared likely, he would refer the case to our firm to conduct that litigation.

QUESTION: Did most of these claims involve product liability – that is allegations that an insured's product was defective and caused injury?

ANSWER: Yes.

QUESTION: Isn't it true that you were the lead trial lawyer in all cases referred to your firm by Mr. Weisenstock?

ANSWER: I believe I was.

QUESTION: You told us at deposition that you in fact were the lead trial in all of those cases – isn't that correct?

ANSWER: [Having learned his lesson, Keislor dropped his head as if to examine his shoes.] Yes.

QUESTION: In the trial five years ago involving Ms. Pavlone's injury – you were the lead trial lawyer, correct?

ANSWER: Yes

QUESTION: And that case was brought to your firm by Mr. Weisenstock, isn't that right?

ANSWER: Yes.

QUESTION: That trial was about Ms. Pavlone's claim that the car in which she received her injury was defectively designed – correct?

ANSWER: Yes

QUESTION: Returning to Mrs. Weisenstock, the former Ms. Reid – did you hire her?

ANSWER: Yes.

QUESTION: When you hired her, were you aware she was on probation from a conviction for prostitution?

ANSWER: Yes.

QUESTION: When you hired her, were you aware that she had been arrested multiple times for prostitution and pandering?

MR.RUUD: Objection your honor. This is not relevant.

THE COURT: Well, I am looking at the Plaintiff's witness list and I find that this very Ms. Reid or Mrs. Weisenstock is on it. Mr. Cleary would seem to be impeaching his own witness before she is even on the stand. But, in any event, I am going to allow it. [Looking at Keislor] Answer the question.

ANSWER: [It was fruitless, Keislor thought, to deny it. Cleary must have the Probation records that document correspondence with Keislor.] Yes.

QUESTION: Beginning shortly after Ms. Reid went to work, you and she began having a sexual relationship. Isn't that correct?

MR. RUUD: Your honor, this is outrageous. Such a question can only be designed to impugn my client's general character and is not otherwise relevant.

THE COURT: Mr. Cleary?

MR. CLEARY: Thank you, your honor. In his answer to the complaint and in answers to questions posed during the deposition, Mr. Keislor denies that he knows anything about the conspiracy to bribe a juror in the 1979 trial of Ms. Pavlone's claim.

But, this very Ms. Reid was a central figure in that conspiracy and she has testified under oath to that fact. Her then future husband, with whom Mr. Keislor 's firm did $23 million a year in business, was likewise a central figure in that conspiracy. This sexual relationship lasted for over two years, including a short time after her marriage to David Weisenstock.

Evidence that Mr. Keislor was so involved is also evidence from which the jury would obviously be permitted to infer he knew about the conspiracy.

THE COURT: You intend to call Ms. Reid as a witness, Mr. Cleary?

MR. CLEARY: Yes, indeed.

THE COURT: Mr. Ruud, does Mr. Keislor deny knowledge of this conspiracy?

MR. RUUD: He does.

THE COURT: [Again to Ruud] Are you aware that Ms. Reid has admitted participation in this conspiracy?

MR. RUUD: Yes. But she did so as part of a plea agreement with the San Francisco District Attorney. She doesn't say that Mr. Keislor was a participant or that he had this knowledge.

THE COURT: What does she say?

MR. RUUD: I don't think it's appropriate to reveal to the jury what she said at this juncture. It is objectionable as speculation and lacks a foundation. May we approach the bench?

THE COURT: No. Mr. Cleary what is your response?

MR. CLEARY: The question pending is whether the witness had a sexual relationship with an admitted participant in the conspiracy to bribe a juror in a trial in which the witness was not only the employer of this conspirator but also the lead defense attorney in that trial. The objection is relevancy and that is obviously not well taken. There is no reason for a bench conference.

THE COURT: I agree. Mr. Ruud you either took Ms. Reid's deposition or you had the opportunity to do so. With that and your cross examination when she takes the stand you have all the right the law allows to attack her veracity. The objection is overruled. Answer the question Mr. Keislor.

ANSWER: Yes. I couldn't end it because I did not want to hurt her. She was very much in love with me.

[No one involved on the plaintiff's side in this case could understand why Keislor added to his answer the belief that Darla loved him. He had to be aware of what she had said on the subject in her grand jury testimony and in her sworn statement before that – that material had all been given to him in discovery. As shall be seen, however, it is consistent with Keislor's mindset as revealed in the testimony.]

QUESTION: During the trial of the earlier Pavlone case, Ms. Reid worked with you – that's right isn't it?

ANSWER: Yes.

QUESTION: And she was frequently in the courtroom during that trial, right?

ANSWER: Yes.

QUESTION: She in fact was there during jury selection, wasn't she?

ANSWER: Yes. I usually have one even two people help keep track of jury answers to questions.

QUESTION: At that time, you also employed another person as a legal assistant with the firm by the name of Drucinda Lacey, correct?

ANSWER: Yes.

QUESTION: And she also worked on the Pavlone trial, didn't she?

ANSWER: Yes.

QUESTION: Ms. Lacey was a law school graduate, wasn't she?

ANSWER: Yes.

QUESTION: She was also in the courtroom assisting you in the Pavlone jury selection, isn't that true?

ANSWER: Yes.

QUESTION: She no longer works for the firm does she?

ANSWER: No, she doesn't. She's dead.

QUESTION: In fact, Ms. Lacey was murdered in her apartment the night she had been released from jail on bail, isn't that right?

ANSWER: Yes, that's my understanding.

QUESTION: It's also true that Ms. Lacey had been indicted by the San Francisco Grand Jury for participation in the conspiracy to bribe Ms. White, isn't it?

ANSWER: Yes.

QUESTION: Do you remember the selection of one Ella Mae White to the Pavlone jury back in 1979?

ANSWER: I had no independent recollection until I reviewed transcripts from that trial about two years ago. When I did that, my memory was refreshed, so that I can say that I do remember it.

QUESTION: Do you recall that Ms. White was black?

ANSWER: Yes.

QUESTION: When she was being considered as a juror, did you have the right to prevent her from being seated – the right to challenge her?

ANSWER: Yes

QUESTION: Why didn't you challenge her?

ANSWER: I don't know. I guess I thought she would be a good juror.

QUESTION: The fact is, Mr. Keislor, that you have strong feelings that a black woman is a bad choice as a juror in a product liability case where there have been serious injuries – isn't that true?

ANSWER: No. That's not true at all.

[Joe turned to counsel table and picked up a small file folder. Opening it, he walked to the clerk's table. Keislor tensed as he looked at Ruud.]

QUESTION: Are you a member of the National Product Liability Defense Lawyers' Association?

ANSWER: Yes.

QUESTION: Have you given tutorial speeches at the proceedings of that organization?

ANSWER: [Realizing where Cleary was going, Keislor tried to get Ruud's attention by a nod of his head.]

THE COURT: Don't do that Mr. Keislor. If you want a break to consult with Mr. Ruud you will have to wait until Mr. Cleary finishes this point.

MR. CLEARY: I think I've got an answer coming from you Mr. Keislor.

ANSWER: Yes, but those are built on hypothetical cases, not real ones.

QUESTION: Then you recall, don't you, giving this tutorial address at the proceedings of this lawyer association two years before the Pavlone trial?

ANSWER: Yes, but I want to explain.

QUESTION: Certainly, but that will have to wait until the jury learns what it is that you said in this presentation back in 1977. I'm handing you a document that is entitled *Proceedings of the Sixth Annual Convention of the National Product Liability Defense Lawyers' Association, June 8-12, 1978, New Orleans, Louisiana. Transcript of the Remarks of Hugh Keislor, Loudon, Mueller & Keislor, San Francisco California.* Have you seen a copy of that before?

ANSWER: Yes.

QUESTION: Does this transcript reflect accurately what you said on that occasion?

ANSWER: Yes.

QUESTION: Would you please read that portion of your remarks that I have bracketed in the margin?

ANSWER: [Keislor looked at Ruud and then at the Judge as if he was seeking help to be relieved of this ordeal.]

THE COURT: Go ahead, Mr. Keislor.

ANSWER: [reluctantly, Keislor read out loud] "Mr. Keislor: The question is: are there demographic factors that I rely on in selection of jurors in product liability cases? There is only one hard and fast rule that I have never broken and probably never will and that is I will not permit a black woman to sit on any product liability jury where the plaintiff is seriously injured. They just don't care about the science – they care about taking care of that injured plaintiff."

THE COURT: [the judge sighed and looked over the courtroom to assess the reaction to what had just happened. He reached for his gavel.]

Ok. This is a good time to take our lunch break. Please be in the jury room by 1:30 – don't be late.

After assuring himself that the rest of the documents for Keislor's examination were in order, Joe grabbed his bag lunch and joined Rick, Pat, Jeannie, and DD in the rotunda. It was decided that Darla would have to be the next witness – she was already on the 24-hour list delivered to Defense counsel. Pat would have to talk to the sheriff's office to make sure she was ready. Ruud might take the chance to examine Keislor today and maybe Woodman, as well. If they did, the day would be shot and Darla wouldn't be needed until tomorrow.

"Maybe we better get David in. He's not getting any better." DD suggested. "Is he on the 24-hour list?"

Pat checked. "He is."

"I've got about another hour of questions for Keislor. Hopefully that inspires Ruud to get active now. Pat, did we order a transcript of Ruud's opening statement?"

"Yep, Woodman's too."

Pat was working off her checklist.

THE COURT: Let the record show that we are reconvened following the lunch break. All counsel are present and the jury is in place. Mr. Keislor is on the witness stand. Mr. Keislor, please understand that you are still under oath. Mr. Cleary?

QUESTION: Before the break, Mr. Keislor, you told us that you refreshed your recollection of jury selection in the first Pavlone trial by reviewing transcripts of that proceeding. Do you now recall why it is that you did not challenge the seating of Ms. White as a juror?

ANSWER: She was initially seated as an alternate juror. When a vacancy occurred on the main jury, she took that place. Yes, I recall that.

QUESTION: Why did you not exercise your right to challenge her – that's the question?

ANSWER: Both Darla and Dru thought I should keep her.

QUESTION: So, in spite of your strong feelings against permitting a black woman to sit on a product liability jury, you decided not to exercise your right to challenge Ms. White – that's what you're meaning to tell us?

ANSWER: Yes.

QUESTION: And there is no argument, is there, that it was your choice, not that of your secretary or your legal assistant?

ANSWER: Right.

QUESTION: Did your secretary and/or your legal assistant explain to you why they thought Ms. White would make a good juror for the defense in that trial?

ANSWER: No.

QUESTION: Was there any discussion between you as to why you should keep Ms. White on the jury?

ANSWER: No.

QUESTION: Do you recall your firm issuing a kind of biographical pamphlet on the partners and leading associates?

ANSWER: [This seeming change of direction was greeted with relief by Keislor, but only briefly.] Yes. It was informational for clients and potential clients...an effort to attract business without crossing the advertising limitations set by the State Bar. Max edited it. Each of us wrote his own biography.

QUESTION: So, you wrote this about yourself in this brochure? "Mr. Keislor is a fierce litigator who rarely concedes even the most apparently minor issues. He is independent and exercises his own judgment in every instance."

ANSWER: [Surprisingly, Keislor blushed.] Yes, I guess I did.

QUESTION: In this instance, Mr. Keislor, you didn't contest the issue of whether Ms. White should sit on the Pavlone jury and you most certainly didn't exercise your independent judgment on the question – did you?

MR. RUUD: Objection. The question is argumentative.

THE COURT: You can answer the question Mr. Keislor.

ANSWER: [Keislor took a long drink of water. When he took the paper cup away from his lips, his hand was clearly shaking. He just didn't look like the old arrogant, self confident, on-rushing Hugh. His answer was barely audible.] No, I didn't.

QUESTION: Mr. Keislor, you acted as lead defense counsel in the case of Branson v Lorraine that was tried in Alameda County, across the Bay, in 1979, isn't that correct?

ANSWER: [Keislor was expecting this] Yes.

QUESTION: In that case, the plaintiff – Eric Branson – had been seriously injured when the tower crane he was operating collapsed, isn't that correct?

ANSWER: Yes. He was a paraplegic.

QUESTION: The plaintiff's lawyer in that case asserted that the crane's design was defective and that this defect caused the collapse and thus the injuries to Mr. Branson. Isn't that right?

ANSWER: [Recovering slightly, Keislor sat more upright and looked at Joe] Well, that's what he claimed. The truth is the wind was so strong that day that Branson should either have not operated the crane, or should have done so with more caution. Whatever defect the plaintiff claimed could not have had anything to do with the accident.

QUESTION: In fact that is what the plaintiff expert testified to at the trial – that the defect could not have caused the accident – isn't that true?

ANSWER: Yes. It was on my cross examination that he made that admission.

QUESTION: The result was that the jury brought back a defense verdict, isn't that right?

ANSWER: Of course.

QUESTION: And you attribute that result to your cross-examination?

ANSWER: [Once more] Of course.

QUESTION: During the deposition of that expert in Branson – a deposition that you took months before the trial – you had asked this expert whether the weather or anything that Branson failed to do had caused the accident, isn't that true?

ANSWER: That's what I remember.

QUESTION: In the deposition, Mr. Keislor, this expert had said that the design defect caused the accident, not the weather or Mr. Branson's negligence – right?

ANSWER: Yes.

QUESTION: So his trial testimony was in direct contradiction of his deposition testimony?

ANSWER: That happens with these experts. They fabricate easily in the context of an informal deposition, but when it comes to open trial with a judge and all, they fold and tell the truth. It's really a matter of a lawyer having the experience and will to make them come clean. [The old Hugh was surfacing]

QUESTION: You've read Mrs. Weisenstock's grand jury testimony and sworn statement haven't you?

ANSWER: You mean Darla's? Yes.

QUESTION: Do you recall reading that Mrs. Weisenstock, your former secretary, says that in Branson she and Dru Lacey seduced that same engineer prior to trial and after he signed his deposition, and filmed the results of that seduction?

ANSWER: I recall reading that, but I really doubt that
is true.

QUESTION: Why do you doubt that Mrs. Weisenstock is telling the truth?

ANSWER: Because she was obviously gilding the lily to persuade the district attorney to take a lighter penalty for her crimes. She was also trying to make me look foolish.

QUESTION: She confessed to several crimes, why would she gratuitously add this if it didn't happen?

ANSWER: I don't know.

Hopefully the jury will conclude that the best evidence Keislor is a fool is his own testimony.

QUESTION: [Joe again went to counsel table and picked up a file folder, removing two sheets of paper from it.] Your honor, I would have marked for

330

identification as Plaintiff's exhibit No. 2 this single sheet of paper dated October 10, 1978. It is handwritten and appears to bear the initials DL. There's a copy for you, and I wish to have the witness review this original.

[Joe handed the marked exhibit to Keislor.]

QUESTION: Mr. Keislor, do you recognize the handwriting on Exhibit 2?

ANSWER: [Looking at the sheet, Keislor coughed and then coughed again. He looked at Ruud and then at Joe.] It looks like Dru's handwriting.

QUESTION: The handwriting of the late Drucinda Lacey – correct?

ANSWER: Correct.

MR. CLEARY: Your honor I move the admission of this document into evidence.

THE COURT: [The judge looked at Ruud and Woodman. Hearing no objection, he intoned] No. 2 is admitted into evidence.

QUESTION: Mr. Keislor, please read aloud for the jury the contents of exhibit No. 2.

ANSWER: [Again looking about for help, but finding none, Keislor read the contents of the exhibit – four questions suggested to Keislor on October 10, 1978 to ask the plaintiff's expert at the trial of the matter of Branson v Lorraine.]

[Again turning to counsel table, Joe picked up two volumes of a transcript, and turned to the Judge.]

MR. CLEARY: Your honor, I'd like marked as plaintiff's next in order a volume of transcript from the matter of <u>Branson v Lorraine.</u> You will note your honor that there is a certification of a public record on the front of this volume. I obtained this from the clerk of the court of appeals where the record had been filed in connection with Mr. Branson's appeal. I'd like to hand it to the witness.

THE COURT: Very well.

QUESTION: Mr. Keislor, please turn to page 447 of Exhibit No. 3, and I call your attention to line 2. Do you see that?

ANSWER: Yes.

QUESTION: This portion of the transcript is recording your cross examination of the plaintiff's expert in that trial, correct?

ANSWER: [Keislor was beginning to realize what was about to happen and he was desperately trying to figure out a way to stop it. He looked at Ruud, who was apparently going through the same feelings.] May we have a break, your honor?

THE COURT: No.

MR. RUUD: May we approach the bench your honor?

THE COURT: No. Answer the question Mr. Keislor.

ANSWER: Yes. It reports my cross-examination of the plaintiff's expert.

QUESTION: Please read aloud for the court and jury each question – just the questions – you posed to that expert at that trial concerning the cause of the accident.

ANSWER: [Reluctantly, slowly, Keislor complied.]

QUESTION: The questions you asked this witness at the trial were exactly the same questions that the late Ms. Lacey had suggested to you in the note that is Exhibit 2 – isn't that true?

ANSWER: That often happens. It was really her role to help me prepare and this is the sort of thing she did.

QUESTION: Did she tell you often, as she did here, that – to quote from Exhibit 2 – "These will definitely work."?

ANSWER: No, I don't remember.

QUESTION: Why would she tell you that here?

ANSWER: I....I don't know.

QUESTION: Have you been made aware of the deposition I took of the former head of metallurgy at the Lawrence Laboratory in Livermore?

ANSWER: Yes. I think I have.

QUESTION: The professor was the individual that had been designated as the plaintiff's expert in the Branson matter – isn't that correct?

ANSWER: Yes.

QUESTION: Do you remember what he said in that deposition about why he changed his testimony?

ANSWER: Oh, yes. It was claptrap. He says that Dru and Darla seduced him and then blackmailed him into changing his testimony. That just couldn't be true.

QUESTION: Why would he lie?

ANSWER: I don't know – maybe just to excuse himself for being such a lousy engineer in the first place.

[Keislor was slumping in the witness chair. He just had not realized how this would happen. Joe permitted a short respite from the hard driving questions. He paused sympathetically – or apparently so.]

QUESTION: How old was Ms. Lacey when she died?

ANSWER: Thirty something?

Question: You wouldn't be surprised to find that she was 32, would you?

ANSWER: No.

[Joe again went to counsel table and picked up a file folder. From it, he removed a photograph, maybe 4" x 6," and turned to the Judge.]

MR. CLEARY: Your honor, I'd like marked for identification as Plaintiff's Exhibit 4 a 4x6, black and white photograph of five women wearing what I would call bed clothing.

THE COURT: [Looking at the photograph] "Bed clothing"? C'mon Mr. Cleary. Even an old guy like me calls this apparel "negligee," maybe even "babydolls." The point, I think, is that they are mostly naked.

MR. CLEARY: Very well your honor. I am showing the defendant Exhibit 4. Mr. Keislor have you ever seen this before?

ANSWER: Only as a result of getting it in discovery from your office in this case.

QUESTION: Can you identify any of the women in the picture?

ANSWER: Yes. In the middle, that's Dru. The woman on the right side is Laura McNeeley. She was a clerk of this court and has since died.

QUESTION: And the black woman in the center, with her arm around Dru?

ANSWER: I don't know her, but I have been told that is Malvina Montrose. The other black woman to the left is Ella Mae White.

QUESTION: Mr. Keislor, do you have any doubt that this photograph was taken before the Pavlone trial?

ANSWER: [Barely audible] No.

QUESTION: And isn't that because Ms. McNeeley died two months before the Pavlone trial began?

ANSWER: Yes.

MR. CLEARY: I would move the admission of this photograph as Plaintiff's next-in-order, your honor.

COURT: The photograph is admitted as exhibit No. 4.

[Again, Joe leaned over counsel table, sorting through file folders and then picking one up.]

MR. CLEARY: Your honor, I would ask the clerk to mark this letter dated November 15, 1979 on the letterhead of this Defendant's law firm as Plaintiff's next in order.

MS. CHIN: Plaintiffs No 5, your honor.

MR. CLEARY: I am handing the Defendant a copy of Exhibit No. 5 and ask that he read it.

QUESTION: Mr. Keislor, having read Exhibit No. 5, do you recognize it?

ANSWER: Yes. I wrote it to Mr. Yamaguchi.

QUESTION: This letter concerns the settlement of a claim against Mr. Yamaguchi and his computer graphics firm brought by Malvina Montrose – isn't that right?

ANSWER: Yes.

QUESTION: Mr. Yamaguchi and his insurer paid a significant sum of money to Ms. Montrose in settlement of that claim, correct?

ANSWER: No.

QUESTION: The money was actually paid to an annuity company on behalf of – not Malvina Montrose, but Ella Mae White – correct?

ANSWER: Yes.

QUESTION: That was because the payment had nothing to do with the claim of Malvina Montrose for a sexual assault, but was for Ms. White's delivery of a defense verdict in the Pavlone case – isn't that true?

ANSWER: I don't know. I didn't negotiate the settlement.

QUESTION: You didn't negotiate the settlement; it was David Weisenstock who negotiated the settlement, wasn't it?

ANSWER: Yes.

Joe's examination of Keislor went pretty much that way for the rest of the day. Although he didn't formally end it, he was essentially done, and so was Keislor. Ruud had barely moved out of his chair while Joe – case by case – pinned Keislor to Dru Lacey and Darla and Weisenstock in litigation that went badly for the plaintiffs. Witnesses had been bribed or compromised by the allure of one or the other or both of the women. A judge had been compromised, one had been killed in a hit and run. The defense in this the second Pavlone trial was unlikely to prevail.

**

CHAPTER TWENTY-SEVEN

Capitulation

By this time, the press in and outside the courtroom had swarmed in increased numbers. "Pools" had been formed, permitting the courtroom to be occupied by a handful of reporters, responsible for alerting the others to any pending action of particular interest. Reporters gathered down the hall from the courtroom to harvest the fruits of the pool while the parties and lawyers made their escape.

Back at Turk Street that evening, getting ready for the next day of trial, DD received a telephone call from Randall Young. It was Young who had seen Roy Lindstrom the night that Gerald Mann died in the San Quentin shooting nearly ten years before. When Jeannie told him Randall was on the phone, DD knew this was going to be a difficult conversation – Randall had brain damage in connection with the injury he had suffered at the hands of the police those many years before and it seemed to have gotten worse. He could barely talk and when he did, it was nearly impossible to figure out what he said. Always, DD had to rely on Randall's wife to figure out his pitiful grunts and moans.

After a few minutes, it seemed to DD that Randall was saying something about a subpoena. He asked Randall to put his wife on – something he hated to do because Randall did not comprehend why DD couldn't just take his word for it.

"This is Brenda,"

"What is this?"

"Dan, someone served a subpoena on Randall. He just handed it to me. It says he is supposed to show up in the San Francisco Superior Court – tomorrow! Shit, Dan, I can't do that. I've got to work. I miss enough time to take care of Randall!"

"Brenda, please tell me what else the subpoena says."

"It says Department 52 and it is signed by...I can't read the signature but the typed part says 'Tyler Ruud, Attorney for Hugh Keislor. ' "

"Relax. Don't go unless and until I call you. As it stands, there is no way they can put you on the stand tomorrow, so it won't formally come up. Go to work. Let me talk to Randall."

DD explained the same thing to Randall and then told Joe and Rick what had happened.

"You are on tomorrow's witness list. They just want Randall there for whatever value he might have to confuse you."

Joe was certain. "I think they want to excite that legendary temper of yours. They have to know that Randall is gorked."

Rick was equally certain. "Sure, they know you're protective and will hopefully blow up. Let's not waste any more time on this."

Joe returned to his preparation.

After a few minutes of looking at Weisenstock's transcript, DD went to Joe and Rick.

"This development of getting Randall Young involved is more interesting than we originally thought. There is one person who certainly knows about what Randall told me as his lawyer, and that is Melanie. There is likely at least one other person who knows that – her father. The defense lawyer from Pan American in Randall's case would certainly know. Of those three people: Robert is as gorked as Randall from that stroke unless he has had a miraculous recovery. The lawyer – Bingston, was his name – died three years ago of cancer in Minnesota. Under this line of thinking, the only person who could have told the defense about Randall was Melanie – a fugitive. What do you say we bring in the posse to discuss this with Ruud?"

Rick stood and laughed, as did Joe. Rick told Joe: "Jesus, I'm glad he's on our side."

The next morning it was immediately obvious that the press had picked up some information about something happening. They were out in force both in and at the door of the courtroom.

Joe and Rick had taken their places at Counsel table, as had Woodman and his young associate and counsel for Pan American, but Tyler Ruud wasn't there.

At a few minutes after nine, Judge Sabatini stepped out of his chambers and onto the bench.

THE COURT: Madam clerk, please call the Pavlone case.

THE CLERK: Pavlone versus Hugh Keislor and others, No. 1984-C02457, jury trial, Honorable Sidney Sabatini presiding.

THE COURT: The record should reflect that we are in the courtroom, out of the presence of the jury. Plaintiff's counsel are present, as is counsel for Pan American Trust and Liability and the law firm of Loudon, Mueller and Keislor, but there is no one present for the Defendant Hugh Keislor.

I received a telephone call this morning from Mr. Ruud. He tells me that he has been detained by the San Francisco police department and is now in the offices of the San Francisco District Attorney. District Attorney Lawrence Harrington confirmed this in a separate telephone conversation. It appears that Mr. Ruud will be held pending a ruling by this Court regarding a matter that may be material to this trial. I've set a hearing on that matter for 1:00 p.m. today. I am going to call the jury in and send them home for the day. This being Thursday, we'll reconvene for the purposes of continuing the evidence at 9:30 a.m., Monday.

Mr. Cleary, if Mr. O'Neil is in the hall, tell him his presence will be required for the hearing this afternoon. Adjourned.

There was a deafening clamor as reporters ran for the door and out into the hall.

"I guess Larry wants to catch Ms. Langley."

Joe was picking up his trial materials.

"Looks like," Rick echoed.

After lunch, the marble hallways of the fourth floor were packed with news people, including television cameras and lights when Joe, Rick, and DD made their way to Department 52. The presence of the video equipment was in violation of Judge Sabatini's order, so two bailiffs were in the process of ordering them removed under threat of arrest.

Then appearing from down the hall were several lawyers associated with the defense in the Pavlone matter. They assembled across the hall from the courtroom and plaintiff's counsel. The District Attorney and an assistant arrived from the other end of the hall. Each ignored the entreaties of the reporters as they approached the courtroom. Except for handshake greetings with the lawyers, little was said. Tyler Ruud, in the company of the prosecutors, was clearly chagrined.

Judge Sabatini was on the bench when the lawyers entered the courtroom.

THE COURT: Call the case please, Ms. Chin.

[She complied]

THE COURT: Present are all counsel – plus I see a couple extra; we'll get to that. Also present is the San Francisco District Attorney Lawrence Harrington and his chief trial deputy, Angelina Bettini. Would you additional lawyers please state your appearances for the record?

COUNSEL: Maynard Jones of the Ruud firm for Mr. Ruud, your honor. Kathleen Murdock, also of the Ruud firm for Mr. Ruud, your honor.

THE COURT: All right, Mr. Harrington, why don't you explain this for the record.

MR. HARRINGTON: A warrant was issued personally by me for the arrest of Mr. Ruud last night. Arresting officers could not locate him for the purpose of making the arrest until early this morning. He is still technically in custody pending a hearing on bail. I am sorry to interfere with this civil trial your honor, but the City and County have an urgent and highly important purpose in securing the presence of Mr. Ruud.

A woman by the name of Melanie Roberta Langley is a fugitive from an indictment and consequent warrant for her arrest for multiple counts of murder and conspiracy to commit murder, as well as for bribery and criminal fraud. She has been a fugitive for more than two years, your honor. Ella Mae White's death is, we allege, a consequence of Ms. Langley's activities, as is the death of Ms. White's lover, Malvina Montrose. We further allege that Ms. Langley is the murderer of Drucinda Lacey. All of these names are familiar to the court, I believe.

THE COURT: Indeed!

MR. HARRINGTON: For your information, your honor, there is also a conspiracy indictment issued in the state of New York, as well as murder and conspiracy indictments issued in the State of Mississippi – all for Ms. Langley. The San Francisco Police Department and the District Attorney's office, along with police and prosecutor's from these other jurisdictions have been vigorously searching for Ms. Langley all this time.

THE COURT: And Mr. Ruud's involvement?

MR. HARRINGTON: Day before yesterday, Mr. Ruud directed the serving of a subpoena on a local citizen, Randall Young. The subpoena commanded Mr. Young's presence in this court for this trial today. Mr. Young is a former client of Mr. O'Neil. He apparently told Mr. O'Neil during the course of that representation that he had seen Roy Lindstrom on the evening following the day Gerald Mann initiated a shoot-out with prison guards near the visitor's building at San Quentin. Mr. O'Neil mentioned that to his then wife – yes, Melanie Roberta Langley. The only living, competent person who knew what Mr. Young told Mr. O'Neil is Melanie Langley – that is to say, until someone told Tyler Ruud. I have concluded that Mr. Ruud has knowledge of the whereabouts of Ms. Langley. Because I know he knows she is a fugitive, I also concluded that he is withholding information as to her whereabouts; that's a felony.

THE COURT: You reach these conclusions solely based on the serving of the subpoena?

MR. HARRINGTON: Mr. Ruud was asked this morning, following his arrest, whether he had any other explanation. He asserted his fifth amendment right against incrimination and refused to answer. As we speak, the San Francisco Police Department is executing a search warrant on his office and we have subpoenaed his telephone records.

By the way, your honor, you should be aware that Mr. Ruud has, more than once, attempted to examine Mr. O'Neil on the subject of Roy Lindstrom and opposed a motion brought before Judge Benjamin to put a stop to it. He seems to be excessively interested in the subject. He even raised the issue in a television interview before any discovery had begun in this case two years ago. I can reach no other conclusion.

THE COURT: What am I supposed to do?

MS. MURDOCK: [A thirty-something-year-old, slim woman with long brown hair had risen to address the court, yellow pad in hand] The first thing that Mr. Ruud would ask your honor is to declare a mistrial here and permit a continuance until this problem described by Mr. Harrington may be resolved.

THE COURT: Why would I do that? We've invested four days in this trial thus far. The plaintiff has been able to exact testimony from Mr. Keislor that would likely not be repeated, except by reading a transcript to a future jury. There is nothing that has occurred here that would require a mistrial and a starting over.

MS. MURDOCK: Mr. Keislor will have lost his lead counsel, your honor. There are countless decisions by higher courts upholding grants of mistrials where a party has suffered the loss of counsel.

THE COURT: No, Ms. Murdock, you don't have that correct. Where a trial judge has granted a mistrial to a party losing trial counsel, the court of appeal won't disturb it. Here, I am not inclined to do that. Mr. Keislor has been ably represented by Mr. Ruud, but also by two or three other counsel throughout the case. I don't see why Mr. Ruud's "problem" as you call it, is so grave as not susceptible of solution by these other present counsel. What is more, there are two other parties in this case defending with very similar interests as Mr. Keislor. Each of those also has able counsel. I am denying your motion for a mistrial and for a continuance.

MR. CLEARY: I would also move to quash the subpoena of Mr. Young your honor. He is severely handicapped from injuries sustained years ago – he cannot talk clearly.

THE COURT: I am going to grant that motion but not for that reason. It has already been held in this case that the subject of the Gerald Mann jailbreak attempt and Roy Lindstrom are not relevant. So, there is no reason to have Mr. Young appear. If this fellow can't talk, Mr. Ruud, why would you want him to appear?

MR. JONES: Your honor, respectfully, Mr. Ruud refuses to answer that question on the grounds that the answer may tend to incriminate him.

THE COURT: [Judge Sabatini sat back and smiled.] What an interesting case. I'll take the question of Mr. Ruud's assertion of the privilege against self incrimination under submission. I may require briefing. In the meantime, this matter is adjourned until 9:30 a.m. Monday for continuation of the jury trial.

Lionel Woodman's nickname is "Trip," inspired by circumstances of his growing up on his father's Santa Barbara estate. Joe never knew or really cared about the detail of the circumstance, but Trip's pedigree of wealth was always apparent in his gentle approach to law and life. For the second time in a week he was dispatched to speak of reason to the plaintiff's mad and wild lawyers.

"Joe?" Trip raised his otherwise low volume voice to get Joe's attention as he walked with his mates toward the fourth floor elevators.

"Yeah, Trip? What's on your mind?"

"Joe, can we sit down and talk about this? It's going to take more than a minute or two in the hallway. How about I buy you lunch?"

Joe haled Rick and DD. "Hey you guys, I'm having lunch with Trip. I need a break from your uncouthness."

He turned to Trip. "How about Tony's?"

Guido was tending bar. Dice cups were up and Trip won the right to pay for drinks. Joe was happy to see Trip in a more relaxed setting and away from Ruud. Sipping his martini, Trip looked directly at Joe.

"This goddamn case has got to be settled this weekend or it will never be settled and it will never be over."

"Are you that supportive of your co-counsel? I mean, didn't Ruud make his own bed here? He's out of the case as far as I can figure. I want to put on some evidence and I want to get all this crud out in the open. I'm tired of reading the guesses of the press."

They got a table and sat down.

"I really don't care about Ruud, Joe. My client – technically the firm – wants to end this so there is something left of a practice. They no longer care about Keislor. The more that comes out about him, the worse off they are. They want to buy him out. The insurer is screaming to get this over and hope to beat other claims arising out the same scheme. They are ready to agree to your settlement agreement conditions and pay serious money – more serious than the million and a half that Ruud spoke of. Pan American, as you know, will do most anything to get out."

Joe ordered a hamburger steak with spaghetti. Trip had veal piccata. When they had finished, Joe asked, "What happens to Ruud? Will he be prosecuted – more importantly – does he know where Melanie is?"

Trip lit a cigarette.

"Right now, Ruud has a couple of smart, green kids giving him advice. They told him he can't be forced to reveal why he subpoenaed Young or who told him about the guy. They believe this stuff is protected by the attorney work-product privilege. I know, that's nonsense and Tyler should know that as well. But he really hates you, Joe, and probably hates O'Neil even more. He will probably realize that's irrelevant by tomorrow morning. He'll also realize he is dead in the water on this issue if the prosecutor comes up with any independent evidence to support the claim that he is withholding."

"Trip, I don't have any doubt that Ruud got the information about Young from Melanie. I doubt she revealed her whereabouts but the circumstances of her contact with Ruud would probably be enough to get him prosecuted. Larry Harrington and my buddy Dan O'Neil very much want to get her arrested, so nothing will work for Tyler short of coming clean. As for settlement, I want to talk to my client and my associates and I'll call you tomorrow. Where are you staying?"

Stubbing out his cigarette, Trip wrote down the number where he was in residence during the trial.

"Is there a chance of getting this done this week end?" he asked.

"Don't know. Can you persuade Ruud? I'm pretty sure Harrington or Angie Bettini will be available at any time to do whatever is necessary to deal with Ruud. But I also think he won't be released."

***

CHAPTER TWENTY-EIGHT

A Form of Justice

By a little after noon on Sunday, what was possible was over. Keislor's entire fortune, with the exception of $1500 a month annuity his mother had bought for him during his childhood, would be divested in favor of Judith Pavlone. That was an estimated $9 million, give or take. The malpractice insurer contributed the policy in the amount of $25 million. Robert and Beatrice Langley became a serious problem as there was no evidence to support a liability finding against either of them individually. The only basis for Pan America's liability was as the owner of the subsidiary that Melanie ran, International Underwriters and Reinsurers. The Pan American lawyers resisted paying anything.

DD had hoped that keeping her parents in the lawsuit with the threat of losing everything would smoke out Melanie. He insisted on not letting Pan American out for anything less than the value of Robert's holdings. The lawyers said they would put up ten million but nothing like what Joe was demanding. He suggested they talk to their client in the hope the message would get back to Melanie.

Sunday morning at about seven, there was a knock at the door of the cottage. DD opened it and there was no one there. However, on the door was taped a piece of paper. He unfolded it and recognized Melanie's elaborate script. The note read: "You've got to be fucking kidding. Right, DD?"

DD later explained to Joe and Rick,"She means she doesn't care about what we take from her parents. The note is to tell me that my insistence on taking it all or any large chunk of it isn't going to bring her into the open. She's just showing off."

"Why is she hanging around? She could be gone. She liquidated something like fifteen million. She could be anywhere."

"Like I said, she's showing off."

"So, what do we tell the guys from Pan American?"

Joe was charged with getting the settlement wrapped up.

"You know, DD, you're going to have to live with the fact we aren't going to get Melanie through this settlement. There's the outside chance that Ruud will give us something, but I wouldn't count on it."

DD let off a big sigh,

"I know. The problem is that when this thing is settled, we can't hold back to go after the phantom of Melanie and collect when we find her. It's over. The fact is that if we get close enough to her to get her money, we'll have her in custody. Money not being the point, I guess I can wait."

The settlement was explained to Judith, who was delighted. She asked if Keislor would be disbarred. Joe explained that his disbarment couldn't be a condition of settlement of the civil case. However, he thought he knew how to satisfy her on the point. She put her barely controllable hand on DD's.

"Hey, I know you want that bitch in jail, but please don't worry your beautiful face about it. She'll get hers – I just know it. You've got to get on with a life."

DD kissed her and everybody laughed.

The remaining hurdle being resolved. Joe, Rick and DD met with the Defense lawyers. Before informing them of plaintiff's agreement, Joe asked the defense lawyers:

"What about Keislor's bar status?"

Ms. Murdock, Ruud's surrogate under the circumstance, said, "There is little doubt that he will be disciplined by the Bar. He may even resign."

"Would you please tell Mr. Keislor that we will make the transcript of his examination in this case available to the Bar, plus what we were going to use if there was no settlement? Tell him, as well, that we will be demanding that he be permanently disbarred."

Ms. Murdock looked down at her yellow pad, replying to Joe in a barely audible voice, "Of course."

"Very well; it's done."

***

Part 6: Elusive Wisdom

We can figure it out, this business of wisdom.
It is the realization of our loneliness, the articulation of
justice.
Another part of wisdom is this truth:
from day to day it is hard to find – it is elusive.

Mathilda Deare, former Public Administrator for Indian County Mississippi,
explaining what she has observed in San Francisco

CHAPTER TWENTY-NINE

The Judge

THE CLERK: <u>Pavlone versus Hugh Keislor and others, No. 1985-CO2457</u>. For confirmation of settlement. Counsel, please state your appearances.

[In turn, save Tyler Ruud, the lawyers made their presence a matter of record. Joe Cleary and Rick Esquivel bravely made their presence known each with a lump in his throat and melancholy in his eyes. Not being counsel of record, DD remained just in front of the bar, behind Joe and Rick.]

THE COURT: I had imagined I would spend the rest of my days on the bench presiding over this case. Since I first met you gentlemen, I dismissed all notion of a settlement. Well, let's make sure there is one and put it on the record. By the way, as a precaution, I have not dismissed the jury. They are in the assembly room. When we get this thing on the record, we'll call them in and explain.

[The Courtroom was packed with representatives of the press and, presumably, the general public, including one Mathilda Deare – although she was for the moment undetected.]

[The lawyers recited the settlement. Judith and representatives of the parties all acknowledged their respective agreement.]

THE COURT: Mrs. Chin would you please have the bailiff bring the jury in and have them seated in the jury box.

[The fourteen people who had been selected to decide the facts in this civil dispute shortly filed in, each – upon entering the Courtroom – realizing that something was up. There had not been this many people present since the first day. DD watched each and couldn't help but recall the day that he first met Ella Mae White, nearly six years ago, and what he thought then. He was reminded that he admired each of these souls for their acceptance of a system that admits of no convenience and only occasional grace. It is acceptance of its necessity – there being no satisfactory alternative ever suggested.]

THE COURT: Ladies and gentlemen, it looks like we won't need you to resolve this dispute – as colossal as it is – because, improbably, the parties have reached an agreement.

[Whereupon the Judge summarized the terms of the settlement amid "oohs!," "awws!" voiced by jurors and press alike.]

This is not to say that you have wasted your time or that your presence wasn't necessary. I've been doing this for 39 years, so I know what I am talking about when I tell you this case would not have been settled if you weren't here, ready to decide it for these parties.

Hundreds of political commentators for hundreds of years have thought the notion of bringing in ordinary people to decide complex matters of civil law was the most daring of the our nation's institutions. They have repeatedly predicted that it would fail. But – here we are, still going strong. There are a lot of reasons for that, but probably the most important is that this is a reasonable and effective way to determine the truth – delicate as that commodity can be. It must be handled with wisdom and you can be trusted to do that.

You are excused with our appreciation and the appreciation of your fellow citizens.

**

CHAPTER THIRTY

And Then This Happened

Mattie had decided not to run for re-election as the Indian County Public Administrator. She had persuaded her longtime assistant, Arlen Johns, to run. As he was unopposed, he was her successor. Being an independent woman with personal ambitions that were inconsistent with a life of subservience as a wife and mother, she long reviled the notion. Long, but not permanently. Once she experienced the unbounded intimacy of DD in San Francisco, her mind's eye could see no future without him.

A date was fixed for the late summer of 1985 on which the wedding would be celebrated at San Francisco City Hall.

Tyler Ruud was eventually persuaded to explain that he had in fact received four calls from the fugitive Melanie Langley. He never met her and never made any attempt to either find out where she was or to report the telephone contact to authorities. Melanie supplied him information about the possible connection of DD to the disappearance of Roy Lindstrom following the San Quentin shootings. Because Ruud knew Melanie was a fugitive and failed to report it, he was guilty of a felony. He was prosecuted and sentenced to probation and later suspended from the State Bar. He never practiced again and retired to Baja California in Mexico.

Rick Baldachre, the former Deputy District Attorney who had taken up with Dru Lacey in the mysterious apartment in Sausalito, pled to possession of cocaine and was sentenced to two years in prison. He served one year in the County jail and was released on probation. Losing his job with the downtown firm, he also lost his license to practice law.

Hugh Keislor resigned from the Bar while disciplinary proceedings were pending. As part of his agreement with the Bar, he agreed never to reapply. He relocated to Arizona, where he joined a firm that staged motivational talks throughout the country. Ed Slator, a newspaperman who had retired from the *San Francisco Examiner*, saw Keislor in such a presentation and wrote and published a story on the <u>Pavlone</u> case. The motivational firm fired Keislor and he has since disappeared.

Joe Cleary, Daniel Dermot O'Neil, and Rick Esquivel continued in the practice of law and fostered more stories, which are yet to be told.

Melanie? Well, her fate is yet to be learned.

THE END

Acknowledgements

Prompted largely by insecurity, I relied on a lot of people to help in this project that began in 1995. Of those, my wife of fifty-one years, Delores, was immediately and always the most encouraging. If this thing bombs, it is primarily her fault that it was done at all – insisting as she did that I was a good writer. Editing, commenting and criticizing was not, however, limited to Dee Dee. In the early stages, the most critical and influential was my late and long time secretary, Pat Pratchios. With a sharp eye and sharper tongue, Pat impressed on me the seriousness of the task.

My daughter and former legal assistant (actually, I didn't have any illegal assistants), Kelly, contributed mightily over the years to the accuracy of the tale. The places are real and where I put them thanks to Kelly. Her suggestions to move the story along...well, moved it along.

Readers of the first draft and lovingly encouraging were my close friends John and Barbara Davids, now of Oakland, then of Decatur Island in San Juan County, Washington. Specific areas of help came from my little sister, Carol Jean Flynn of Washoe Lake, Nevada, confirming this and that about horses – a subject never more than thirty feet from her existence. Similarly, my college classmate and soul buddy, John Lewallen, did what he could to discourage the publication of this complicated story. A primary influence was my old law partner, Keith Roberts and his wife, Verna MacCornack, of New York City. Keith persuaded me to spend some time with a New York editor who, like other New York editors and literary agents, could see the book succeeding only if it fit the shape of things as New York literati see them. Nonetheless, it was helpful and I am thankful to Mr. and Mrs. Roberts for that.

Finally, but not least, was the incisive criticism of one of San Francisco's most famous and demanding teachers, Sara Trelaun. Notwithstanding that we were longtime neighbors, she brought this work into the perspective of an uncompromising and demanding teacher and linguist. Trimming the final version by fifteen thousand words was a product of Sara's reading. You, as a reader, ought to thank her.

About the Author

Joe McCray is seventy years old. Some might think this is an age where one really shouldn't be launching a writing career. But maybe it's a better time. His has been a long life – a long, eventful, and revealing life. Maybe others could have come across what he did without living it, but, if that is so, there seems to be a value in actually doing it

His most important years were spent in San Francisco – forty of them. The center of those years was his thirty-two years as a practicing trial lawyer, beginning April Fool's Day, 1971, and ending in January of 2005. It was on the latter date that the California State Bar placed him on "inactive" status. At that point, he and his wife returned to the Portland, Oregon, area, where they had attended high school. There, they took over a failing little farm and took to raising two Labrador pups. Finding farming very hard and hunting season short, he began to spend some time mulling over and writing about his practice as fiction. After all, being in San Francisco from 1965 until 2005 was like trying to enjoy a good bottle of wine and some pasta in the middle of a battlefield.

BOOKS BY JOE McCRAY

Murder at the Thorn Tree Hotel
Elusive Wisdom
The Wisdom of Rain

Connect with Joe McCray online:
http://elusivewisdom.com
http://joemccray.com/blog

Facebook:
http://www.facebook.com/profile.php?id=100002557424812

Cover design and book formatting:
Linda Wisner, Wisner Creative

"Snapshot" photo on cover derived
from an image ©photographykm - Fotolia.com